D1403136

Yannick Hill was born in 1980 and is a graduate of the Creative Writing MA at the University of East Anglia.

Versailles is his first novel.

VERSAILLES

A Novel

By Yannick Hill

unbound

For Milena

This edition first published in 2016

Unbound
6th Floor Mutual House, 70 Conduit Street, London W1S 2GF

www.unbound.co.uk

Text Design by Ellipsis

Art direction by Mark Ecob
Cover illustration by Yehrin Tong

A CIP record for this book is available from the British Library

ISBN 978-1-78352-230-9 (trade hbk)
ISBN 978-1-78352-231-6 (ebook)
ISBN 978-1-78352-301-6 (limited edition)

Printed in Great Britain by Clays Ltd, St Ives Plc

1 3 5 7 9 8 6 4 2

For now she need not think of anybody. She could be herself, by herself. And that was what now she often felt the need of – to think; well not even to think. To be silent; to be alone. All the being and the doing, expansive, glittering, vocal, evaporated; and one shrunk, with a sense of solemnity, to being oneself, a wedge-shaped core of darkness, something invisible to others . . . and this self having shed its attachments was free for the strangest adventures.

Virginia Woolf, *To the Lighthouse*

Prologue

Somewhere in America, at the limits of a silver city, a giant monitor lizard is making his way through Versailles, a one-hundred-room mega-mansion set back from the ocean. The human that tends to him was fired for not wearing her complete uniform. In her absence, the six-foot monitor made his escape from a makeshift cage of chicken mesh and rough cuts. His lizard eyes dart from thing to thing but there is no meaning really, only forward movement and a hunger that is fast turning a tame animal into one ready to bite the exposed flesh of those not feeding him. Most of the people living in the residence do not know the monitor exists. The yellow and blue-black scales that make up his hide reflect the low light coming in through a window. He is in the Grand Ballroom now, his lizard brain detecting the change in texture from soft to hard under his belly. He makes a decision on direction based on faint smells and the distant sound of clinking, metal on porcelain.

Elsewhere in Versailles, Casey Baer is waking up. He is the man of the house, CEO of the internet's pre-eminent social network. A man for his times. His dreams were of mass murder, the silk sheets under him lightly damp with clean sweat. But there is no lingering guilt. Casey slips out of the bed, careful not to disturb his beautiful wife, former chief design officer to the world's leading tech company. Standing up straight, he extends his left arm out at ninety degrees to his torso and makes a fist. A charisma without witness. His tall, lean, forty-two-year-old body is that of the modern sprinter, youthful, uncanny in its construction. With his right hand he finds an invisible bow string, draws back, left eye closed, right eye focused on a target somewhere well beyond the bedroom wall.

His daughter, Missy Baer, turns sixteen today, but her birthday won't be announced on the network because first thing this morning she deleted her online profile forever. That was her first act. Her second was to run away from home, never to return. Versailles is missing its princess.

PART ONE
Escape

1

Missy walked the beach alone, sword angled down in line with her mesh skirt, black baseball cap pulled over her eyes like she's feeling the future. Waves broke gentle, the sun rising. All summer long she'd practiced on the sand, boys watching through their phones from the low dunes, boys drinking vodka till the fade. They always kept their distance. Saw a girl preparing for battle. The war inside.

Today was her birthday. Sixteen candles. But Missy wasn't coming home. She thought about the gleaming palace, her sleeping parents king and queen, twin brother deep in the west wing, four out of seven screens telling him the same thing. River didn't sleep. His room so big you could play hide-and-seek and win. Her little brother, younger by ten seconds. Missy remembered. Magic candles. His tears when the flames kept coming back.

Facing the water, she made a circle in the sand with the tip of her sword and struck her first pose. Eyes closed. It was like slow motion. No one to see this now. This time alone was molten, an arc of quicksilver. Second pose, the blade passing close by her left cheek, her long blonde hair and skinny wrists tied with black ribbons. Her mind played the right music. Third Pose.

Missy sheathed the sword like a pro, relaxed the muscles in her shoulders. She walked back through the gardens to her car, a crystal black SUV, unbirthday gift from her father. The PX8 paint was the blackest on the market. She remembered the monitor lizard, wondered if someone thought to feed it with Leticia gone. Nanny Leticia was like a second mother, singing lullabies in her own language. Missy turned the key in the ignition. The engine vibrated through her bones. The car telling her it would be okay. But she had a bad feeling all the same. She made sure to frown to herself just in case. The electronic gates opening at their own pace. Versailles in the rear mirror. Her car moving out of frame.

The link turned up in her email back in June. No sender, no subject. A video of Missy's favorite singer, pop princess Scout Rose. But this was crazy. Scout had been missing for almost a year. The most downloaded artist of all time had disappeared without a trace but here she was, in a new video. Missy waited for the music but the music never came, just the sound of wind moving past an unprotected microphone. She was dancing in a desert with her eyes closed, gray mountains in the distance. The sword made it ritual, a rite of passage, but she was dancing, enjoying herself, taking pride in her every move. There were other figures in the background. They wore plastic animal masks, the kind you saw at kids' parties. But they were out of focus, their attention on Scout and her performance.

Missy watched all seven minutes. According to the counter, she was the first person to ever view this video. Her impulse was to share it to her network, but something gave her pause. This was a new feeling. Of wanting to keep this close. A secret crush. *My inspiration.* She knew it would blow up in no time, but she would always be the first, the very first person to see this video. She watched it again. And again. There was something about it, seeing her hero without the music, this newfound grace, like courage, her command of a new language. But why? And what did this have to do with her disappearance? Missy noticed Scout's black baseball cap had a white star over the peak. All Missy knew was she loved what she saw, and wanted more.

capturethecastle 5 seconds ago

If this is the future, I want to leave now

In the days after watching the video, she hadn't slept too well, dreaming in wide neon beams of pink and green and blue, no story, no control, like falling in love. Next thing a package arrived with her name on it. A long wooden box from New Zealand. Missy didn't know anybody in New Zealand but she loved getting packages in the mail so she ran up the stairs to her bedroom, locked the door and knelt on the pink carpet. When she saw what was inside she had to cover her mouth to stop herself squeaking. A sword. But not just any sword. *The* sword from the video. It was perfect. She balanced it on her knuckles and couldn't stop smiling. So lucky!

Since then she'd practiced every day on the beach, switched her phone to silent, muted all her group chats, told friends she was with other friends. They were used to it by now, Missy not hanging out like before. She'd been like this for a while, finding more time to be alone. She'd lost a lot of followers this summer, but she didn't care, not really.

Her dreams were of falling, falling upwards into a dark,

dark sky, and when she opened her eyes the fading light from outside would tell her it was late, too late for Saturday, for swimming or seeing friends. Her friends told her she'd changed; they didn't understand. There were rumors it had something to do with her mom. Missy stayed silent. The sword came at the right time. She felt alive again. Going to the beach every day. Practicing her moves. It felt so great to be doing *something*. By late summer she was better than the video. Now she needed a new routine. Her own moves.

And right on cue another late-night email. No sender, no subject. The message itself was two words:

Level up!

She clicked the link and nothing happened. Then out of the corner of her eye she saw her phone light up on the bed. It was downloading an application out of nowhere. The icon was a white star against black. She touched it. Custom GPS. Her location marked by a blue dot. Then a voice from the handset. A man's voice.

Congratulations, Missy, you leveled up. Gather your things, your sword, your thoughts. Be ready to follow in Scout's footsteps. Your adventure begins tomorrow, at first light.

Missy felt the sun pass across her face and for three or four seconds she was driving blind, the world beyond her eyelids rendered in a dark, coral pink. The summer was almost over and she might never see her friends again, her brother, her mom – her mom would be so upset when she found out, so upset, and that made Missy upset. Missy didn't know what would happen, she didn't want to think what her mom might do, she really didn't know. The thought nearly made her turn the car around, her mother still asleep, still asleep and not knowing she was gone, then waking up on her daughter's birthday, waking up in her dark, dark bedroom, the late morning light pressing on the heavy curtains. Her beautiful mother, all the unworn clothes in her wardrobe. Her mom was always elegant, her voice low and slow, the words she used, like an actress in a movie. These perfect words, as though they'd always been there, before she even spoke. And now. Her mother was still calm, but in a different way. Those pills in the white boxes. Not calm. Lost.

The thought nearly made Missy turn around but she didn't, her car traveling at high speed with her in it, her car, her car, her journey into the unknown, away from the past, from Versailles, and into the future. *If this is the future, I want to leave now.* She'd been ready to go for some time, even before the video. Her father's betrayal. What Casey did. What Casey did had cast a shadow over Missy. The sword video had shown her there was light behind the black curtain. And now the voice on her phone guiding her out of the city, like a robot voice but more real. It was like someone calling from the other side of her reality. The start of a video game. Her sword, the sense of being chosen. She was like, *Yes!*

She was out of there, away from Versailles, and everything looked different: the tall palms and city streets, it all played like a movie outside her darkened windows. All these years. The police escorts to and from school. Bodyguards outside classrooms. Boys too scared to talk to her after a kid nearly got his arm broke for asking her to prom. All these years. Versailles itself, house of a thousand cameras. Her every move recorded and now, here she was, out of frame, out from under watchful eyes, music up loud on the 5.1, cruising like there was no yesterday. Missy put on her sunglasses and for a split second her mind's eye is a camera outside the car, pointed in through the windscreen. In that second she is watching herself like on film. The speed of the car, the thrill of escape – she gave a scream of delight that cut through the music like a silver coin into a deep swimming pool.

This was all so *perfect* and *gorgeous*, the landscape playing like a movie outside her window. If only they could see. Her millions of followers. Missy Baer. #RunningAway. If only they could see her, with everything that was happening, right now, the passing seconds, minutes . . . One last status update . . . But she'd deleted all her profiles. Her father's network gave you thirty days to reactivate. Her father . . . CEO of the world's fastest-growing social network and here was his daughter, running away from home. What a story. It would break the internet! Missy took the phone from its cradle and swiped for the camera. One last picture, her eyes in the rear mirror. She took off her sunglasses. #NoMakeup #MissyMissingNow. Snap. Filter. Share this moment. All she had to do was log back in. It was all still there, the glowing embers of her user data: every photo, every like, every comment.

No. Missy put her sunglasses back on. She hadn't posted anything in months. So why do it now? This was her. This was escape. Escape from everything. Under the radar. Going dark. Offline. The space between. Missy missing. She tapped *cancel*, returned the phone to its cradle. This was her, no one to see this, an arc of quicksilver, a dream in neon beams of pink and green and blue, no story, like falling in love. This was her, all her. Away from Versailles, no cameras on her now. *Missy at the controls!*

Pretty soon it was time for breakfast. No one to tell her she was late. She pulled into a truck stop, wondered if it was too early for a cheeseburger. Yeah, she could do a cheeseburger and soda right now. Come to think of it she'd never been this hungry in her life.

Turned out this was a great truck stop. It had a good feeling for some reason, everybody in there chatting away and friendly. Missy noticed two young dudes by the window eating pancakes with their tops off and painted faces. Not like clowns but sort of like clowns. Kind of handsome in a weird way. She overlapped her hands on the counter, leant forward and ordered a coffee.

'You'll have to speak up, honey.'

'I'd like a coffee, please.'

'Coffee. Coming right up.' The nice lady with the turquoise eyeshadow placed the cup in front of Missy and gave her a second look. 'You come far today, sweetheart?'

'Not far.' Missy raised her eyebrows in anticipation of the next question, but when it didn't come, she was quick to close the gap: 'Can I please get a cheeseburger, or is it too early in the day for that?'

'Darlin' you can have a cheeseburger whenever you want.'

Missy smiled. This was so nice. Everybody being so nice to her. 'Where am I right now? I mean, am I still in the city?'

The nice lady took a beat to answer, lips slightly parted. 'Highway 5, honey, you out in the country now! You sure you're okay? Anyone you need to call? We got a telephone out back if you need.'

The kindness of this stranger. 'Oh, no, that's okay,' Missy said, showing the lady her cell. 'I have this, thank you though. I. . . I never left the city before, I—' She was saying too much. She saw the lady's name badge. 'I think you have beautiful hair, Nora,' Missy said. 'And I love your smile. You smile with your eyes.' She saw Nora's wedding ring and pictured a Disney prince ascending a white marble staircase, a bouquet of flowers in his arms. 'Your husband must be very happy he found someone like you.'

'Why, thank you, what a kind thing to say to a person. What's your name, sweetheart?'

'Scout,' said Missy, 'My name's Scout.' She sipped her coffee. Why did she have to lie? She felt like saying something true to make it right. She could say it was her birthday. No, that would seem silly. She wasn't a kid anymore. She wasn't a kid, but she did miss her mom, the way she kissed your forehead when she said goodbye. 'This coffee is delicious!' Missy said.

She looked over her shoulder for the shirtless clowns but they'd gone already. The coffee really did taste good. The film of light brown foam and dark liquid underneath. So alien and adult. She took a picture in her mind and sent it to her mom. #coffee #delicious. She shifted focus, the clowns walking to their car outside the window. A big, wide, beat-up car from the 1950s, she didn't know anything about cars but it looked cool, there was no roof and they drove off in the direction she was heading. Some kind of music festival maybe?

Sixteen years old today. She looked down at her bare arms, hands, her fingers, but they didn't look any different. She felt it though. She'd always felt a little older inside. She looked over her shoulder again and that's when her food arrived.

Leticia had told them bedtime stories when they were kids, made them up as she went along. There was this one about a white dog. Woof woof. It was Missy who woke to the sound of barking outside. She went over to the open window and saw a big, white, fluffy dog waiting in front of the house. Woof. She put on a cardigan over her nightdress and went downstairs to see what the dog wanted. She followed the dog until they reached the edge of the gardens belonging to Versailles. Woof woof! The white dog had led her to a place where he'd been digging. He'd dug a deep tunnel right under the fence and next thing Missy knew, the dog disappeared inside. Well, of course she had no choice but to go in right after him. Once outside Missy saw that the dog had grown much bigger, so she climbed on his back like he was a little pony and off they went, due north toward the forest. Once inside the trees, the dog introduced Missy to a pack of wolves and that's when she realized he'd been a wolf all along. But instead of eating her up, the wolves took care of Missy and showed her their way of being, and that's where she remains to this day, living wild in among those dark trees.

Missy couldn't eat all her cheeseburger but it was so good. She thought about calling her mom but decided it wasn't the right time, not yet, better to get back on the road and put more distance between her and Versailles. She missed her mom. She missed her little brother. Nora stopped her by the door as she was leaving, put a hand on each of Missy's shoulders and kissed her on the forehead. 'You're a good girl, Scout. I want you to take care now, you hear?'

'I will,' Missy said. 'Thank you.'

Outside, she turned to wave goodbye a final time but Nora was already taking someone's order. Missy got back in her car and opened the new app on her phone. It took a moment to triangulate her position and told her to continue north-east toward the mountains. Was she really following in Scout's footsteps somehow? For now it didn't matter. She was free. A free Missy.

2

As the sun rose above the horizon, River typed words into a binary translator.

River Baer

01010010 01101001 01110110 01100101 01110010
00100000 01000010 01100001 01100101 01110010

River Baer likes girls

01010010 01101001 01110110 01100101 01110010
00100000 01000010 01100001 01100101 01110010
00100000 01101100 01101001 01101011 01100101
01110011 00100000 01100111 01101001 01110010
01101100 01110011

River Baer likes boys

01010010 01101001 01110110 01100101 01110010
00100000 01000010 01100001 01100101 01110010
00100000 01101100 01101001 01101011 01100101
01110011 00100000 01100010 01101111 01111001
01110011

Hornier than a 4-balled tomcat

01001000 01101111 01110010 01101110 01101001
01100101 01110010 00100000 01110100 01101000

15

```
01100001   01101110   00100000   01100001   00100000
00110100   00101101   01100010   01100001   01101100
01101100   01100101   01100100   00100000   01110100
01101111   01101101   01100011   01100001   01110100
```

River wasn't himself this morning and it felt good. It wasn't just his new bear costume that fitted him like a dream. He'd been up all night again on the internet, generating fictional profiles for the social network. It was his art, his thing, pretending to be different people, dreaming other lives online. Some were never more than a name, others he took all the way, finding them real friends, real enemies, in and out of love, sparkle and fade. His favorite profile of the night was a mom of one named Jenny. She'd majored in English at college but had to give up her dream of becoming a writer after getting pregnant with her first kid. She had long red hair, green eyes (just like his mom) and a husband she thought was having an affair. River came up with Jenny at three in the morning while watching a documentary about overfishing in the East China Sea on mute with some under-ground Finnish hip hop playing so loud the bass sent a glass show-jumping trophy smashing to a thousand pieces on the floor.

There was nothing unusual in the conception, Jenny came to him as they always did. First as an emotion, not his but real. Colors. A play of light and sound. Then her voice, at first as heard through a wall, then right there in the room with him, like she was in his head. He decided to go on with Jenny. He ordered breakfast in bed on his phone and started streaming the second in a series of films about human trafficking in the former Soviet Bloc nations. He would work on Jenny all day, take her on some forums. No better way to discover who she was than to *be* her, go through her motions. He knew just the place to start. He found a message board with mothers exchanging baby tips. Perfect. Then he paused. Something he had to do first. It was like a ritual, part of his creative process. River walked across his bedroom to the tennis ball cannon, got up on the high stool, spread his legs, ran his fingers through his longish brown hair and took a deep breath. He pressed the green button on the plastic remote.

Thung, the yellow tennis ball hit him right boom in his private collection. The pain wasn't pain, it was a dull paradigm shift, a sad dragon in the mist, a deluxe gray curtain falling lazily across his consciousness, it was exit stage forward, a thousand oncoming headlights but no blood. The sounds he made in the aftermath were those of a sea lion shrugging off the powerful advances of another male. River collapsed on his knees and inadvertently licked the floor like it was a block of ice on a hot summer's day. Muscle memory. He was ready now. Totally ready to be Jenny. He slowly got to his feet like a ruined hero and stumbled back to his workstation, a concave semi-circle of seven vertically oriented monitors framing an endless cascade of live social interactions.

Okay, baby forum. He made his first post as Jenny in an active thread about whether to give your baby milk heated up or at room temperature:

jenny78
I make the bottles up ahead of time and store them in the refrigerator, then warm up when needed. My boy likes it warm but I think it depends on the baby. Hope this helps. :)

A little further into the discussion someone addressed Jenny directly.

bubblegurl

Haven't seen you here before, jenny78. We welcome you to the forum and hope you are enjoying your baby!

jenny78

Thanks bubblegurl. I have a gorgeous 4-month-old boy named Buddy. He's just the most wonderful thing that ever happened to me. I'm so so tired but of course I'm in heaven.

While River was waiting for a reply, a gentle chime and pulsing green LED told him breakfast was served. He opened the hatch in the wall and removed the tray. Sleepy Bear pancakes (yum) and hot chocolate with marshmallows, his favorite. Well, it *was* his birthday. He refreshed the page.

bubblegurl

Buddy sounds like a darling. I remember those sleepless nights well. He could be teething mine started when he was 3 months.

jenny78

Yes he must be teething. Last night he managed about two hours sleep. None of my usual tricks are working I've tried cuddles, car ride, movie, lullaby. Not a happy camper.

cathyasmom

Have you tried taking him to bed with you? Mine is six months and likes her space now. I know it's not a long-term solution but it saves you getting up every time.

jenny78

That's what we did I had him between us and he was okay after that. When he settles like that his breathing actually sends me to sleep quicker than anything. I'm so happy right now. I know you know but it's this feeling of your life meaning so much more. It's like waking up and the room is full of sunlight. Sure the endless nights have left me feeling like a zombie, but then one of these days Buddy will say something and it's because of me, you know?

bubblegurl

I know exactly what you mean and you sound like a wonderful mother, Jenny. So happy to welcome you to these boards. Don't hesitate to check in any time. You're never alone!

jenny78

Likewise, bubblegurl. It's a real comfort to know I can go online and share like this. Things can get kind of isolated at home when my husband's at work. I know that sounds terrible because of course I have my baby but, I don't know . . . I'm sure you ladies understand.

River was flowing now. Feeling the character. It was like Jenny saying these things just before he typed the words. It wasn't always this quick but there was something about her. He could see her at a bureau of dark, varnished wood, the kind with a panel that folds down into a desk with drawers and compartments. She inherited this piece from one of her parents, her father – no – her mother. It was where she wrote her first novel about a spiritual journey to the Arctic north by nuclear icebreaker. It was where she still wrote letters by hand to her old friends and opened her laptop when she needed the internet, which was more often these days. She could lose hours online, adrift in a sea of celebrity trivia, baby forums and male-on-male hardcore. The search was for nothing in particular. Oblivion. She loved her son. Her baby boy. She wasn't lying to those people on the forum. It was only that this reality, *real life*, felt more like a dream now, and when she closed her eyes, when she finally did sleep long enough to dream, that's when it all felt tangible and her world came back into focus. The internet was another such dimension. Browsing, she could almost achieve a kind of dream state. She always made sure to delete her search history before her husband came home late at night.

River could hear her baby crying upstairs. He followed Jenny from her desk, across the moss-green carpet to the foot of the stairs. She paused only momentarily and they ascended together as one. He took Jenny into Buddy's room, which smelled like strawberries and freshly laundered towels. She reached into his cot and lifted out her baby, bringing him close to her bosom and kissing him again and again on his warm head, whispering, *Yes, yes, my darling, it's alright, Mommy's here now, did you have a bad dream, bunny, did you? Well, you're awake now and it's all okay again. I'm here, I'm here* . . . Jenny slowly danced and talked like this until Buddy was quiet again, but instead of returning him to his bed she took him with her back downstairs where she could keep a closer eye on him.

River bit down on the strawberry lollipop and swiveled in his chair to face into the bedroom. He only knew it was his birthday because his twin sister had come by late last night to say hi. Or had he dreamed it? Either way, he couldn't remember much about the conversation. And according to one of his screens, he was about to get another visitor. His mother. She was in the corridor, approaching his room. She was wearing her long nightdress with a suit jacket over her shoulders. River cursed under his breath before triggering the deadbolts and opening the door.

He met her eye for half a second before seeing her bare feet. The rush of anger was unexpected. He wanted to take her in his arms but couldn't even look her in the eye. Like knowing there's a ghost, right there. Her perfume mixed with something else. His own mother. Mom. His blood. Hers. He remembered. It seemed like long ago. The time they used to spend together. The two of them. Side by side as he played video games.

She'd watch him for a while with raised eyebrows, ask him what his mission was in her deep, deadpan voice, and once he was convinced she wasn't making fun, he'd explain (and she was always quick to learn. It wasn't long before she was punching the air when he did good and bossing him around, telling him she'd take the M-16 over the AK-47, every time). He liked it, her attention, her watching made his progress a performance, the controller in his grasp designed by her, he liked the way it fit inside his hands just perfect. *Human factors,* she would say, *ergonomics.*

He liked her there, her smell, those questions in her low, slow voice. But something changed. Her voice wasn't quite the same. And she moved different. Her face. It wasn't her, not quite. Her smell. Her perfume masking something. The drugs masking everything. Those pills in the white boxes. She didn't come to visit anymore, not even for a goodnight kiss. This appearance was the first in weeks, no, months. He felt the sting in his nose. He missed her. The time they spent.

He missed her even now, with her standing right in front of him in the corridor. He wished his sister could be here, she always knew the thing to say. 'Hi, Synthea.'

'River, have you seen your sister this morning?'

'No, I haven't.'

'Well if you see her will you tell her to come see me in my office, I want to wish her—' Synthea Baer broke off when she realized. First Missy, then River, ten seconds after. *My darling River, I didn't forget, please don't close the door. I didn't forget your birthday, you're my son. Let me see your face, you look so tired, and it's your birthday. I knew it was your birthday and I didn't forget. Let me sit with you a while and watch you play. Spend some time together like we used to do.*

She remembered. River offering her the game controller each time and her saying no, she liked just being there. Her son, the deft movements of his fingers over the color-coded buttons, the rapid twitches of his thumbs over rubberized analogue sticks. Her design. Form and function. His form, the shape of him. And how she loved him. Her son beside her, her blood, his eyes flickering like jewels as he played, a kind of dreaming, the violence on the screen fading into the deep background. How different she was from him. This time was something she could share in. He'd offer her the controller but she'd say no.

Synthea went to kiss her son's cheek but he moved away before she could. 'Happy Birthday, River,' she managed to say, and the door was closed again. The cool, steel surface gave her a light electric shock.

River woke his computer and watched his mother in the corridor. Something about the way she carried herself. Her bare feet. In the past she was always dressed to perfection, by day in pale, futuristic suits of her own design, by night in dresses dreamed in strip-lit Paris ateliers. She used to look like a movie star. Nowadays it was always this nightdress and business jacket ensemble, and never any shoes, her bare feet silent on the carpets as she wandered the corridors like a stray spirit. This woman in the corridor was not his mom . . . He felt the sting in his nose like he was about to cry but he didn't cry. This is how it was. A kind of grieving.

He watched her touch the door and then recoil. She turned to face the camera and held its gaze for a minute before turning and disappearing out of shot. By the time the monitor lizard entered the frame not long after, River had minimized the window and resumed his role-play as Jenny.

3

The mountains loomed and Missy turned left onto the northbound highway. The sky was cartoon blue. Her first time alone outside the city. It was like a dream. #AllMe.

I'm running away – I'm running away from home – I'm flying – Like an arrow – My black feathers fluttering in the wind – My wings fluttering with black feathers – I'm flying, away from them, away from everything. And the boy at school, the boy at school who told her she was beautiful. If only he could see. If only she could share this moment. All she had to do was log back in. Status update. Break the internet. No. This was her. Her escape. No more internet. No more Versailles. No more Casey. Missy missing now. She tapped *cancel*, returned the phone to its cradle.

What Casey did. She almost wished it was one thing she could bury deep inside, like a specific memory of a bad event. But this wasn't like that. What Casey did was more like finding out you were living on top of a giant ant colony. Under the carpets. Teeming. First it was two, three ants crawling up the power cable to your computer, up your little finger. Then they're in your clothes, in your bed, crawling in your mouth when you're asleep. Continuous. What Casey did was – a betrayal, but Missy wasn't interested in finding the words just yet. First she had to live her life, follow her broken heart while it was still open. The music loud on the stereo, sword on the back seat. #OpenRoad.

A convoy of bikers overtook Missy. The roar, the vibrations, it was kind of scary but she wanted a part of it. More painted faces. There was definitely something going on. She'd drive till she got tired then find a motel, new sheets, fresh sheets, get some beauty sleep! It was weird because she didn't miss any of the people she'd left behind, except her mom . . . and her brother . . . and Leticia . . . Okay, those guys, but that didn't mean she wanted to go home. No way. Maybe it was too early to say, but right now? She felt she could handle her business just fine.

She thought about flooring the accelerator to keep up with the bikers but she was happy cruising at this speed for now, following the gentle instructions on her phone, the landscape outside her windows playing like a movie all day, the highway disappearing under her car, appearing and disappearing, the rush, rush of tarmac and the landscape outside her windows, wide, wider than anything she'd ever seen, wider than a dream, this landscape like a movie outside her windows, moving through and then across, a rush of tarmac and the thrill of escape. Away from Versailles, no cameras on her now. This time alone was precious. She played the right music. And the boy at school. The boy at school who told her she was beautiful.

She thought about checking in on her mom but decided it wasn't the right time, not yet, better to put more distance between her and Versailles. She missed her little brother too. River would have loved this. He couldn't drive but he would have loved this, the road disappearing under the hood like in a video game, him jabbering at her from the passenger seat about the latest developments in virtual reality, making her listen to his Finnish hip hop on the stereo, knowing every word but not knowing what they meant. She thought about messaging him right now, but no. This was all her, this time alone was precious. Eyes forward, she took a picture with her mind for later, a blink against the sunlight streaming in the forward windshield.

4

It took Synthea seven minutes to walk between River's bunker and her office in Versailles' East Wing. The elevator opened into a work space defined by a single pane of curved glass framing a view of the ocean so total it sometimes felt like being at the bridge of a great ship headed elsewhere.

Casey had built this studio to her precise specifications, equipped and furnished it to the highest possible standards. It was the only way he could persuade her to bring her work home. *To be closer to the kids . . . Because they miss you,* he had said. *Because I miss you.* It was the view of the ocean that finally convinced her. Those first days she felt she could reach out and touch the glittering water with her fingertips. Those first months were among the most productive of her life. It was here she created some of her best-known designs, concepts for an order of iconic technology that would become *the* delivery devices for Casey's ever-expanding social network; the windows to a billion souls. Watches, phones, tablets, laptops, desktops, cars . . . Synthea's designs had helped define the direction for personal computing throughout the developed world. *Time* magazine called Casey and Synthea Baer the King and Queen of Silicon Valley, the power couple to end all power couples.

And, yes, she had seen more of her kids. River coming by to watch her work, quiet as could be, resting his head lightly on her shoulder, gasping now and then as he remembered to breathe, his clever questions about what she was doing. Missy bringing her mother lunch on the Chinese dragon tray, lovingly prepared with Leticia's help in Versailles' kitchens. And, yes, for a time Synthea had loved this space, a view of the ocean so total that on wilder days she half expected the waves to crash against the glass. But as the years went by the water seemed to have receded, a tidal retreat independent of the moon's influence. *Because I miss you*, Casey had said.

These days the view gave her no pleasure, the glass a vast reminder of her imprisonment, curving by degrees of separation from the outside and everything she'd known. She couldn't remember the last time she turned on her computer. She couldn't remember her own face as she no longer looked in the mirror. She couldn't remember the name of her company, or even why she hated her husband so much. She had lost entire days in this room, and that is how it would be today.

Versailles, the ocean seemed to say, *Versailles*.

A fortress for his family. And everything they needed, right here. Versailles. House of a thousand cameras. Their every move recorded. Versailles as fortress, the choice of stone, walls within walls, the miles of cable and the levels of control. *You can have anything you want*, Casey would tell their children. *Like Disney World, but no Mickey Mouse.*

Her precious children. Their birthday. She had almost forgotten their birthday. Her first pill had eased the nervous tension in her chest and neck enough that she could at least breathe more fully now. Synthea sat at the angled desk, closed her eyes and placed her palms face down on the cool, brushed-steel surface. She inhaled deeply through her nose and out again through pursed lips. She was like an actress on film, waiting for a kiss that never comes.

Synthea loved to swim. She especially loved to swim early in the morning, when her husband was asleep. Versailles had two swimming pools, but Synthea had not set foot in either for some time. In the golden days, when she'd first started working from home, she'd go with little Missy and swim in the waters off Versailles' private beach. While Missy paddled, Synthea would swim way, way out into the open ocean, so far she could barely make out her daughter anymore. Then after a time she'd return to the shore and put Missy through her paces in the shallows. Missy was a strong swimmer, just like her mom. It was in her blood.

Synthea couldn't remember exactly when the changes started. The break in her routine. Every morning she would enter the walk-in closet, intending to put on her swimsuit, and emerge wearing her work clothes. It was automatic. Like sleepwalking, the imagined ribbon of light guiding her out of the closet, out of her room, and back up to her office.

Once there, sitting in front of her desk, the trance only deepened, the numbness spreading to her lips and fingertips. And there she stayed, sometimes for hours, not moving a muscle. The journey to her son's room this morning had been a deviation from the designated path, this pattern of non-existence, and the effort had left her with barely enough energy to breathe.

But breathe she did, and swim. She swam great distances in her mind, out, out into the ocean, away from Versailles and out of frame, until there was no land in sight and then downwards, diving deep and deeper still, until there was no light, no one, nothing but her.

Memory as dream. Her boss telling her it was okay, she would be *welcome back, any time*. His mouth telling her to *stay in contact*. She couldn't remember his name. The name of her company. She couldn't remember any of it just now. Her designs. Her designs were all still there, not so much in her mind's eye as feeling part of her, as familiar as any part of her body, her hands and feet. Human factors. Ergonomics. Symmetrical balance.

Her children. Her children she remembered perfectly. The first time Missy made her laugh, not infant Missy (and the way she pronounced 'anteater') but teenaged Missy, making a joke, a good one, and Synthea laughing. She remembered her children perfectly. Shouting at River and River shouting back, and then his knock on her bedroom door much later to apologize, and her solemn apology to him because they'd both been wrong. Symmetrical balance.

She remembered her children perfectly. And she loved them for how different they were. From her. From Casey. From each other. And finally from themselves, as they grew older and became their own people, making jokes and answering back. How different and exotic and strong and full of potential. She remembered her children perfectly, pills or no pills.

It was hours before she surfaced again, she could not tell how long, but the sky had darkened outside her window. Time for her second pill. Versailles roared beneath her like a vast, buried spaceship. Missy's birthday. For several moments she couldn't remember her daughter's age. She made a calculation. That's right. Her Missy was sixteen years old today. She realized there had been no promises. Nothing planned for Missy's birthday. Not even a cake with candles. She remembered. Magic candles. River's tears when the flames kept coming back. She never bought them again. Her two children, her Little Baers, both taking a big breath and blowing out the flames at once. The flickering image. Their happy birthday. Missy first, then River ten seconds after. But Missy was big sister, always looking out for little River. The two of them together, their playing. The water pushed beyond the edges of Versailles' outdoor pool and onto the grass, an unexpected gust of wind across. Flying crocodile. Flying crocodile. She couldn't remember what it meant just now, the memory escaping her like eggshell in the viscous white. Her children. Their birthday. She had almost forgotten their birthday. Sixteen candles, the magic gone. Sparkle and fade and then. No picture.

Synthea opened her eyes. An unexpected adrenaline rush allowed her to stand up from her chair. She picked up the smartphone from the desk and selected Missy from her favorites. It was ringing. It was ringing but Missy didn't pick up. Synthea couldn't bring herself to leave a voicemail. She touched the metaphor of a red button on the capacitive screen and let the device fall to the floor at her bare feet. She looked down and saw the diagonal crack. Her toes were turning blue. She hoped it was a trick of the light.

Time to break the rules.

She put the pill back in its plastic bottle and screwed the lid until it clicked and clicked again. She turned to face the elevator and walked towards it. Like one of River's video games. First person perspective. She pressed the button in the wall and the door opened. Time to find her daughter.

5

Until now the voice had told her where to go next. Which turns to make in the city, which exits to take on the highway. Like satellite navigation but better, because this was her adventure. Around four in the afternoon, the landscape playing like a movie, the voice on Missy's phone said to stop at the next gas station and take something that wasn't hers.

Whatever happens, the man said, *do not hesitate. Do not look back, Missy. It does not matter what it is, but you must. To move to the next stage, you must take something that is not yours.*

Right away she turned the music off, the landscape now a different movie outside her window. She felt sick. Controlling the car was suddenly a very difficult task, like the whole thing might break apart at any moment. Like riding a roller coaster. There was no way. No way was she going to steal. This wasn't a video game, this was real life, and stealing was wrong. She thought of her mother again, the comb passing through her long red hair, a cache of birthday presents somewhere. Sixteen candles. A birthday cake made with lemons and her mother waiting in the electric blue dress, the choice of outfit, her careful make-up. It was Synthea who taught Missy how to drive, and she was a good teacher. Patient. Her voice low and slow and careful . . .

What was she doing out here? Taking orders from some random voice on her phone, all the way out here in the middle of nowhere? Her mom needed her. Missy suddenly wished she'd taken Synthea with her, away from Versailles. The two of them, out on the open road, singing songs from the radio. Missy remembered. A rare trip into the city. *I'm taking you to my favorite place,* her mom had said. *Just don't tell your daddy.*

The aquarium. Missy remembered. The rippling blue light on her mother's white clothes. Being hugged close as the shark swam by the darkened glass, their breath held as one, and then their whispered words and celebratory dance of fear and excitement. The car ride home with the radio on, her mother's voice, singing songs from long ago and knowing all the words. Her mom's hands on the wheel, the muscles in her arms moving under her freckled skin as she steered the car home. Versailles. The electric gate and Casey waiting at the top of the stairs to the mansion.

Missy remembered. A family dinner. Casey asking about the aquarium, what Missy saw. But when Missy got to the part about seeing the shark Casey interrupted and asked Missy what she wanted for her birthday. And when Missy said it wasn't her birthday for a really long time Casey said he could get her anything he wanted. She could have her own theme park, right here in Versailles. Roller coasters, cotton candy, the whole thing. *It'll be like Disney World,* he said, *but no Mickey Mouse.*

Missy remembered. The muffled roars from the master bedroom hours later. They never went into the city again.

She and her mom. Side by side in the car as they sang old songs from the radio. Her mom's hands on the wheel, the muscles in her arms moving under her freckled skin as she steered the car home.

Missy looked down at her hands, more like her father's. She should never have left her mom, but she could not go back. Not now, not ever. This wasn't a video game, this was real life, her life, her decision to run away, out of frame, Versailles in the rear mirror. And then it hit her: bouncy ball.

Aquarium shop. She'd stolen a bouncy ball from the aquarium shop, taken it home. Bouncy ball . . . thinking about it now, she didn't know if she'd ever actually *bounced* the ball, just remembered River using it as some kind of code, like: I'm gonna tell on you (not that he ever did). So, okay, she *had* stolen before. But that didn't mean she was going to steal something now, just because some random voice— and there it was, still a ways off but close enough to know: the spinning blue and white sign of a gas station.

The sharp air conditioning set the mood. Missy hooked her arm through the handles of her basket like, *look, this is me, walking down the aisle, shopping for myself.* She realized she'd never done this before. All the food, drink, clothes, make-up, whatever she needed, it was there before she even asked. Versailles was a dream she was only just waking up from, here in this convenience store.

Right now she needed supplies. Something to eat, something to drink. Apple juice, she liked apple juice. Orange juice, she liked orange juice. Iced tea. She *loved* iced tea, especially with lots of ice, by the pool. There was lemon iced tea. Raspberry. Green tea iced tea. All different kinds. Missy had never been this thirsty in her life. She held one of the cold bottles to her cheek, the condensation leaving a patch on her skin. Then she cracked open the lemon iced tea and took a hit. She was paying for it so why not, right? Wait, this was too many drinks, the basket was already too heavy. She put back the orange juice with pulp and the diet sparkling green tea with strawberry kiwi iced tea, and kept the rest. Next. Cereal. Most important meal of the day they said. Two boxes of Cap'n Crunch and her basket was full and almost too heavy to carry. Missy felt suddenly very tired, ready-to-go-to-sleep tired.

She set the basket on the ground and took a second to compose herself. Shopping was really *hard*, she decided. Missy gave herself a second. But in that moment something happened, the world shifted on its axis. Twinkies. Twinkies happened. Right in front of her, at eye-level, she saw them, or rather, they saw her. She didn't even like Twinkies, but in that moment she knew. Flying crocodile. Versailles in the rear mirror. What Casey did. She suddenly had the strangest sense that this bunch of Twinkies was the answer, her escape. She plucked the packet from the scratched white shelf and scrunched the cellophane till it tensed like a balloon.

She closed her eyes and she was high above the earth, suspended there from a brightly colored air balloon and rising, Versailles too small to see, the ocean waves unmoving, areas of blue, patches of green, yellow, brown and then . . . Missy opened her eyes and started walking, reality left behind with her basket full of cold drinks, the condensation forming a small pool on the ground now they were out of the refrigerator. Next thing she knew she was through the automatic doors, a slow flash of glass catching the neon and the sun, a blast of warmer air from outside. The automatic doors and her act felt automatic, her shiny black SUV waiting for her in the parking lot across the way, the closing distance and the man calling her back from inside. The man was calling and she started running, closed the distance to her car and climbed inside. The thumping bass of whatever music played last.

She chased herself for miles afterwards, every car in her mirror, the pine trees growing darker to the right, taller somehow and the looming mountains behind. She thought of him. The young clerk who hadn't made eye contact. She saw him on the way in – a little heavy around the edges, his curly hair a murky blond. She thought of him in his glass box, as the tarmac passed underneath her car she worried he might get in trouble with his boss, their different-colored shirts, the pine trees growing taller somehow and the thought of cameras, grayscale security footage of her crazy act.

Twinkies. She laughed out loud at this, but didn't dare glance at the shiny cellophane packet on the passenger seat, the feeling in her belly blossoming with new guilt, the laughter turning to singing when Scout Rose came on the radio, her favorite song, a song she'd had on a loop in the weeks before she ran away, away from Versailles, across America, Twinkies on the passenger seat and the soft roar of the SUV, the muscles in her arms flexing under her skin as she turned the wheel, minor adjustments translating to giant swerves, the thrill of escape and the blue unknown.

If only they could see. If only she could share this moment. All she had to do was log back in. The glowing embers of her user data. Thirty days to reactivate. One photo.

#Twinkies ... No. This was her. Missy missing now. She tapped *cancel*. But there was one person. She had to make contact. This wasn't about likes or comments or follows. This was different. She opened her messenger app and spoke a text.

6

Flying crocodile. Like *bouncy ball*, it meant different things. When they were little kids flying crocodile meant, like, you wanna play? Flying crocodile? A proposition. Let's go play outside. Let's do this. Nowadays it was more if you saw something random on the internet or in real life then it was *so* flying crocodile. An acknowledgement. By doing something unexpected or risky, you could also *be* flying crocodile. Like when the two of them took their father's speedboat so they could go look for dolphins and got grounded for a month? They were being totally flying crocodile. A badge of honor. But like this, as a text message, with no context? This was new territory. Missy was taking flying crocodile in a new direction, and River wasn't sure how he felt about it. Could it be some kind of birthday greeting? He could work with that he guessed.

Where are you? he texted back – No reply. *Fine then*, River said out loud. He bounced a fluffy tennis ball off the wall and caught it again. Bounce, catch. Bounce, catch. Still no reply. Very unlike Missy. Their texts, like all their conversations, were always rapid-fire. This delay was unheard of. It wasn't a twin thing, but he was worried.

Usually it was Missy worrying about him. Always hassling

him about something, trying to introduce him to her friends, not that she was seeing all that much of them herself. Now that River thought about it, his sister had been wanting to hang out a lot more, trying to get them to do stuff together, play co-op video games, go out in the speedboat again, whatever. But it wasn't like when they were kids. He didn't need her to protect him like before, he could protect himself. He didn't need her friends. He had friends. Sure they were a motley bunch of freaks he'd met online under various guises – moms on baby forums, chainsaw enthusiasts, random NASA personnel, phone-sex workers, around-the-world yacht racers, cheating husbands, cheating wives, bored elite Navy SEALs, America's leading expert on big cats, his worst enemy at school, several errant algorithms – but what difference did it make? They liked him and he guessed he liked them. He didn't need her protection. He could take care of himself. He remembered. Then he shook his head, canceling the memory. Bounce, catch. Bounce, catch.

River ran a search on Missy's phone, trying to get a fix on her location. Nothing. That was strange. His sister was smart, but not tech smart. What was she up to? He didn't like it. It felt out of sync.

Was this flying crocodile some kind of birthday riddle? Bounce, catch. He took a second look at the tennis ball. Too fluffy. New balls, please. Bounce, catch, curveball across the room, so hard River might have dislocated his elbow. He watched as the tennis ball slammed right into the cage containing his mynah bird, Money. He didn't mean to do that.

'I didn't mean to do that,' called River.

'*Squawk!*' Money flapped his wings, his feathers brushing

violently past the metal bars. Money was a mimicking bird, but right now he was just pissed.

'Sorry, Money, I didn't mean it. Sorry, dude.' River turned his attention back to Jenny. Blinking cursor. Blink, blink, blink. Flying crocodile. He couldn't stop thinking about flying crocodile. It was like a trigger. It made him want to do stuff. Play outside, jump in the pool, take the speedboat. The open waves. But he wasn't a kid anymore, and besides, River wasn't doing outside at the moment. *Inside* was more his jam. Inside this room was where the magic happened. Well, maybe not in that way, and not in this room, per se. No, but inside his *head*. *Creativity*, that was his way out, his outlet. River was an *artist*, his medium anonymity, the internet his canvas, a glittering ocean of possibility. Yeah. Blinking cursor. Flying crocodile. River turned his smartphone face-down on the desk and clicked 'Play again' on the retarded horse video.

7

There was no one else around. The early evening sun made everything seem gold. Swoosh went the cars on the highway – swoosh, swoosh. Missy dived into the motel swimming pool and swam three lengths underwater. By the time she surfaced, the guilt had changed color, and these were new smells to her. She still felt badly, but as she pushed away from the side of the pool with her feet and swam some more, there were other feelings, mixed with memories, of playing with her brother in the water, their endless games, the water pushed beyond the edges of Versailles' outdoor pool and onto the grass, an unexpected gust of wind across. Flying crocodile. She still felt bad about the Twinkies, but swimming always brought her into the present, she found it relaxing. This time alone – there was no one else around just now, her phone inside her bag inside her room, locked away and almost forgotten – this time alone was precious.

Away from Versailles, her father, his cameras. The guilt changed color again. Her mother staring in the mirror, all the unworn clothes in her wardrobe. Staring in the mirror and no one looking back. She would call her mom tonight. If only to hear her low, slow voice, wishing her a happy birthday. She would call her after this, make sure she was okay. Missy turned underwater and pushed off the concrete wall. She was an excellent swimmer. They said she could turn professional if she wanted. Could have. A natural talent. It was in her blood. Synthea had always been a strong swimmer. Missy remembered as a kid. Watching her mom swim out into the ocean, so far you couldn't see her anymore, as though she'd swum over the edge of the world. Missy would play in the shallows, but always with an eye on the horizon, waiting for her mom to reappear.

She'd always wondered what her mother thought about on those long swims out into the ocean. Deep, private, adult thoughts. Secret. Strange. Important. Thoughts Missy herself had never had. Once out of sight she imagined her mother transforming, not just into a different person, but another creature altogether. Returning from the shallows to the beach, Missy would wrap herself in a towel, shivering on the warm sand, not with cold but foreboding. The thought that her mom might come back still somewhat changed, different in a way only Missy could see.

Years later, after Missy stopped sleeping with the light turned on, she asked her mother outright: *What do you think about, Mom, when you're swimming out there, with the white horses?* Synthea smiled and said it was when she dreamed up some of her best designs, out there. She said swimming into those depths was calming, but also frightening, and it was the fear that really cleared her head. The icy water below the surface: it made her feel alive. Missy remembered her mom's tone of voice when she said these words. The fear, her feeling alive, the cold water around her feet. Something about her tone made Missy want to avoid her eye. Almost like it was her mom talking about sex or something, it was weird. Her mom had *secrets*. And Missy didn't think she liked secrets. She never lied. But was keeping a secret the same as lying? She thought about the Twinkies in the footwell of her car.

Missy turned underwater. The coolness of this water under open air. She turned and pushed off again, propelling herself forward like an arrow. Swimming was dreaming. Swimming was freedom, flying away from Versailles, her father. Out of sight. Her millions of followers looking elsewhere, sparkle and fade. The dying embers of her user data. And then a roar above the surface, the sound of engines above the surface of the water, like something from a neighboring dream.

Missy came to the edge, slowly peeked over the edge of the swimming pool. It was the bikers, maybe not the same ones as before, but they had the same painted faces. They were pulling into the parking lot on their shiny motorcycles, one by one alongside each other, like in a movie. And they were staying at her motel, all these other people. Missy kicked her feet with excitement, bringing her head higher out of the water. She took a picture with her mind, saving it for later. She ducked back down with a small splash. Too shy, too shy to show herself just yet. Some time later maybe, when it got a little darker. Missy dived underwater and swam some more. Swimming was dreaming, swimming always brought her into the present, Twinkies in the footwell of her car, all but forgotten.

Meanwhile, inside her locked motel room, at the bottom of her soft, tan leather backpack with the cowboy tassels, her phone began to ring. It vibrated like a trapped insect, lit

44

up and demanded her attention, but her attention was elsewhere. And then the room was quiet again, a voicemail recording Missy may never hear, the notification telling her it was Synthea Baer who was missing her. Synthea, her beautiful mother, far, far away from here, roaming Versailles' corridors like a ghost. The gleaming palace. Versailles, Versailles. House of a thousand cameras. The house that Casey built. Loving father, CEO of the world's pre-eminent social network. The dying embers of her user data. Thirty days to reactivate. And what a story it would make.

8

She had to find her daughter. She wasn't in her bedroom. She wasn't with her brother. She wasn't in the kitchens looking for a birthday cake that did not exist. Early evening on her sixteenth birthday and nothing planned, no cache of gifts, no kiss on the cheek. Her princess. Synthea suddenly had a sense of great distance, horizontal distance. She could not remember the last time they had spoken. It could have been days, or even weeks. Time torn free of the mast, her ship lost, her soul was lost. But Missy wouldn't leave the house without saying something. She wouldn't leave the house without saying goodbye.

Perhaps she was outside. The garden, the swimming pool. That was it. She would find Missy outside. She was outside by the pool reading and drinking iced tea, or taking a stroll on the beach. That had to be it. She could see her walking along the shoreline, collecting shells for her room. She loved to decorate her bedroom with sea shells. She'd been doing it since she was a kid.

Synthea descended the marble staircase in her bare feet. The effects of the medication were wearing off. She could sense the world coming back into focus, the difference between a bad dream and a nightmare. It could have been weeks since she last spoke to her daughter. She didn't know, not for certain. The past was a great horizontal distance. The future vertical, the sheer unknown, a depth measured in fear. But back to the present. She had to find her daughter. The garden, the swimming pool, a walk along the beach perhaps, the glittering ocean. She turned the handle to the front door and pushed. It was heavier than usual, like there was someone on the other side preventing her from leaving the house. Like someone in a neighboring nightmare. She leaned with her shoulder against the door and it opened, the wind subsiding long enough for her to close it again, a strong north-westerly from the ocean, pushing hard over the uncut grass, the blue water of the swimming pool. Tall palm trees swayed in the background, the tallest palm trees Synthea had seen in her life. She was taking all this very carefully. Every step, every movement. A world of hidden traps, everything set to spring and cause pain.

The swimming pool. Something about the swimming pool, and it wasn't just the wind. Something happened here not so long ago. Something very bad, but it escaped her, like the memory of a dream. Missy was nowhere to be seen. It could have been weeks since they last spoke. She wouldn't leave without saying goodbye. She wouldn't do that, it wasn't like her daughter to just leave without saying goodbye. Synthea stood at the edge of the swimming pool, at the very edge with her toes over the water, so that she had to rock back on her heels to stop herself falling in. She stepped back onto the grass and began to walk deeper into the garden. She did not look back. She did not look back at Versailles. She walked across the grass, grass that needed cutting, but was gleaming gold just now in the twilight.

She could see Missy walking along the shoreline, collecting shells for her room. She loved to decorate her bedroom with sea shells. She'd been doing it since she was a kid. Or what if . . . A rush of anxiety that hurt her fingertips. What if Missy had gone swimming and . . . What if Missy had gone swimming in the ocean and she was still out there? What if . . . Synthea passed through the garden like a day spirit, a silver-gray suit jacket over a long, white nightdress. Bare feet over grass and then sand, between the tall palms and onto Versailles' private beach. No Missy. She looked up and down, up and down, again and again in case her eyes deceived her. White horses out there. But her daughter wasn't here. Missy was a strong swimmer, but this ocean . . . White horses. She was a strong swimmer, just like her mom, but— Synthea walked toward the water's edge and closed her eyes. They'd told her Missy could turn professional if she wanted. A natural talent. It was in her blood. Eyes still closed, Synthea removed her jacket and let it fall into the lapping waves.

She hadn't been in the water in what seemed like a long time. Something stopping her from going all the way in. *Because I miss* you, Casey had said. She loved to swim. She especially loved to swim early in the morning, when her husband was asleep. But there was something stopping her. Her boss telling her it was okay, she would be *welcome back, any time*. His mouth telling her to *stay in contact*. And then her husband's voice again: *Because they miss you. They tell me all the time how much they miss their mom. Come home to us, my love. I'll get you anything you need. A view of the ocean. A window so big it will feel like you're outside. We always talked about that. A house in nature, windows in place of walls. We always talked about that. I can make it happen. They tell me all the time how much they miss you. We can have the best of both worlds. What's all this money for if not to live our dream? Come home to me, my love. Because I miss you.*

Her hate for him a perfect thing, its edges softened to infinity by her forgetting why.

But she remembered this: sitting with her daughter inside a circle of candles. It was outside, the sky was dark and full of stars. She was warm after a long swim in the ocean, still in her swimming costume, and Missy finding her like this, in a circle of candles, the dark grass of the vast lawn all around them, Versailles across the way, floodlit and gleaming like a spaceship ready for take-off. She remembered. She and Missy inside the circle of candles, but it's a memory with no soundtrack: her daughter's mouth opening and closing but there are no words. Her Missy. She has her father's long limbs and delicate fingers but she is strong. So strong. She cannot hear the words coming from her daughter's mouth but she can see her anger. Anger from love. Missy looks like she is going to cry but she doesn't cry. Her Missy. She remembers. Leaving Missy in the circle of candles and making her way back to the mansion. No longer like a spaceship. Clouds moving across the stars like a heavy curtain, a cold wind on her naked shoulders. Then looking back at Missy and Missy blowing her a kiss, candles flickering in the breeze. But this isn't memory. This didn't happen. This is something new.

An adaptation. Missy's kiss was now, right there in her mind's eye. A cosmic gesture, daughter to mother. Like seeing her through water, like seeing her through blue water. And that's when she knew, standing in the shallows, that Missy was still alive somewhere. Not out there in the ocean. No, but she wasn't here either, anywhere near Versailles.

Missy missing on her sixteenth birthday. She wasn't out there, but there was something wrong. Synthea gathered the skirts of her nightdress and made her way quickly back to the house. Her husband would be home soon. Clouds moving across the blue sky like a heavy curtain.

9

Missy wanted to go ask them where they were going but they were set up around their motorcycles in the parking lot with their music playing, eating off a barbecue and drinking beer and whatnot, she didn't want to bother them because what was she going to say: Hi, I'm Missy Baer, daughter of infamous internet entrepreneur Casey Baer, and I ran away from home today!

Actually they'd called her over to join them but she was too shy she guessed so she came in from the balcony and switched on the TV in her room, first thing she did. It wasn't hooked up to cable so there weren't too many stations but that was okay. Missy settled on a reality show in which people literally had to survive on an island without any supply drops. She hadn't watched this show before and was shocked when two men got in a fist fight over a girl and drew blood on camera. It was streaming over one of their mouths and down his neck and he was hitting for the camera to get out of his face. So ugly, he had to be ashamed. It's what made Missy fall for the sword video. That wasn't reality at all, more like a dream of what the future might be like, her future, like being a superhero with no violence. The guy on the TV spit out what looked like a tooth and sure enough they cut to him being interviewed under studio lights with one of his front teeth missing. She didn't think they allowed that kind of stuff on TV.

She pressed the mute button on the remote and flopped back on the mattress, listened to the voices and music of the clown faces downstairs. She glanced at her bag with the cowboy tassels and thought about getting out her phone. She hadn't checked it since seeing the missed call from her mom. She knew she should call her back, but now that she had time, there was something stopping her . . . Synthea, so far away, still wandering Versailles' corridors in her bare feet. Those pills in the white boxes . . . Something about her mother's voice, so different from before. Missy realized now that she couldn't bear to hear it. Her own mother. The time they used to spend together. They could talk about anything . . . Her phone was switched to silent, no vibrations or notifications, but Missy could sense it in her bag, still as a dead insect, its sting still active.

Those voices outside. She wanted someone to talk to, tell people what was happening to her, where she was going, but she didn't know where that was just yet. Her millions of followers. If only they could see her. In her own motel room, car parked outside, the engine still warm from her long journey. If only they could see her now. One picture. One last picture. Her lying on the bed like this, hair still wet from swimming in the motel pool, sword by her side. Status update. Break the internet. #MissyMissingNow. Snap. Filter. All she had to do was log back in. The glowing embers of her user data. Her millions of followers looking elsewhere.

She reached for her bag. Why did she do this? Because

sharing made it feel more real, this journey north. Her escape from Versailles.

For years it was all she knew. Her home, Versailles. The corridors, the kitchens, her room, River's room, her mother's studio, the gardens and the beach. For a long time she knew nothing of the outside world besides the distant sounds of the city floating in over the fences bordering the estate. Sirens. People yelling. A gunshot now and then (one time she remembers some kids launching a bunch of fireworks at the mansion from behind the fence. Then the sirens and heli-copters and Casey taking them into the den like it was war). A soundtrack to a life she and her brother only got to see on television, or on the internet. And when they finally were allowed to go to school, like, with other kids, it was under the kind of security usually reserved for the First Family. Versailles (some journalists had actually started calling it *The Other White House*) was Missy's life for as long as she could remember and now that she was free? She didn't know what to do with all the new information. Sharing would make it feel more . . . One last picture. All those millions of followers and she hadn't posted anything in weeks . . . All those millions and she could count her real friends on one hand. The ones in between, the kids she'd met at school? They only talked to her because of her second name. Because of who her parents were. And yet . . .

Missy stared at her bag, knowing the phone was in there, waiting for her. She reached inside and the phone felt cold, but still familiar. She felt its beveled edges, the uncanny velvet of the unbreakable glass, her mother's design, dreamed up on one of her long swims out into the ocean, transforming, transformed, yet still familiar. She felt the beveled edges of this thing inside her bag. She should call her mom, let her know she was okay. But then someone calling her name from outside. At least she thought it was her name. Missy bounced herself off the bed, opened the door and looked out over the parking lot at all the bikers gathered there.

Not her name, but one similar. 'Cassie!'

She tried to make out Cassie, but there were too many people, all the talking and laughing and Missy couldn't take it anymore. She had to tell someone. All of them. She leaned over the balcony and shouted, 'Hey! It's my birthday!'

It played like a movie. The crowd in the parking lot whooped and cheered. One of the women, totally naked except for a pair of leg warmers and panties, got to her feet and held up a red plastic cup for Missy. 'Come on down here, girl, I got something for you.'

Despite her clown face, the lady looked friendly so Missy gingerly made her way along the balcony and down the stairs, her phone forgotten.

The woman threw her arms around Missy and handed her the drink, which was a deep pink color. Whatever it was it tasted *strong* and Missy told herself to take this slow. But these people were relaxed, they carried on laughing and drinking and Missy got to talking with the naked lady.

'So, how old are you, girl?'

'Nineteen,' Missy says.

'Nineteen, well. You don't look nineteen, but I was always young for my age, I know how that is. Come here, sit down.'

'Can I guess how old you are?' Missy says.

'Sure, why not.'

'Twenty . . . three?' The lady laughed a big laugh and had

to grab hold of Missy's arm to stop herself falling backwards with her camping chair. 'What's wrong?' Missy said, 'You're really pretty!'

'Oh, my goodness, you're so sweet, but no. I'm not gonna tell you how old I am, but I guess I still got great tits, so . . . Cass by the way, my name's Cass.'

'Hi, Cass.' Missy smiled and took another sip of the pink liquid. She felt a lovely warm rush of blood to her throat and mouth and cheeks and realized she was having the time of her life. 'So where're you guys headed?'

'It's a gathering,' Cass said. 'There'll be music but that's only part of it. We all know each other. All the people you seen today on the road? They're my brothers and sisters. We're all connected. All of us. Why? You wanna come with us, Missy?'

Missy looked up and saw the moon. 'I'd love to but I got this thing I got to do first.'

'Mystery girl. You're cute. Seriously, how old are you?'

'Sixteen.'

'More like it. What you doing out here all on your own, little Missy?'

'I'm not alone, I'm here with you.'

'You know what? I don't wanna pry. I don't do that. But you seem like a sweet kid and this world is full of – how do I say this?'

'Men.'

'Right, men.'

'I know men,' said Missy.

'You do?' The naked lady laughed again but not for long and she took Missy's hand in hers and pulled her close. 'Listen to me, Missy. Listen. Pretty girl like you? Long legs, pale skin. *I* know men.' She glanced sideways. 'And I don't want you getting hurt.'

'I can take care of myself,' Missy said. She licked the sugary pink drink from her lips and looked Cass right in the eye.

'You're right,' Cass said, 'I don't know you. You're young is all, I seen things. Check this out.' Cass dipped her right shoulder to reveal a tattoo. 'Can you see it?'

'Not really.'

Cass twisted in her seat so Missy could take a good look. The tattoo was of a wolf howling at the stars. The stars went all the way up her neck, getting smaller and smaller.

'I think it's beautiful,' Missy said. She really thought so. She'd seen tattoos before, but this one was special. She couldn't think why, but she had tears in her eyes, her heart ready to burst.

'You really like it?' Cass said.

'I do, I do,' Missy said.

'You got any tattoos?'

'No, but I always wanted one. I saw one once on this kid's profile? She's a friend of mine – well, not really a friend she just follows me online – but she had this picture of her arm, it had these tattoos all the way up, right over her shoulder and up her neck like you have, all different symbols with different meanings, but they kind of linked up and told a story, *her* story, and I saw it and I realized . . . I don't really have that – a story, of my own. So that's why I'm here, out under the stars with you guys, that's why . . .' She was saying too much. She had to stop doing this. *Secrets.* She thought about the sword lying on her bed in the motel room. No one knew about the sword but her. Leticia saw the package, but never saw what was inside.

'I do know what you mean and you should do it, Missy, you should just do it,' Cass said.

'I can't. I mean, I want to, but I can't.'

'Why not?'

'My dad wouldn't let me,' Missy said. 'He says if I ever get a tattoo he'll never talk to me again.'

'He doesn't mean that.'

'Trust me, my dad means everything he says. He's—'

'I'm sure he's just protective.'

'Fuck him,' Missy said. It didn't feel right, coming out of her mouth, like, she wasn't the cursing type. But right now she meant it. She was glad she didn't have to see him again. Glad to be gone. Out of that house, all those cameras. Out here under the stars. I mean, fuck *him*, right? He didn't rule her life, not ever. She was out of reach for now. Missy emptied her cup and stared for a second at the white circle at the bottom. Her mother, her mother all alone somewhere. Missy felt the alcohol all through her body and it made her feel alive. She was here and nowhere else. The millions looking elsewhere and she didn't care just now. And then she caught the eye of a boy sitting on the other side of the group. He wasn't wearing any face paint but his expression was difficult to read. She'd seen that look before from men and she didn't like it. He broke eye contact briefly and said something to the older guy sitting next to him. Missy had to check an impulse to call the kid out. It wasn't her, but she hated that, the control men thought they had. She closed her eyes and moved to the music. When she opened them again the kid was on his feet, acting out a part in a movie. The group laughed. She changed her mind. This wasn't a bad guy. Matter of fact, he was kind of cute.

'You sure you don't wanna come with us, Missy?' Cass said, tweaking her left nipple.

'I want to, but . . .'

'You running from someone, girl? You can trust me. I'm a good person.'

Missy wanted to tell Cass the whole story, the video, the sword, the messages, but something told her no. 'I want to come, I so want to come,' Missy said, 'but I can't just now. I'm sorry. I really like you guys.'

'Don't be sorry, girl, I just want you to be happy.'

'But we only just met,' Missy said. 'Why are you being so nice to me?'

'Sure, we only just met but that don't mean a person can't have their intuition about another human being, and I happen to think you got a magic about you, Missy, like you're gonna do something special with your life, you know? And it's gonna make a beautiful story. Not like me. You don't ever want to be like me. Promise me that. Promise me, Missy. Till I met these guys I was on this dark road to nowhere, and then I found these people and they showed me how to love again, myself, each other. I go to sleep at night. I have my eyes open when the sun is out. You? You're different to begin with. You've got your whole life spread out in front you like the open ocean, wider than a dream, you understand what I'm telling you, Missy? I'm sorry, I know I'm drunk, I should just stop talking now.'

'No, don't stop,' Missy said. 'I like it when you talk, it makes me... I don't have a sister at home. I have a brother. I love my brother but he doesn't say too much these days. He stays in his room most of the time. He's, like, always on the internet.'

'That's the world we live in, Missy. Does your brother know you're doing this?'

'Doing what?'

'Running away from home.'

Missy's heart skipped a beat. 'No, he doesn't,' Missy said. 'Nobody knows except you and—'

'And who?'

'That's what I want to find out. Yeah. But my brother, he used to be my best friend. We're twins but he's still my little brother, even now it's like that but he wouldn't admit it. We used to . . . Wait, is this boring, am I being really boring right now? I tell stupid stories sometimes, my friends used to tell me I talk too much; you can tell me to stop talking whenever you want! I don't mind, I'm just so happy all of a sudden, being here with you, you seem like such a nice lady, and I love your tattoo and you and your friends all seem so cool, and when I saw you earlier? I was swimming in the pool and I saw you turn up on your bikes and I just knew I had to say hey, I just knew and . . . oh, no I'm talking way too much, just tell me to shut up, I just get so excited when I meet new people—'

'Missy, Missy, Missy!' Cass said, taking hold of Missy's shoulder and giving it a little shake. 'I like to listen to you. Tell me about you and your brother.' Cass leaned back again.

'Okay, so me and my brother used to play the best games. I don't mean video games I mean like *real* games, around the house, outside in the garden. One time. One time we stole my dad's speedboat!'

'You did?' Cass said.

'Yeah we took it way, way out into the ocean. My brother loves dolphins so I said to him let's go look for dolphins, and that's what we did, we took the speedboat way out, switched off the motor and just waited. I remember the sky being so blue. Like in a cartoon but it was us there. We talked about a bunch of stuff, everything, we talked like we never did before, like two best friends, not brother and sister. He told me secrets and I told him some of my secrets, things I've never said to anybody, not online, my friends, not even my mom.'

'What's your brother's name?' Cass said.

'River,' Missy said. 'My brother's name is River.' Missy felt the sting in her nose like she was going to cry but she didn't cry. 'River's cool, don't get me wrong, he's actually really smart, he could do anything, but when it comes to our dad it's like . . . it's like my brother is a superhero but he doesn't know his superpower yet, and until he figures it out, he'll never defeat the bad guy.'

'So how about you, Missy, you know your superpower?'

'Sure! But it's a secret!' Missy laughed again and Cass laughed with her. 'No, I don't have a superpower. I'm not talented like the people in my family, I'm just . . .'

Something about Cass. She was different from the others. All the people at school, her friends, it was like – they all chose *her*. She was always popular with the other kids but here was somebody. Missy choosing this time. 'It's like we're friends,' she said out loud.

'Totally,' said Cass.

'It's like I've known you,' Missy said, and she finished her sentence with a toast of her empty plastic cup.

10

River had spent his whole birthday online as Jenny. He knew there was something kind of wrong about that. He just didn't know what it was.

Jenny was fun to be. Jenny was kind, Jenny was gentle. Jenny was thoughtful, Jenny was a good mother. Jenny made milk choc chip cookies, Jenny wore a checkered apron around the house looking hot. Yeah, Jenny was pretty, Jenny was fine, and Jenny liked online porn quite a bit. Jenny. Jenny was strong, Jenny was weak. Jenny was a happy person, Jenny was real angry inside. Jenny had bad thoughts sometimes about her husband. Ugly thoughts. She was full of resentment, a shadow of her former self. Moving between rooms like a vengeful ghost. Some days she took a pair of scissors to her husband's clothes. Little cuts, little cuts, nothing you would notice unless you were to look real close. Jenny reminded him of someone, he couldn't think of who just now. Being Jenny made River feel . . . being Jenny made him feel . . . like a better person, like he was becoming a whole person, a whole other, someone other than himself. Being these people: it was running over inflatables on the surface of a swimming pool and not falling in, reaching the other side and rolling on the grass, a long, soft fall, all hands and the loss of perspective. He could almost say it made him happy.

But it was getting late, or early, whatever, he needed some sleep to get him by . . . One more time couldn't hurt. One more run as Jenny and he'd let her go, or was it the other way round? He was never quite sure. And what better way to say goodnight than with some good old-fashioned, anonymous IM filth? River pulled his swim cap on for this one.

jenny78
What's your name, honey?

unknown_user
No names

jenny78
No names. So what do you want?

unknown_user
What don't I want. I want video

jenny78
No video, cowboy, just words

unknown_user
Measurements

jenny78
34B-25-34

unknown_user
Tell me what you're wearing. I want brands, fine details

jenny78
Embraceable Cool Nights Delicate Chemise from Soma

unknown_user

Tell me more

jenny78

It's ultra-feminine and ultra-comfortable, with a satin charmeuse front strap, pleated neckline, and delicate ivory lace embellishment

unknown_user

Are you mocking me?

jenny78

Never

unknown_user

Is that everything?

jenny78

Vanishing Edge Microfiber panties, also from Soma. The pattern is a stylized floral print in the pastel spectrum. The panties themselves are lightweight, breathable and comfortable all day long

unknown_user

Take off the panties, lay them across the keys, and type the following through the fabric: You know me so well

jenny78

You know me so well

unknown_user

Again

jenny78

You know me so well

unknown_user

How well do I know you?

jenny78

You know me so well

unknown_user

That's good. One more time

jenny78

You know me so well

unknown_user

You can put your panties back on now

jenny78

Thank you. Is that it?

unknown_user

Your turn

jenny78

What a gentleman. Alright. What are you wearing?

unknown_user

Jeans and mask

jenny78

What kind of mask are you wearing?

unknown_user

Lion mask

jenny78

*Lion mask. You feel like a lion inside, unknown_user?
You feel strong?*

unknown_user

I guess I feel like a lion, yeah

jenny78

What is it that makes you feel that way?

unknown_user

Wearing the mask. Wearing the mask makes me feel like a lion

jenny78

You like to play dress up, unknown_user?

unknown_user

Too much talking. Switch on your camera

jenny78

I said no video

unknown_user

I want to smell your skin. Is Jenny your real name?

jenny78

You said no names

unknown_user

That was before

jenny78

Jenny's my real name. Now you

unknown_user

Lions don't have names

jenny78

They do if they live in captivity

unknown_user

I roam free. Matter of fact, I could come to your house

jenny78

You'd like that, wouldn't you?

unknown_user

I know where you live

jenny78

Lol

unknown_user

You think I don't know?

jenny78

I don't think

unknown_user

I know where you live, River Baer

jenny78

Who the fuck are you?

unknown_user

The lion king

jenny78

Fuck you

unknown_user

I look forward to finally meeting your sister. We've been watching Missy for a long time. We think she's ready to join us now, River. Girls only, I'm afraid

jenny78

I know where you live, too, motherfucker. I'm looking at your IP right now

unknown_user

You're going to have to do better than that, River. We were living here before you were born

jenny78

Living where?

unknown_user

On the internet, River. You don't find us. We find you. And by the way. You so much as think about announcing Missy's disappearance on the social networks and we'll do more than delete her profile. No reactivation period. Same goes for the cops

jenny78

So there's more than one of you

unknown_user

We're a family, River

jenny78

Fuck the police, I'm coming after you myself

unknown_user

That's the spirit, River Baer, that's the spirit

The moment unknown_user logged out of the conversation, River took his laptop and threw it hard as he could at the concrete floor. This wasn't anger, this was protocol. If he'd been hacked he needed to start again. He got hold of his skateboard and whaled on the laptop some more till the outer casing came apart completely. After that, he got his shiny claw hammer and went at the motherboard till it was in little pieces, some of them flying so far across the room he was finding them in his bed and everywhere else in the days after. Okay, there was some anger there too. He took his drill and drilled into the SSD. Finally, he took a blow torch and incinerated the NVRAM until it was a bubbling globule of brown and black plastic.

When River had caught his breath, he did the same thing with every other computer he owned, all except the brand-new, air-gapped laptop he kept under his bed for just such an occasion. But what occasion was this? Had his sister been *kidnapped*? River looked at the hammer in his hand, gently put it to one side. Then he got the brushed-steel suitcase out from under his bed, removed the air-gapped laptop, hooked it up to his monitors, mouse and external keyboard, and got to work.

11

The monitor lizard makes his way along another empty corridor. His teeth are bared but he is not angry. His yellow eyes look mean but he is not mean, he is simply a monitor lizard who has not eaten in several days. Just then he passes a white door. As with the majority of Versailles' one hundred rooms, the door is locked. To look inside would be to know a little more about our host. For who is Casey Baer if not a sum of his endeavors?

Room 5 contains a different kind of monitor. Three custom-built LCD screens occupying every inch of three adjacent walls. The resolution of these panels is so high as to give the images a liquid, hyper-real quality. The warmth generated by the technology in this room gives it an almost tropical feeling, like visiting the reptile house at the zoo. But the smell is of new computers, of brand new electronic equipment.

Three walls, three pictures, three Baers. Look left and you see Synthea as she is at this very moment, naked in her office, smoking a filterless cigarette at the window and staring out at her ocean. The room is in darkness, but the moon outside, and the hidden camera's ability to make use of all available ambient light, render the image relatively clear.

Look right and you see River. His face lit up white-blue by his computer screen. He looks tired. He has his mother's eyes. He looks more like his mother, but as he grows older, by his late twenties, he will come to resemble his father in ways he finds hard to define. His face disappears. He has shut down his computer. The intelligent camera switches to night vision and tracks River as he crosses his room on a skateboard.

Look straight ahead. Look straight ahead and the image quality is not so good. This is a different kind of picture. This is not Versailles, but a security feed from a parking lot outside a motel. Motorcycles. There is no one in the frame just now, but look closely and you see evidence that people were here, and not so long ago. Plastic cups, paper plates stained with the grease of cheap barbecued meat, an empty bottle of vodka. People were here and they were drinking and having fun.

While Casey has made certain he might view these images over live stream on any one of his multiple devices, this room serves a different purpose. This is not surveillance. This is the most private of cinemas, a place where the master of the house can spend time and reflect. He considers it to be sacred ground, his chapel, his shrine to family and what that means to him.

12

Twinkies. She laughed herself awake, and then the swoosh, swoosh of cars on the northbound highway. The sword lying in the bed next to her made it real again. Missy smiled and turned on her back, the ceiling unfamiliar. The walls, the light coming in through the open curtains, the sword lying next to her in the bed. This was not a dream. She was really here, far from Versailles. No cameras to see this now. This time alone was precious.

And this was her taking a hot shower in a motel, her body lit from above by the cold light in the bathroom, but it was her light, her light and the pleasure of the water on her head and arms, her arms, this time alone, this time alone was precious, no cameras to see this now, this time alone was precious but she was missing now, missing Missy now, she never came back, never came back last night, never came back on her birthday no less and now they'd come looking in their cop cars and their have you seen this girl, have you seen this girl, she ran away, far away from her family, from Versailles, but right now this was her taking a hot shower in a motel, and it was still morning, still early morning light, her light and the pleasure of the water on her body, her body, her blood, her heart, her future, the sword in the bed was who she was now, the sword in the bed was who she was and there was no turning back, her arms, her arms, this time alone was who she was now, sixteen candles, an arc of quicksilver, her light, her light, and the pleasure of the water, of swimming, of swimming upright, far from the ocean, across America to another ocean, this was like slow motion, the sword passing close by her left cheek, the sword on the bed was who she was, the cold light on her body but it was hers, this body was hers and the boy at school, the boy at school who told her she was beautiful.

The parking lot looked empty now that the clowns were gone. She rotated her left arm and saw Cass's number written there. It had faded in the shower but you could still make out the digits. There. The impulse to type them in her phone, add the number to her contacts, try find Cass on the network, her profile, pictures, her likes. No need. She just had to remember. Hold the number in her mind. Remember her face, her eyes. The things they talked about.

Missy climbed back in her shiny black SUV and closed the door behind. *Thunk*. The sound of engineered perfection. She breathed the newness deep. Her own car, ready to convey her to the next adventure. She touched the place on her forehead where Nora had given her a kiss and then turned the key in the ignition, the powerful engine vibrating through her bones. It made her nose itch. She turned the wheel, the tires crunching stray rocks on their way round, the stillness of the blue swimming pool outside her window. *Swoosh* another car goes by, *swoosh-swoosh*. And now – a gap in the traffic, her chance to get back on the highway, the long road north.

13

When Leticia went to the supermarket she had a system. It didn't have to take so long. She had a list of everything she needed, and she knew the layout of the aisles by heart. Today the cart had a bad wheel and she was having trouble keeping it from knocking into all the items on the shelves. So many items to choose from. It still made her upset inside sometimes. But her life was more simple now. She could do what she wanted. No more rich people craziness like before. Just Leticia. She had her apartment, her stupid car. It was a crummy apartment, but better than her room at Versailles. As a matter of fact, it had a bigger bathroom. Synthea Baer let her take a couple chairs and a table, she was a good woman. And a good mother to her children. Two great kids. Leticia loved them like they were her own. She left the Philippines as a young woman and found work at Versailles almost right away.

It brought tears to her eyes to think that she might never see Missy again. After she got fired, she never got a chance to say goodbye to her Missy. It all happened so fast. Missy was such a wonderful girl, so kind, thoughtful, honest. Even as a child she had shown how she could feel for others. Empathize. Very unusual for a young child, and one with all she'd ever wanted in the world. But Missy was more interested in playing outside, exploring the gardens outside, it was true! Feeding the ducks in the lake, being in the open air, hiding behind trees, climbing, running, jumping, stealing speedboats with her brother, oh my God! Yes, but she was always so protective of her River. Leticia remembered, when they were little kids, Missy always holding her brother's hand, leading him into trouble but taking all the blame when they got caught. Because Missy was the favorite with their father. That was the sad thing. Missy was always the favorite with Mr Casey.

River was a good boy, but always in his room nowadays, like a lonely prince in his castle. Leticia remembered when he was just a cub, River following her everywhere, asking her questions. This was when he was maybe four years old, such a cute kid. So many questions. But when Leticia answered wrong, River set her straight! You better believe he knew all the answers already! He just wanted to hear it from an adult so it was hard sometimes because she didn't have all the answers, of course not, but he was a good boy. Not mean, not like his father at all. Leticia knew River would make a wonderful young man some day.

Those poor kids. Sure, they had everything they wanted, all the toys and clothes and candy, but they were never allowed outside the fence. Their whole childhood was Versailles. The mansion, the gardens, the beach. It was only these last years they were allowed to go to school. Right up until sixth grade, their whole childhood, they were at home, home-schooled, it was only because their mother *insisted*. She got so mad with Casey that eventually they were allowed to go. Those poor kids. Missy had done okay, made some friends. River not so much, but Missy sure. Missy would have friends over sometimes, but Leticia could tell. Some of those kids: they only came to visit because they'd heard about the mansion, the famous Baer family, read stuff online about what happened behind those closed doors and they wanted to see for themselves. When all Missy wanted to do was play, watch movies, go swimming in the ocean, and you could see her friends were disappointed, because all they wanted was to see inside Versailles, the biggest private home in America, share pictures to their networks. Leticia remembered. The kids' faces when they found out they had to leave their smartphones at the door. Yes, Mr Casey ran a tight ship. And sometimes Versailles really felt like a ship. All the strange sounds at night. Vibrating walls. Like somewhere deep inside there was a great engine, roaring, dreadful, and dripping with black oil.

Leticia remembered. Missy and River's thirteenth birthday. Handing out non-disclosure agreements to everyone along with their party crowns and slices of cake. Nobody ever saw anything of course. One hundred rooms and only Casey had a master key. Nobody knew what really happened at Versailles, but there were always rumors. A secret dungeon, equal in size to Versailles itself but below ground, its purpose unknown. A fire-breathing dragon (and dragons don't even exist!). Mountain ranges of discarded toys. Time machines. Reanimated celebrities living on kitchen scraps. An aquarium of great white sharks. Lions, tigers and bears. Magic mirrors. Stupid stuff. But people's imaginations went crazy because Casey knew how to keep a secret. As CEO of the world's pre-eminent social network, he had dedicated his life to connecting the world, but the world knew nothing of him.

Leticia herself spoke to him only once or twice, she had spent most of her time at Versailles with the two children and their mother. But she did not like this man. The way he talked to his wife and the way he didn't talk to his kids. This was a bad man, this Casey Baer. Too tall. Like someone you find out later is a robot.

She looked in her trolley and realized she had too much stuff in there, she didn't know how it happened. She had to tell herself: life was simple now. Her small apartment, not so much stuff. Only her teddy bears! Yes. She loved her little bears (some of them were big). And she had a lot of them, a lot of teddy bears. They kept her company, mostly at night. They kept away her nightmares. Leticia had terrible nightmares, and every time she had a nightmare, she would buy a new teddy bear from the store, and for a while it would be good, her dreams were of better times, but then they would start again and – that's right – another teddy bear for her team! She had so many now. But who cares, right? They were like her welcome party when she came in the room! Hi, teddy bears! So friendly, so cuddly, so nice. When she moved to the apartment, she threw some things out. Old clothes. New start. But not her bears. No way, she could never throw them out because then, well, what would happen? Leticia didn't want to find out. She wanted only good dreams.

Her good dreams were of her home country, the Philippines. The green mountains, her parents' farm. These dreams did not have any story, they were about the landscape of her childhood, Laguna Province in the Philippines. She had come to America to make enough money for her family who were very poor. She had heard being a maid in the United States was a difficult job, she knew all the news about Filipina maids. Suicide, abuse, no paycheck. She was scared about coming to America because they told her it was hard. But she went, and at first it seemed she was lucky in a way. She landed a job at Versailles and most of the money she made she sent home to her family. The money wasn't great, but she could get by okay. She'd loved those kids like they were her own.

Leticia's nightmares were about Versailles. The corridors, the doors, the rooms. Those cameras everywhere. The rumors on the internet about what went on in Versailles were one thing, but the stories among the staff were worse. They too had signed the non-disclosure agreements, but that didn't stop them talking among themselves. Leticia knew deep inside that the dreams would never go away, no matter how many teddy bears she brought home from the store. Because, somehow, Leticia believed the stories might be true. In her nightmares, Leticia always had a key, a master key for all the rooms in Versailles, and every nightmare was a different room, opening another door and the horror inside.

Leticia loved the movies because they were another kind of dreaming. At the movie theater she could pretend she was a whole other person dreaming. She loved to watch the actors and actresses on screen, saying things to each other and getting into trouble! She loved all kinds of movies, even horror movies, it didn't matter what they were about or who was in them. And when she left the theater or the credits rolled on her TV, she wanted the dream to continue.

That's why, every chance she got, Leticia liked to research movie stars (okay, all the celebrities) on the internet. All her spare time on the internet, searching, reading, chatting, posting. She knew God would not be happy at all with her for spending so much time on celebrities, but she couldn't help it! Once she started, she couldn't stop. She had one of River's old laptops he was going to throw out anyway but it still worked just great. And she was good at her research, really good at it. Want to know where a celebrity is right now? Ask Leticia. Want to know their favorite food, where their kids go to school, allergies, rap sheets, how many cats, how many teeth, first love, last seen with? Ask Leticia. She kept folders on the computer. On each celebrity she researched. All the things she found out, she put in the folders. Web archives, pictures, video, sound files. She was very proud of her collection, but at the same time she was ashamed. She never wanted anyone to see her folders, they wouldn't understand. There was one time. Her first boyfriend in America. Romeo. He worked in the kitchens at Versailles. He saw her folders and he got real angry. She had to sleep at the hospital that night.

Leticia watched her items get checked. The checkout lady was handing her the smaller items. That was nice of her. She appreciated it when people were kind. She was not used to it. Her phone, her phone was vibrating in her pocket. She couldn't answer it just now because she had to pay for her items. She handed over the money and the checkout lady wished her a nice day and she wished her a nice day also.

It was only when Leticia got back home that she remembered the vibrating phone. She checked her voicemail. It was Synthea, very upset, almost crying. Something about Missy not coming home last night. On her birthday. The message was distorted, but Leticia knew, she knew right then that this was bad, Missy not coming home on her birthday, but not as bad as Mrs Synthea not picking up the phone. Missy was young but she was strong. Leticia was sure she would make contact soon. But Mrs Synthea not picking up gave her a sick feeling in her stomach. Because Leticia loved this woman.

Synthea Baer. She had known this woman for many years. Synthea taught Leticia how to speak English when she first arrived in this country. She was patient, generous, calm, always smiling. *You ever need anything*, she would say, *you come to me*. Like a mother sometimes, but also like a sister. She'd even paid for Leticia to fly home and see her family once in a while. Synthea had always been so kind to her, and in exchange Leticia had taken care of her children like they were her own, so that their mother could continue with her work, designing the technology in everybody's hands, in everybody's homes: their phones, their cars, the watches on their wrists. She had so much love for this woman, so much admiration. And when all that ended, when Synthea was forced to leave behind her precious work and became this ghost that walked Versailles' corridors, Leticia did her best to make sure the kids were okay, that they understood what happened, that their mother was only human. Underneath those smart clothes and behind all her clever words and kindness, she was a human being. *And like all of God's creatures*, Leticia would say, *we have our limits*.

Those pills with no name. Those evil pills in the white packaging. If only she could return to Versailles and talk to her friend one last time, remind her of the life she had before. Wash her hair, some make-up, dress her in some of the gorgeous clothes in her wardrobe and take her out in the city, somewhere high up, have a drink and talk about what was and what could be again, the lights spread out below them like those thingies in the ocean. What did they call it? *Bioluminescence*. Mrs Synthea had always loved the ocean. The ocean was somewhere she could be free.

She called Mrs Synthea once more but it went straight to voicemail. She said a prayer to God for Missy, and the prayer was, *Please bring Missy home because she is a good girl and we love her, such a sweet, kind girl, so please bring her home safe*. And then Leticia gave a hug to her biggest teddy who was so big he really needed his own room.

14

The crash happened so fast it left reality behind. Opposite lane she saw the vehicle swerve then flip – a flash of surface and sunlight – roll twice and spin a quarter turn on its roof. Almost immediately Missy had to apply the brakes as cars in her lane slowed right down to take it all in. There were flames, a column of black smoke. It played like a movie in her mirror. Special effects. Then the explosion, louder than expected. It shook the bright August day out of alignment.

In the minutes after, Missy realized she didn't feel a thing. #CarCrash. She turned off the music on her stereo and played back the crash in her mind, frame by frame. Nothing. She'd read about this on the internet. This exact thing. Lack of empathy. Psychopathy. One out of every hundred. The article even used the example of a car accident. How the psychopath didn't process these kinds of events like the rest of us. First the Twinkies, now this. Could she really be a psycho? Then why'd she feel so sad when Leticia lost her job at Versailles? All she'd thought about that day was Leticia, all on her own somewhere with the teddy bears. Missy felt a tear roll down her cheek. Yay, not a psychopath! Music!

Without warning the man's voice came through her smartphone, telling her to take the next exit. It occurred to

Missy that maybe these directions weren't pre-recorded at all, that this was someone speaking to her in real time through some kind of voice changer. She exited the highway and the instructions became more frequent, turn by turn. She drove slowly along a wide road flanked by trailer homes. Some were big, some small, she saw clothes out on the line, American flags hanging heavy, but no people, no movement. This was a trailer park.

The voice again: *You have reached waypoint alpha, Missy. Look for Silas.*

Say what? Missy brought the SUV to a standstill and turned the key in the ignition, bringing her music to an end. She looked at her watch. Midday in the middle of nowhere. She checked her make-up in the mirror and saw that she looked like her mother, like seeing her through water, diving from the highest of three platforms and seeing her through blue water, they could talk about anything but now she was swimming, away from her mother towards the fall, no one to see this now, she always told her everything before, and the boy at school, sword on the back seat of her brand new car, the blackness of the PX8 and the boy at school, the boy at school who told her she was beautiful.

She checked her make-up in the mirror and saw herself, the sun across her face was her now, an arc of quicksilver, her light, her future, far from the ocean, sword on the back seat, this was who she was, across America to another ocean, late afternoon and she was somewhere. She opened the door to her car and breathed swamp air. She was far from home, no one to protect her, no one to protect, and out of nowhere a young kid approaching like he just took off his invisibility cloak.

They stood looking at each other. The kid wasn't a day over seven. He had a white bunny rabbit under one arm.

'What's the matter?' Missy said. 'Never seen a princess before?'

'You ain't no princess,' said the boy, spitting on the yellow grass, one hand on his hip.

'Who says I ain't?' Missy said, flicking her long blonde hair.

The kid almost smiled, then said, 'Cus I know a dirty-ass skank when I sees one.'

'That's rude,' Missy said. 'Why would you want to talk to me that way? We only just met. Didn't your parents teach you any manners?'

The kid did this thing where he wiped his face hard with the palm of his hand and stamped his foot like he was mad about something. Then he shrugged. The rabbit closed its red eyes and moved its triangle nose up and down, up and down.

'Cute bunny,' Missy said.

'He likes you,' the kid said, 'and he likes apples. Sliced apples, he likes them pretty good.'

Missy changed tack. 'I'm looking for someone named Silas. You know him?'

'Yeah, I know Silas.'

'Great, could you show me where he is? I'd like to meet him.'

'He inside.'

'Inside?'

'Inside my house. Silas my father 'n' shit.'

'Okay.'

'My rabbit'll sniff you if you let him,' the boy said.

'Good to know,' said Missy. 'What's your name, by the way?'

'I ain't got a name.'

'Well that can't be true. Everybody has a name.'

The kid looked bored.

'Well, mine's Missy.'

'That's a stupid name.'

'I happen to like it,' Missy said, which was the truth.

She followed the kid as he showed off, kicking trash cans and balancing the rabbit on his head. He was quite good at it actually, and the rabbit didn't seem to mind too much. They stopped in front of one of the bigger trailers at the back of the park and the boy with no name banged his fist twice. Right away Missy saw the insignia on the door: a white star against black. There was movement inside, a shift in dark color behind the plastic window. The door opened but no one looked out. It stood ajar, no light in the gap. The kid with no name gestured for Missy to go on inside. Whoever Silas was he was expecting her.

15

The chat with unknown_user had River so freaked he lost his hold on the climbing wall and fell backwards onto the blue gym mattress. He hadn't slept much last night but his dream was of lions. Tiny lions, giant lions, tiny lions, giant lions, all marching with computer-generated uniformity toward and through him across an infinite savannah of purple grass. River stared up at the fake, multi-colored rocks of his beloved bedroom climbing wall. He was an excellent climber (had never seen a rock face). He totally never fell usually. River bounced himself to his feet and jogged over to the heavy leather punch bag, delivering a furious volley of punches. Left-right-left-left-right. River was the kind of monk to stay in shape. He had his father's frame: lean, and broad across the shoulders. Left-right-left-left-right. He felt the sweat run down behind his ears. It was this damn bear costume. Always making him run hot. Left-right-left-left-right.

He'd always taken great pride in his anonymity online, taken every precaution to remain as close to invisible as possible: he was a lone wolf, he'd never used his real name, always used anonymous currency, proxies, VPNs ... His system of tunnels beneath the surface web was second to none. And yet . . . this unknown_user character had found a way in.

Profiling . . . That's how they got you: the way you talked, your political views, typos . . . Basically any of your idiosyncrasies would eventually give you away. In other words, unless you were an actual robot, you could never be truly anonymous. River had always thought differently. River was a shape-shifter, he'd assumed countless identities online, and no one had ever made the connection. Until now. Someone was watching. And not only were they watching: they knew where he lived! Versailles' security was pretty tight. All those cameras had to be good for something. And Angel, their head of security, was ex-Special Forces. Offline River felt pretty safe.

Online was a different thing. He'd had to start again. Close off one tunnel and start digging new ones. No typos this time. He'd spent half the night with a black blanket over his head trying to get a fix on this clown on his air-gapped laptop using military-grade tracking software. But unknown_user was the real thing. Untraceable. Bona fide anonymous. It made River so mad he almost set light to his 1:1 matchstick sculpture of a bottlenose dolphin consisting of 100,000 matchsticks. Almost.

He was *this* close to leaving his bedroom to look for Missy, but what was he gonna do? Fly in a custom one-man electric helicopter? Completely silent and more than capable of traveling up to sixty-two mph? Okay, fine, that was actually an option, but no, right now he was more use to Missy on the ground, right here in his bedroom. Right here in this room is where he had the internet and the internet was his zone, his stage, his summer palace. Right here in his room is where he had his machines, so many machines, his computers, his screens. They hurt his eyes sometimes, a dull ache in his eyeballs when he went to sleep at nighttime. But his seven monitors were his windows onto the true world, the better world, more than real. Better. Data. Flowing, popping, scrolling like the shore of an endless ocean. Streams of information. And his bedroom was the observation deck. He was all up in this place like a master criminal, with his crazy-new machines, mad surveillance skills and pimped office chair featuring a tri-panel mesh backrest and mechanism-free, self-adjusting recline technology. That's right, he was way more use to his sister on the ground, on the ground like ground troops, like a herd of panther cats. Hmm, maybe not panthers, they hunted solo, but even still, unknown_user better watch out because . . . unknown_user better watch his back cus River 'bout to make him *known* user, that's why. River 'bout to flip the switch on this fool, catch him like a coyote in his lights. Left-right-left-left-right.

'I'm *bored*,' screeched the mynah bird.

'Shut up, Money, this is serious.'

River and Money had practically grown up together. He mimicked things that River said. But he could mix it up too, catching River off-guard now and then with a natty formulation that almost rang true.

Left-right-left-left-right.

'I'm *bored*,' screeched Money, actually sounding bored this time.

'Wait,' River said, holding the bag still for a moment, 'who taught you to say that? I don't remember telling you I was bored. I'm never bored. Ever.' Bored people, dude. Line 'em up and – Left-right-left-left-right.

'Missy missing now,' crowed Money, blinking with his creepy little eyelids.

'What did you say?' River stopped punching again and rounded on the bird, bringing his glistening face right up to the cage, the bag swinging out of focus. He repeated the question: 'What did you say to me?'

Money gave his master a random sidelong glance and flapped his black wings a couple times for extra effect. 'Missy missing noooow, *squawk*.'

'Who told you to say that? Hey! Money, look at me.' River had goosebumps. Had someone got to Money?! All those cameras throughout the mansion, Angel on the gates . . . It couldn't be. River spun around. A room so big you could play hide-and- seek and win. But he'd been here the whole time. No way someone could be in here with him. He hadn't moved in days. River squeezed his eyes shut like when he was a kid, scared there might be nighttime monsters in his wardrobe. *There's nothing there. There's nothing there.* Man, this unknown_user character really had him spooked!

Missy missing now. What, had Money read his mind? He'd heard of pets being able to sense their master's moods, but no bird was that smart. Money could say a bunch of stuff, but none of it meant anything.

More flapping from Money and then: 'Missy mail. Missing Missy mail.'

WTF! River dropped the skateboard in front of him and carved across his bedroom to the computer console, flinging himself into the ergonomic office chair in the same movement and spinning round three times before settling into his mouse and keyboard routine.

A remote hack of Missy's computer gave River access to

all her data. Right away he found an email confirming deletion of her account on the social network, date-stamped the day before yesterday. She had thirty days to reactivate, but River had a feeling that wasn't going to happen. There was another email from a day earlier. No sender, no subject. *Level Up!* He clicked the link but nothing happened. Level up . . . River was thinking some kind of AR game, maybe a treasure hunt? But the hyperlink was coded for a one-time-only download, so it was a dead end. He did a search of her archive. There. Three months ago. No sender, no subject. The email contained a link.

The video of Scout Rose with the sword. He remembered this thing had caused a sensation because it was her first appearance since her famous disappearance. When the video ended he watched it again. It was only on his fourth play that River realized he wasn't doing this for Missy anymore, he was watching because he wanted to, because he'd never seen anything like this. Stuff about it he hadn't noticed before. There was something alien about it, the onlookers in their animal masks, like a broadcast from another planet. Scout Rose. Her performance was fear, it was fearful, the future unfolding. And River was falling. He scrolled the comments.

pinkandgold 37 minutes ago
Perfect :)

ewanmee 1 hour ago
strong and sexy

ursula9000 1 day ago
I want to wield a sword in the desert!

m-16fan 3 hours ago
> *What did I just watch . . .*

dead_mickey 7 hours ago
> *I'm gonna go do a whole bunch a drugs to this later on*

compassrose 17 hours ago
> *Nothing but love, Scout.*

Animals 17 hours ago
> *My penis is confused*

border 1 day ago
> *Iguana magic*

golden 2 days ago
> *sex*

dothevoice 2 days ago
> *this has been flagged as spam*

litvak 2 days ago
> *kids*

harmony 2 days ago
> *The director is the artist*

He found her at the very beginning. Hers was the first comment.

capturethecastle 3 months ago
> *If this is the future, I want to leave now*

He knew what his sister meant, but it hurt to read this, not knowing where she was, not knowing she was safe. Sure it was kind of flying crocodile, but he didn't like that whatever was happening was happening without him. First comment. That could only mean . . . Whoever sent Missy this video had something to do with its creation. But why would she want to leave like that? Where was she headed? That desert could be anywhere, so what did Missy see in the video that he couldn't? It had to be the second email. If this was AR she was probably following some kind of virtual breadcrumb trail. Waypoints, portal hacks, all that good stuff. But this looked like an invitation-only type deal.

More flapping from the cage. River let Money out once every day, let him fly around the room a while until he got sleepy. He reached into the cage and took Money gently between his palms like, well, like a living thing, and released him into the air. He returned to his desk as Money began to circle above. '*Squawk*. Missy missing now.'

There'd been something up with her all summer, he'd hardly seen her in the house. *What have you gotten yourself into, Missy?* unknown_user had made it sound like a cult, like Missy was being recruited . . . The video was uploaded back in June by ruhin, registered to the website since its inception, but he or she had only ever uploaded this one video.

He soon tracked ruhin to *scoutfan.net*, a site dedicated to none other than Scout Rose, but the trail ended there. ruhin was no longer active but appeared to have had moderator status at one time. Okay, big leap but could *scoutfan* be some kind of recruitment portal? For a cult?? Only one way to find out! Go a little deeper. Play dress-up. The forum was members-only, but it didn't take him long to bypass the vetting process, generate a profile and sign himself in as *pr1ncess*, a sixteen-year-old girl excited to make some new friends on the internet. River hesitated. He remembered unknown_user's words on chat: *You don't find us, we find you.* He fought the impulse to take the claw hammer and smash his new laptop to smithereens.

Okay, so maybe he'd gotten cocky over the years, not taking so much care to cover his tracks. Those days were over. Starting today. He'd taken every precaution. No typos. If this unknown_user freak could be anonymous, so could he . . . And yet, this feeling there was someone watching him, right now. Someone in the room with him. But that was impossible. He'd been there the whole time. River looked over his shoulder. No movement. He went and got a mirror and set it up on his desk to act as a rearview. Then he squeezed his eyes tight shut. *There's nothing there. There's nothing there.* He wished his mom was here to tell him it was okay, he was safe, and Missy was safe, that they would all be together again soon, under one roof.

16

He was a big guy, built strong like a tree. When Silas stood to shake her hand he towered over her, two heads taller than she. He was dressed in black biker leathers and an orange neckerchief and his gray beard and sunburned face made him look like a drunken wizard, though she didn't think he actually *was* drunk. Missy didn't know this guy, but she liked him all the same. His deep voice and patient way. His trailer was bedecked with wood paneling and there was a stuffed cat's head – swear to God – on the wall. Not like a lion's head or something like that, this was like a house cat's head, right there on the wall above where Silas was sitting in his high-backed chair, conducting this interview. Because that's what this was, like it or not: an interview. This morning Missy had felt free as a bird, like the world belonged to her. This felt a little different, like summer camp – not that she'd ever been to summer camp! She was nervous, but for right now, she figured she was still on an adventure.

Silas looked at her askance, but it was just him thinking twice. 'I was going to do this sitting down, Missy, but I changed my mind,' he said. 'What do you say we take a turn in the woods near here? It's a pleasant day outside. We can walk and talk.'

'I'm cool with that,' said Missy. 'I like trees – I think!'

'Excellent,' Silas said.

It was a pine forest. A little cooler than Missy expected. The only trees she'd known so far were the tall palms that lined Versailles' private beach. This was a real forest, the kind with bobcats and mountain lions and bears. She pulled the sleeves of her sweater down over her wrists and turned the collar up on her polo shirt. The forest was very still and the early afternoon sun was only allowed through the canopy as fans of blinding light. The boy with no name ran ahead, hiding behind trees and staging the occasional ambush armed with small pine cones, all the while carrying his white rabbit in a small backpack with its head and ears sticking out. Despite her best efforts to keep up with Silas's tall strides, Missy answered most of his questions to his leather-jacketed back and rough, sunburned neck.

'The car crash you witnessed, Missy, how did it make you feel?

Missy nearly tripped over a tree root but kept her balance, arms spread wide like an airplane. 'How could you know about that? There's no way you could know about that.'

'Answer the question,' Silas said, his tone remaining easy.

'It made me feel . . . It made me feel . . . nothing,' Missy said. 'But I wanted to, I mean – I'm not a psycho or anything – like, I cry all the time! Seriously, when I was a kid? I nursed a little bird back to health and it flew again. And this other time? Me and my brother River raced our pet tortoises, but they kind of went in circles so we built them this racetrack so they would go in a straight line? And that worked for a while but they were really slow, so River figured out this way of fixing wheels on the back . . . wait . . .' Missy stopped in her tracks. 'I'm a psycho, aren't I? I just told you a story a psycho person would tell. Can we pretend I never said any of that? I have empathy, mister, I honestly do. Like, sometimes, when I'm talking to my mom, I'll say the right thing and make her feel better. And I once posted a video of a baby elephant trying to get out of a paddling pool and it got 7000 likes!'

Silas laughed heartily but didn't turn around. 'I know you're not a psychopath, Missy. The question wasn't diagnostic. I merely wanted to hear what you had to say on the matter. Let's go back further. I want you to think about somewhere that makes you happy; a place that when you're there, you feel good. Can you do that for me, Missy?'

'Sure, a place I feel happy. The swimming pool at my parents' house made me happy, but—' Missy interrupted herself and started again. 'I'm outside, the sun's shining, I haven't been in the water yet, but I'm about to. The wind rustling the palm trees . . . Is that the kind of thing?'

'This might seem like a strange question,' Silas said, 'but how old are you as you're imagining the swimming pool?'

'I . . . I guess I'm the age I am now. Sixteen,' Missy said, 'No, wait.' She came to a standstill and closed her eyes and set the scene again. The outdoor pool at Versailles. Saturday sun reflecting off the water, River diving from the lowest of three concrete platforms, knees bent, arms out, palms down, a hesitation so slight but Missy saw it, and that was it, that was what Silas meant. It was like he read her mind. Missy nearly opened her eyes, but not yet. River. He was there and she saw him hesitate. This wasn't now, this was memory. This really happened. She and her brother, playing together in the swimming pool, their parents elsewhere, an afternoon with no end, the unexpected breeze across the water. Flying crocodile. River running as fast as he could after their inflatable crocodile as it rolled away from them into the air, flipping and flipping again until it almost reached the ocean, but he got it.

Missy remembers the relief that River got there in time, but also the unspoken wish that the crocodile had gotten away from them after all, blown out over the ocean and floated away on the current, along the coastline and then inland again, picked up by some other kids, a boy and a girl just like them, but dressed in different swimming costumes, playing different games, speaking in their own made-up language and answering to different parents. She remembers wishing the crocodile had gotten away and knowing that River felt the same way. They'd returned to the swimming pool and gone back to playing their game, but something had changed, something that made their playing less fun. They had stopped soon after, gone back into the mansion to watch a movie, Missy didn't know which movie, but she'd felt closer to her brother than she ever had, that twin feeling they talked about, the talking without words, a shared secret. Flying crocodile. Missy opened her eyes as from a dream of dreaming. She had to run to catch up. 'I was younger. I was a kid when I thought about the swimming pool.'

'I see,' Silas said, and somehow Missy thought he did see. 'And how much time do you spend online on the internet would you say?' he continued. 'Average? Above average? You should feel you can be honest, I'm not going to judge you.'

'Before it was, like, all the time,' Missy said. 'Every day, every minute pretty much, any time something happened that I thought was cool or if I saw something I liked? I'd wanna post it to the network because, why not, right? If I see something beautiful I want my friends to see the same thing. I know, I know, it's unhealthy but whatever, sharing things is fun.'

'You said *before*. What changed your mind?'

Something about Silas, this walk in the forest, the kid with his white rabbit. It made her want to tell him everything, but something else was holding her back. She didn't want to lie, but the whole truth? That belonged to her, and in a way that was her answer right there. 'One day I saw something and, like, I don't know, I wanted to keep it to myself.'

'Something online?'

'Yeah, online.'

'Why did you want to keep it to yourself?' Silas cut in. 'Tell me more about that.'

'Because keeping it to myself made it precious . . . like shells on the beach,' Missy heard herself say. The ground underfoot was beginning to slope upwards, towards the mountain. 'Sometimes I'll find something on the beach near my house and I'll want to take it home with me, back to my room, and taking it home in my pocket kind of makes it even better, even more precious. Because it's mine and no one else's, I guess.'

'I understand,' Silas said.

'So, anyway, I stopped posting so much because I liked that feeling. Of keeping things close. It makes me feel—'

'More like yourself?' Silas said. When Missy didn't answer, he continued. 'Before I ask you any more questions,

Missy, I think it's important that you know something, that I explain a few things. You're here because you've been chosen. You were chosen out of millions of other people because you possess certain qualities, and it's these characteristics that we think will stand you in good stead for the next phase of your journey. I know all this must seem rather extraordinary, rather mysterious, but the very fact of your coming here and finding me is proof that, at the very least, you are willing to try something new, to live in the moment, as they say. As you may have gathered, it's my job to interview prospective candidates, and while that role brings with it a certain degree of formality, it's of great importance that you try to relax. You're not in any kind of danger, you can come and go as you please. Should you decide to stay, I will be more than happy to explain why I have a domestic cat's head mounted on the wall back in my trailer.' Silas was chuckling as he said this and Missy laughed with him, drawing up alongside.

'Why do you have a cat's head mounted on the wall?'

'Mickey, for that was his name, was a dear friend of mine,' Silas said. 'I found him on the side of the road as a kitten and he'd ride with me on my motorcycle all day long without a care—' But before he could say any more, the boy with no name came crashing into his father, throwing his arms around his waist. 'A bear, Dad,' he said breathlessly, 'I saw him. Big ole bear right over there, behind those trees, Dad.'

Without looking behind him, Silas put out his arm across Missy's path to stop her in her tracks, and there it was, less than twenty feet away, emerging from behind a tree, its giant head swaying from side to side as it made its way. A big brown bear. Ambling toward the mountain, a steady afternoon climb for a furry killing machine.

17

'MONEY, GET DOWN HERE!' River switched to good cop: 'Come on, enough with the flying in circles already.' It was no good. Money wouldn't stop flying in circles. He was being super naughty today for some reason. Discombobulated. 'Come on, Money, quit being a douche and come and chill in your cage, I'm working here.'

Until Money stopped flying in circles like this above his head, River couldn't concentrate on the task at hand: finding out what had happened to his twin sister these past few days. He'd spent the morning lurking on *scoutfan.net* looking for clues, any sign that there was more to the fan site than met the eye. If *scoutfan* really was recruiting young girls for something other than Scout Rose appreciation, they were doing a damn good job of hiding it.

River leaned back in his office chair and watched as his pet mynah bird continued to circle the room in long, relaxed, arcing swoops. His morning exercise routine was going on longer than normal. It was surreal when it got like this because you couldn't reason with a bird, you couldn't talk him *down*, in that sense. You had to be patient, let him do his thing till he was done doing it . . . Except there was this one trick, it didn't always work, but it was worth a try.

He'd had Money since he was a little kid. Too little at first to be allowed to keep him in his room like now. Mom was scared he might peck River's eyes out, and she was probably right. You couldn't call it friendship, River guessed, but there was no question Money had *character*, meaning he was something of a motherfucker, but anyways, River loved this bird like other people loved their teddy bears. And there were things he could do to elicit a response. Fun stuff. The mimicking was one thing, but there were other tricks, and one of them was how to get Money back in his cage. River's preferred method: sing to him. No kidding. There was this one song, a favorite pop song from both their childhoods. All River had to do was sing it out loud, only gentle like a lullaby. It didn't matter that he couldn't hit a note if someone had a gun to his head.

The effect was subtle at first, a slight adjustment to the angle of his wings, a couple wider circles to begin with and then smaller than before, a series of plaintive squawks, like he was doing right now, like the song was touching his tiny, stupid bird heart. And then the final descent, a dramatic flapping of wings as he hovered for a moment in his peripheral vision, and this time, to River's great delight, Money alighted on his shoulder, a wing tip briefly caressing his right ear as he found a place to settle down. 'Hello, sweetheart,' River cooed, craning his neck to make eye-contact. 'Fancy seeing you there.'

'*Fancy*,' Money squawked, with little or no regard to what it meant.

'Well,' said River, 'Haven't you been a good boy?'

Squaaaawk!

'That's right,' River continued in dulcet tones, 'you good

for nothing mutt, you want me to flush you down the toilet? Huh? I could flush you right down the toilet and watch you disappear down the hole and then I wouldn't have to weather your pointless existence any longer now, would I?'

The mynah bird tilted his head to one side: 'Down the toiiilet.'

'That's right, Money, down the toilet,' River said.

But Money wasn't done talking. What the mynah bird said next sent a chill the length of River's spine: 'That's the spirit River Beeear, that's the spii-rit.'

River's reaction was pure impulse. He grabbed Money from his shoulder like a grenade, tossed him into the open cage and shut the door. 'What did you say to me? Tell me what you said, Money, or I *will* flush you down the toilet, you hear me?'

'We been watching Missy for a loooong time,' drawled the bird, 'we think she's ready to join us now – *squawk*!'

River punched the cage with his fist and immediately felt bad for doing it. The bird looked rattled. 'I'm sorry, Money, it's not your fault.' But if the mynah bird was rattled, River was shaken. There was no doubt about it now. Someone had gotten to his bird and filled his tiny skull with those same words unknown_user had used on chat . . . But there was no way. No way someone had entered this room without his knowledge. He hadn't moved in days. Almost a week in fact. River had everything he needed in this room so there was no way someone could have come in here. This was like one of those locked room puzzles, but in reverse. This place was his bunker, his refuge. Angel on the gates. River ran through all the possibilities in his head. Maybe unknown_user had hacked one or more of his devices and had it speak out loud while River was asleep (River was a deep sleeper), or in his en suite. Unlikely, but possible. He had to think. He eyed the tennis ball cannon, the boxing gloves, the climbing wall. No, he couldn't waste any more time. He had to post something on *scoutfan*. *Anything*. Find a way in.

River grabbed a blanket from his bed and threw it over Money's cage. 'Sleepy time, little buddy.' There were no squawks of protest, only silence.

In reality Versailles was never silent. Brown noise they called it: a low, soft roar, the sound of a nearby city, a storm within a storm, some unnamed horror still to come, one hundred rooms and the majority were locked. He'd worked for years to find a hack, unlock the doors, find out all his father's secrets. He'd fantasized for years. Open every door and he could show the world who his father really was, reveal the true colors of the man who set them free. He'd get there, it was just a matter of time.

For now, River had to get back online as pr1ncess, trawl the *scoutfan* forums for clues. He closed his eyes and thought of her, his lovely sister Missy: her eyes, her voice, her kindness. He wished they had a twin thing, like, all the time, some kind of live telepathic link-up. That would be sweet. Even in peacetime that would be awesome. All he knew is he missed her like crazy, she was in trouble, and she needed him to bro the hell up. River removed the headpiece of the bear costume. Too hot to think. This was his chance. Reverse the roles. Sure, he was born ten seconds after Missy, but he was taller than her (just). He got that from his father. His father. He'd called him Casey for as long as he could remember. You say *Dad* enough times with no response and the word starts to lose meaning. So he started calling him *Casey*. His father was a jock. His father was a bully. Just a thug with a website. Nothing but a bully, too old for his creepy hoodies and thousand-dollar runners, too young to be CEO of the world's pre-eminent social network, telling everybody how to think and how to be.

No wonder Missy had gone AWOL. River would have jumped ship years ago if it wasn't for . . . If it wasn't for . . . He didn't know why. He could walk out of here right now. Take that one-man helicopter and make Versailles a pixel. But first, he needed to find his sister. Bro the hell up. Show this unknown_user creep who was boss. River eyed the tennis ball cannon, his rearview mirror, pursed his lips, spun round three times in his office chair and settled into his mouse and keyboard routine.

Trust no one. Be anyone but himself.

Rearview mirror.

There's nothing there. There's nothing there.

18

Silas gripped Missy by the sleeve of her sweatshirt and told everybody to stand completely still, stay together, and not make eye contact. 'If he charges us, we must stand our ground. More likely than not it's a bluff and he'll back off.'

Missy couldn't help herself. She had to get a better look at this thing. Silas and the leather jacket. She pushed up on her tiptoes so she could look over his shoulder. And there it was. A real, live, brown bear. Like seeing a celebrity. Was it a grizzly? She kind of hoped so. It wasn't moving at that moment. So real it was unreal. She had to get a picture. Before it disappeared. She had to get a picture. Prove to everyone back home she'd seen a real, live bear. Missy reached for her phone and when she found it wasn't there, she lost her balance, just a little, had to put her right foot out to stop herself from falling. But she made a noise, her black sneaker scraping the ground just enough. The bear heard it and started moving forward. Silas had stopped breathing. She looked at the back of his head. She could feel his anger. She was angry with herself but there was no time. This bear. One paw swipe and it was all over. She'd seen a video. The internet seemed so far away just now.

The bear moved closer, but not for them, maintaining its

course, a path mapped out a hundred years before by other, younger bears. It paused again, bobbed its head slowly up and down like it was sniffing the air. It was looking right at them. Missy closed her eyes against its amber gaze. She closed her eyes and saw only darkness, no pictures of past events, no highlights from her life so far, and no color. Only a blossoming darkness, the sound of three people breathing through their noses, the smell of biker leathers mixed with pine needles, a scent at once unfamiliar but always having been. And then, with her eyes tight shut, she saw the bear, right up close, like HD camera close, every last hair making up its massive, furry face, those amber eyes that told them nothing, only seeing, no meaning, right through them to the empty universe beyond.

When she opened her eyes the bear was gone, exit stage right between the trees, somewhere to the higher ground. They stood awhile like statues, terrified.

'Well done, both of you,' Silas said. 'You were very brave. It's not every day you see a grizzly bear.'

'So it *was* a grizzly?' Missy said, delighted because grizzlies were like, really famous. 'But I thought there weren't any left in this part of America?'

'Indeed,' Silas growled.

They made their way back in silence after that, the boy with no name keeping close by this time, his white rabbit disappeared somewhere inside the backpack.

They'd only been away an hour or so, but it felt like a lot longer, like it should be darker by now. But when they got back to the trailer it was so hot in there, Missy had to take off a layer of her clothes to stay cool.

'Well,' Silas said, opening all the windows. 'I don't know

about you two, but after that I'm hungrier than a cannibal in a mosh pit. You like eggs, Missy? My son cooks a mean three-egg omelet. You game?'

'That sounds great,' Missy said. She couldn't remember ever being this hungry in her life. Something to do with facing down a grizzly bear in the middle of the afternoon she guessed. She went to check her phone and then remembered . . . It wasn't in her pockets. It wasn't in her handbag. Missy got to her feet and turned once on the spot, scanning the trailer.

'Looking for something?' Silas said.

'Oh, yeah, have you seen my phone? I must have . . .'

Silas put his hands on his hips and took a look around. 'Hmm, must be here somewhere, can't have gone far. Tell you what, why don't you relax, and I'll keep looking. I'm sure it'll turn up.'

Missy could smell the eggs now. The boy with no name was so small he had to go on his tiptoes by the cooker to see what he was doing.

'I hope you don't mind,' Silas said, 'But we like to eat our meals in front of the TV. I know it's not something everybody likes, but it's how we do things around here. You don't mind?'

'Not at all,' Missy said, stroking her pockets one last time. She tied her hair up in a ponytail and thought of the sword on the back seat of her car. She wondered whether Silas had any more questions.

'You take the armchair,' Silas said. 'Watch out, though, you're liable to drop off quicker than a lost sheep over a cliff.'

Missy lowered herself into the armchair and it was true.

All this adventuring was catching up with her. Silas turned on the TV, gave Missy a wink, and disappeared into another part of the trailer.

This was the first time Missy could remember being without her cell for more than minutes at time. Even as a kid, she and River had had these pretend plastic phones that made dialing and ringing sounds (River had a whole call list of imaginary friends), and they were still pretty young when Casey gave them their first smartphones (designed by Mom), complete with ready-made profiles on Casey's social network. Missy closed her eyes and saw the brown bear, its amber eyes staring right through her. She opened her eyes and saw the TV, but she couldn't concentrate on what was happening on the screen. She looked down at her bare arms, hands, her fingers, and they looked different somehow, still part of her, but different. She felt older. Sixteen candles. She felt stronger. She thought about the sword on the back seat of her car, her sword, her inspiration, the key to her freedom, to the future. *If this is the future, I want to leave now.*

'You mentioned your house before,' Silas said, appearing out of nowhere and flopping down in the armchair beside hers. 'Have you lived there all your life?'

'Me and my brother were little kids when it was being built. I remember playing hide-and-seek in the foundations. My dad . . . He named it Versailles, after the palace in France . . . I'm sorry to be annoying, but did you happen to find my phone?'

'Sure, sorry, no, I didn't see it. You wanna go check your car?

The thought of leaving the trailer was overwhelming for some reason, her car seemed so far away. Impossibly far. So tired. She would check later. 'Oh, no, don't worry, I'm sure it's somewhere.'

'Tell me, Missy,' Silas said, watching the TV, 'as you sit here now, do you feel homesick?'

She thought for a moment, but only a moment. 'No, I don't feel that. I feel . . . excited.' She sat up in her armchair. 'Like being at the airport.'

'Yes,' Silas said, leaning back deeper into his own chair. 'The airport. Anteroom to the unknown.'

'I guess I just love airports, or I love the idea of airports, I never actually flew in a plane before!' said Missy. She suddenly felt like she was giving too much away. She hardly knew Silas, but she was telling him just how she felt. She missed Cass for some reason.

'The reason I ask,' Silas said, 'is because once you start on this journey of ours, there's simply no turning back. There's no going home. Does that frighten you, Missy, when I say those words to you?' His eyes were fixed on the television screen as he said this.

'No,' Missy said, 'it doesn't frighten me.'

'You don't sound so sure,' Silas said, switching channels.

She thought of her mother, all the unworn clothes, walking between rooms like a day spirit. She missed her mother, their conversations about just anything. But most of all, right now, she missed Cass, the tattooed stars all the way up her neck, getting smaller and smaller (*You've got your whole life spread out in front of you like the open ocean, wider than a dream, you understand what I'm telling you, Missy?*). And she missed Nora, the nice lady at the rest-stop (*I want you to take care now, you hear me?*). These new people in her life. Right now they meant more to her than anything.

'You don't need to ask me again,' Missy said. 'Whatever this is, I'm ready. I don't want my old life anymore. I want a new life. Forget the past, live in the future.'

The boy with no name brought Missy a tray with her omelet, along with a refrigerated soda in a glass bottle, the cap already off. The omelet was great, the kid had done a really good job. The cold soda cut through her something samurai, but it wasn't enough to wake her up. She finished her meal and set the tray to one side, watched the television screen with half-closed eyes. A bear encounter in the middle of the afternoon, middle of nowhere. The leathers creaked like an old ship as Silas shifted in his seat, eyes fixed on the television screen in front of them. But he didn't say any more. On her other side, the boy with no name stroked his white rabbit, top to tail, top to tail. A little too rigorous, but what was Missy going to say? A bear encounter in the middle of the afternoon, but it wasn't enough to keep her awake.

She fell asleep in the comfortable armchair watching an interview with Scout Rose. She was talking about falling in love. No, it wasn't any one person, she had fallen for an idea, a system of ideas. *Deep Sky*. No, she wouldn't call it a cult so much. Something about a Deep Sky, but Missy was falling, falling asleep like a lost sheep over a cliff, and into an ocean that was ready to carry her away, far away, her body passing through the salt water, the pleasure of the water on her body, her body, her heart, her future, her fate, the sword still on the back seat of her car outside, but it was too late. Missy tried opening her eyes. She felt so far away. Impossibly far . . . The soda in the glass bottle. They must have put something in it. They must have put something in it, but it was too late.

110

Down, down she went, down deep, and deeper still, until there was no light, no one, nothing but her. A Missy-shaped core of darkness.

Versailles is missing its princess.

19

A view of the ocean so total it sometimes felt like being on the bridge of a great ship. But right now, Synthea's attention was elsewhere. Here: the cracked cell phone resting on her otherwise clear desk, the conversation over. A blank, blank screen. He told her not to call the police, not yet at least. He told her to calm down. He had it under control. He asked her if she was taking her pills and she lied yes. She said *Yes, Casey, I'm taking the pills.* And he said *Good, that's good, Honey.* He told her why not take a walk on the beach, calm her nerves, breathe some of that ocean air. She said *I already took a walk on the beach, Casey. I am calm.* But that was yesterday. Or was it today? She could feel the sand between her toes, her bare feet were a little cold under the angled metal desk. She should really get dressed, put on some make-up. The minimum. She stopped taking the pills but the effects were still present, like pressure before a storm, and some time after. The conversation with her husband was over, just like that. One minute they are talking, the next there is silence and this thing in front of her, this small device of glass and metal. Dead, just dead. A blank, blank screen.

She could feel the sand on her feet. An incoming tidal wave of deep silence that she must escape. He told her to calm down. What *was* that? Calm down? What did it even *mean* in the context? Their daughter missing and she was meant to take a breath. A pill. She wanted to take the phone and destroy it further, shatter it against the opposite wall, but there was no sense. No. This crack would do for now. A reminder that she was still here, that not all of her belonged to him. She took her right hand from inside her jacket pocket and traced the line of fracture with her index finger, bottom left to top right along the diagonal. On reaching the beveled edge, she continued tracing with her finger, sensing the shape of the device by touch alone, the subtle perfection of its forward profile. Yes. All her best designs came to her in the water. Underwater, where thoughts and dreams might form together. This phone on her desk. An old design of hers, one it seemed that had stood the test of time. She wanted to take it in her hand and hurl it hard at the opposite wall, smash it out of existence, but it would do no good. Her daughter was the thing, her beautiful, smart, charming daughter, so full of life. A lifesaver. But she had this feeling, this ugly feeling inside of her that something was very wrong, that her daughter was far from safe, far away somewhere and out of reach. Synthea took up the phone and selected her husband's name from the list of recently dialed numbers. It rang. It rang but he did not pick up. She let it ring until it gave up automatically. The conversation over before it had begun.

And this is how it was. Even if they were in the same room. She'd say his name and nothing. *Casey*. The continued staring at whatever screen. When they first met she could laugh it off. She even admired it: his single-mindedness. Less talk, more action. His ruthless determination was what first attracted her to him. But as time went on it lost its charm, until eventually she came to hate him for it.

Casey . . . Casey. Synthea remembers. One time she said his name, and when he didn't answer she walked behind his desk and saw that the monitor was switched off, that he was simply staring into a black screen, the glass acting as a mirror. She remembers. Their four eyes in the dark reflection. A look she will never forget, a look no amount of pharma could erase. Dead, just dead. No meaning, just seeing right through her to the other side of the universe. Like a reptile. Like a lizard.

20

The monitor lizard makes his way along the empty corridor. His teeth are bared but he is not angry. His yellow eyes look mean but he is not mean, he is a monitor lizard who has not eaten in several days. Just then he passes another white door. According to Versailles' schematics, this is Room 15, and it, too, is locked, though there is no way the monitor lizard could know that.

Room 15 is haunted, but not how you might think. A seven-year-old River is talking to his father, Casey, who is hard at work at his computer desk. They appear to really be there, in this room, but something isn't right. Their skin, their clothes, they seem to glow, as though a light was shining through them. Like ghosts. But Room 15 is a trick, a nineteenth-century optical illusion. A high-definition projector casts footage from Versailles' family archive onto a sheet of angled glass, scenes captured by the myriad cameras hidden throughout the mansion. Every conversation, every fight, every whisper.

The trick is forced perspective. You open the door and see only what you're meant to see, these scenes played out as though in three dimensions. Every breath, whisper, every fight. Room 15 is how Casey remembers. One thousand cameras recording everything that's ever taken place inside these walls. Versailles as witness. Right now, Room 15 is a conversation between father and son. The last recording selected for playback. A young River attempting to solicit his father's attention.

'Dad . . . Dad, look at my horse . . . Dad. Look at my horse, Dad. I drew a horse, Dad, I—'

'River.'

'—wanna show it to you, Dad, you gotta see this.'

'River, just stop talking for one second and do something for me.'

'But, Dad.'

'*Stop* – talking. Excellent, now take a breath. Take a breath through your nose, River. And out. Good. Now I want you to take a look around and tell me where you are.'

'It's your office upstairs.'

'Right, my office. And what does Casey do when he's in his office upstairs? Can you answer that for me?'

'Working on the website.'

'That's right, working on the website, working on the website. Working, River, on the website, and when I'm working on the website, I can't be distracted, not by you, or anybody else. You understand? Now, I'll take a look at your drawing just as soon as I've finished what I'm doing here.'

'It's not a drawing, Dad, it's a painting, a painting of a horse.'

'I'll take a look at your painting when I'm done here, River. Go play with your sister or something.'

'But it's good, Dad, it's a good picture. Miss Perez? She told me it was a good picture and I should be very proud of myself. She even gave me the pink button to prove it. I wore the pink button all day. It's a horse, Dad. Miss Perez said I did such a good job with the picture, Dad. She told me it looks just like a horse she remembers riding when she was a kid like me. When she was my age like I am. She asked me if I ever rode a horse before and I told her no because I haven't rode a horse before but I would like to. And I was thinking since Missy was allowed to go to the aquarium with Mom I figured maybe I could go horse riding because I love horses and that would be so neat if I could ride on one.'

'River.'

'Look what I can do with my tongue now I don't have my two front teeth. Dad? I lost my teeth and the tooth fairy gave me money for my teeth and I spent the money on some new software for my computer cus the old software wasn't as good as the new software? And now I'm working on a new game cus I like making games and when I get older I wanna—'

'OH MY GOD RIVER I THOUGHT I TOLD YOU TO SHUT THE FUCK UP. I THOUGHT I TOLD YOU TO SHUT THE FUCK UP RIVER AND LEAVE ME ALONE.'

The trick is forced perspective. No one to see this now. The footage ends, a fade to black, the recording set to loop until a new selection is made from the database. A fade to black, but River bears the scars. His father's words like deadbolts fired *out*, deep into his flesh. These bruises in their purple phase, blood just under the surface.

Room 15 is how Casey remembers. This recording is one of many of its kind. River in a room with his father. These recordings form a playlist. His son at different ages. The playlist expresses a pattern. A pattern Casey wishes to break, but never will. Casey looking at River and telling him he's no good, that he's a good for nothing, and why can't he be more like his sister? Sometimes he tells River these things in a raised voice, other times so quietly it's almost as though Casey were talking to himself. And River listens, never making eye contact. These recordings form a playlist. His son at different ages. The playlist expresses a pattern. In some of the recordings Missy will enter the room. She will enter the room, stand between her brother and her father and tell her father he can't talk to River this way. She'll tell Casey he's a coward and a bully and one day he's not going to have any kids because they hate him and they've run away. Room 15 is how Casey remembers. Of all the rooms in Versailles, it's the one he visits most. All hours of the night. The space filling with the smoke of his filterless ciga-rettes, one after the another, the projections taking on the appearance of ghosts, their looped enactments tantamount to a haunting.

21

She is sleepwalking again. In her dream, Synthea is searching for her Missy, her darling girl. In the waking world, she has found her way out of Versailles into the open, her long nightdress torn from other summer nights like this, the thorns of rose bushes, always the same path, the fresh ocean air moving across the garden, filling her lungs but she still does not wake up. Through her closed eyes she can see her daughter, far away at the other end of a long stretch of beach lined with unnaturally tall palms.

A mist as wide as the dream is rolling in from the ocean. As it reaches the shoreline, Synthea sees that this mist consists of nothing but ones and zeros. A googolplex of digits has made it impossible to see, the ice-cold air sealing her mouth tight shut and that is when she hears the voice behind her. It is Missy, she can make her out in silhouette, her baseball cap, long hair and skinny frame. She takes her daughter in her arms and this is flesh and bone, her blood, her love. *I carried you, and in my arms, and later when you told me stories, I listened to the end.* She wants her daughter to remember, but cannot move her lips to form the words. Missy comes in close and whispers something in her mother's ear. A terrible secret. She always knew, she always knew but never dared believe.

In the waking world, Synthea has walked into the black of the ocean in her nightdress. She feels the cool water on her belly and wakes up slowly, lets herself fall sideways and swims a little way along the beach, enjoying the feeling of her body passing through the salt water, this precious time before her feet must find the sand again.

Versailles vibrates inside the line of tall palms, its southern edifice illuminated by the waxing moon, the sickening non-architecture of a fever dream. Versailles. A brand of monster to be viewed by satellite, its gray foundations plunged deep into the shifting, bubbling marsh. Versailles. Its towering A/C stacks breathing out, only out, ever out into the wider world. Versailles — Versailles. Ever-expanding, ever there, never dark, no windows open to the night just now, the ocean framed and framed again. Versailles, a stranded ark. A tidal retreat independent of the moon. *Versailles*, the ocean seems to say, *Versailles*.

Versailles as mission control. Mission Missy now. She is on the move again. Kidnapped. Taken out of time, this story, out of reach for now, our reach, for there is another agency at work – the choice of camera, a blue dot on the map, arti-ficial light glancing off a capacitive screen, *his* screen. The man of the house, King of Versailles. Casey Baer. A man who knows what we want, what his daughter wants. But what she wants and needs are different things. She may be his daughter, but what Missy needs is to be taught a lesson. His birthday present: a final fantasy. This journey north. A rite of passage. A roller coaster rebellion. Destination: Deep Sky,

America's most enigmatic cult, the last people left on earth who can keep a secret. Casey swipes for an update. Her reality in pictures, captured, moments witnessed before they elapse, a dream of life. The ocean framed and framed again. *Versailles*, the ocean seems to say, *Versailles*.

PART TWO

Search

22

Missy falling asleep in the comfortable armchair watching an interview with Scout Rose . . . something about a Deep Sky, but Missy was falling . . . into an ocean that was ready to carry her away . . . the pleasure of the water on her body, her body, her heart, her future, her fate, the sword still on the back seat of her car but it was too late . . . A dreamless sleep.

What Missy doesn't know is this: we always dream, only sometimes we forget. A memory as dream:

Walking along one of Versailles' many corridors, hand in hand with her father. His hand is warm and he uses the other one to open a white door, one she's sure she's tried before and found locked.

He tells her it's an aquarium, but she doesn't see any water, only these concrete structures that remind her of what lava looks like when it cools and solidifies deep under the ocean. But there is no water, not even any glass, only these friendly men in florescent jackets and hard hats, waving and greeting her by name.

Casey tells her it's an aquarium, that he's gonna fill it with all kinds of weird and wonderful creatures, that it'll be the most magical place on earth. He's describing the movement of a shark with his arms and the wiggle of little seahorses with his index fingers.

Missy can feel a giggle in her chest, and then her throat, and then she's laughing out loud in real life but she doesn't know it, she's still asleep in the trailer as it speeds along the highway, Silas at the wheel of the car out front telling his nameless son a story about a man whose only chance of redemption is delivering a rough diamond to a stranger who lives in the middle of a desert.

But in the dream, Missy runs to give her father a hug. He smells like a computer when it's running too hot. Melting plastic and circuitry. He tells her the aquarium is their secret, that she mustn't tell her mom about it, not yet. It'll be a surprise.

23

Leticia had also watched the program with Scout Rose, and for her it was very interesting because this was Scout's first interview since her disappearance. Leticia had always liked Scout Rose, always respected her very much as a human being. She was an amazing singer. Amazing! So pretty, so talented, ambitious, she wrote all her own songs and those green eyes. Gorgeous! It was her eyes that made her a superstar because eyes were the windows to the soul and Scout had a great heart, that was what Leticia loved about her. Such a nice person, not like the other celebrities, so friendly in her interviews, always happy to answer all of their questions, invite them into her wonderful home and share her secrets about the bedroom and how she loved to work out in her fancy gym and watch movies with her friends. This is what Leticia loved the most about Scout Rose. Her openness. Her honesty about life.

But then, one day last year, she disappeared. For a long time there was no music, no new photographs or videos. Nobody knew where she was, not even her family, think of that! It was the biggest story on the internet for a long time. They thought she had to be dead. Such a famous girl, it was like the earth had swallowed her right up! One year. She was gone for a whole year and then she turned up again, just like that. A new video of Scout dancing in the desert with a sword. But no music; it was strange. And after that, images of her with the sunglasses getting in her car and driving away down the street, camera flashes in the black windows. Like all the other celebrities, not answering any questions and getting in their cars with the dark windows. Not the same Scout as before.

Something changed, and this was her first interview since the disappearance. Wearing sunglasses and very careful with her answers. *I won't say where I was. It doesn't matter where I was. What matters is who I am now. I fell in love . . . No, it wasn't a boy, it's not any one person, it's an idea, a system of ideas . . . Not a cult, no. Deep Sky is a state of mind.* She touched the side of her sunglasses, her hand was shaking a little. *I can't say anymore about it, I've already said too much.* After that, the interviewer asked Scout about a new album. She smiled nervously, said that she *was* working on new material, but asked her fans to please be patient. *It will be worth the wait, you guys, I promise.* But Leticia wanted to know more about this Deep Sky. She searched the net for *Deep Sky*, but there was no information about it. Only scary stories. Very strange. Scout Rose talking about Deep Sky and nothing about it on the internet. How could this be?

That night her dream is of her parents' farm, a view across the rice fields towards the deep, deep forest. A creature just inside the trees, a big cat but strange, its body not reflecting any of the sunlight coming through the leaves, not gleaming but shining, not fur but hard plastic, black plastic inside the shadows, moving very slowly but always inside the line of trees, the hot sun reflecting off its plastic armor. This is not a bad dream, it is a dream of childhood, not hers, but this is her parents' farm, the rice fields bordering the forest, a creature just inside the trees, the darkness of her childhood, the forbidden forest, so deep her imagination cannot reach, the screech of cockatoos and wet earth beneath the fallen leaves, the glint, glint of the mawmag's eyes, the rain sounding in the upper canopy, growing heavier, and now she feels it on her face, in her hair, the forest of her childhood and she's well inside the treeline, the creature tracking her, but this is not a bad dream, Leticia does not feel afraid, and this is not a good dream, not gleaming but shining, rain beading on its surfaces, black plastic in place of shadows.

She was woken by an electronic bell sound. She knew that sound, but wait, how could it be here in her apartment? Leticia rubbed her eyes like in the cartoons. This wasn't her apartment. This was her old room at Versailles. Then she remembered. Synthea had sounded so bad on the phone. A broken woman. She had asked Leticia to come to Versailles, forget about Mr Casey, he was out of town on business anyways. She had asked her to please come over, she did not want to be alone at this time. She had sounded very upset on the phone and so Leticia left her apartment and got in her car right away. She found Mrs Synthea in her office and she was a mess, saying things that made no sense, so Leticia took her to the bedroom, put her in her bed like a child.

And now the electronic bell that told her Synthea was awake and wanted something. She picked up the handset clumsily and put it to her head. 'Yes.'

'I had a dream last night,' started Synthea. 'It was Missy

129

on a beach, a strange mist coming in from the sea. She always told me everything, Leticia, she always did, but something changed. Our relationship changed and now she's gone and I don't know why. It's all my fault, Leticia. I should have been there for her and I wasn't. Missy always told me everything and something must have happened because she didn't want to talk to me, not like before, like when she told me her problems, we talked about everything, Leticia, and now she's gone and I know it's got something to do with my husband, I just know it has something to do with fucking Casey. It's all him. I just know he did something. Call it a woman's intuition, a mother's intuition. And get this, he won't let me call the police because . . . and he won't tell me where she is. Can you believe that? He says he has the situation under control, that she just needs some time and not to worry. Then where is she, Leticia? It's been two days. Where is she, where's my daughter if it's all under control? Why won't he tell me? I know why. Because he's lying, Leticia, to protect himself. He doesn't want me to call the police because of the attention it will bring to the family. I think he's lying to protect himself and his precious network. Over our daughter! Our daughter has gone missing and all he cares about is the fucking company! Oh my God! And it's always been like this, Leticia, you've seen it, you've seen the way he shuts us out. His family. You've seen the sacrifices he's made. You know what he's capable of.'

'Yes, but I don't understand you, Mrs Synthea, I don't understand everything you are saying, but I will come upstairs and you will tell me again. Stay where you are and I will come to you and we will talk some more. Would you like some food, Mrs Synthea? Would you like me to bring you something from the kitchens? Some yogurt, some blueberries?'

'Blueberries, yes,' Synthea said, 'but no, no thank you, Leticia, I couldn't eat. I really couldn't eat. And, anyway, you don't have to bring me anything, not after what happened. I asked you here as a friend, Leticia. You don't have to bring me anything. Somebody else can bring me blueberries. But not now. I asked you here as a friend because I trust you and you know my daughter, I think you love my daughter. I have to find my daughter. And River. My River. He's so angry with me. He's so angry with me and I don't know why.'

'Okay, but we don't need to talk like this on the phone if we are in the same house! Please, Mrs Synthea, calm down and I will come to you and we will talk. Don't worry, we can work this out. Together, we can work it out, alright?'

By the time Leticia got to the bedroom, Synthea was gone. When she opened the heavy curtains, such terrible, heavy, black curtains, she saw the chaos. Horrible. There were clothes everywhere, all over the floor, the bed, it was a big mess, almost scary in a way, like the mess left by an angry spirit. Leticia remembered other times like this, Mrs Synthea acting like a crazy person, walking naked in the house, sometimes sleepwalking, other times just like that because she liked going naked! She'd scared the kids a couple of times, turned up outside their rooms, knocking on the doors. They should never see their mother like that. They should see her as she was, as they knew her before, as Leticia knew her. Leticia was angry. Leticia was scared. Leticia wasn't used to this chaos anymore.

It was not her job, but Leticia felt like cleaning up the

clothes. Even when she worked here it was not her job, but she wanted to help somehow. Maybe Mrs Synthea would feel better if she cleaned up her clothes, so she could see everything in the right place and then she could decide. Maybe decide to make another mess, but never mind, she would try! Maybe Mrs Synthea could decide who she was after that because it was time she recognized what was important: her responsibilities! Her children! Her future! This Casey Baer. But Leticia did not understand about the police. Why not call the cops? That was their job: to look for people, bring them back safe. Why would Mr Casey do that? Mr Casey did a lot of things, but he would want his daughter safe. He was Missy's father, whatever Mrs Synthea said. Nothing could change that. He was her father, and a father would not let his daughter go like that.

All the beautiful dresses, all these beautiful dresses. White dresses with grass stains, her shoes full of sand from the beach . . . A lost woman, yes. Leticia closed the door to the wardrobe and went looking.

24

River replayed the Scout Rose interview a third time. It was the top trending story on the internet right now. Deep Sky. It sure *sounded* like a cult! unknown_user. ruhin. *scoutfan*. River was sure they were all connected. And if Deep Sky *was* a cult, then maybe it was them who had his sister.

The fan site was still River's best lead, but he needed to stop lurking and start intervening, posting, even start some threads, gain the attention of the moderators, but his persona had to be right. *Just be Missy. You can do that.* He signed into *scoutfan* as pr1ncess, clicked the first thread he came across and hit the *post reply* button. Blinking cursor. Again River hesitated. Again he checked the rearview mirror for movement. Again he remembered unknown_user's words on chat: *You don't find us, we find you.* River clenched his fist till it hurt. This feeling that someone was watching, looking right through him. It was giving him that thing. What did they call it? *Writer's block.*

It was like that time he fell off his skateboard and cracked his head open. The doctors said the fracture was along the suture lines in his skull, the areas between the bones that fused when he was a little kid. Missy was the one to find him unconscious and she told him later she could see his brain peeking out. There was no damage but this idea of his head being open had stayed with River . . . His sister seeing inside his actual head. Even after he was healed, it took him weeks to want to get back on a skateboard, and even then he'd had to relearn some of his most basic tricks, and not because he didn't know what to do. It was a confidence thing. Then one night, he had this weird dream. He was lying on the beach outside Versailles at night, the water lapping gently around him, and someone was filling the cracks in his head with wet sand. It didn't hurt, it felt good and loving and when he woke up he was like a different person. He felt new.

River stared into the monitor. Blinking cursor. He hesitated . . . Fuck it. This was his art, his thing, pretending to be different people, dreaming other lives online. He wasn't going to let one hacker stop him doing what he did best. No way. Versailles was locked tighter than the White House. He'd taken every precaution online. Now he just had to get back on the board. No typos. If this unknown_user freak could be anonymous, so could he.

Just be Missy.

Blinking cursor.

River thought he knew his sister, her way of thinking. But *being* her was a different thing. He leaned back in his chair and closed his eyes. When they were younger they pretended they were telepathic. Because they were twins the other kids believed them. They called it their pirate frequency, but they just had stuff worked out ahead of time (*What am I thinking about, Missy? / Crocodile!*) But in real life they did have a special connection. River just *liked* his sister. They were friends. And now she was gone and River had to do

134

something. Best case scenario, somebody was using *scoutfan* to recruit teenage girls to join a cult. River had to get the attention of *scoutfan*'s moderators somehow. But before posting, he had to have his act together, he had to have this pr1ncess character perfect. River figured having a sixteen-year-old twin sister was a good start. He could just pretend to be Missy. Couldn't he?

He kept his eyes closed, imagined her in the room with him, her endless excitement about whatever, acting out what she was saying in wide, arcing gestures, like a ballet dancer, like a ballet dancer that is making up her routine as she goes along, that was his sister, writing her name in the dark with a sparkler, M–I–S–S–Y, but then also shooting fireworks straight ahead of her into the darkness to see how far they'd go, that was his sister, talking, talking it up like time was running out but then giving, giving you as much time as you needed to say what you really meant, listening, she was a good listener, that was his sister, her imagination, her ideas for games when they were kids, running through the corridors of Versailles like a wild animal, always moving, always dancing, acting like a nerd in your peripheral vision to make you laugh, that was her, her need for your attention but then her power over you, that was her too. He imagined her in the room with him, talking about this and that, trying to get his attention and him not listening really, caught up with something he was doing online, and then her leaving, telling him she loved him and then leaving, and he realized this was memory, this really happened. The night before she disappeared she had come by his room to say hi, and now he saw she was really trying to say goodbye, trying to get his attention and him not listening. *River, wanna play a video game? River . . . River . . .* He played it back but the memory wasn't all there, fragmented because he hadn't listened to her, hadn't even looked up from his computer screen, too caught up with some random shit he was doing online, some stupid fucking meaningless internet shit and now she was gone, somewhere he could not follow. He remembered. That moment when he got ahold of the inflatable crocodile and how he wished – how they'd both wished – it had got away. That twin thing they talked about in books and movies. The speaking without words. River squeezed his eyelids. She was out there. Somewhere he couldn't follow. It made him want to get that thing, that crocodile, and shred it to pieces with a knife, shred it into ribbons until . . . until it was *nothing*.

River opened his eyes, checked the rear mirror, pulled the black blanket over his head, and started typing.

25

Leticia couldn't find Mrs Synthea anywhere. So many rooms in this place, she'd worked in Versailles for ten years and had not seen inside most of these rooms, strange to think. To live in a house for so long and not know what was there, behind that wall, and all the other walls, it always gave her bad dreams, even nightmares. But Leticia knew by heart which doors were locked, she'd tried opening all of them at some time.

She had searched for her former mistress in every other room, the doors that opened without a key, calling her name, even looking under tables sometimes! She wasn't in her office. The indoor swimming pool. She tried the Grand Ballroom, the dining room, the kitchens. Nobody had seen Mrs Synthea, although they were happy to see Leticia, thinking she was coming back to work, but she told them no, only for today, she had her own apartment now and she was quite happy, thank you for asking.

She took the elevator down to the den. This was where the family had watched movies together when the kids were much younger, movies and TV on the big cinema screen, played all the latest board games, so many rules, so much plastic, so many fights, but it was a happy time in a way, when the family could spend time together, laughing, arguing. But over the years, as the kids got their devices around them, their TVs and computers and phones, they didn't want to go down to the den anymore, they wanted to stay in their rooms and play video games and text their friends and post pictures. Now the den was like a big cupboard full of junk! Boxes, cardboard boxes, outdoor equipment, colored ropes, surf boards, skis, bicycles, more bicycles. This was where everything ended up that the family did not want. Some of this stuff was still in its packaging, not even opened! It was a shame, really.

The den was also where they kept Louis, a rare forest monitor lizard Casey bought as a Christmas present for the family, but they forgot about him, like everything else down here in the den, they forgot about Louis after a while, but not Leticia. She loved him, she *loved* Louis. Such an amazing animal, with his shiny armor and perfect, perfect face. Like a handbag! Leticia had felt so sorry for Louis down in the den all on his own, he should have been outside like other animals. And he was Filipino like her! No kidding! Louis was all the way from the Philippines! She cared very much for him and after the Baers forgot about Louis she carried on feeding him, looked after him, talked to him every day, every single day she talked about her life, celebrity news, gossip around the house, her job, her plans for the weekend. Sometimes she even talked to him about the Philippines, like she was sharing memories with him, haha!

She wished he could talk sometimes, but she enjoyed being with Louis because he listened to her, with his cute little yellow eyes and teeth like he was angry all the time. But she knew he couldn't help it if he looked that way, he wasn't angry with her, he was just Louis, eating mice like they were candy! Yummy, squeaky snacks! He also ate fish, shrimp, crab meat, turkey, chicken, and eggs – all raw – just like that. Hungry boy! Louis. It was her name for him. They never gave him a name but she gave him a name. She named him after Louis XIV, the king of France who lived in the real palace of Versailles in Paris. Right? Because Louis was a very special lizard and he deserved a special title like that. Nobody else knew his name but she did. Wow, the den was even more full of junk than the last time she was here. Leticia had to climb over some boxes to get to Louis.

She let out a shriek when she saw the enclosure. The wire mesh on one side had been ripped away from its plywood frame from the inside. Louis had escaped. She had seen him try before and told him no, to leave his cage alone, that if he ever escaped they would kill him. *They will not hesitate, Louis. They'll shoot you like a dirty dog if you ever get out of there, I'm telling you that right now.* But he was determined. Louis had escaped, but where was he? *Oh, my goodness, it's my fault.* She realized right away that she forgot to tell somebody. She forgot to tell somebody to feed Louis when she left Versailles. She was so upset when she lost her position, her contact with the kids, she had forgotten all about it and now he was hungry, her poor, poor Louis. She wanted to cry. He was hungry and looking for food. Hunting somewhere! That made her laugh for some reason, but this was not funny at all, no, no, no, no, no! Louis had lots of teeth and maybe now he was angry, maybe after all this time of just looking angry, he really was angry! First thing she thought was call his name. '*LOUIS! LOUIS!*' She called him again and again, but what was she thinking? He didn't really know his name was Louis, and even if he did he wasn't going to come to her like a little doggy. She had to find him *and* Mrs Synthea, and Missy, everybody, she couldn't believe it, she couldn't believe it. Really. Everybody was disappearing, all around her. But Leticia didn't panic. She was not a panicky person. Breathe, Leticia, calm down. Right, Louis first. She had to find Louis first because this was dangerous, somebody might get hurt even if he did not mean it. '*LOUIS! LOUIS!*'

26

scoutfan > forum > scout > scout thoughts

Why does Scout wear sunglasses?
Started by kitsuun

kitsuun

Is it just me or has Scout started wearing sunglasses, like, all the time? Ever since she showed up again she's always wearing them. All through that interview she was touching her sunglasses, it reminded me of people who are hiding something, like when a woman gets beat up and she doesn't want anyone to see she's got a black eye, you know what I mean? Call me crazy, I just thought it was a little strange . . .

catpeople

Seriously I think you are reading too deep into the whole sunglasses thing. Celebrities wear sunglasses for fashion because it complements their outfits Scout wears them to look perfect and she looks perfect so why not wear sunglasses it looks cool. Last time I checked she was totally rich so she can do whatever she wants.

neonlove

kitsuun's right though Scout always had the best make-up it was part of her personality plus she has the most beautiful eyes so take off your sunglasses Scout we wanna see your face girl for real!

pr1ncess

Hi, I'm new to the forum and so excited to be here! Personally I can understand Scout wanting to protect herself from all those people around her all the time, wanting to take her picture and talking to her. Maybe she doesn't feel confident in her looks although I think she's gorgeous I would totally understand that because she's a human being like you and me and we all feel badly about ourselves sometimes, right? I know I have days when I don't want to talk to anyone, when I just want to be by myself, have time to think. I might be a ways off base with this but I'm just thinking out loud I guess!

catpeople

There are no confidence issues with Scout, you're crazy to even think that, pr1ncess. I don't want to be harsh but you need to chill the hell out and listen to her music and then maybe you'll lighten up and feel better about yourself.

InnerFame

First of all welcome to the forum, pr1ncess, we're always happy to see new people on here and you're obviously an intelligent person with something to say about Scout. You make some interesting points in your

post and catpeople everybody is entitled to their
thoughts and opinions so go easy on the new girl.

pr1ncess

Thanks InnerFame but catpeople is right, I don't know
Scout at all, I was just thinking out loud like always,
that's just me.

catpeople

It's okay, I forgive you, pr1ncess ;) Any fan of Scout is a
friend of mine xx

ineedscissors

I would wear sunglasses if I were high all the damn
time . . .

catpeople

Scissors running with scissors once again. I thought
your ass was banned girl. Why you always got to hate
on Scout like that? An why you have to be so angry all
the time scissors? Scout just wants people to be happy
so why can't you be happy? I hate negative people they
make me so depressed sometimes it's like kill yourself
already!

ineedscissors

Scout's not herself right now and you people are too
blind to see what I see. She disappears for a year and
now she's back and everything goes back to normal?
Fuck that shit. Did you even watch the interview with
Scout? That was some creepy shit right there. Deep Sky?
Say what? I saw that and I thought this girl's either high

on drugs or she's spent the last year hanging out with some dark-ass cult. All I know she's in trouble and you clones don't want to admit it because you're goddamned hypocrites and all you care about is the release date for her next album. I was listening to Scout right from the start, before this forum even existed, I was listening to her music and now she's in trouble and she needs her fans more than ever. You know I'm right, and pr1ncess is right too, Scout's a human being, start treating her like a human being because that's what she is. Out.

InnerFame

Three strikes, scissors, three strikes. You know the rules.

catpeople

Stalker alert.

ineedscissors

Fuck the rules, Fame, and fuck you too. What, did I say too much, like Scout said too much in her interview? Fuck you, Fame. You're probably one of them. You think just because you get to ban people from some random board on the internet you some kind of mini boss and shit? Well you're not. You used to be one of us. I got nothing against Scout, you know that better than anybody, you know I respect her as an artist and love her music but why does that mean we have to pretend like she's perfect all the time? Something's going on with her right now. She needs our help. You call yourself a fan, Fame? You stopped being that the moment you became a moderator. For all I know your part of this cult that's got Scout all brainwashed and shit. Go ahead and ban my ass, it wouldn't be the first time but it sure won't be the last. I'll be back under a different name and you'll have to ban me again because I'm not giving up till the truth comes out, and the truth will come out, Fame, I guarantee you that. I know who you are, bitch, I know what you represent. I'm on to you, Fame, all over you like a cheap suit.

catpeople

RIP scissors, you one messed up kid.

InnerFame

She's gone now, gone for good. What a shame. And let that be a lesson to y'all. This forum is a fan forum and when we talk about Scout we do so with the respect she deserves. The people still standing are her real fans, you guys are her real fans because you know who she really is. I'm sorry you had to see that, pr1ncess, scissors always was one for conspiracy theories, it's sad really. I hope she didn't put you off visiting us again. The forum could use somebody like you, someone with a little sensitivity.

pr1ncess

No need to apologize, Fame. I'm just happy to be able to get to talk to other fans about my favorite recording artist. Her music has got me through some hard times . . .

kitsuun

I gotta admit the interview was a little weird, to say the least. I mean, come on, I'll bet there isn't one person on this board who hasn't searched Deep Sky and turned up *some dark material. You look hard enough and the same things keep coming up. I read they remove your eyes and replace them with uncut diamonds. That was just one thing. I don't know if I believe it but it creeps me out all the same. Hey, maybe that's why Scout wears sunglasses all the time! D:<*

InnerFame

You want to be next, kitsuun? I'm not afraid to wield the hammer twice in one day.

kitsuun

What did I do?

neonlove

Let the games begin.

InnerFame

I don't have to explain myself to you, kitsuun, but for the benefit of those not familiar with our ethos here @ scoutfan. This is a fansite, not a gossip site. We're here to celebrate a great artist while at the same time respecting her right to privacy. Are we clear?

Moderators. They were all the same, always making with the small-town power trip. But InnerFame knew something. Could *scoutfan* really be a recruitment portal for Deep Sky? That stuff about diamonds for eyes. River had to believe it was all nonsense. He had to because his sister . . . it didn't bear thinking about. Whatever Deep Sky was, InnerFame was in on it somehow.

He'd tried hacking InnerFame and some of the other members posting on this board and had mixed results. Most of these guys were just real boys and girls, fans of Scout with nothing to hide. InnerFame though. Like unknown_user, InnerFame was untraceable. A dead end. And dead ends made River very nervous. But he was playing the role, keeping it loose (no typos). He was *pr1ncess*, a sixteen-year-old girl excited to make some new friends on the internet. unknown_user may have won round one, but River was going for the knockout. Left-right-left-left-right.

Anonymity was his art. Anyone could be themselves. But what was the fun in that? Being yourself was for amateurs. Being yourself was for suckers. Who needed honesty when you could have duplicity? River never felt more alive, more centered, than when he was pretending to be someone else.

But this wasn't a game. This was about River finding out what happened to his sister. It made him sick to think of her in the hands of some *cult*. He threw his mouse across the room and watched it smash into not enough pieces. He was wasting his time with this forum nonsense. He needed to get out of this room. Only way he was going to make a difference was if he actually *did* something. No cops, unknown_user said. River cast his eyes around the room for something else to break. When nothing good enough revealed itself, River thought of something he hadn't thought of in years. Okay, so it wasn't going to help him find Missy, but maybe it would help him relax, get his head straight. River hesitated. *Fuck it.* He pushed off from the desk with both feet, sending the expensive office chair careening across his bedroom in the direction of his bed. Next to his bed was a safe. He held his thumb to the scanner, triggering a satisfying *chunk* sound that told him the safe was unlocked. He reached inside and pulled out a scrunched-up brown paper bag containing something soft.

Here was the deal. When River was a kid and he got sad or upset he'd do this thing. He'd lock his door, set up Croc the dinosaur on the bed and dance at him. Basically Croc was River's favorite soft toy and he'd had him since he was like, four years old. His name was Croc but really he was a pea-green dinosaur with purple tail spikes. He had one eye missing and his tongue sticking out of his mouth like a dog, but somehow he managed to look serious in his expression, almost like he was worried or something. Plus, Croc dropped these dino data bombs every time you squeezed him (Croc: *'The heaviest dinosaur was Argentinosaurus, at over one hundred tons. It was the equivalent to 18 African elephants.'*/ River: *'Hey, I didn't know that, Croc, tell me more.'* etc.). So anyways, River's thing was to dance as hard as he could in front of Croc and try to make the dinosaur move somehow. Like a dance-off. And Missy was in on it. She'd walked in on River dancing at Croc one time (before his bedroom got upgraded, Fort-Knox-style) and from that day made her brother swear to text her whenever it was happening so she could watch. Actually, having Missy watch was kind of great because he loved to hear his sister laugh. The harder River danced at Croc, the harder his sister laughed till she was crying. It was in the trying that River usually started feeling better, forget about whatever bad was happening. But today wasn't about forgetting. Today was about *focus*, getting his head straight so he could save his beloved sister from harm.

River reached inside the brown paper bag for Croc and got his second big shock in twenty-four hours. This one was a body blow. It wasn't Croc in the paper bag. Croc was gone. These were clothes, rolled up neatly and tied with a blue ribbon like a fat scroll. Embraceable Cool Nights Delicate Chemise from Soma. It still had the labels. Vanishing Edge Microfiber panties, also from Soma. River had never seen these items before in real life, only on the computer screen when he loaded up that random lingerie site for inspiration during the chat with unknown_user. Something dropped to the floor from out the lacy scroll. A white key. Old-world. Ornate. Wait. It was made of chocolate. A white chocolate key. A fancy label attached by a line of black thread, it read: *byte me*, the handwriting somewhat familiar.

Heart thumping hard, River did as he was told. He ate the key then and there, and like it was only natural he chased it by holding the panties to his nose and breathing deep. They smelled brand new. This could only mean one thing. The knowledge gave him an adrenaline rush so complete he was ready to walk the ceiling. There was someone in here with him after all, besides Money under the blanket. Someone stepped out of the internet and trolling him in real life, in his own home. His own bedroom. A room so big you could play hide-and-seek and win.

27

Versailles was her nightmare, the corridors and locked doors, and in her nightmare Leticia had a key for all the rooms. But this was not a dream, she had to find the monitor before he hurt somebody. Anything could happen. Louis could be dangerous, even if he didn't mean it he might bite somebody and then they would kill him in cold blood. She called his name again but knew he wouldn't understand, stupid lizard with no ears. In fact it wasn't true, monitors were actually pretty smart, she read on the internet that they could count all the way up to six. 'I'm sorry, Louis,' Leticia said out loud, 'I know you got ears, they're just not on the outside of your head like other animals, but that's okay, Louis, that's okay . . . LOUIS!'

She entered another corridor, walked slowly down the middle like she was on a tightrope, listening for movement. But how could she hear when Versailles roared like an ocean? About three quarters of the way along the corridor Leticia saw that one of the white doors was slightly ajar. That wasn't right. Leticia knew all the doors by heart, and this one should be locked. She took a step back, nearly losing her balance on the tightrope. This was like her dream. This was like her dream and it wasn't right, the white door ajar and she knew it should be locked tight, like all the other doors in this corridor, locked tight, white on white.

Leticia suddenly felt very cold, the door was ajar but there was no light in the gap. She tried to move but she could not, it was all she could do to keep her balance. She closed her eyes and thought about her teddy bears, so friendly, so cuddly, so nice. She pictured them on her bed at home, her welcome party. Hi, teddy bears! She managed a smile in the corridor. She pictured them on her bed and all their faces. She thought about how she cut each label off after bringing them home from the store, cutting the fabric label with the washing instructions, real close to the stitching so the rest disappeared in the fur. That way the bear was born, that way it was *her* bear and nobody else's. She thought of how they smelled, when she put her nose in their bellies! She pictured their faces looking up at her when she came in the room, all friendly and fluffy, waiting for her on the bed, ready to protect her from all the bad things in the world. Her smile faded in the corridor. The door ajar when it should be locked tight. But she knew she had to look inside this room. She had to go inside because maybe then the dreams would stop, maybe then she would have only good dreams, the ones about her home country, the green mountains of her childhood in the Philippines. She was very cold, frozen to her spot on the powder-blue carpet in the corridor, the door ajar and no light in the gap.

28

River turned his room upside down looking for this real-life troll (he wasn't talking to Money right now). Scariest game of hide-and-seek ever. After working through his vast wardrobe consisting mainly of customized caped crusader costumes, River decided to get into his fencing armor, complete with rapier, to continue the search (better safe, right?). He looked in all the obvious places. Under the bed. Behind the black-out curtains. Inside the full-scale replica of the lunar landing module (so *that's* where he left his chainsaw). Beneath the wooden structure of his indoor skate park. Nothing. WTF. He had to be here somewhere. How else could this shape-shifter have gotten to Money or switched out Croc for ladies' nightwear and a chocolate key?

River climbed the rope ladder to his tree house. He had his library up here, all his books and comics too. He had, like, ten e-readers, but River was all about the real books still, loved the smell and weight and all that good stuff about bendy books. The hard ones not so much, but, yeah, he loved to read and there was no sign of the troll in the tree house so he took his position and zip-lined back down into the ball pool below, the rapier between his teeth. Except for his long-lost copy of Robert Louis Stevenson's *Kidnapped* and a bush knife disguised as a bunch of flowers, the ball pool was empty, so he took a token ride on his ghost train, just to be sure he wasn't in there either.

Casey had the ghost train installed after Synthea overheard River request a ghost train for Christmas in his sleep aged seven. In reality, River was totally awake at the time and knew exactly what he was doing. In fact, River's whole room – the climbing wall, lunar module, tree house, zip-line, ball pool, ghost train, tennis ball cannon – *everything*. All of that was post-Missy getting to go to the aquarium in the city with their mom that time. Next thing River knew he was sleeping on his sister's floor for like a month while all this epic new shit was installed in his room. An *upgrade*, his father called it (they called him Alt Disney). River never really saw the logic in the whole thing, but he was just a kid at the time, so . . . Besides, these kinds of developments weren't uncommon at Versailles. It depended on their father's mood. For months, life would go on as normal and then suddenly it was all go: white vans, men in fluorescent vests and plastic hats filing into Versailles' service entrance, and then the listening at walls and doors as the work was carried out.

These days the ghost train wasn't scary so much as a way for River to relax, a throwback to the halcyon years of his shitty, anonymous childhood. River did a lot of his most productive thinking in the ghost train. But there was no troll in there either. Weird.

River set down the rapier so that it was flush with the edge of his desk and stood with his fists on his hips. Time to say it how it was. 'Hey, listen, mister, just so you know? I ain't scared of you, not even a little bit. So you can carry on doing your thing, hiding out here or doing whatever you're doing from a remote location or whatever, I don't care cus I'm ready. I'm a black belt in Karate. That's number one, but you should also know I'm working on a martial art right now of my own design that'll fuck you up real special if called for, real subtle at first so that you think you're okay for, like, a while, but two minutes later when you're going to the bathroom and your arm falls off while you're, like, trying to wipe your ass or something? Don't come crying to me cus I warned you. This is my warning. You have been warned. Peace out, bitches.'

The part about being a black belt was true, the rest, well, let's just say River was working on some things. He stood his ground a few moments longer. The seven vertically oriented screens behind him were giving off a pleasant heat, the warmth of an early morning summer sun on his back and neck. River breathed a sigh and turned to face into his workstation once again. The cascades of live social interactions, dynamic news sites with their ever-shifting narratives, animated new-message indicators and looped advertisements with the volume cranked, everything vying for his attention, his intervention, his volition. It was like a jungle chorus, all of it calling for him to step inside again, cross through into another world. He took his seat in the comfortable chair, grabbed an old cable mouse from his desk drawer and blink-blinked his way back in.

Deep Sky. The internet glittered like an open ocean, reflecting on the possibilities. *#DeepSky*. The words had continued to gain currency on the social networks, but no one really knew what it meant. Satanic cult? Suicide cult? Some kind of cult. There was no concrete information anywhere on the internet. Only hearsay. Scary stories. Whoever these guys were, they sure knew how to keep a secret. And yet it was all *scoutfan*'s community wanted to talk about. ineedscissors' post on the sunglasses thread had apparently started a shitstorm of rumor and speculation over Scout's mentioning of the words *Deep Sky*, and there was nothing the moderators could do about it. To enforce the rules pertaining to Scout's right to privacy would have meant banning the entire community. The forum raged like a child left at the supermarket.

River would have found it all very amusing were it not for the fact that his sister was missing and *scoutfan* was still his best lead. This ruhin character who uploaded the sword video had been an active member of the forum at one time, but there was no sign of him, online or in his bedroom! River had to assume he and unknown_user were the same person. But it could just as easily be two people, or a thousand. River had to think.

He took the thick rubber band from around his wrist and flicked it hard at his tin robot toy, knocking it to the ground where it smashed into several pieces. Nice shot, but also a little bit sad face. Oh, well. He spun round and round in his chair till he wanted to throw up. Then he got on his skateboard and tried to do a laser flip but totally bailed from being too dizzy and hit his head on the floor. He curled up like a baby for a minute. The pain was white sparks rising upwards as from an open fire. *Deep Sky*. *Deep* Disney motherfucking *Sky*. Scout's mysterious disappearance. And now his sister. There had to be a connection. River got to his feet and back in front of his screens. He could hardly believe his luck when he refreshed the page and saw InnerFame's new competition thread at the top of the list:

scoutfan > forum > scout > scout thoughts

New Competition
Started by InnerFame

InnerFame

I know it's been too long a time since we ran a competition for you guys, so it gives me great pleasure to announce what will undoubtedly be our most popular contest to date. Why? Because we've never had a such an exciting 1ˢᵗ prize. Fasten your seatbelts, ladies, because one of you is going to be given the opportunity to chat with Scout one on one. That's right. The winner of our biggest-ever competition will be allowed to spend a few precious moments with the star in an online chat hosted right here on scoutfan. But it gets better. The real prize is you will be allowed to ask Scout a question, any question, as personal as you would like, and she will have to answer it honestly. This is a once-in-a-lifetime opportunity to ask one of your heroes anything you want, nothing off the table. DM. Personal. Your question, her answer, your secret. So that's the prize. To enter just log onto our competition page and submit your email address along with a brief description of the last dream you remember. We'll pick a winner out of a virtual hat this time tomorrow and post their name on this thread, along with our favorite dreams ...

River remembered all his dreams. Last night he dreamed

he was a black panther hunting a man wearing only a diamond tiara in a twilit jungle. He'd woken in the middle of the night so aroused he had to jerk off in the shower to calm down. But it didn't matter what he dreamed about because River didn't need to enter this competition to get to Scout. If *scoutfan* was hosting the chat themselves, hacking their server and gaining access to Scout's profile was a piece of cake. Get to Scout and he could ask her what she knew about Deep Sky, and what they might want with his sister. On second thought he would enter the competition anyway. He had a feeling *scoutfan* wanted their dreams for a reason, that there was more to this than a chance to meet Scout over chat, something less random than a virtual hat. He opened the word processor application, glanced over at the tennis ball cannon, shook his head no. He'd go with his instincts on this one:

> *A girl is dancing in a desert with her eyes closed, gray mountains in the distance. The sword makes it ritual, a rite of passage, but she is dancing, enjoying herself, taking pride in her every move. There are other figures in the background. They are wearing plastic animal masks, but they are out of focus, their attention on the girl and her performance. I am one of them. Mine is the lion mask.*

He clicked submit and leaned back in his chair. Twenty-four hours till they announced the winner. What the hell was he going to do till then? Sleep? That'd cut it down to around sixteen but still, time sucked ass sometimes. How could he relax or do anything with the thought of his sister missing?

157

He couldn't call the cops. This competition was his best hope. He just wished he could hit fast forward on this thing. He could go outside, he guessed, he could try leaving this room, but outside sucked even harder than time.

He could call Levon. Levon was River's best friend but also a fuck-up. Last time he got together with Levon they both broke their noses failing at pretending to punch each other in the face. Levon was always trying to get River to come out, not just out of the house, but the city, go camping and surfing and shit like that. But River preferred indoors, their indoor activities, their nature documentary marathons and recording sessions together. River and Levon had recorded an entire hip hop album in whispers. They called it *Hushed Bones*. River selected Levon from the favorites on his phone. Levon had dated his sister and Missy was missing and that was a secret and River didn't want to lie to his best friend. He switched his phone off. If he called Levon, Levon would want to get together and that meant maybe leaving the house.

Outside meant people and people meant talking and talking meant having something to say to people and he had nothing. To be more accurate, he had nothing to say to people as himself. For that matter he had nothing to say to people when they were being *them*selves. That's why the internet was so perfect. On the internet you could be whatever you wanted, and, more likely than not, you were talking to people thinking the same damn thing, meaning everybody's fronting on everybody and who cares right because at the end of it all you still got to shut down your computer and go back to your real life. Nobody gets hurt. Anonymity. It was River's drug of choice. Fuck it, it was his art.

River had one hero. He wasn't a hero type of person but there was one kid he had to admire, someone who really knew how to play the internet, someone who inspired him in his art. Marchpane. Dude was a hoodlum. The ultimate troll. Dude was totally out of control but totally in control at the exact same time. Coming at the internet like a human meteorite, burning up across the sky. He was a troll, but not like the others. Trolls caused trouble, tried to upset people. Marchpane was different. His posts and comments were always fresh, always positive. Sure he was off-topic, but always in a way that seemed to make sense, if only in his world. If River had to have a role model it would be Marchpane. Dude had his shit locked tight, too. No one knew who he was, all this time. It was an unspoken thing amongst trolls on the internet. Unmask Marchpane and you become Marchpane, you take his crown.

But River wanted his own crown. An upside down crown with all different-colored gems. How to kill twenty-four hours. That's another thing the internet was perfect for. Go online. Out of time. Off-topic. In the zone. But first, something to get him there. There was one post by Marchpane that always got River flowing. He'd cut and pasted it from some random forum years ago, printed it out and stuck it up on his wall. He couldn't remember the context of the thread, but it didn't matter. Marchpane had blazed in from leftfield as always:

Marchpane
I want to wear a top hat, a black suit with tails, shoes

so shiny you have to close your eyes. I want to stand atop a moving car, my chainsaw buzzing, buzzing at the sun. I want to climb skyscrapers like a spider and fly the flags of forgotten sons. I want to know a panther cat, teach it to hunt in a pack of four. I want two yellow motorcycles for sport, one reflected in each eye. For every man I meet to know my darkest secrets and to find no meaning. For everywhere I sit to be a golden throne, mined from mountains where the dragons lie, their serpent tails swishing slowly side to side like my volition. My motivations locked away like rocket codes. I want to lurk in cold channels in a private submarine, down periscope, no need to give the word just yet. I want to ride inside a wooden horse, thrice as large as it should be, roll into town and turn it upside down. I want my heart to beat strong, to last as long as you will have me. I want to be a one-man riot, for language to run out, for you to stop paying in gold coins, and for black on white to matter like it did before. I want to tell you stories told to me by giants, not all of them were tall. I want my father in the mirror where he belongs, for the things I choose to say to be forever, and for thoughtlessness to do for now. Bring me your doubts, forget what you tell yourself, we will make fire from all this, a bonfire unworthy of the guy, flames licking at the deepest sky. I want to land on Mars, travel north in a car encrusted with photovoltaic diamonds. I want the first interstellar spaceship to put people in mind of a dark curtain of rain off an urban coastline. And I should be the one to commandeer the craft, my satin-gloved hands passing without contact over controls that

*to the untrained are a shallow pool of water reflecting
an alien sun. For this is the future, pull your sleeves
down, make sure to cover your wrists, for appearances
are everything, nothing to see here, everything to want,
nothing in its place on my watch. Your musculature
should be that of a career criminal, the sinew woven in
a pattern known only to the worst of us. You will have
received your combat training from none other than he
who play-fights with polar bears. You will know when
you are ready. You will know because I will be there to
murder the idea in cold blood. For I am the contender,
the original soldier with an industrial complex, ready to
jump, lean forward and over the edge, your parachute,
not mine.*

29

Synthea threw herself against the one-way glass and screamed at the top of her lungs, but it made no difference, Leticia could not hear or see her inside the box. The former nanny was close enough that Synthea could see the holes in her lobes where earrings should be. But Synthea was trapped. Positioned in the middle of the room, her prison had the dimensions of the old pay phones, its walls constructed of a thick, utterly soundproof glass and you could only look out. Synthea let herself slide to the floor. She was half-naked, she was cold, her shoulder bruised.

How did she get here? That's right: the ringing telephone. She was walking the corridors and heard a ringing. An old-fashioned ringing, and it was coming from somewhere inside Versailles. *Ring-ring, ring-ring.* It reminded her of a movie. A telephone sounding in an empty house, loud and drenched in silence. She had followed the ringing in her bare feet, feeling her way along the walls until she was right there, on the other side of a white door. This door. One of the locked rooms. She tried the handle and it opened. A sick feeling of doing something she shouldn't, like when she was a little girl, stealing moments inside her father's office when he wasn't there. But the door opened and she had ventured in.

Ring-ring, ring-ring. Three levels louder than it should be. A dark glass box, same dimensions as one of the old pay phones, but this wasn't that. This was something quite different. She approached the glass and one side had opened to the slightest touch. It was a door, deathly quiet on its hinges. *Ring-ring, ring-ring.* She stepped inside, there was no phone but it was too late, the door slammed behind her like a coffin and she'd been there ever since.

Now she watched Leticia's small feet as they circled the box. She was wearing new shoes. She'd never seen Leticia wear such nice shoes before, they had to be brand new, she must have bought them right after leaving Versailles, after she was fired. She was pleased for her friend, glad she was treating herself for once. She missed Leticia, missed having her around at the other end of the intercom. Leticia was her friend and confidante, like a sister, more like a beloved aunt. They were the same age but Leticia was the older soul, wise and unafraid to impart her wisdom. She watched Leticia's shoes as they paused right by the box. Such pretty shoes, the kind a girl might wear on her first day of school, the bright gold buckles, patent black crocodile leather and natty white socks with the frills.

Synthea began to cry again. She had been such a good girl. Her first day of actual school, outside Versailles' perimeter fence, and Missy had been so brave, better than brave, her daughter had come home the very same day with a new friend. And the next day. As a matter of fact, by the end of that first week, Missy had her very own entourage. Her Missy was such a good girl, so kind and thoughtful and generous. Whatever could have happened? Such a sweet, happy girl, what could have driven her away like that? She blamed herself. Synthea blamed her husband. She knew something had happened, some unholy thing, she had felt it but did nothing, and now Missy was gone, and *oh my God, he has his wife in a glass box, he has me in a glass box like an animal. This can't be happening, this doesn't happen in real life.* She looked down at her bare arms, hands, her fingers, and they looked different somehow, still part of her, but different. She felt younger, not in a good way. She was frightened. The fear a child might feel at hearing her father on the stairs. The inevitable crash as the door swings open . . .

It was a bad dream, like a scene from a horror movie but this *was* real life, the smear of blood on the glass told her so, the pain in her shoulder from trying to break out, the goosebumps all over her body. *Like a lizard.* Leticia's patent shoes. She was walking away from the box, toward the door. Synthea tried to scream but nothing came, the box closing in like sick magic, and then his voice. Casey's voice, the fidelity was crystal, like he was right there with her, whispering in her ear under the covers.

'Don't cry, darling, I'm here.'

'WHAT THE FUCK, CASEY, WHAT THE FUCK IS THIS, CASEY, HAVE YOU GONE TOTALLY INSANE?'

'Don't raise your voice, Synthea, there's no need. Unlike the nanny, I can hear you perfectly well. Let's talk about this like grown-up adults.'

Synthea breathed hard through her nose as she composed herself. 'What did you do, Casey? What did you do to our daughter that's so bad she had to run away? What did you do that's so bad you have to keep your wife prisoner so she doesn't call the goddamned cops for help. Tell me what you did, Casey. Tell me what you did to our daughter.'

There was silence for ten seconds before she heard his voice again. 'I don't know what you're talking about, darling, you're very upset. I need you to calm down and think about this. You really think I would ever do something to our daughter? Look into your heart and ask yourself that question. You know how much I love Missy, you know I would do anything for my daughter, that I'd do everything in my power to make her happy, and that counts for the rest of my family. I'm nothing without you guys. Look into your heart and ask yourself, Synthea. You know how much I love Missy, that I'd do *anything* to protect her *and* River. So how could you even say that to me? How could you think that I would do anything to hurt our daughter? She means everything to me, as do you.'

'Then let me out of here.'

'I can't do that, Synthea. Not until you promise.'

'Promise?'

'I know about the pills, Synthea.'

'I don't know what you're talking about.'

'I know you stopped taking the pills. And you're out of control. I thought we were making progress. I thought we could put the past behind us. But you're out of control, Synthea. It's no wonder our daughter ran away.'

Synthea didn't know her husband anymore, but she recognized the mode of discourse. His meaning was inexorable. There was no room for discussion. She knew Casey was manipulating her but there was no point arguing, it would lead nowhere. It was like telling a screaming infant to stop screaming, like holding up your hand to an articulated truck as it charged down the road towards you. It was this relentless determination that got him to where he was, the most influential man on the social internet, a man whose ideas about human interaction became the modus operandi before anyone had time to question their merit. No one to say no. Every day his hacker disciples at the network's campus turned his word into code while society forgot how to opt out. Universal trust. Openness. Faith in each other. But really their faith was in Casey and his company. Openness was the grand illusion. A glass box.

Synthea knew the only way she was getting out was if she went along with everything her husband said, or at least gave the appearance of doing so. There was no safeword with Casey, only complicity. And she was a good actress, years of pretending she loved him. 'You're right, Casey,' she said. 'I'm out of control. Missy needs both her parents. Let me out of here and I give you my word. I promise to resume the medication. I promise I'll find my feet again and step into the light.' Synthea took a deep breath, as though she were about to go underwater. Her hate for him a perfect thing: for now, it acted as a diving bell, airtight, reflecting no light. 'We want the same future,' she said 'we always have. To be a family. To change the world. We've always been a great team, you and I. There was a time we were invincible, the Queen and King of Silicon Valley, two beautiful children, a beautiful house. We were the blueprint. The American Dream.

'I don't know what happened to us but I know we can be that again. The four of us. Happy, productive, loving each other. I just want us to be together again. I just want to get our daughter back. Our children. Our greatest creations. I know we feel the same. I know we both want what is best, and that you wouldn't do anything to hurt them.' Synthea looked down at her hands again and saw two clenched fists, the knuckles white as bone. In that moment she thought she might actually break the glass. But instead she unclenched the fists in slow motion, the effort causing her to shake so violently she nearly lost her balance.

'I love you, Synthea,' her husband said, his voice seeming to crack, 'You know that, right? I've always loved you. And I believe in you just like you believed in me when we first met. Things are going to be better, I promise. Our family—'

'I know you love me, Casey, I know you want what's best for me, and our children.'

'Let me see you take the pill, Synthea. I know you keep one in the locket around your neck. Let me see you take the pill and this can all be over.'

Synthea touched the heart-shaped silver locket resting on her chest. That's right, she always carried one pill. Just in case. She opened the locket and let the small white pill fall into the palm of her hand. She knocked it back with a jerk of her head, it was hard to swallow but she managed, felt it travel slowly down her throat and further inside. Then she stuck out her tongue for Casey, showing him there was nothing there. It would be several hours before the pill would take effect, but already Synthea felt she had thrown the key away forever this time. She closed her eyes and saw whiteness in place of blackness, like being caught in a breaking wave as tall as a house, and pulled down, around and down, around and down, and down, and down, while on the surface her ship would stay becalmed forever, time torn free of the mast.

'Thank you, Synthea. Thank you,' Casey said, 'The door is unlocked, you are free to go.'

'Casey, wait. There's something I still don't understand. If you've known all this time where Missy is, why haven't you brought her home? I've just been so worried about her.'

'I know you're worried, but you've got to trust me on this one, Synthea. All I can tell you is Missy's safe. She needs some space, that's all, some time to clear her head. I know it's hard but I need you to be patient a while longer. Rest assured the situation is under control. Trust in my judgment, Synthea, as your husband and her father.'

'I trust you,' Synthea said. She nearly threw up when she realized she was telling the truth.

30

Leticia reached out and touched the glass. She had a strange feeling, like there was something living inside there. Some kind of animal. The room was quiet and cold like a church. But she knew that smell, Leticia closed her eyes to remember. Synthea's perfume. She had been here, in this room. Not knowing why, Leticia spoke her name out loud. *Synthea.* But she wasn't there to hear it. Leticia hugged herself against the chill. She didn't like this place, it felt all wrong. Haunted. She took one last look at the glass cabinet and closed the white door behind her.

Leticia walked to the end of the corridor and turned a corner. Another corridor, and, halfway down, another door left ajar. Maybe Mrs Synthea was in that room. She had to try at least. She pushed the door and it was heavy like the last one, she had to use both hands this time. It was dark except one wall, lit from below. Masks. A wall of masks. All different kinds, hundreds of them. There were some really scary ones, but Leticia didn't want to look at them, not yet.

Plastic animal masks, like you get at parties for younger kids. An elephant, a tiger, monkey, zebra, panda, always the same animals. Friendly, fun, but not like this, on a wall like this and mixed up with all the others. Then there were the soft ones, like you get at Halloween time: goblins, former presidents of the United States, monsters, clowns, but these weren't the really scary ones. In random places there were other masks, very different from the others. She made herself look. They were like real people on the wall there. So much like real-life faces. It was like they were in the room with her. No eyes, but she still recognized some of them. They were people Mr Casey worked with, and famous people, like actors and other celebrities. She looked at the faces and the faces looked right back at her. River. There was River's face. And Missy. Synthea. The whole family was there on the wall. Except Mr Casey, she couldn't see him anywhere. But there was something. A gap. A space on the wall where a mask should be. She thought she understood, and the idea made her feel very cold inside. Leticia suddenly felt weak in her body. She looked at her hands and the fingertips where white, numb, and her feet. She opened and closed her hands, continuing to back away from the wall of masks. This wasn't funny anymore. It was never funny but now it wasn't funny at all. Then the voice behind her. Her name spoken quietly. It was Mrs Synthea in the doorway. She was naked and falling. Leticia caught her in her arms before she could hit the ground.

31

As River is typing, causing trouble on the boards, flaming just to see what burns, he has his mind elsewhere. He's been able to do this since he was a kid. Do one thing while concentrating just as hard on something different. This other thing. It's like a dark shape at the edge of his consciousness, a figment, but this isn't imagination. River is beginning to understand. What happened to Missy. What's happening to him. The sword video. unknown_user. Croc. Hide-and-seek. Come out, come out. The chocolate key. Versailles — Versailles. What all this means – his life, her life – what it's all for. A shape at the edge of his consciousness. It could be human, but he isn't sure just yet. Or maybe he just doesn't want to look, to understand. But there is something happening in this house. One hundred rooms and only Casey holds a master key.

The intuition almost stops him typing. He knows that opening even one of those white doors would bring him closer. For most of his life he's lived in this house, inside these walls, and never once has he set foot inside a room he wasn't allowed to. For years he looked for the hack. The things happening in this house. This house he calls home. *Like Disney World, but no Mickey Mouse.* But right now

River feels like he can do anything, like he has to do *something*. One hundred rooms and only Casey holds a master key. Bullshit, River thinks. Just one of those white doors. He stops typing. Clicks *post reply* on a 500-word put-down designed to make this vindictive bully of a troll he's been stalking stop and think for one minute about the consequences of his actions. Not all trolls are created equal.

River closes his eyes. Sees his right hand enter the frame like in a first-person video game. He's reaching out to open one of the white doors. The door swings open, no light in the gap. River takes a step forward, deeper into his daydream, across the threshold of the forbidden room. He feels for a light switch, the room too dark to see. But there is something. Deep inside the space. A pinpoint of light, like a distant star but right here in the room. River moves towards the light, the darkness closing in. And then the door slams behind him. His eyes open because the bang isn't in his daydream, it's in his room.

He grabs the rapier from the desk and shouts *en garde* in time to realize it's his skateboard fallen over. It rolls toward him like it's a ghost about to bust an ollie. River lowers the rapier and laughs, that same adrenaline like before, enough that he was ready to kill just now. Ready to kill someone. He clocks the tennis ball cannon across the room. An overwhelming feeling of being in love. A boy he hasn't met yet. Leaping dolphins. A girl he hasn't even met yet. A tunnel of rainbows. A feeling of being in love, of wanting to make babies, see his sister again, her endless excitement about whatever, acting out what she was saying in wide, arcing gestures, like a ballet dancer, like a ballet dancer making up her routine as she goes along. River laughs. He's about ready to— he lets the rapier fall from his grasp and clatter to the hard floor. Hornier than a four-balled tomcat. River jumps on his skateboard and pulls a perfect casper 50-50 like he's saying hi to a pretty girl/boy. He can taste the white chocolate in his mouth, he's about ready to pop, show the world what time it is. River Baer, breaker of codes, white knight about ready to bust some white doors. Open wide like a dream, wide like a nightmare.

Out the corner of his eye. *New Message.* Screen six, a personal message from someone on *scoutfan*'s Instant Message server. River swiveled slightly in his chair and single-clicked the notification before it could disappear. It was from Inner-Fame.

InnerFame
Hi, pr1ncess. Saw you online and thought I'd say hey.

pr1ncess
Hi there, Fame, what's happening?

InnerFame
I wanted to tell you I read your dream submission just now and thought it was really interesting.

pr1ncess
You did? It's strange, right? I never had a dream like that before.

InnerFame
What's strange about it is I had the exact same dream.

pr1ncess
No kidding? Like, exactly the same dream?

InnerFame

I think it means something, pr1ncess, I really do. And you know what's even freakier? When I set that competition, I had this feeling. I had this feeling one of you was going to come back with the same dream. And I was right. It's you, pr1ncess. You're the one. I just wanted to let you know that, pr1ncess, because I think this means something. I shouldn't be telling you this but that competition? The chance to speak to Scout herself over chat? I think we have a winner.

pr1ncess

squeals

InnerFame

That's right, but pr1ncess? Don't tell anyone, it'd only cause problems. I can't announce officially till tomorrow.

pr1ncess

Your secret's safe with me, Fame. Thank you so much. I can't tell you what this means to me. Scout Rose has been my inspiration for as long as I can remember.

InnerFame

I know, sweetheart, I know.

River spun around on his office chair. This was it, this was it. He was being recruited. pr1ncess being groomed for Deep Sky. A bone fide cult and they chose *him*, just like they chose his sister. It was almost too easy . . . And then a cold chill came over him as he remembered Money speaking unknown_user's words and the underwear scroll in his safe.

What if he *wasn't* a step ahead of Deep Sky? He'd taken every precaution online but maybe he'd allowed his arrogance to get the better of him. What if he wasn't a step ahead? What if all his precautions hadn't worked and Deep Sky was just playing him for a fool? They could all be the same person: unknown_user, ruhin, InnerFame. Everybody. *scoutfan* itself: it could all be one dude . . .

Had they seen through pr1ncess all along? Had Deep Sky known all this time? Was River headed into some kind of trap? Only way he was gonna know the answer to these questions was by catching up with these freaks or getting caught. And the only way that was gonna happen was if he played along. So InnerFame and unknown_user were probably the same person. So what? So maybe it was impossible to be anonymous from these people and they were watching him at this very moment, both online and off. So what? All River cared about right now was finding Missy, and whatever Deep Sky had planned for him – pr1ncess or no pr1ncess – he was pretty sure it would mean seeing his big sister again.

32

A sense of floating, as on the surface of an ocean, except this light is not the sun. The sun is warm and this light is cold. And Synthea is moving, floating on her back. But this is not the ocean. These are walls. These are artificial lights. A long ceiling. She is inside somewhere. These walls. Versailles. She wants to scream, but no sound comes. The effects of the pill. She lifts her arm into the frame, her skin, her surfaces are turned to white plastic. Or so it seems. These pharma companies. Their sick magic. Four faces. One of them Leticia. It feels like water. She is being carried. The effects of the pill but her heart is full of love for her children. Missy and River. Her children. When Missy told her everything before. The water only pink with blood. And River in his room, hidden in his room, a game of hide-and-seek gone on too long. Her missing daughter. But Casey knows. He says he knows what's best. A wave of nausea.

Her room, their bedroom, she knows this ceiling well. Hours gazing through this white ceiling, past it to the empty universe beyond. Well beyond the bedroom walls. They carry her to bed, the silk sheets smelling lightly of clean sweat, Casey's scent. She loved him once, before all this. Before Versailles. She loved him. This young man with all the vision and good intentions. A charisma without witness and he let her in. And he loved *her*, he loves her still. She feels the cool sheets, silk sheets being pulled up over her naked body. This feeling of being put to bed. Like a child being sent away to sleep. She feels her eyelids close, two soft switches *off*.

She remembers. Casey's words in her ear, when they were still students, their relationship long distance, travelling across America to sleep in one another's dorms. She remembers, one night, lying in his narrow bed, her head on his shoulder, his roommate already asleep.

His words, low tones: 'I'll build you a house—'

Her words, interrupting him: 'Not if I build you one first!'

His: 'I'll build you a house by the ocean, right on the ocean. You'll be able to walk out of the house and dive right into the water . . . I can see you, I see you, you're naked, and you're walking right out of the house without your clothes and diving into the ocean. I want to . . .' His words. ' . . . I want to have kids. More than one . . .' His words, whispered now, ' . . . I want to build you a house by the ocean . . . I want us to have kids. I love you, Synthea.' It was the second time he'd said it in as many months, and again she didn't answer him in turn. Even then she'd felt . . . a feeling she was sinking, being pulled down, around and down.

She remembers. Versailles being built, their *house by the ocean*, the biggest private residence in America. The kids playing hide-and-seek in the foundations, her walks along the beach with Casey by day, their swims in the ocean by moonlight.

They lived in an RV for a whole year. The social network's IPO was the biggest in the history of the internet. Synthea's design for the word's bestselling touch-capacitive smartphone was being heralded as a classic. They were billionaires. More money than most people would know what to do with, but Casey seemed to know exactly what he wanted. The RV meant he could oversee as much of the mansion's construction as possible. One hundred rooms and only Casey and one or two essential figures involved in the project had access to the blueprints.

Synthea remembers it as a golden time, those early days and months. The ocean right there, evening meals under the blue awning, Casey reading to the kids every night. Every. Night. And every other weekend they'd take the RV on these adventures, drive out into the mountains, endless picnics and hikes and impossible views, card games in the evening by the warm glow of a 12V light bulb, and when the kids were asleep she and Casey would put out a couple of folding chairs and talk and talk under the millions of stars, a sky so dark you could see the Milky Way, a vast, shimmering band, like bioluminescence.

She can't remember now. What they talked about.

And the kids were young, so they probably don't remember much about that time.

They wouldn't remember that when Versailles was finally built, its Pentelic marble glowing gold in the sun, everything changed. That very first night in the master bedroom, beneath the silk sheets, something felt different. She'd felt a shift in Casey. It happened during sex. Nothing violent. No, but more than once she had to ask him to go slow. That he was hurting her. And she remembers how sorry he was, saying he didn't know what was wrong with him, that she knew he wasn't like that, and it wouldn't happen again. And it never did.

But it wasn't just that. When Versailles was built he was not the same, always distant. These great distances inside the mansion. It was too big. All those rooms. She'd ask him what was in those rooms and he would never tell, except to say it was a work in progress, and that one day he would show her, one day he would show her everything. She remembers coming home from work and not being able to find him anywhere. Asking the kids, the staff, if they'd seen Casey and they'd say no. It was like Versailles had swallowed him up.

Then one day. She remembers. She was in their bed and just fallen asleep. She woke to him coming in the room. He was breathing fast, like he'd been running, or seen something that had frightened him. She remembers. Him slipping under the sheets, catching his breath, and the words in her ear: *I miss you, darling. I miss you.*

She'd pretended not to wake, heard his breathing slow as he fell asleep. But then it happened the next night again, and the one after that. His coming in the room, out of breath and telling her he missed her like that, whispering it in her ear. Soon it became a mantra, one that found its way into their waking hours. *I miss you, darling*, he would say. *But I'm right here, Casey*, she would reply. It was like comforting a child sometimes. And then the mantra extended. He wanted her to start working from home. He brought the kids into it, telling her, *They miss you. They tell me all the time how much they miss their mom. Come home to us, my love. I'll get you anything you need. A view of the ocean. A window so big it will feel like you're outside.*

It became a mantra and it found its way into their day-light hours. It was seamless. He started saying it in front of the kids. And eventually they joined in, begging their mom to come home, to work from home. You repeat something enough times to a young child and they'll start saying it themselves.

And so Synthea came home. And for a time it was wonderful. Being closer to the kids. River coming by to watch her work, quiet as could be, resting his head lightly on her shoulder, gasping now and then as he remembered to breathe, his clever questions about what she was doing. Missy bringing her mother lunch, lovingly prepared with Leticia's help in Versailles' kitchens. And she was productive, and her designs were a great success. And Casey had what he wanted: his family together, all under one roof.

And when the kids were old enough to go to school, Casey said they couldn't go, that they were to be educated at home. And when Synthea said no, said her kids needed to be with other kids, play in the sunshine, see the world as it really was, something happened that had never really happened before. Casey raised his voice. And not like people raised their voices in a heated argument. He started shouting at her like nobody ever had. Roaring about his kids, *my kids*, like suddenly they belonged only to him.

She fought hard. Day in, day out, Casey roaring at her about his kids and what was best, his own childishness turning to something monstrous. He had become a monster. A Versailles monster. And eventually she had to say yes, and her saying yes was the end. Not just of her love for him, but something else. Saying yes was the beginning of the end for Synthea. She'd look out of the window of her studio and the ocean seemed so far away, a tidal retreat independent of the moon's influence. Versailles, Versailles. A fortress for his family, and everything they needed, right here. Versailles. House of a thousand cameras. Their every move recorded. Versailles as fortress, the choice of stone, walls within walls, the miles of cable and the levels of control. *You can have anything you want*, he'd tell his children. *Like Disney World, but no Mickey Mouse.*

But by the time the kids were old enough for junior high she had an idea. She thought of the worst thing and threatened Casey with it. She thought of the worst thing and told him she would do it if he didn't let her kids go to school. She threatened him and he bowed to her threat.

He bowed but never let her forget. He thought of his own worst thing and threatened her with *that* every day. His punishment for the one time she got her way.

Something about Versailles. These rooms. At some point she'd lost her husband to this mansion, the man she fell in love with, so full of promises. Something about Versailles. These rooms. She imagined each one was an experiment, a locked test-chamber. And this bedroom was no different. This house. His family. They were all part of one big experiment, and only Casey knew why.

Synthea tries to open her eyes. She has to find her daughter, her little Missy. She can hear Leticia moving around her in the room, singing one of the lullabies she used to sing to the kids at bedtime.

Leticia draws the black curtains, those terrible black curtains, and now the room is dark, dark as night on a moonless night. But she will not leave her side. Leticia will sit here, in this comfy armchair beside the bed, and wait. So when Mrs Synthea wakes up she will be right here. Leticia has her phone. She will play games on her phone with the sound turned off. She likes the one with the falling jewels. Falling, falling, and Leticia must keep up or she will *lose!* She could play that one forever. She loves the sparkly animations, and the nice explosions when she's doing really good. But she will not leave her side. When Synthea wakes up she will not be alone. First thing she sees. For Leticia knows, she feels deep, she understands. No one likes to be alone for too long, and Mrs Synthea has been alone for too long. She loves this woman sleeping here, quiet like a child underneath the beautiful sheets that are the color of pearls. And she hopes her dreams are only of good things, for all the badness in the world, let her dreams be good dreams, of white unicorns, big rainbows and colorful jewels everywhere, falling from the bright blue sky like candy, millions of them sparkling in the sunshine forever and ever.

33

We rejoin Missy where we left her last, fast asleep in the northbound trailer, Silas at the wheel out front, telling his son a story of the Cahuilla Indians, of an older boy who must climb a mountain and become a man.

Missy sleeps a dreamless sleep. What Missy doesn't know is this: we always dream, only sometimes we forget. A memory as dream:

A trip into the country, she's very young but she remembers now. Her whole family, Mom, Dad, River and her, all packed into their RV and on the open road. They're going on another adventure and she's out back with her brother, reading and playing video games and fighting and sleeping and eating snacks and looking out the window.

When they arrive they're right in the mountains. A view of their city in the great distance, glittering and silent in the late afternoon sun. Missy says can they go play, she means inside the treeline, but Casey tells them to stay close, not to go out of sight or earshot. It's Synthea, already collecting kindling for a fire, who tells them it's okay to go a little further, just be back in time for dinner, and *play nice*.

Missy wants to see a bear, like the one she saw on TV. That would make her very happy. River wants to see a bear too, but he's scared. Missy takes him by the hand and they stand inside the pine forest. They take a few steps forward, out of the sunlight.

They never see a bear. In real life, they find some sticks and have a sword-fight. Missy draws her brother's blood and gets in trouble, but is still allowed to join in later when they sit around Synthea's sparking fire toasting marshmallows.

In Missy's dream things play out differently. She doesn't see a bear but she does see something else.

In her dream she is suddenly alone and she sees a man, half-hidden behind a tree in the middle distance. *Come out!* she yells, the anger unexpected. The man comes out from behind the tree and . . . it looks like her dad, only older. It looks like it could be Casey but that's impossible because Casey is back at their camp. *Who are you?* Missy says, and then the man is much closer, like he took a blink to close the distance. It's Casey, her father, she can see that now, but he's older, the age he'll be when Missy is awake again. She's never seen her father cry before, but she's not scared. This is not a bad dream.

She sees he's wearing a sword by his side. All his other clothes are like the ones he wears now – the hoodie, slacks and the white sneakers – but the belt holding the scabbard is from another time. It's wide and made of leather, scorch-marked with intricate patterns, like ocean waves and lizard scales and human eyes without the iris or the pupil. But Missy isn't scared, this isn't a bad dream. Because this Casey isn't scary, he's sad. And when he unsheathes the sword she doesn't flinch. And when he brings it horizontal she holds out both her hands, palms up. A ritual. Her father's love so strong but when she looks up again he's gone. And as Missy begins to wake she can feel the weight of it, her sword, her key to the future.

The ground was moving. Missy woke from a dreamless sleep in the comfortable armchair but everything was different. The ground, the walls, everything was moving. It took her several seconds to remember where she was, and several more to work out what was happening. The trailer park in the middle of nowhere. The boy with no name. The bunny rabbit with the red eyes. Silas. The bear in the dark woods. Scout Rose. Oh my God, Scout Rose giving an interview! But how? Why now? She tried to recall details. Deep sky. Something about a deep sky. But she couldn't remember anything else. Just blackness. A dreamless sleep. It didn't matter right now. They were on the move. The trailer was on the move, and she was in it. A new feeling . . . This was it. This is what it felt like to be in danger.

She leapt to her feet and moved to the window. It was nighttime outside, pitch black. How did she not wake up? Then she knew. The soda in the glass bottle. They must have put something in it. They must have put something in it and now they were moving at high speed along an expressway, away from anywhere she knew, the trailer park, her car, her car, the sword, her phone. Oh God, her sword! The phone she could replace but her beautiful sword . . . Missy's confusion turned to panic and then anger in a split second. She screamed in frustration. Her instinct was to go for the door, but where was she gonna go? She had to think. She had to calm down and think.

PART THREE
The Idea of North

34

Versailles vibrates inside the line of tall palm trees, its rain-slicked southern edifice illuminated by the silver moon, the sickening non-architecture of a fever dream, its gray foundations plunged deep into the shifting, bubbling marsh. Versailles, USA. Palace to an American King, a man for his times. Casey Baer. His command our wish. Versailles. A family fortress. The choice of stone. Pentelic marble shipped here from Greece, pure white by night and glowing golden in the sun. The choice of stone, the choice of glass, glass that curves by degrees of greed. Versailles. All-consuming. Versailles vibrates inside the line of tall palms, no windows open just now, the towering, ocean-liner A/C stacks breathing out, only out, ever out into the vanishing world. *Versailles*, the ocean seems to say, *Versailles*.

Versailles vibrates, its oscillations widening with every passing hour, every passing day that Missy isn't here, an exponential deepening of frequency that bears little relationship to the goings-on inside its rooms and corridors, the activities of those human beings who ... the activities of those human beings who are living here just now, their little hands and feet, their little mouths and deft articulations. The shiny buckles on their shoes, their painted faces. Their little hands and feet, like ceramic dolls, their delicate features reflected back at them in blank screens, so many screens, these mirrors reflecting back their delicately painted features again and again. The surveillance total. Versailles — Versailles.

A white fortress for his family. His wife and their dynamic, beautiful children. Missy & River Baer. His pride & joy. Versailles. The house where they grew up. Versailles as witness. So many memories. The miles and miles of cable, the choice of cameras, motion sensitive, the choice of lock, unbreakable. One hundred rooms and the majority are under lock and encrypted key. Will River find a way, will River flow again, between and around the many obstacles? One hundred rooms and only Casey knows. The goings-on. A secret combination, the choice of lock. The castle, the keep. His secrets safe for now, but will River find a way? Versailles as fortress, the choice of stone, walls within walls, the miles of cable and the levels of control. Missy missing now. Versailles as Mission Control. The view from space. The God angle. Cameras tracking Missy on her journey north, her final fantasy, following in Scout's footsteps, the idea of north, the levels of control, what Casey doesn't know.

What Casey doesn't see: the fullness of her anger. What Casey doesn't see is that his daughter stole the Twinkies. It was under his instruction but it was *her* who carried out the act. *Her* anger, her impulse, her choice – flying crocodile – her pulse, her path, the journey north, her north, wherever that may be. This newfound confidence. Character. Rebel before cause. What Casey doesn't know will hurt him. The sheerness of this youth. A youth synthesized like none before, their mirrors reflecting back again and again. Her generation witnessed like no other, their every action reflected on the social networks, the internet as molten mirror, a primordial balm. Yes you are, *yes you can*. You are, you are, I am, I am. The determination of this youth. To be somebody. Like and unlike. A brand of monster. You, you, you, me, me, me. Acting up and *out*. The fuck *out*. Fuck yeah, fuck *yes*.

What Casey doesn't know. His daughter's anger. Her hate for him. A perfect thing, its edges softened to infinity. Her love of life. She wants to live. His daughter loves, has loved. Her youth, her future unfolding, dark to light, affect not effect. The boy at school. Such beauty in the world, the world beyond Versailles, the doors thrown open.

So much he doesn't know, but this is Casey Baer, the most powerful man on the internet and he knows what we want, what Missy needs. She may be his daughter, but what she needs is to be taught a lesson. His birthday present: a final fantasy and it's only just begun. This journey north. Her rite of passage. Her roller coaster rebellion. Destination: Deep Sky, America's most enigmatic cult, the last people left on earth who can keep a secret.

What Casey did. Will Missy tell the tale? Realize her fate, break free? For now, the monitor lizard makes his way along another empty corridor. His teeth are bared but he is not angry. His yellow eyes look mean but he is not mean, he is a monitor lizard who has not eaten in some time. Just then he passes a white door. According to Versailles' schematics, this is Room 57, the throne room. Let us enter, let us see. The white door. Locked yet unlocked. For who is Casey Baer if not a sum of his endeavors? He swipes for an update.

35

The texture of the road had changed, tarmac smooth to dirt track rough. For the first time in a while Missy wished she knew where she was, wished she had her phone so she could see herself as a blue dot on the map. Now and then the trailer went over a bump in the road and something fell off a shelf. Missy liked things to be tidy so she was on her feet picking things up and putting them back where they belonged. It was a losing battle, but it gave her a job to do. She looked at her watch. Ten p.m. Seven hours since she ate that omelet. There was a fridge with food and drink but she didn't want to risk it.

Since waking up she'd had some time to think, and not being in control of where she was going next had made it difficult for her to focus on the future, so her thoughts had turned to the past, to all the things she was trying to escape. Her father's betrayal had cast a shadow over Missy. Before that she'd been happy, happier than she'd ever been. The boy at school who asked her to prom and ended up in a headlock. Levon. River's best friend. The only person at school she really cared about. The only one of them who felt real to her. Levon. Missy's first love.

She told her parents he was her study partner. They'd

shared their first kiss on the beach of the desert island in her bedroom, by the light of her tall palm tree lamp. The next day Missy told her mom she had a boyfriend. *In a relationship*. Levon. The boy at school who told her she was beautiful. He'd grown up in the city, in their school on scholarship. Between making-out in her room and actual study she would ask him endless questions about everything, the world outside, what it felt like to walk down the street, go to a concert with your friends, eat ice cream at an ice cream parlor, go walking with a dog, cross at traffic lights. She'd ask him if he'd ever seen someone sleeping rough, or witnessed a fight, or if he'd been mugged, seen a gun, bullets, murder, a murder scene, someone dead, a car crash, plane crash, train crash, funfair, zoo, bonfire, any kind of fire, what it felt like to sleep under the stars, drink water from a river, catch a fish, eat sushi from one of those moving belts with all the colored plates. All the colors in the world. She imagined it all looked so different, beyond Versailles, the tinted windows of the cars driving her to and from school. And Levon would do his best, tell her all his stories, his friends' stories, their friends' stories, all the things he'd seen so far, he'd show her photos on his phone, videos, try to explain, and when he couldn't he would kiss her eyelids and her mouth, their kisses long, then smaller and smaller until she gave him one last one and asked him something new, and on and on. Levon, the boy at school who told her she was beautiful. Missy's first love.

What Casey did after that had turned her world upside down and inside out. She stopped seeing Levon. She saw less of her friends, didn't answer as many calls. That was in the spring. Then early summer, the link to the video, the sword, the instructions to head north, and the rest was now, here in this trailer with the disembodied cat's head staring down at her from the wall.

They were slowing down. They were stopping. OMG, finally. Missy hadn't spent all her time thinking about Levon. She'd planned for this moment, when Silas or the kid with no name opened the door to the trailer. She was ready for them. She held the giant paperweight in the shape of a brilliant diamond high above her head and waited. She heard a car door slam. Then another. Two sets of footsteps along the side of the trailer and coming to a standstill right outside.

Silas spoke. 'Now, Missy, I know you must be pretty mad in there. It's been a long day and you've been cooped up in this trailer all that time and for that I am truly sorry. I also know that you're probably standing right by the door with a heavy object over your head more than ready to send it crashing down on mine. I'm going to hazard a guess it's the oversized diamond paperweight from my desk. Good choice, but I myself am holding something in my two hands that might change your mind about how this is going to shake out. It's not a gun if that's what you're thinking. We may have given you a little something to help you sleep, but we're not violent people, are we, boy? No, Missy, I'm offering you a trade. Your sword for my diamond. How does that sound? Missy?'

Missy lowered the paperweight and held it against her belly. Her sword, her amazing sword, forged on the other side of the world. Her sword, her key to the future, whatever that may hold. All that time practicing on the beach back home, she'd formed an attachment to the sword like no other object she owned, and that included her phone. And it wasn't a weapon to her, she didn't see it that way. Missy was the least violent person ever. She could never use her sword to do harm, no, it was how it made her feel holding it. The shadow she cast, her long silhouette against the evening light. Wielding the sword brought her into the moment and beyond in a way that nothing else could. Her time alone on the beach had been precious, not thinking, just being, casting shapes in the evening light and losing herself. Losing yourself made finding yourself so much better! Her sword, her inspiration. And then Missy remembered! Scout's interview! Had that really happened? Or was it just a dream? Was Scout really back? And from where? She wanted to check the internet so bad. But she didn't have her phone, and besides, right now she was in negotiations with a giant biker and his nameless son over a hero sword forged on the other side of the world. She placed the diamond paperweight at her feet and opened the door to the trailer.

Silas looked ceremonial, the sword held out in his open palms and a smile on his big, bearded face. 'It's a splendid sword,' he growled. 'Whoever made this beauty knows their craft. You'll be the envy of everybody at Deep Sky.'

Deep Sky. That thing Scout mentioned on TV. Missy stepped down from the trailer and stood in front of Silas in the gloom. 'How do you know I won't take this sword and cut you down where you stand?' she said. She had to keep reminding herself: this was a kidnapping, no two ways about it.

'There's many reasons I can think of but the main one would be because you want to know what comes next, and I'm the one who's going to take you there. We've got a long road ahead of us, you need to keep your strength. And you need a guide.'

Missy reached out and took her sword, unsheathed it from its black leather scabbard and angled the blade so that it caught the light of the moon. 'Thank you,' she said.

'I want to take this opportunity to apologize,' Silas said. 'We had to get you out of there. They were closing in on our location at the trailer park and we had to make a move right away, no time for questions. I could tell you were feeling a little homesick . . . we had to get you out.'

'Who's *they*?' Missy said, 'You mean the cops?'

'Not the cops.'

'My father then,' Missy said. 'You're wrong, by the way. I'm not homesick, I never was, not even a little. I meant what I said back there: whatever this is, I'm ready. Forget the past, I want to live in the future.'

'That's good to hear, Missy, it truly is. Well, now we're friends again, me and the kid could use some help setting up camp. You know how to build a fire?'

Missy squinted with embarrassment and shook her head no. Levon had once explained it to her, but saying and doing were two different things.

'Well, that's not a problem because I'm going to teach you,' Silas said. 'Boy, take the head torches and go with Missy to find us some wood.'

'What about Bob?' said the boy with no name. 'He told me he so hungry he could eat the south end of a northbound skunk.'

'Bob can stay in the car for now. You can take him one of those juicy carrots we picked up from the store just as soon as you've got us some firewood. Now, scoot!'

They sat in silence for some time, all three enjoying the warmth of the fire, sausages sizzling in a hanging pot. The night sky was so very, very dark. Missy had never seen so many stars, she had this sense that she was looking *into* the sky for the first time, deep into space, so deep it felt like falling. And the shooting stars. They came every few minutes it seemed, always seen out of the corner of her eye.

They sat in silence and Missy enjoyed the fire, looking into it as the flames danced ever upwards, the heat almost too much but she didn't want to back away, and the kid with no name stroking his bunny rabbit, a little too hard she thought but with a steady rhythm, head to tail, head to tail, its triangle nose moving up and down, and Silas with his eyes closed, cross-legged with his arms out to the sides like he was meditating. He'd taken off his leather jacket to reveal a leather waistcoat and nothing underneath. Across his collar bone and down his arms, shoulders to wrists, everywhere you could see skin, there were tattoos. Really it was one tattoo. An entire forest, and in amongst the trees there were animals, all the animals you might find in a real forest. By his right shoulder was an owl, and on his left forearm a bear had appeared from behind a fallen tree trunk. It looked just like the bear from before, it was weird, like a snapshot of what happened. It was like this tattoo was alive, and Missy was fascinated by it. She wanted to ask what it meant to him but at the same time she didn't want to seem too interested.

Silas said yesterday there was no turning back, but did that mean she was being held prisoner? She wanted to call her mother, to hear her voice one last time. Her mother was lost, but it wasn't her fault. She wanted to call her on the phone, hear her voice, not the words, just her voice, her voice, her hands, her hands stroking Missy's hair as she went to sleep, stroking her hair and pausing to touch her on the cheek. But this was memory, this was when she was still a little girl, her mother's hands stroking Missy's long blonde hair, the perfume lingering long after lights out, Leticia's lullabies in words she came to understand as she grew older. She wanted to call her mother on the phone but her mother was lost, moving through Versailles like a ghost. The way she carried herself. And her voice. It was like a different person.

Missy looked down at her hands in the light of the fire. They were dirty from collecting wood, and they smelled of dirt. She'd smelled dirt before. Went through a period of burying her dolls at the bottom of the garden at Versailles, explaining to her worried mom that *they were going to sleep for the winter*. But this dirt out here smelled different somehow, and Missy decided she liked it. The boy with no name had shown her the different kinds of kindling. *Kindling*, she loved that word, it was like it was already burning. The names and explanations for the different kinds of kindling sounded funny coming out of the kid's mouth, but Silas had been a good teacher. *Extra fine kindling* ('Like matchsticks, but it's gotta be dry, Missy, it's gotta be dry or it's no good.'). *Fine kindling* ('Thicker than a match, but thinner than a pencil. You got that, Missy? Hey! You listening to me?'). *Small fuel* ('Thicker than a pencil but not thicker than your thumb. Ha! Thumb rhymes with dumb and you're dumber than a box of rocks!'). *Main fuel* ('Sticks thicker than your thumb that you can break over your knee, but that's my job. That's my job breaking the sticks cus I like doing that. You got a problem with me breaking the sticks, Missy? Cus even if you do I don't care cus I'm breaking them sticks.').

There was a loud *crack* from the fire that made Missy jump. Silas slowly opened his eyes and caught her wide-eyed expression. 'That's just moisture in the wood,' he said. 'It turns to steam and explodes. Nothing to worry about.' He smiled. 'You must be hungry, Missy.'

She nodded.

'Well, I think these sausages are just about done. I've pre-sliced buns, there's tomato ketchup and mustard. You like hot dogs, Missy?'

'I love hot dogs.'

'Good then.'

Missy had three hot dogs. #yum. The sausages were kind of burned on the outside but they tasted good, like eating a hot dog for the first time, but then pretty much all of this felt like a first. When she was done she licked her fingers. She rubbed her hands together then held them closer to the fire. She wasn't cold but it was a nice feeling. She had helped make this fire, made the spark that caused these flames. This warmth, it was her warmth, she was here because she wanted to be. And she didn't want her phone anymore. Something great about not knowing your location.

She wasn't sure she trusted Silas, but then again, who did she trust anymore? She trusted River. She didn't know half the stuff he got up to on the internet, but he would always be there for her when she needed him. That's why she regretted not telling him what happened. What Casey did had cast a shadow, and Missy had gone inside herself. She hadn't wanted to talk to anyone about it, not even her own twin brother who she told everything, and now she might never get a chance to explain. She hated the thought of having abandoned River, but her brother could handle himself. He had an imagination as deep and wide as an ocean. He was creative, and creative people found a way to survive, they could go inside themselves and find something new every time. Like diamonds in a cave.

Missy wasn't sure if she was a creative person. She was a friendly person, she had friends and they seemed to like her. But there was something missing. She didn't *make* anything. She thought she might want to design clothes. She loved fashion, she loved experimenting with different clothes. Years of watching her mom get dressed in Versailles' master bedroom, emerging from the walk-in wardrobe in her extraordinary outfits, half of them her own making, looking and smelling like an empress from another world. Missy dreamed of having her own perfume one day, like Scout Rose. But Missy didn't know. She didn't know if she had the creative thing her mother and brother had. And her father. Was his work creative? He called himself a hacker, a coder, but she knew different. One hundred rooms and only Casey had a master key.

What happened with her father had changed things for Missy. She couldn't talk to anybody about what had happened, not even Levon, so she went inside herself, spent less and less time with her friends, and more time alone, and when she closed her eyes she could explore inside herself, explore the cave. Every night before she went to sleep, Missy would close her eyes and explore, going deeper every time. And there she found her own kind of treasure: crystalline fragments of memory, of desire, hope, anger, all different colors, all different shapes, but they were beautiful and they had *weight* and they felt important, more important than anything else. She'd wanted to bring them back into the waking world, assemble them into a new whole, like a new armor for herself, a new look for her waking life. She wanted to tell Levon. Just like he'd told her about the world outside Versailles, she wanted to tell him of her own discoveries, these things about herself she never knew before. But something told her she had to hold these things close. And anyway, it wasn't something that was easy to put into words.

The sword video came at the right time. Scout dancing with her sword in the desert in the dying light. Her look, the dance, her silhouette. She had the right *shape*. This is what it would look like if Missy assembled all those fragments of herself in the right order. The right shape. When Missy watched the sword video she saw herself, a strong girl who could overcome anything, hell, who'd already left everything behind and was striking out on her own, tearing through the invisible curtain with her sword and stepping into the future.

'Deep Sky,' Silas said, interrupting her thoughts. 'That's where we're headed. It's in the far north, we have a long road to travel, but when we get there, everything will be different for you, Missy. I can promise you that. You'll meet people, young people such as yourself who are looking for the same things. We live in a world of attachments – the information age – of the online social network, of triangulation, perpetual connectivity, frictionless sharing and our insatiable appetite for affirmation. But the people who live in that world have forgotten that where there is light there must also be darkness. We all have secrets, Missy, but what those people don't understand is that we need secrets, because without that private, inner life, we lose the ability to distinguish ourselves, we lose the sense of who we really are. You ever heard of *true dark*, Missy?'

'I haven't,' she said.

'There are still places in the world, far from any human settlement, where the sky is truly dark. It is the sky that once was. They talk about the dark ages. Millions upon millions of stars visible to the naked eye. It's all there still, only we can't see it. We build, we expand, we cast our light on everything and everybody, we eat the darkness. I've seen it, Missy, the night sky as it should be, and when I saw it I knew who I was, I knew my purpose in life. True dark. I was there when he built Deep Sky, his monument to the true dark. I was there, Missy, and soon you will see it for yourself.'

'Who is he?' Missy said. 'Who built Deep Sky?'

'You will know in time.'

'But I know *your* name.'

'Ah, yes, but I was never chosen. My role is to choose.'

'What about your son, does he have a name?'

The kid with no name didn't look up from stroking his rabbit. 'My son will have his time,' Silas said. 'He will have his time in Deep Sky. For now, he helps me in my work, he helps me choose.'

'Did he help choose me?' Missy said. They were speaking about the kid like he wasn't there.

'Why, yes, he did,' said Silas. 'As a matter of fact, he wouldn't stop talking about you in the car. He thinks you're a real life princess . . . Don't you, kiddo?'

The kid with no name got to his feet without a word and walked away from the fire into the darkness. It looked for a moment like the white rabbit was floating in mid-air before they both disappeared.

'You embarrassed him,' Missy said.

'Perhaps, but then what are fathers for? He'll be back in a minute.'

Missy lay on her back and waited for a shooting star. 'Can I ask you something?'

'Ask away.'

'That video. I mean, have you ever met Scout Rose? Did you ever, like, talk to her?'

'Sure I did,' Silas said, 'Matter of fact, I was the one brought her in, just like I am you.'

Missy sat bolt upright. 'Are you serious? You know Scout Rose? You really talked to her? She's like my favorite recording artist of all time! I've been downloading her music since I was a little kid.'

'She's certainly a talented young woman, there's no doubt about that. And one of the best students Deep Sky ever had.'

'So it's really true,' Missy said, 'All that time she was away, when no one knew where she was, she was with you guys, at Deep Sky?'

Silas chuckled. 'Man, oh, man, you really got it bad, don't you? Damn thing is, you remind me of her a little bit. Her enthusiasm, her curiosity for life. I'm sure the two of you would have got on just fine.'

Missy lay back down again, one hand under her head. The stars in the sky seemed to have quadrupled since she last looked. Scout Rose. Deep Sky. Something about it still didn't seem right, but she couldn't help feeling a little excited. She was totally on an *adventure*, following in the footsteps of her hero. Her millions of followers looking elsewhere and . . . she didn't care. Her phone somewhere, the battery gone, the velvet of the unbreakable glass. She ran her thumb over the leather binding around her sword's hilt. Her key to the future, whatever that may hold. She closed her eyes and played the sword video in her mind; Scout in the desert, dancing slowly to a hidden soundtrack, casting shapes, perfect shapes, in the twilight. She played the video until it went to black, and when Missy opened her eyes again she saw only stars.

'Clouds are coming in,' Silas said. 'An hour from now all these stars will be gone. It will be like somebody turned the lights out. You're tired, Missy, and it's late. I've made up the bed in the trailer. We can sleep out here by the fire. You need a good night's rest in the bed. Tomorrow will be a long day and you need your strength.'

'Are you sure?' said Missy.

'I'm sure,' Silas said.

The kid came and sat back down by the fire. Went back to stroking his bunny rabbit real hard, head to tail, head to tail, so hard Missy nearly had to say something, but she kept quiet, the deep sky above pulling her upward, something like gravity, so powerful she felt a tingling up and down her neck. So far, so far from home, no one to see this now. No one she knew. Right – out – *here*. Wherever here was, but, yeah, she felt alive, she felt undone. She thought of Cass, the tattoos of stars, wolf howling. She felt the chill of the desert on her back, held her hands out to the fire one last time, the amber flames dancing ever upward, the warmth of this fire that she'd helped build, a skill to take away with her, on to the next place. She glanced over at Silas once more. She wasn't sure she trusted this man. *Let's see how this goes*, she told herself. *I can build a fire. I can drive a car. I can handle myself.* Sword by her side, her heart still open, her heart, her body, her future. Far away from Versailles, out from under all those cameras. Even the dirt smelled different. Her millions of followers looking elsewhere and she didn't care. These stars, these millions of stars. The open road was who she was now. Destination: Deep Sky. If her father only knew. His princess hooking up with the last people on earth standing up to the social internet and Casey's brand of freedom. If only her father could see her. But she was glad he couldn't. The sky darker now. Clouds coming in like Silas said, drawn across like a heavy curtain.

36

Room 57. The throne room. A cathedral space, the gloomy heavens above Versailles displayed in ultra-high definition on the vast screen above, millions upon millions of stars lost in the synthetic mix, the skyglow of a nearby metropolis. The throne room. An absent king. A cathedral space rendered in black marble, the silver light of the captured moon. A steep flight of steps leading to a platform. The throne itself. A high-backed chair built of non-reflective glass. Nearly invisible.

The throne room is empty just now, but Casey was here not so long ago. There is evidence that he is sleeping here. An orange ridge tent, the one you see in your mind's eye when you think *tent*, the very same, pitched a short distance from the glass throne, a stone's throw you might say. An orange ridge tent, lit from within by a lantern. A glowing tent. Two triangles of canvas, two rectangles. A scene from childhood. The start of an adventure. Outdoor equipment spilling from a brightly colored backpack by the tent entrance. An expensive, chrome-housed torch, no batteries. A goose down sleeping bag of the highest quality, tightly repacked inside its compression sack. A folding gas stove, scorch marks resulting from more than one failed ignition. A scene from half-remembered childhood. An open packet of Twinkies, infinitesimal crumbs visible against the dark granite floor. His time alone is precious. A scene from Casey's present. Half-remembered skills taught him by his father. Shavings from an unfinished wooden spoon, the carving knife flecked with blood, a trail of blood to the white door. There are signs that he is sleeping here from time to time, a scene from childhood, the taste of beer years later, a college camping trip, and Casey was the one to build the fire, a hunter's fire, the skills taught him by his father, the taste of weak beer and the mutual respect.

The throne room. His time alone is precious, away from it all, the light of the moon and the sense of adventure. A scene from his youth. His friends' happy faces captured in the glow of a fire he built with his own hands, strong hands that now are cleaner than most. Most other people's hands are dirty, Casey thinks. Most people's hands are greasy, their smelly fingers, the smell of other people, too human, like and yet so unlike himself.

The throne room empty just now, but he was here not so long ago. A scene from childhood, the brand-new orange ridge tent lit from within by a nine-hour candle lantern. Evidence that Casey Baer is sleeping here from time to time. His time alone is precious. Away from it all, alive by the light of the silver moon. An adventure just beginning. Such beauty in the world, the world beyond Versailles, the starry sky above, millions upon millions of stars. He remembers. How every other weekend he would take his family away into the mountains. Versailles in the deep background, rising from the shifting marsh, brick by white brick, until one day it was complete. Their home, his pride, their *house by the ocean*.

An American Dream. A dream turned to nightmare. Casey Baer, CEO of the world's pre-eminent social network. A man in free fall. And the black box of his soul. The black box found among the wreckage of a forgotten life. And yet.

Outside the monitor lizard makes his way along another empty corridor. His teeth are bared but he is not angry. His yellow eyes look mean but he is not mean, he is a monitor lizard who has not eaten in some time. Just then he passes a white door covered in colorful stickers: pop idols, some favorite cartoon characters, skull and crossbones, some of River's old skating decals. According to Versailles' schematics, this is Room 70, Missy's bedroom.

37

The bed inside the trailer smelled fresh, these were fresh sheets, and the mattress was on the hard side, just how Missy liked it.

In her dream she is back in Versailles. It is nighttime but the corridors are brightly lit, like in a cheap hotel. And as she walks the powder-blue carpet she becomes aware of something, the knowledge creeps up on her like a cupboard monster: all the doors are unlocked. Every last room in Versailles is unlocked.

She walks between the white doors and it's like everything's vibrating, so slight you almost can't tell. But Missy feels it as an itch in her nose, the whole of Versailles vibrating, like a long-buried spaceship readying itself for vertical take-off, the upward fall. It's her fear of what's inside these rooms. That's what this is. It's Missy's fear feeding the engines. Everything vibrating and Missy closes her eyes against the bright light in the corridor to make it stop. And so it does.

She continues across the carpet with her eyes closed, she will walk like this until she finds her way. She is looking for something. What Casey did has cast a shadow, but there are no shadows in the dark, and Missy feels her way along the corridors, knowing she will find what she is looking for if she can bear to keep her eyes closed.

Missy senses something behind her, following closely, but she must not look back, she must keep her eyes tight shut until the time is right. There is someone right behind her but there is no sound, only the high-frequency buzz coming off these bright lights. *You have young ears,* her mother said, *I can't hear it but you can because you have young ears.* Her beautiful mother, her voice low and slow, all the unworn clothes in her wardrobe, her perfume lingering in the air.

The thought nearly makes Missy open her eyes but she doesn't. No shadows in the dark. Feeling her way along familiar corridors, this darkness is her light, if only she can bear to keep her eyes closed. A flight of stairs. She feels the cold marble on her bare feet. Versailles' entrance hall, but the doors are closed, shut tight. Beyond these doors is another kind of darkness, black on black. She leans against the wooden door. It's heavy on its hinges, like the door to a bank vault. She has to lean right in with her shoulder.

And as she passes through the frame into the open air it's like a firework fired straight ahead into the dark. Bang. The big reveal. This is where it happened. Outside – her first sensation is a smell. Dirt. She can smell wet earth. Chlorinated water. There is still darkness when she opens her eyes. The firework still burning out on the short grass near the swimming pool. The water only pink with blood. And then a scream, a child screaming no, but this is not the dream, this is real life, this is now.

The boy with no name is screaming and Missy is out of bed. She throws open the door to the trailer. Day breaking over the desert. A bobcat has Bob, the white rabbit with the triangle nose. Silas takes a shot with his rifle. Bang. The shot rings out. The lynx continues running, its fur makes it difficult to see, a moving target. Bang. Another miss. The boy screams no, his only friend is lost forever. Missy puts her arms around him and the boy lets her. He buries his face in her side, he hugs her tight. Missy finds a place for his head in the arc of her neck. She and Silas watch the bobcat run, the white rabbit floating away in the half-light.

They continued on the northbound highway. Missy looked out the passenger window at the mountains as they moved slowly past. And now she remembered. An extended flashback. Her family's trips into the mountains when she was a kid. The RV. The fights with River, looking out of the windows. The blue awning, marshmallows over the fire, a view of the city, their parents talking into the night. And these were good memories. Seeing Mom kissing Dad and Dad kissing Mom. She didn't think of them as parents so much anymore, more like individuals. Casey. Mom. Missy looked out the passenger window at the mountains as they moved slowly past. The sky was no longer blue, it was gray, the sun somewhere deep in the background. The boy lay in her lap with his eyes closed, but he wasn't asleep. Missy stroked his short, bristly hair with her fingers. She had her father's hands. But she was her mother's daughter, her flesh and blood. She wondered if her voice might deepen, if some day she might form her mother's perfect sentences, say all the right things, like an actress on film. Synthea . . . Synthea. She'd never thought about her mother's name before. Even the spelling . . .

Before Leticia, when her mother was the one to say

goodnight, it was Missy told the stories, not the other way around. She made them up as she went along, her mother lying by her side, falling asleep before the end. Her breathing, it was her mother's shallow breathing that sent Missy to sleep, but when she woke Synthea would be gone, her perfume still there, the coolness of the bedclothes where she had been. She had her father's hands, and she felt older, no longer a child. Her hands, her blood, her heart. And now it was coming back. The RV. Casey telling them stories every night, sometimes reading from books, sometimes making things up as he went along. Yes. She remembered now. His voice. The way he told the stories. A different voice for each character. She couldn't believe it. She couldn't believe she'd forgotten all these years, these trips, her father's stories. Every night, even back in Versailles. He would read to them. This is when she and River shared a room, River in the bunk above hers. Yes. They'd gone through this brief phase in the newly built mansion, after living in the RV all that time, where River had wanted to sleep in the same room as his sister, bunk up like before . . . It actually hurt how much she missed her brother right now. She looked down at the boy in her lap. This boy was like a little brother, someone to look after, to tell stories till they fell asleep.

'We'll get you another rabbit,' Silas said.

'I don't want another rabbit, I want Bob.'

'You know that's impossible, son, Bob's gone, but I promise you we'll find a rabbit for you to love, just as much as Bob.'

'I don't want no other rabbit. Never ever. Bob was *special*. Bob could *talk*. I talked to him and he talked right *back* to me. You don't believe me but I'm telling you the truth. There's no other rabbit 'cept Bob can talk. He the only one in the wide world.'

'I wish I could bring him back, son, but I can't, I—'

Their conversation was interrupted by a roar out of nowhere. The bikes overtook them either side, eight hogs in convoy, eight mirrors framing eight clown faces. Missy's stomach did a flip. She could have sworn that last one was Cass, her naked friend from the motel. She let go of the boy's hand and clapped her own. 'Oh, oh, I know those guys, they're my friends!'

'You know those bikers?' Silas said.

'I think so, I think so, that last one I think I recognized her, her name's Cass. Can we follow them? I think they're headed to a music festival or something like that.'

'Right now we have no choice,' Silas said. 'This road's the only one for miles, but if you mean can we go where they're going, the answer's no, Missy. We have a destination, and that destination is Deep Sky. No time for fun and games, I'm afraid.'

The anger shot through her like electricity, right through to her fingertips and toes. Anger, followed closely by fear, a realization of what this really was, this journey really *was*, the car travelling at high speed with her in it, this journey into the unknown, a stranger at the wheel, but it was her danger, her choice to say yes. The anger was unexpected, but she kept it under control when she spoke the words. 'I've done everything you said, I've played along so far, but whatever this is, whatever lies in store for me at Deep Sky, I think I deserve the opportunity to see my friend, to make the choice to see my friend one last time, one last choice before I give myself to Deep Sky, whatever and whenever that may be. I'm a human being, and as another human being you should allow me this, one last choice.'

They drove in silence. The road stretching ever northwards. The boy had his eyes open now, he was waiting for his father's reply. Silas glanced over at Missy but she didn't catch his eye. He shifted in his seat, hands tight on the steering wheel, the small adjustments that kept the car and its trailer steady on the road.

The boy with no name started jiggling. 'I want to go, Dad. I want to follow the clowns. Please, Dad? I just talked to Bob and he says he wants to go too.'

'You talked to Bob?' Silas said.

'Yeah, it's when I close my eyes I can talk to him. He's right there when I close my eyes. Bob's a rabbit that can talk and he told me he wants to go with the clowns. Please, Dad?'

Silas stared ahead through the windscreen, but he had loosened his grip on the steering wheel, his knuckles turning from white to pink to red. 'Alright, look, I have a pretty good idea where these bikers are headed, and if I'm right, it isn't so far out of our way that Deep Sky can't wait another day. But, Missy, know that this is the last time. I asked you back at the trailer park if you were sure, I told you once this journey has begun there was no turning back, and I meant what I said . . . But if Bob wants me to follow the clowns, I guess I have to do what Bob says, right, son?'

'Right!' exclaimed the kid, banging both his fists on the dash. 'Follow the clowns, Dad, Bob says follow the clowns. Yeeeehaw.'

So Silas kept the bikers in sight.

'Dad tell your story about the boy and the mountain, I wanna hear the story.'

'Ah, but that's not my story, son, that's an old folk tale.'

'Yeah, but I like you telling it, Dad, I wanna hear the story about the boy and the mountain.'

'But I told you that story, like, two seconds ago!'

'But Dad!'

'Alright, alright, I'll tell it. Okay . . . Well, here goes – the Cahuilla Indians. The Cahuilla Indians made their home just south of a range of mountains that today we call the San Bernadinos.' Silas paused to stroke his beard with the full flat of his palm. 'One night, in the fall season of that year, the chief of the Cahuilla tribe called the boys of the village together for a meeting. "Boys," he said. "Boys, the time has come. Behind me stands a great mountain. It may be invisible now, under cover of darkness, but you know it well, for you have grown up in its shadow. It has always stood there, since before we built this village, and it always will, long after we are gone. But the time has come. Tomorrow morning you will set out from the village and climb the mountain. You will climb until you are too tired to go any further, but on turning back each of you must take a twig from whichever tree stands nearest."

'The boys went to bed that night too excited to sleep a wink. The next morning, they all set out, each more determined than the last to reach the top of the mountain and return to the village a hero.' Here, Silas turned to look at his son with raised eyebrows.

The boy with no name started shaking Missy by her arm. 'The fat kid? He's so fat he doesn't even make it across the desert. Ha ha ha, he's so fat his cereal bowl comes with a lifeguard.'

'Son, I thought you wanted *me* to tell the story,' Silas

215

said. 'Missy hasn't heard the story before so maybe no more spoilers.'

'Sorry, Dad.'

'That's okay, so, yes, the first boy to return was a little out of shape, shall we say, and when he opens his hand for the tribal chief it's a piece of green Beavertail Cactus.

'"My boy," said the chief, "I can see that you did not even make it to the foot of the mountain. Never mind."

'An hour passed, and the next boy to return presented the chief with a twig of Black Sagebrush. "Well," said the chief, "you may have reached the foot of the mountain, but you went no further. What a shame."

'Another hour passed, and the third boy to return held in his hand a sapling of young Cottonwood. The chief smiled for the first time that day. "Well done, my boy, you got as far as the springs. I'm proud of you."

'Time passed. Another boy returned with some Buckthorn in his hand. "Very good," said the chief. "You must have reached that first rock slide. You've worked hard today. Well done."

'Later that afternoon a boy returned with a frond of Incense Cedar. The chief was very happy. "You got halfway up! To the very heart of the mountain. You will sleep well tonight."

'The sun was low and the sky was beginning to darken when the next boy arrived in the village with a branch of Ponderosa Pine. The chief congratulated the boy, telling him that he nearly made it to the top of the mountain, and that surely next year he would succeed.'

Silas sighed a deep sigh before continuing.

'The sun set below the horizon and darkness descended

over the land. The chief began to worry. There was still one boy left who had not returned to the village. The chief knew the mountain well, he himself had made the ascent more than once. He knew the dangers, thought the boy might have crossed paths with one of the hungry grizzly bears he knew roamed these mountains. The boy may have lost his way in the dark, or worse still, fallen from a precipice to his death. The chief was ready to gather the men of the village when at last the boy emerged from the darkness. He stood before the chief and opened his hand. It was empty. It was empty but his heart was full of joy, for this is what he said: "My chief, where I have been there are no trees, no twigs or any other living thing, for I have been to the very top of the mountain, and when I looked out and up, I saw a deep ocean of stars. All around me, everywhere I looked, I saw stars, and for a moment I thought I would fall, not off the mountain but up, up into the deep sky forever. I have returned, but only to tell you what I saw, for tomorrow I wish to climb the mountain once more, to look upon the heavens as they truly are, to be among the stars."

'"And climb you will," said the chief, "but know this. As you close your eyes to dream this night, it will be as it was at the top of the mountain, an ocean of stars as deep as deep, and that is the true dark, the true light, inside of you, for you have seen yourself as you truly are, a star among other stars, here long before we built this village and long after we are gone. You carry the darkness with you."'

They drove in silence for a while after Silas had finished the story. The desert road stretching ahead, the mountains drawing ever nearer.

'You changed it,' the boy with no name said. 'It doesn't end like that. Why'd you change it, Dad?'

'It's a folk tale, son. Folk tales are stories passed down from generation to generation. The world changes, people change, and the stories change with them. I'm just telling it like it is, son, I'm just telling it like it is.'

Silas flipped the indicator and they exited the highway. They'd lost sight of the bikers but there were signs every now and then for *Troll Meet*. Strange name for a music festival, but Missy could already hear the bass pushing through the trees, she felt it tickle the fine hair on her arms. Soon they were passing half-pitched tents by the roadside and people, groups of people with painted faces and all headed in the same direction. *Troll Meet*. They smiled at Missy through the windscreen and Missy smiled back. All ages, all races, their painted faces, all headed in the same direction and *excited*, triple piggy backs and gonzo gymnastics. There were half-pitched tents and smoke rising. She could smell burning food, hear the bass pushing through the trees. She'd seen pictures of festivals before. On other people's profiles. Pictures of kids having fun in the sun. The kissing, the dancing, the drinking. #endlesssummer. But nothing prepared Missy for the reality.

The hundreds of painted faces, smoke rising, people walking, fairground rides spinning crazy in the daylight, this canvas city shifting in the summer breeze, the bass pushing through her body now. Missy closed her eyes and breathed deep. This was real, this place felt real, her time with Silas already like a dream. She had to get out of this car and breathe the real air outside.

Her millions of followers looking elsewhere and she didn't care. She was right *here*, living the dream, no phone, nothing tracking her location. No status update. She was under the radar, and no one need know. Her being here. This adventure: she might tell someone about it one day, but she'd do it just with words, spoken out loud, like her mom did sometimes, conjure a picture with a careful choice of words, a tone of voice, a gesture. And she wouldn't tell just anyone. Maybe her brother, maybe Levon. And then again she might *never* tell. All this – the sword, the journey north – no one need ever know. It could be her secret. She had to get out of this car.

She looked at Silas and found that she hated him, hated how old he was, he was an old man and she was a young girl, she missed her friends, she missed her friends back home, she was a young girl and he was some creepy *old* guy who kidnapped young girls. Deep Sky. It sounded like a cult. Cut off from the rest of the world, everything that was going on. Her friends, their friends. Levon. River. All of them. And here she was, a young girl, getting in cars with strangers.

She was waking up too late; how had it come to this? They parked up and right away Missy opened the door to the car and nearly lost her balance on the grass. Flying crocodile. She stood under the open blue sky and breathed deeply through her nose, right to the bottom of her lungs. This place, the cool summer breeze rippling her T-shirt, this is where she belonged. She caught his eye through the windscreen. Silas's face in shadow but she could see his eyes, the realization – hers. Twinkies. Her impulse was to turn and run, disappear into the crowd of painted faces, find Cass and tell her everything, lose herself in the sunshine, lose herself in the light, disappear among the crowds of painted faces, forget everything else, what Casey did, it wouldn't matter anymore because she was young and she could find a boy to kiss it all away. His face in shadow, but she saw his eyes. Twinkies.

Then she was running, running as fast as she could through the crowd, her sword on the back seat of his car, but it didn't matter anymore, the future didn't matter, this place was who she was *now* and there was no looking back, the sun high in the sky, her light, her light, and the crowds of painted faces closing in, the smell of other bodies all around, sweat and smoke and dust, all these people here for the same thing, all these people and she was one of them, none of them, her heart pumping blood as she ran as fast as she could away from the car, her sword on the back seat, but who cared about some random sword when she had her youth, the rest of her life spread out like the skirts of a gold-sequined infinity dress of her own design, the Saturday sun reflected back a million times, a million billion times until there was only light, her light and the pleasure of being lost in a crowd. Missy missing now.

38

Room 70. Missy's bedroom.

Before the sword. Before the sword, her room was what you might have thought. A young girl's dream, fit for any princess. There were balloons, all different colors, always blown right up and ready. Her beloved white and gold rococo dresser with the oval mirror, turned now to face into the wall. Her walk-in wardrobe with catwalk, filled with clothes designed for her by the world's most gifted couturiers. Her own desert island: a tall palm tree lamp, surrounded by clean white sand, a small beach with shells, special stones, and plastic starfish. Her doll's house was a replica of Versailles, a doll for every member of the family. There was Synthea, gazing from the window in her office, River in his bunker, sitting on a chair in front of his computer screens, and Missy herself, playing with a miniature doll's house, complete with dolls so small that one time River put his sister in his ear and had to go to the hospital to get her out. But what really struck those who entered Missy's room was all the photographs. Every inch of her vast wall space was covered in pictures of her and her friends. One for every day of her life since she got her smartphone, an ocean of smiles, teeth, sunsets and spilled alcohol, dyed hair, pierced tongues and half-closed eyes. Her friends, their friends, all looking into Missy's room and reminding her that she was loved, that she was loved by all of them and more.

That was Missy's bedroom before. The day the sword arrived, everything changed. The day the sword arrived, something clicked, like a camera pointed up into the blue, blue sky. What Casey did had cast a shadow over Missy. She didn't want to get out of bed, listen to music, go swimming, nothing. She just wanted to crawl under the covers and return to sleep, to dream of better things. The day the sword arrived Missy woke right up. She placed the sword on her dressing table and stared at it awhile. It was that feeling of wanting to tidy your room around a new device, make it birthday ready, but deeper than that. No balloons this time.

Missy put her favorite Scout song on repeat, turned it up loud and got to work. First thing was taking down all her photos. All these people and she realized now she didn't know any of them, not really. Every single photo on her four walls, she took them down and tossed them in her monster, leopard-print suitcase. It took her a long time but when it was done she zipped the suitcase and wheeled it into her walk-in wardrobe, out of sight. Next came the balloons. She took a long, shiny hat pin and went round her room popping every one of them. It was actually a lot of fun, running around her room and popping all those shiny balloons, bang, bang, bang, bang. Next up was the desert island. She got one of Versailles' industrial vacuum cleaners and sucked that beach right up into the transparent cylinder. She picked the shells and stones out first but the rest of it she vacuumed right up until every grain of sand was gone. She put the palm tree lamp in the wardrobe along with the suitcase of photos. Out of sight. Out of sight for now.

She'd stood in the middle of her room then, to admire her work. Those white walls, those vast, white walls where all the photographs had been. They seemed to vibrate with possibility. Potentiality. She glanced at her brand new sword lying on the dressing table. *Inspiration.* No colored balloons. Nothing to distract her now. Standing there, Missy had this weird idea, this vision for how her room should be. Before she knew what she was doing she was busy. It was hours and hours of work but she loved every minute. She must have listened to that Scout track like a thousand times before she was done. But when she was finished she was very happy. She was very happy, but she also knew that if anybody saw this they wouldn't understand; her so-called friends wouldn't understand what all this meant. And for once, she didn't care.

Room 70. Missy's bedroom. Before the sword, her room was what you might expect: a young girl's dream, fit for any princess. Since Missy ran away, nobody has set foot inside her room, so it remains just as she left it. Four vast, white walls. Her bed is made, not a crease in the silken sheets. The curtains are wide open, letting all the bright sunshine in from outside. There is very little in this room besides the main furniture. The effect is of a modern gallery, a large, open, rectangular space. It is like an art gallery because the thing defining this space resembles a work of conceptual art. Exactly half of the pink carpet on the far side is occupied by an army of dolls. These are all of Missy's dolls. Every Barbie, Sindy, plastic, porcelain, tears, no tears – every single doll of Missy's since she was a little girl, all arranged to look like they are marching, an army of dolls, rank upon rank, all marching in the same direction toward the giant window at the end of the room. But that's not all. Every one of them is armed with a sword across their backs, razor shells collected from Versailles' beach over many years. All marching in the same direction toward the giant window at the end of the room, a window looking out onto the glittering ocean.

39

Missy had to find Cass, but first she needed a disguise, something to help her blend into the crowd.

The girl in the face-paint tent was wearing a one-piece coral-pink swimming costume over fishnet tights, matching lipstick and a dirty white bow tie. She applied the face paint to Missy's skin with her fingers. The human contact was giving Missy shivers. Missy laughed at the sensation and Crystal laughed too. Crystal was seventeen and made up to look like she was crying blood. She was making Missy up to look like a leopard.

'You have nice eyes,' Crystal said.

'Thank you,' Missy said. A rush of goosebumps.

'And a great smile. You look more like your dad or your mom?'

'My mom,' Missy decided.

'I'll bet she's real pretty,' Crystal said.

'She is.'

'I never saw you here before . . . I'm good with faces.'

'This is my first time,' Missy said.

'Oh, yeah? Who you here with?'

'Er, Cass. Her name's Cass.'

'Always-naked-Cass?' Crystal said.

'Yes!'

'Oh my God, you know always-naked-Cass, that's so awesome!'

'I know!' Missy smiled.

'How long you known Cass, if you don't mind me asking?'

'Not long, we met on the road, actually.'

Crystal didn't say anything as she applied the leopard markings to Missy's face with her index finger. Missy turned in the orange plastic chair to ask, 'Why, is something wrong?'

'Oh, it's nothing, really, I just know some of the guys she hangs out with . . .'

'What about them?'

'It's none of my business,' said Crystal. 'I just know they're into some really weird shit.'

'What, like sex weird?' Missy said.

'That too,' Crystal said.

'Oh,' Missy said. She remembered Cass's tattoo, the wolf howling at the night sky, the stars getting smaller as they went all the way up her neck. 'Is this going to take much longer?'

'I'm almost done,' Crystal said. 'Why, you gotta be some-where?'

'No, I mean yeah, I . . . I told Cass I'd meet her.' Missy hated lying, especially because Crystal seemed like such a nice girl. She felt like saying something true to make it right. 'I feel so happy right now! I've never been to a music festival before.'

'You're kidding me! That's so cool! I mean it's not cool but you've come to the right place! This place, these people. They're like the most amazing people, not like anyone else.

There's no one fake, everyone's so real and friendly and honest . . . I've been coming here since forever and I can't think of anywhere else I feel this . . . free. Just enjoy yourself, girl, you're going to have the best time . . . There, you're done.' Crystal held up a mirror.

'Oh, my goodness, you did such a great job. Thank you. Thank you so much,' Missy said, standing up. She felt very different, unlike herself, and more like herself. It was a warm feeling, like that time right after her first kiss with Levon. Crystal was doing something on her phone and Missy almost asked her to take a photo but there was no need. She'd remember this moment and it would be a part of her story. No need to share this now.

'That's no problem, Missy. Maybe see you at the fire later?'

'The fire?'

'You don't know about the fire? This really is your first time, huh? The trolls are burning an effigy of Casey Baer at dusk. It's been our tradition the last couple years, but this time we've got a special guest as our master of ceremonies.' Crystal's eyes brightened.

Missy had that feeling again that she was dreaming. She glanced at Crystal's phone again. 'Why would they do that?'

'Why? Because he's the mortal enemy of the free internet, that's why. We trolls have to keep a united front, stop the Casey Baers of this world from turning the internet totally social! Pretty soon there won't be anywhere left on the net that isn't his. Casey Baer's like the Antichrist around here.'

'Is that what this is, this place? You guys are all internet trolls?'

'Are you serious?' Crystal said, 'You must know that, otherwise why would you be here? The name's kind of a giveaway.'

'I guess I always thought of trolls as like, all out for themselves,' Missy said, 'making mischief, out to upset other people. This place – it's like you said – everybody seems so friendly.'

'That's because we *are*! What, did you think we all look like monsters or something like that? We may be trolls but we're also human beings! Troll Meet is like the one place where we can come and feel the love, share our stories of mayhem and upset, get away from our computers, have some fun in the sun! You should come tonight, Missy, see for yourself. The fire really brings everyone together. It's a great atmosphere. Please come, it's not every day you get to watch Casey Baer go up in flames surrounded by, well, flamers!'

Missy pinched her own arm above her elbow. 'Okay, I'll be there,' she said.

'Yay!' said Crystal, and gave her a kiss on her leopard cheek.

'Listen,' Missy said. 'I forgot my sunblock and have sensitive skin. Do you have something I could borrow to cover my arms?'

Crystal went to the back of the tent and picked a hoodie off a pile of other clothes. It was black and covered in small gold stars. 'Here.' She watched as Missy gathered her long hair in a swirl under the hood and zipped up the front. 'Girl, I don't know why, but you make that look sexy as hell.'

'Thanks,' Missy smiled, hands in pockets. 'I guess I'll see you at the fire later.'

*

228

It took Missy nearly all day to find Cass. She couldn't relax, couldn't stop looking over her shoulder for Silas and the kid with no name. They had to be looking for her and she didn't know about her disguise. It was cool *having* a disguise though, she actually felt like a cat, prowling the festival in search of her new friend. She started in the middle and worked her way outwards in ever-increasing circles. Knowing all these guys were trolls made her kind of happy, it felt familiar, like a dream.

No, not a dream, it was that she thought her brother would like it here. Yeah, River would like this place, all the kids with painted faces. Not that she would call her brother a troll. River went online looking for companionship, even if that meant hacking someone's email and pretending to be the horny wife of a marine commander stationed overseas. But he'd still like it here. All the boys and girls. Some of them had to be gay, right? Missy knew there were different kinds of gay. She didn't know what kind River was, but then she was still the only person in the world he ever came out to. She remembered. Out on the speedboat, waiting for the dolphins to appear.

She looked up at the blue sky and sent him love with her mind, hoped he could feel it on their pirate frequency, wherever he was. What was she thinking about? There's only one place he could be. Versailles. In his bedroom, on the internet, playing at being other people. He always said it was more than playing, but maybe if he spent more time as himself he might realize he was an amazing person with so much to give the world.

It was some way into her sixth circuit of the festival, as she was approaching the outer edges, that she saw Cass, and what she saw gave her an adrenaline rush so intense it hurt her hands and feet. But this wasn't excitement, this was fight or flight. What she saw made her sad and scared at the same time. Nothing to compare this to, not in her past, and she hoped not in the future. Missy took a picture with her mind, then wished she hadn't. No way to unsee. No way to delete.

There was a group of them, standing in the shade of some trees, away from everybody else. There was a guy, he looked young but on second thought he could have been older. He was short and skinny. He was really muscly but in a compact sort of way, like Missy imagined soldiers to look when they took their shirts off. He had no expression and he was leaning back on his heels like a water skier, suspended there by seven lengths of thick wire. Each strand of wire ended in two large meat hooks, and they in turn were hooked into the skin either side of the upper spine of seven women.

Three of them looked too young to be called women, but all Missy cared about was that one of them was Cass. She took it all in, then a step towards them. She opened her mouth to scream but no sound came. The guy holding the wires had no expression, but then nor did the girls. They too were leaning, only forward, their eyes closed, their faces relaxed. Missy said her friend's name, it came out too quietly for anyone to hear. But maybe she did hear because now Cass was opening her eyes. Their eyes met but there was no recognition. It was like Cass was in a very different place. Missy could see that her pupils were fully dilated. She'd seen that expression before.

Every day Missy had dreaded the sight of the black sedan with the tinted windows pulling up outside her school because it meant she was going home, and going home meant seeing her mom, or someone who looked just like her. Those black eyes, her pale lips. Every day she'd walk through the front doors of Versailles and Synthea would be there to greet her, and Missy would see what she was seeing now: Cass's expression. It was something she thought she'd never have to see again. She would see her mom in the hallway and want to run up to her room and cry. Her beautiful mother, all the unworn clothes.

Just then something changed in Cass's face, she squeezed closed her eyes and opened them again like she was trying to focus. Missy heard her name. She felt a tear roll down her painted cheek, the smell of face paint melting in the sun. Cass was saying her name. 'Missy? Missy, is that you?' But it was too late, Missy turned from the group by the trees and started running again.

This was going to be a big fire. Missy was sitting on the ground at the edge of a big group of boys and girls who were drinking and talking and smoking weed. She was beginning to think she'd seen the last of Silas. Bobcat. She brought her knees up to her chin, tugged down on the peak of her hoodie and watched the preparations. The wicker man didn't look like her father, but that didn't make the sight of him any less weird. You could see daylight through the loosely woven materials that made up his body, but the figure cast a mighty shadow that seemed to grow longer with each passing minute.

Missy's eye was caught by a row of fire helmets on the ground. The helmets were colored gold and glowed in the late afternoon sun, giant synthetic sea shells on the shore of an alien world. What Casey did. It had turned her world upside down and inside out. His betrayal. It had changed everything. The way things looked and sounded. She'd be talking to somebody, like, one of her friends, and find herself zoning out, just watching as the other person's lips moved, forming the words. It was like all the darkness in the world, all the shadows, were gone. No outlines, no borders. No meaning. Everything bleeding into everything else. *No.* Missy bunched her fists inside her sleeves, tasted the metal of the hoodie's zip in her mouth. She was still here. *She* was still *here.* Her anxiety made it real. The helmets were not shells, they were protective, for the firefighters to wear should the fire get out of control.

She suddenly felt out of control but she didn't change her position even an inch, her arms around her knees, biting down on the metal zip of her hood and tasting blood. Her father's name. She was saying his name in her head, over and over, the way she used to when she was trying to get his attention, the way they all did, her mother, her brother, everybody. Saying his name, over and over again until his silence swallowed you. Casey . . . Casey . . . *Casey* . . . And when he finally looked up from what he was doing, acknowledged you were even there, it was like you wanted to tell him everything, because in that fleeting moment his attention felt like the sun coming out from behind a cloud. You stood there, basking in the warmth of the light, and then he'd look down again and it was over, and you were on your own again.

Missy shivered. The fire. She wanted to be the one to start the fire . . . *she* wanted to be the one, she *would* be. Missy got to her feet. The movement was automatic, beyond

232

her. She scanned the scene like an android and saw the guy in charge. That was the guy she had to talk to. Right now. She walked over to the fence surrounding the pyre and called to him. 'Hey, you! Hey, kid with the crown.'

He was around her age, maybe a bit older, dressed in a black Lycra jumpsuit and what looked like a real gold crown. He turned and took a look at Missy. The attraction was instant. The way he carried himself.

'Hey,' Missy called again. 'Will you come here a minute? I want to ask you something.'

The kid looked over his shoulder at the wicker man, then joined Missy by the fence. He was wearing a plastic panda mask over his face.

'Hi,' said Missy.

'Hi.'

'What's your name?'

'Marchpane,' said Marchpane.

'That's an interesting name.'

'Yeah, I guess.

'I'm Rachel.'

'You're lying,' said Marchpane. 'It's not nice to lie.'

'I . . . how did you know that?'

'I recognize you from your profile. You're Missy Baer.'

'But I—'

'Deleted it,' said Marchpane, 'I know.'

'How?'

'I see everything that happens,' said Marchpane

'So I guess my leopard disguise isn't as good as I thought,' said Missy.

'Why, are you hiding from somebody?'

'Yeah, it's a long story, I came to—'

233

'Ask if you could be the one to set your dad on fire?' finished Marchpane.

Missy burst out laughing.

'Sure,' said Marchpane.

'Oh my God, really? You'd let me do that?'

'You ever throw a Molotov cocktail?' said Marchpane.

'I am Marchpane,' Marchpane said through the megaphone. 'And I love the internet.' There was a cheer from the crowd so tremendous it gave Missy chills. 'I love the internet because it lets me be who I want to be.' Marchpane continued speaking through the cheers. 'The internet is freedom. Freedom of expression. The internet is open. No doors, only perception. But there are those that seek to change the landscape, the mindscape, to put up walls where there was open ground. Closed structures. One entrance, one exit. Log on, log off. Forgot your first pet's name? Fuck you. The revolution won't be televised, it'll be charted on a social graph. Closed structures, walled gardens, whatever you want to call it, the skyline's changing, and the keys to all the castles are encrypted. Casey Baer. Casey Baer, erstwhile inventor and entrepreneur, now just a middle-aged man playing God with porn on the other screen. Casey Baer thinks he holds the keys to the kingdom. We're here to tell him that kingdom is not a place, it's *us*. No doors, only perception, only us, only forward. Trolls, let the flames begin.'

Another cheer from the crowd.

Marchpane gave Missy a look. It wasn't a signal so much as a flirtation. They both turned to face the wicker man. All the eyes on her right now and she didn't care. Thirty days reactivation. Marchpane struck a match and set light to the kerosene-soaked rag. No time for hesitation. Flying Twinkies.

The moment the glass bottle left her hand and began arcing through the air was a moment caught on film, not only by a thousand smartphones in the crowd, but by the camera fixed over her left shoulder, her camera, her experience of the action as it played out, this was now, her story, her moment, so public yet so secret, a moment only she would truly know and understand, her arm throwing the flaming glass bottle, her arm and the pleasure of the fire as it exploded before her like a special effect, but this was real life, her act, her fire, her story, her father going up in flames, sparks rising into a night sky now aglow with the light from the burning man, her father, the old man, Alt Disney, Daddy, Dad, Casey, what Casey did, for now it didn't matter, as she felt the heat emanating from the fire, the pleasure of the heat as it burned away her edges, her past and future tense. She felt it as a kiss on her painted cheek. She turned expecting Marchpane but it was Crystal, and then her lips, kissing on the lips as the fire raged, a kiss rendered in silhouette, this moment was her moment, no film left in the canister, flicker, out, only now, only perception.

40

Back in his bear costume, River maximized the live stream of the burning man at Troll Meet. This was unbelievable. *Unreal.* He'd been trying to keep his mind off things, spent all evening on the internet, channeling his hero on the boards, and now here was Marchpane himself, *in person,* giving a speech about internet freedom in front of a towering wicker effigy of his father, Casey Baer. Fucking *YES!*

River was on his feet in front of his screens, doing karate moves along to the things Marchpane was saying. When the crowd cheered he roared with them, jumping up and down with closed fists. When Marchpane had finished speaking, someone in a black hoodie threw a Molotov Cocktail. Kaboom. Just wow! He wished he was there to feel the heat, smell the smoke and sweat of the crowd. He wished Missy was here to see it play out on video. The fire actually looked pretty cool at the lower frame rate. Either way it had River in the best mood *ever.*

Best mood ever

```
01000010   01100101   01110011   01110100   00100000
01101101   01101111   01101111   01100100   00100000
01100101   01110110   01100101   01110010
```

Binary style, that's right. He knew he should go to bed, catch up on some sleep, but he was ready to bounce off the walls right now, do some damage (to himself, for fun!). Tomorrow they announced the winner of the Scout Rose comp. If he could get the audience with Scout, he knew he had a shot at tracking his sister. The prize was getting to ask Scout one question, and there was only one question he needed the answer to. He needed a location for Deep Sky. Find Deep Sky and he would find Missy. Fuck it, he might even take the helicopter. A really stupid plan where anything and everything could go wrong right out of the gate, but it was a plan, and he had a good feeling about this one for no reason. He knew he should go to bed but seeing his father burn over live stream had him floating on air.

Yeehaw
01011001   01100101   01100101   01101000   01100001
01110111

River skated across his room and pulled out his *box of tricks* from a low shelf. Ahh, his box of tricks. Rope, blades, all different types of blades, more rope, pliers, rasps, a nineteenth century flat iron (hot!), a little gunpowder, a gun (potato gun, it didn't belong), pins, needles, lots and lots of needles, no syringes, just very thin, hard, pointed lengths of metal, non-lethal poisons . . .

River specialized in a school of self-harm that barely left any marks, at least not for very long. A release of endorphins was all very well, but how to *sustain* the rush, grammaticalize it, give it structure. The only answer was pain. Not suffering. Pain. Short bursts of pain, like commas in a sentence, like sentences in a paragraph. It wasn't that River *liked* pain, pain actually sucked pretty hard, no, it was the moment *immediately* before and *immediately* after that he lived for. Like the stitching on a fine suit. It made his nose itch just thinking about it. There was a difference between being in a good mood and *harnessing* that goodness, riding it out like riding across an open plain on a stallion. Brown horse.

He stopped what he was doing for a second. He had to ask himself *why*? Why was he in such a fantastic mood? Why did watching an effigy of his father go up in flames make River feel like he could take over the world, beat the universe at its own game of quantum tennis (River glanced at the tennis ball cannon, shook his head, no, wrong vintage). Because. Brown horse. Fuck you, so it was a stupid elementary school painting of a brown horse, fuck you, so it was a long time ago, but *fuck you*, it had never been any different. His father's rejection of him had been total. Brown horse was just one thing, one time. Dad, look, Dad, listen. Dad – Dad, I'm right *here*. He said it out loud. 'Right *here*.'

The connected world. A sharing world. Openness. All that garbage Casey talked in public, when in real life, behind closed doors, he was the most secretive person you could imagine, a regular Dracula up in his castle. When River wanted an update on his father's life, he hit up Google, no joke. There was nothing on the internet about Versailles, btw. Versailles, France, sure. But Versailles, USA? Nothing. Rumors, but nothing concrete. That's because this place was locked down tighter than the goddamned White House. All those rooms. Dark secrets. Probably a bunch of sex dungeons and God knows what else. One day, one day River would crack the code, blow those doors wide open and show the world who his father *really* was.

River picked up the jump cables like they were a pair of delicious lobsters, but he wasn't feeling electroshock tonight so he returned them to the pot. His box of tricks. At one time the box had been where he kept his Lego. Oh my God, Lego. But he was real specific about what he built as a kid. No buildings, no castles, no spaceships, no make nice. Instead he built these ridiculous suits of armor, basically giant tubes of Lego of varying sizes, four for the arms and a kind of box open at one end so it fitted over his head. And he built them kind of loose so that when Missy beat the crap out of him with a plastic baseball bat they smashed to pieces in a really satisfying way. Yeah, they played that game a *lot*. River always regretted not having a use for the little plastic flowers . . . Oh, well, his box of tricks but oh God, he could feel the mood lifting, he was taking too long over this, if he didn't hurt himself a little in the next minutes or so it would be too late, and then who knew where the next high would come from?

The problem was River didn't do drugs. Fuck weed because he was too busy for that shit, too much on the menu. Fuck the tropics because he didn't need no pills to achieve an altered state. He could do that shit pretending to be other people on the internet. He rolled back the sleeve to his bear costume. River didn't need drugs because actually what he wanted was what everybody else wanted: to be happy. :) And not happy as in, like, transient – like hearing something funny or jerking off in the shower – but *sustained* happiness, something from deep inside, acting and reacting like a sun, like a warm sun from behind a cloud . . . like a sun . . . like a sun – River continued inserting the long, very thin needle through the skin of his forearm. He let go of the pinch of skin and took a moment to admire his work. Subdural, no blood, and just enough pain. He took a second needle from its sterilized wrapper and began the insertion, making only tiny adjustments to make sure it was flush with the first needle, an inch and a half further up his arm. When he was done there were seven needles total, elbow to wrist.

For a moment he thought about what would happen if his mom saw him like this. Not his mom now but Mom from before, the Synthea that would come sit by him sometimes while he played his video games. For a moment he imagined being her, coming in the door and seeing her son like this, seven long needles inserted in his arm, elbow to wrist. Her child, her little boy, her River Baer. The same boy who rested his head against her arm as she worked on her designs, the same River who wouldn't let her leave his childhood room before telling him there was no monster in the cupboard, and even if there was, *It is the good kind, there to protect you from the bad.*

She always knew the thing to say. Her voice low and slow and wise and she could always make him laugh . . . River thought about what that would be, for her to see him like this, seven long needles inserted in his arm, elbow to wrist. But that's what the lock was for. We lock our doors to be alone. To not be seen. To be as we are, not as we are perceived. In reality, of course, he was a combination of the two: the River out there and the River in here. The River with the needles in his arm was who he was now, but there was a River who wished he could see his mom, have her take him in her arms and tell him it was all going to be okay, that even if there were monsters, they were good monsters, there to protect him from the bad.

He lay back on the concrete floor and closed his eyes, the sting in his nose but he didn't cry. What pain remained manifested itself as a light burning sensation across his forehead, similar to the feeling of someone you were really attracted to entering your personal space. That tingling at the edge of your lips and across the forehead for some reason. Weird. River smiled to himself. It was a smile that came from relaxing the muscles in his face, relaxing the *eyeballs*. River laughed quietly. He fell asleep where he lay, on the concrete floor.

On the other side of the room the live stream continues, the burning man has lost his outline. He is no longer a man but a fire, the crowd has dissipated. But there are those that remain, leant up against the fence surrounding the pyre. Lost souls of the internet brought together in the physical world, the warmth of the fire under a starless sky, a dark sky that grows ever darker as the fire dies, the glow growing weaker with each passing hour.

41

Missy looked around for Marchpane but he was gone.

'Is everything okay?' Crystal said.

'Yeah, everything's great,' Missy said. 'It's just, I never kissed a girl before.'

'It's okay, me neither,' Crystal said.

'Really?'

'I just saw you throwing that Molotov. I don't think I've seen something crazier than that in my life. You were amazing.'

'Oh my God, it was so fun,' said Missy, catching her breath. 'I don't think I've ever had this much fun.'

'And you got to meet Marchpane!' exclaimed Crystal. 'That's like, *in*sane.'

'Why, what's the big deal?' Missy said.

'You mean you don't know who Marchpane is? Come on, he's like the most famous, the most badass troll on the internet. He's also probably the greatest hacker for a generation.'

'He was kinda cute,' Missy said.

They were walking away from the fire now. Missy looked over her shoulder a last time. You could still see the outline. A burning man against the deep sky. 'Where are we going?' Missy said.

'I wanna dance,' Crystal said. 'You wanna dance?'

They walked towards the source of the music holding hands. Missy felt like herself for the first time since before it happened. She only wished Levon could be here to enjoy this with her. People her own age. It made such a difference to how you saw everything. They stood at the entrance to the tent, waves of bass breaking over them, drowning out all thought. She started dancing, they danced together, falling laughing into one another, but then Missy closed her eyes, closed her eyes and let go, first of Crystal's hand and then herself, the music in her ears, the kiss still on her lips, her eyes closed, the lights beyond her eyelids rendered in darker shades of violet.

She is floating now, up, up into the darkness of her open mind, away from everything, from memory, from time itself, far from Versailles, the present taking over, bubbling to the surface like a river, a flowing river headed elsewhere, away from Versailles, across America to another ocean, the glittering ocean, wider than anything she's ever seen, wider than a dream – but there is something, a tiny point of pressure on her open palm, her left palm, she looks down, Crystal's warm hand folding something into hers, their eyes meet and Crystal smiles a strange smile. Her lips move to form words, the music drowns them out but Missy thinks she understands. *A little something, a little something to help you wake.* Missy opens her fingers and sees the black pill. This would be the first time. She always hated the idea. Her mother's endless pills in the white boxes. Uncanny. The ghost effect. This would be her first time taking drugs. She didn't like the idea, but the waves of bass, her youth, the swish of the infinity dress and gorgeous Crystal crying painted tears of blood. She took the pill between her thumb and index finger and turned it over. And there it was. A tiny white star against black.

It was the sick feeling of waking from a wonderful dream. This. This and every other moment. Everything. Crystal. Marchpane and the Molotov. The burning man, the kiss. Everything. Deep Sky. This was all Deep Sky. Silas and the boy with no name. They were watching her right now. Their watchful eyes. Her every move— Not everything. The time before she pulled into that trailer park. White rabbit. White star. She had to get away, find Cass again, find Cass and she would be okay. The sick feeling of waking from a dream of a better life. She angled her hand and let the black pill fall on the ground between them, looked into Crystal's eyes, long enough to read something like relief, then shouldered her way into the crowd, the waves of bass crashing, crashing overhead. Twinkies again. Twinkies on her mind.

Find Cass again and she would be okay. Cass was from before, she had said all those nice things back at the motel on her birthday, made Missy feel real special inside, like she had something to give back to the world. Find Cass and she would be okay. Her friend. A heart shaped like a heart. Cass was from before, when Missy still had her own car, music loud on the 5.1, the wind in her long blonde hair. When it was still *her* adventure, the changing landscape outside her window, the rush of tarmac and the thrill of escape. #RunningAway. She had to find Cass again, find Cass and get *drunk*. Wasted. Yeah. That's what Missy wanted. To get really fuckin' drunk and forget everything that had happened. But she needed alcohol to get drunk. Like magic she saw a pair of boys, they were two skinny boys with painted faces standing way out from the main stage, way out on their own, dancing mainly with their arms, taking alternate hits off of a clear glass bottle with a red and white label. 'Hey,' Missy heard herself say, 'can I have some of that?'

'Sure thing,' the one kid said, handing her the bottle but still dancing with his other arm, dividing up the incoming beats with the flat of his hand. She'd never seen anyone dance like this, thought he was cool in a goofy kind of way. She took a hit but held her ground, gave the other kid the bottle and wiped her mouth with the sleeve of her black hoodie. She felt the blood rush to her throat to meet the alcohol, a quick, delicious warmth to her fingertips and toes.

For a moment she thought about what would happen if her mom saw her like this. Not her mom now, but Mom from before, the Synthea she could tell anything, her best friend. For a moment she imagined being her, coming through the crowds and seeing her daughter like this, her arm around a random boy and drinking liquor straight from the bottle. Her child, her little Missy, her Missy Baer. The same girl who would bring her lunch on the Chinese dragon tray, prepared with love in Versailles' kitchens with Leticia's help. The same Missy who told her mother everything. Just like Synthea told *her* everything, all her secrets and regrets, doubts and desires. Things about Casey, things not meant for Missy's ears. And Missy always knew the thing to say, her mother's head resting lightly on her shoulder.

Missy felt the alcohol taking effect, the anger unexpected. All those years. When she was still just a girl. Trying to make friends at school, still sleeping with the light on in her room. She remembered. How much she wished her mom could just be Mom, even for one day, one night. Not her best friend, but someone to tell her it would all be okay . . . Most times it had been the other way round. Even before what happened with Casey, before the pills and the walking Versailles' corridors at night. Her mom was so unhappy. Casey asking her to work from home. Her mother said she felt like a prisoner. A prisoner in their own house. Missy remembered. Coming up to her mother's studio one time with the tray of food and seeing right away from her eyes that Synthea was drunk – right in the middle of the day – drunk enough she barely noticed Missy there.

The memory made Missy want to get more drunk herself. She took another hit on the vodka, closed her eyes and breathed deep. She hadn't talked to her mom in what felt like a long time, but in reality it was a few days. Anyway, she didn't want to talk to her mom right now, she didn't want to hear how worried she was. Missy didn't want any of that. She wanted this, this right now. This was real, this place, this festival, these people felt real, her life in Versailles was already like a dream. She was dancing now. Her hands, her heart, her blood, her anger. The fullness of her anger with her parents, her self given new shape, hoodie pulled down like she's feeling the future, this dance, this dance was who she was now, the smell of bodies all around, sweat and smoke and dust, all these people here for the same thing, all these people and she was one of them, none of them, she was floating now, up, up into the darkness of her open mind, away from everything, from anger, memory, her parents, Versailles. *If this is the future. If this is the future. This, this, this* . . .

She opened her eyes and the boys were still there, and it was cool, so great, so funny, so nice to be dancing with boys her own age – but she had to find Cass. Find Cass and it would all be okay. Cass had been so nice to her. Missy was about to kiss the first boy on the cheek goodbye when it happened. A familiar voice coming out of the speakers either side of the main stage. Special surprise guest. It couldn't be. Missy climbed on one of the boys' backs to get a better look. It really was. Black baseball cap pulled low but it was her. Scout Rose.

42

Off the rails. He hasn't had an update on his daughter in four minutes. No sound, no picture. Nothing. Casey expresses his displeasure through dangerous driving. Once in a while he will drive himself to and from the network campus because he likes the feel, the constant hum of the engine, the vibration in his bones, the flash of sunlight and surface. These are residential streets. Casey drives so quickly he could kill, even fantasizes one or two bodies rolling up and over the forward windshield like wild animals caught off-guard, their elbows and knees, the blood splatter glowing pink in an oncoming high-beam. 4m 47sec and still no news. She is. Under the radar. He senses the weight of the car in his biceps and flexors, a sensation that he is at one with the machine, this journey home, this journey home should be a pleasure, the dark road disappearing under the hood of the sedan like lava, the whiff of lightly burning rubber in the open window. Casey expresses his displeasure through more dangerous driving, bites down on the metal zip to his hoodie and hits eighty miles per hour on the bend, this time alone, inside the beautiful car, street lights reflecting off the PX8, the blackest paint on the market. Casey wants the best, the very best. Streetlights off the PX8. He wants the best for

Missy. 5m 24sec and still no signal, not a peep. This is not what he paid for. He would like to take this Silas character and— The blood splatter glowing pink.

Casey keeps a pair of king cobras in the trunk, likes to keep the danger close. Death as discreet stereo system. This car is his car. This custom model was two full years in development, his personal vision machined into existence by reprogrammed industrial robots and capable human hands that no longer bleed. This car is his car. The faint creases in the leather hide upholstery are *his* creases, left by the rearrangement of muscles inside his new clothes, his entering, driving and exiting of the car. Man enters car. Man drives car. Man exits car. A vision caught on photochemical film, the grain giving off its own perfection. This car is his car. The horror-green readings on the dash include up-to-the-second heart-rate and blood-pressure counts. The values rising. This car is his car. Six minutes. An impulse that feels predestined, as though everything were building to this moment. Casey continues steering with his left hand for a second as he coils his right fist for the strike, a mean uppercut that catches his lower jaw so hard that at first he thinks he's knocked it off its natural hinge. It takes everything he has to correct the swerve, but it is too late, the front right tire hitting the curb at seventy miles per hour, pitching the car on its side in a long, halting skid, painted metal over tarmac, sparks reflected in the lenses of no less than seven closed-circuit cameras positioned along the street.

Casey releases his seatbelt, completely unharmed save for his jaw, takes his automatic handgun and sunglasses from the gaping glove compartment and climbs out of the car. He stands atop the gleaming wreckage for a moment, surveying the scene, his body language that of the apex predator. He jumps nimbly down and strides to each of the seven cameras in turn, shooting out every lens with unflinching accuracy, the gun reports doing nothing to interrupt the main soundtrack of field crickets and distant coyotes. Casey removes the sunglasses and hooks the gun inside the waist of his jeans, concealing it from view with an adjustment to the loose material of his hoodie. He whips his smartphone from his pocket and swipes for an update on his daughter. Still nothing. He keeps his cool this time. He must return home, to his base of operations. Mission control. Mission Missy now and there's no turning back. A roller coaster rebellion gone off the rails.

He starts on the long walk home through the city, street-lights reflecting off the upward-facing screen of his phone, this dark, velvet window telling him nothing just now, only that his daughter is somewhere out there, outside the map, passed through his invisible walls into another realm, her world, her game, and the idea nearly makes him drop his phone on the concrete sidewalk but he doesn't, he grips more firmly, his fingers growing whiter as they close around the device, this dark window into every reality but his own. This world is his world, his beautiful car on fire now, the trunk sprung open in the crash, a pair of seventeen-foot king cobras continuing on their way.

43

Missy caught glimpses of her hero as she pushed through the crowd, but by the time she reached the front, Scout's guest appearance was over. She watched Scout turn from the stage with a perfect smile and disappear behind a black curtain. No way, not like this, not after everything. Missy puffed her flushed cheeks like a boxer. The vodka meant no hesitation. Her new mission: meet Scout Rose. Deep Sky or no, this was her favorite singer in the whole world, and she had to meet her. Right here, right now.

What happened next did not take place in slow motion. As she clambered over the metal barrier, ducked the security guard and vaulted onto the stage, Missy was a leopard cat, her make-up faded but she didn't know. She turned once on the spot, crouching low to the scratched black floor, taking in the crowd for only a second. Twenty thousand souls, all eyes on her, the dream logic of her actions. The camera in her mind. But this was not a dream, this was reality. She made this happen. Giant men in black T-shirts running at her from the sides, but Missy was too quick, scrambling away on all fours and finding the divide in the heavy black curtain.

Backstage was a maze of stacked equipment, miles of

cable and the rows of drums and other equipment. Kick drum. Kick drum. Keyboard. Keyboard. Speaker. Speaker. Black box. Where next? Rough black boxes with the heavy-duty locks. Missy sprinted along a corridor of speakers and turned a corner, heard Scout's voice among others. There, across the way. A door closing. *Click*. Green sign. A way out.

Missy found herself outside again, only there was nobody here, an expanse of moonlit grass, almost like a lawn before a house, the thrum of the main stage like the weight of an ocean behind her. Any second now they would find her, catch her. Any second now and the waves would crash around her, the backwash carrying her all the way home, to Versailles. Where next? Where next? There, in the middle darkness, two rectangles of soft yellow light, the sound of laughter. Missy tore across the grass, realized it was a trailer and for a second she thought the very worst and skidded to a halt. But this trailer was different, no white star against black. A Winnebago they called them, the metal housing polished to a surreal shine. More laughter. Scout's voice from inside. But it was too late.

'YOU, STOP!' The men in black T-shirts closing in, their arms out to the sides like they were ready for a big hug. And for a crazy instant Missy actually felt like a hug, for some-one to take her in their arms and tell her it was going to be okay, that this really *was* all a dream. But this was not a dream, this was real. Her story. Flying Twinkies. She made this happen. Her current mission: meet Scout Rose. The vodka fading but Missy didn't know.

She shouted at the top of her voice. 'SCOUT! SCOUT ROSE!' The laughing in the trailer stopped. The men in black T-shirts looming over her. No one to help her now, her brother far away in Versailles, four out of seven screens telling him the same thing. No time for teddy bears. Flying fucking Twinkies. 'SCOUT! I NEED TO TALK TO YOU. SCOUT ROSE!'

The men in black T-shirts closed in and got a hold of Missy, their hands clamping her shoulders so hard she fell to her knees. 'SCOUT!'

'Wait!' Scout's voice again, her speaking voice, so clear in real life. 'What's happening here?' Scout said. 'Hey, Cassius, Jean-Pierre, take it easy. HEY! I said take it easy. Look, she's just a kid. Let her go.'

Missy couldn't bring herself to make eye contact, not right away. She studied Scout's sneakers for a long moment, the newness of these sneakers, the factory-white laces tied in two perfect, perfect loops. Like the idea of sneakers in someone's mind. Did Scout tie her own laces? No, she probably got Cassius or Jean-Pierre to tie her laces for her, right? The newness of these sneakers, box fresh, the windowed soles pumped to max. Max air, Scout's wrists tied with ribbons, black baseball cap pulled low like she's feeling the future, her arms, two arms, her hands, Missy's leopard make-up fading but she didn't know. 'Scout, I need to talk to you,' she said, catching her breath. 'I need to talk to you.' She looked up at Scout and saw the sunglasses, those delicate features but the sunglasses hiding her eyes, probably Cassius who tied her laces, Cassius or Jean-Pierre.

'Hey, don't cry,' Scout said, holding out her hand and helping Missy to her feet. 'It's going to be okay.' She held Missy at arm's length, gently lifted her chin so she could get a look at her face. 'Oh my God, it's you. You're the one – you threw the Molotov. It was you, you started the fire back there.' Missy turned to run, but Scout held her arm. 'No, don't go, it's okay, it's okay. That was the coolest thing. Don't cry, sweetheart, you're safe with us, Cassius didn't mean it ... Hush now, listen, why don't you come inside and we can talk. Just the two of us. I can't believe it's you.' Probably Cassius tied her shoes and Missy almost blacked out. This time right here was precious. She had to stay awake for this. The vodka fading but the adrenaline making her shiver inside the black hoodie. 'You're cold,' Scout said. 'Let's get you inside.' She took Missy's hand in hers and led her up the stairs into the trailer, into the soft yellow light, Cassius and Jean-Pierre standing guard outside on the moonlit grass.

44

In Versailles' master bedroom, Synthea lay with her head in Leticia's lap. She had blacked out, Leticia told her. Three members of staff and Leticia had had to carry her to her bed. She had slept right through the evening and Leticia hadn't left her side. On waking up Synthea was very talkative. The pill was wearing off. All she wanted to do was talk about her two children, Missy and River.

These two women had known each other for some years now. They liked each other very much. They loved each other. There was trust. Their words overlapped. Their words overlapped because there was always something to talk about. Not the future, nor the past, not even the now. They needed each other. Sometimes Leticia played the mother. Sometimes Synthea played the mother. They were always sisters, they shared secrets. They never lied. They could tell each other anything but in reality they didn't. This was important. There remained a darkness between them, around them, like the opposite of light cast by a lampshade, these skirts of darkness that swished around them, and that is how it always was and always would be.

There were parameters, unspoken rules established when Leticia signed a contract to work at Versailles as a nanny to the two children. Leticia would never get angry with Synthea, but Synthea might lose her temper with Leticia because she put something somewhere. But Leticia had never gone to sleep thinking badly of her mistress. They might bicker. They were always sisters. Leticia remembered being at the toy store with Synthea and putting toys back on the shelf. Synthea got very angry but Leticia just kept doing it, taking the brightly colored boxes and returning them to their place on the shelf, saying the kids didn't need two of everything for Christmas. Synthea had wanted to slap Leticia across her face, but she just stood with her hands on the trolley, watching this little woman put the boxes back. She was right, of course, her children didn't need so many things.

She lay with her head on Leticia's lap and they remembered the time River taught Missy how to ride a bike when she already knew from being at summer camp but pretended because she didn't want to upset her little brother. It was true, although they were twins, River had always been the little brother. Missy looked out for him. At school. She fought for him. Sometimes the fights were physical. And it worked, they left him alone after a while. She protected him from Casey. She protected him from Casey again and again. Telling her dad he was being too hard on River.

They remembered how much the kids loved playing in the swimming pool when they were younger. Being inside and hearing their voices outside, their endless games. Their play had always been collaborative, Synthea thought. No winners, no losers. She told Leticia she could remember everything about their lives, her children's lives, but found it hard to remember the details of her own. 'Sometimes I forget what I look like, but I don't want to look in the mirror. Sometimes I think I'm losing my mind, Leticia.'

Leticia's way was to say nothing in response, only stroke her mistress's hair like she would a child.

Synthea continued: 'I remember everything about their lives, Leticia, but sometimes I think I've spent so much time just watching them: from behind glass, from across a room, hearing them through the walls, these terrible rooms, I always hated how big all the rooms are in this house. I sometimes think I've spent so much time . . . She could tell me anything, we talked about everything and now . . . It's my fault, Leticia, it's all my fault. My darling Missy. I should have protected her. I should have protected her . . .'

'From what, my dear? She was fine, she was fine, what would Missy need protecting from?' Leticia paused, wanting to choose her words carefully. 'Mr Casey?'

'From myself, Leticia,' Synthea said. 'It's all my fault. I should have protected her. She's my daughter. She saw things . . . she heard things . . . no daughter should have to . . .'

'You are their mother,' Leticia said, stroking the long hair of her mistress. 'And the children love their mother.'

'Sometimes I think she loves you more than she loves me,' Synthea said.

'You know it's not true,' Leticia replied, very calm. It wasn't the first time she had heard this, and she knew what to say. 'You know the children love you in a way they could never love me, you know that, Synthea.' It was rare that she used her mistress's first name. She looked down at Synthea's face, upside down, the faded make-up around her eyes, the lipstick still perfect. She loved this woman, and it was not out of pity. No, she had been at Versailles for long enough to see the bigger picture, everything that came before, the way her husband treated her, or the way he didn't treat her like anything because he was always away from the house, and when he was here there were the arguments.

Leticia was not proud, but she had listened at the door to this bedroom more than one time. More than one time she had listened at the white door to this bedroom and heard the way he talked to her when he thought there was no one to hear and, oh, my goodness, she had never heard anything like that before. Never, not even in any movie, it was so bad how he talked to her, as his wife, but also as a woman, like an animal he talked to her, with no heart. Leticia loved this woman, but it wasn't out of pity. She admired her strength after all these years as his wife, on her own in the house, all her talent wasted because she stopped believing, and how could she still believe if her husband, who was meant to protect her, was the one telling her she was nothing. You hear it enough times. You hear these things and it is all you hear.

The faded make-up around her eyes, the lipstick still perfect but there was no one to see it, no one except the cameras installed throughout the house, she couldn't believe it sometimes, all those cameras picking up every single thing that happened in that house. It was not right. Sick, in a way. And what did Mr Casey want with all the footage? Why did he want to film everything like that? His family, he could see his family if he just knocked on the door and talked to them, it was all so strange in a way, so strange. She stroked her mistress's long hair and began to sing the song her own mother sang to her at night when she was a young girl.

Synthea closed her eyes and listened to the singing like

listening to water. She was lying on a beach, the ocean breaking gently on the shoreline, so gentle she almost fell asleep but for the gracious refusal of her mind, her mind continuing to work like a projector, going over and over what had been today, and all she saw was color, and all she heard was sound, flashes of color from a single point and out, unfolding like a folding fan flicked *out*, folding back and then *out*, and then no sound, only the splayed visual, of metal and glass and silk and skin, clean-shaven skin, her husband's face, angular, triangular, always clean-shaven, so clean she could not remember his smell, far across the room from her, asleep facing away from her, his back smooth and muscular as a teenaged boy.

She couldn't understand how she had ever found him attractive. Her hate for him was a perfect machine, but the perfection was surface. Inside the casing, under the hood, her hate for him was a dirty thing, more of a contraption, the workings glistening and dripping with black oil that was almost blood. On the surface her hate was perfect. Like one of her designs. It woke her up in the morning and kept her awake. Industrial design was as much about dreaming as the waking work towards perfection. Her hate for her husband was perfect until they shared the same space. She looked at him and saw her children. Their flesh and bones. Blood and oil. She looked at him and saw what she had become, because when you were in a room with Casey you saw things only from his point of view.

He's one of those people that when he walks in a room you . . . she despised this idea, that charisma should mean anything at all, that it should allow a person to succeed in convincing those around him that his point of view mattered more than anything else, to the exclusion of everything else. There were times when she tried convincing herself that it was his work that had changed him, the success of the network. She was only human, looking for correlations. The truth was she *had* at one time found his determination to be an attractive quality. The man she fell in love with had been an idealist. He really believed his social network would set us free. His code would bring people together, allow them unprecedented access to one another, wherever and whenever. The more we shared, the deeper our understanding, in each other and ourselves. Perhaps beyond. His code. There's the rub. *His* code, *his* website, *his* terms. It *had* changed him. Not the money, but the power. He had become more than us. We were his customers. More than human, but far less.

Synthea remembered. Their year living in the RV, Versailles rising from the marsh like a waking kraken. Their trips into the mountains, views of the city in the great distance, toasting marshmallows over the fire and Casey's voice telling the kids their stories as they went to sleep last thing. That's what he'd do. Instead of reading to them from books he'd make up stories about the kids themselves, the adventures of Missy & River Baer. Sometimes they were stories about what they'd done that day, with new parts about bears and talking rabbits and doors in trees to other worlds. But toward the end of their year in the RV, Casey's stories were more about Missy and River when they were older. These stories had less magic and more audience participation, with Casey letting the kids chime in for key plot moments and twists. Synthea remembered, or rather she couldn't remember, when the bedtime stories stopped.

The Casey from those days seemed as fictional to her now as his character in the news media and his social networks. Those photos on his profile of the family together, smiling for the camera with Versailles gleaming in the background. Versailles, house of a thousand cameras and a majority were pointed inward. His fortress, their prison. The ocean framed and framed again, a grand illusion. A family in name alone. Four Baers. But this was no fairytale. Her hate for him a dirty thing, workings glistening and dripping with black oil that was almost blood. All their blood.

Leticia was uncomfortable in her position on the bed but didn't dare move. She looked down at Synthea's face, the faded make-up on her closed eyelids. She was sleeping now but Leticia would not stop singing, not yet. These songs. These songs she had sung to the children when they were much younger and it always worked. With both of them. Leticia smiled at the idea of River falling asleep to her singing. She imagined singing to him now and almost laughed out loud, but she didn't want to wake Synthea who was sleeping now. She needed to sleep, so important to give her strength for the next day. We humans needed sleep because without sleep we go crazy, we forget who we are. Her eyes were open again. Leticia stopped singing. 'You were asleep,' she said. 'Go back to sleep, Mrs Synthea, it is time for you to rest. Rest, rest, rest.'

'I wasn't asleep, I had my eyes closed but I wasn't asleep,' Synthea said. 'I want to talk to my son. I want to talk to River and tell him goodnight.' She sat up in the bed. Leticia put a hand on her shoulder saying she should lie back down. 'No, I want to talk to River. I want to tell him goodnight and that I love him and that it will all be okay.'

'But it is late, Mrs Synthea, very late and River is sleeping by now.'

But Synthea was already off the bed, her bare feet on the carpet in the master bedroom. She walked across the room to her walk-in wardrobe and disappeared inside. She emerged some time later wearing a dress, nothing too formal, just a dress, not too young, not too old, a nice, normal dress a mom might wear to go and see her son and tell him goodnight, tell him she loved him and that soon his sister would be back and everything would be okay, she promised.

45

Missy untwisted her long blonde hair from under the black hood and Scout moved back in her seat like she'd seen a ghost. 'Oh my God, you're *Missy Baer!?* No freaking way, dude. No. Freaking. Way. I didn't recognize you under the crazy make-up, which I'm *loving*, by the way. Missy Baer up in my trailer, I can't believe you're really her! . . . Wait, I heard you deleted your profile. And oh my God, you threw that Molotov, you—' Scout Rose suddenly burst out laughing. 'Whoa, girl – Daddy issues much?!'

'About that,' Missy said, 'this can't come out online, you can't tell anyone you saw me. Truth is I . . . I ran away. From home. I think the cops are after me. The cops, my father . . .'

'Oh my God, are you serious right now?' Scout waited a beat before holding up her hand for the high-five. They high-fived, just like that. She was really here with Scout Rose and they just high-fived. If only they could see. If only she could share this moment, it might feel more real. She took a photo with her mind for later. #ScoutRose. 'Look,' con-tinued Scout, 'don't worry about that stuff, all my people have to sign something. I run a tight ship. Nothing gets out. When you're with me, you're with me, you know what I'm saying? Under the radar. Don't sweat it, Missy Baer, you can relax.'

'But what about Deep Sky?' Missy blurted. 'How come we heard about that?'

'Ah, now that's different,' Scout said, removing her sunglasses for the first time. 'Deep Sky,' she smiled. 'Deep Sky was cover. Image control.'

So strange to see her without her sunglasses. Two eyes, her nose, her delicate mouth and perfect teeth. She was a real person, breathing the same air. Missy suddenly saw why people sang songs. Such a pure form of expression. Emotion. Meaning. Scout Rose was just another girl trying to be heard. 'Cover,' Missy said, 'You mean you never joined a cult?'

Scout unconsciously touched the brim of her baseball cap. 'Truth is, Missy, I needed a vacation, fall off the face of the earth, out the public spotlight, from under all those cameras. Paparazzi were driving me crazy. So, yeah, one day this package arrives at my house. Hand delivered. A sword. I'm not kidding. There was a message too, an address. Sounds crazy, but I took my bodyguards and went along. I was curious. I'm a curious person. Anyway, it turns out it was these guys calling themselves Deep Sky. They told me I was chosen, that kind of thing, that they intended to expand their operations, bring more Americans into the fold. They invited me to visit their facility somewhere in the north of the country. And I was sitting there in this meeting thinking, oh my God, this is like, some kind of freaky-ass cult and these guys are trying to recruit me. This is *perfect*. Cults are a good look right now. Dark, dangerous, you know what I'm saying? Plus, these guys know a thing or two about how to keep a low profile. I mean, I'd never even heard of Deep

Sky till I took that meeting. So I figured: maybe I can meet these guys halfway, come to some kind of arrangement where they get to use my brand and I theirs, all while taking some time out from my career. I'd disappear off the face of the earth for a year and then name check them in my first interview back. They weren't interested at first, but I brought my lawyer along with me to the second meeting. He knows how to talk to these types of people . . . Let's just say Deep Sky were adequately compensated. But, no, to answer your original question, I never went all the way, I never actually *joined* any cult.'

'They sent me a sword too,' Missy said.

'Get out.'

'No, I'm serious. I don't have it with me, but I totally have one of those swords. I saw your video, the one without music, and next thing I get this long package delivered to my house, same as you. That's why I'm here. I'm on my way to Deep Sky right now, or I was until I ran away . . . It's a long story.'

'Missy, tell me you're messing with me,' Scout said. 'Because if you're not messing with me, I have to tell you something.'

'I'm telling you the truth,' Missy said. 'It was Silas brought me here. I was with Silas until this afternoon. But I ran away because—'

'Silas?'

Missy felt her throat close up. 'You don't know Silas? He said he knows you.'

'It's possible,' Scout said. 'I'm no good with names, and these meetings . . . there were a whole bunch of them there. It was freaky, actually, a whole room of black suits. Sunglasses.

These perfect, white shirts buttoned right to the top. No ties. I know how it sounds, but it's true. I don't remember any Silas, but that doesn't mean this isn't real, that you're not in danger. Missy. Deep Sky. From what I heard, these guys play for *keeps*!'

'Why, what did you hear?'

'It's gonna sound so dumb saying it out loud,' Scout said.

'Tell me,' Missy said.

'All I know is Deep Sky's brand of redemption doesn't come cheap. I mean, they don't send those swords out to just anyone. Check it out, the two of us. Most downloaded recording artist of all time and daughter of internet royalty ... Look, I don't pretend to know everything about Deep Sky, but before I took those meetings I had my people look into it and they turned up some dark, dark material let me tell you.'

'Like what?'

'Okay, you're not going to believe this but someone got hold of the blueprints for their main facility, the one I was telling you about, somewhere up north. You'd be surprised what money can buy if you know where to look. Deep Sky. It's an actual building, like their headquarters. We never did get a location on this thing but it's somewhere in the far north, maybe even Alaska. But there was one detail in these blueprints, a series of rooms whose function matched another story we'd heard, and actually it's a story that's since made it onto the internet, in one form or another.'

Missy was nearly off the edge of her chair.

'These rooms,' Scout continued. 'It was an operating theater. Like at a hospital. The real deal ... So, I'm guessing you haven't heard this story. Like I said, it's out there online, there're different versions but the basic details are always the same. It's the last stage of your journey. If you go all the way with these guys, they . . . they take out your eyes. I'm totally serious. They remove your eyes and replace them with a pair of rough diamonds. Uncut diamonds. Something about *true dark*. I don't understand the whole thinking behind it, but it seems these guys are equipped to do this thing. I told you it sounded crazy. But it makes you think about those celebrities who wear their sunglasses all the time, and I mean *all* the time. I started doing it to look the part, like I was really in with these guys.'

'But if they're blind, how do they—'

'Bodyguards,' Scout said. 'Ever notice how these celebrities are always holding onto their bodyguards? I'm telling you, girl, Deep Sky is no joke.'

Missy looked pale.

'I shouldn't have told you,' said Scout. 'You don't need to be scared, Missy, it's over now. It was a close call, but you're clearly smart enough to have gotten away in time. And now you're here with me, you're safe. I have to ask, though. They may have sent you the sword, but there must have been something else, something that made you want to run away.'

'Something did happen,' Missy said. 'I had to get out of that house.'

'*Versailles*. I heard about that place. Biggest private residence in the United States? I mean, I got a big house, I got more than one, but that place . . . Didn't your dad, like, *invent* the internet?'

Missy laughed. 'My dad's not who everybody thinks he is.'

'Tell me more.'

Missy was cold, but this shivering wasn't the adrenaline. This was something different. She missed her mom. Cassius outside with his big arms. She missed her mom, the smell of her perfume faded almost to nothing, the choice of lipstick, her head resting against Missy's shoulder as a tear rolled down her cheek. She wished she had her phone again, not to go online, but to feel the velvet of the unbreakable glass, her mom's design. The whiteness of Scout's sneakers and Cassius outside. Cassius with his big arms and small ears. Big like a bear and he tied her shoelaces, the muscles flexing in his big arms as he ties her shoelaces. Missy nearly passed out again, tucked her hair behind her ears and tried to breathe. #ScoutRose.

'You don't have to tell me anything if you don't want to,' Scout said.

'I love your music,' Missy heard herself say. 'I love your music so much. It's been my inspiration for as long as I can remember. I think you have the most beautiful voice.'

'Thank you, Missy, that means a lot,' Scout said. 'You're a cool girl, Missy Baer. I still can't believe you threw that Molotov. What does that even feel like?'

'Do you have any alcohol?' Missy said, like she was asking for water.

'Why, you wanna get messed up? Scout Rose and Missy Baer getting wasted in the middle of nowhere. I like that.' Scout opened a cabinet and held up a dark brown glass bottle. 'I got this moonshine, I don't know what it is. My bodyguard makes it on the bus, he's like a chemistry major in real life. It tastes like apples, I swear to God.'

*

Missy doesn't remember everything but she remembers this, these moving pictures, scrolling up and past like looping GIFs:

Slipping out the skylight of the Winnebago, a crazy-far jump to the grass below, too drunk to feel the pain, Cassius none the wiser, Cassius and Jean-Pierre standing guard outside an empty trailer. Funniest thing ever. They enter the crowds arm in arm, two drunk girls in sunglasses showing everybody else what time it is. Scout is smaller than Missy expected, she smells like her perfume. Running, laughing, dancing, falling, triple piggy backs and gonzo gymnastics. Boys here, boys there, the boyz, the boyz, nothing bad, a kiss here, a kiss there, everything given rhythm, the sheer joy of this youth brought together by a shared love of hate, all love, all love, all now and for never. Two drunk girls in big sunglasses and Missy's fading make-up but she doesn't know; Scout's disguise destined to fail and pretty soon they have an audience, the randomness of everyone around them turned less random, less good, boyz will be boys. A crowd of people all around, watching Scout Rose dance with that chick who threw the Molotov, the fading make-up. The mutual feeling, two girls not too drunk to know what's happening, Missy takes Scout's hand and pushes her way through the audience, boys here, boys everywhere, Missy wide awake now and Scout's fame like a force field until her sunglasses are crushed underfoot and a boy makes eye contact and it's too much for him to bear, Scout *Rose* right there and he'll never get this chance again. He grabs her T-shirt in his fist, but Missy keeps hold, pulls her friend behind her and they make it through, and now they are running, not too drunk for the rush of adrenaline as they break free of the crowd and make a run, people calling after them, wanting them to play, they run away, tripping on the lines of half-pitched tents, out to the edges of the festival, where the grass grows longer and then trees, young trees and darkness.

They run into the trees, into the darkness of the trees, the moonlight out of frame. They run into the darkness, two drunk girls, deep into the forest, the music faded right into the background. Time to rest, time to rest, some moonshine still left in the bottle, two girls getting drunk by the dim light of the moon, the stillness of the forest winning out against the music, the bass still pushing through the leaves, but these girls are deep, their laughter muted like buried glass, crystal fragments buried in the loose topsoil of the forest, laughter giving way to sleep, the deep sleep that comes after too much excitement.

Missy doesn't remember everything but she remembers this: her eyes flickering open, first light streaming in low through the young trees, Scout's hand touching her hand and she turns to say hey but it isn't Scout, it's the boy with no name and he's saying hers. *Missy. Wake up, Missy Baer.*

Scout was gone and he was saying her name, again and again, telling her he was lost, *I went looking for you, Missy, and I got lost.* 'I'm lost and I want to go home, Missy. Can you take me home, Missy, back to the trailer? Can you help me find my dad?'

46

In his dream, River is back in the jungle as the black panther cat. This has become a recurring dream and his latent awareness of this lends the sequence a lucid quality, but not so much that he cannot enjoy it as one enjoys a movie in the cinema, playing out in front of you as someone else's fantasy might just. And this fantasy has him as a panther prowling through the undergrowth in pursuit of a young man with deep brown skin wearing only a diamond tiara.

The feeling of the dream is a breeze pushing its way through the trees, the rustling of long leaves, the paths of ants as they crawl along up and down the hard spines and limbs of all the plants. The feeling is of anticipation. Intense calm before a perfect storm. For River is in complete control. At this very moment he could sink his white teeth into the flesh of his prey. At any moment. This isn't a hunt, this is pursuit.

River is following the man deeper and deeper into the jungle. His bright yellow eyes never leave the man's body, how the musculature rearranges itself again and again as he navigates the dense undergrowth, ducking, moving forward on his haunches, occasionally breaking into a reckless sprint and disturbing other, smaller, but no less dangerous, creatures.

This isn't a hunt, this is pursuit, an anticipation that has River moaning quietly out loud in the waking world, his penis so stiff it has lifted the waist of his shorts clean away from his belly. The man in the diamond tiara is growing tired. River begins to circle his prey, increasing his speed exponentially in a wide flanking maneuver. His yellow eyes never leave the man's body. The dream has never lasted this long. River doesn't know what will happen next.

When the man emerges into the clearing River is waiting for him. Their eyes meet and the man turns to run but River is so much faster and brings him down with two mighty front paws, no claws. His claws remain retracted. River uses raw power and repeated snarls to suppress his victim. With his prey pinned to the ground, River settles down, almost bored. He yawns and blinks against a shaft of sunlight coming through the canopy above. He looks down at the man and sees the tiara, although he doesn't really see a tiara because he is a black panther cat and doesn't know what one is.

What next? At this very moment he could sink his perfect white teeth into the flesh of his prey but he doesn't. Instead he takes his big cat tongue and licks the man's face slowly, neck to ear, neck to ear. His brown body undulates with involuntary pleasure, his left hand slowly opening to reveal a white key, the chocolate key turned overnight to bone, and River knows. This is the answer. All these years looking for a hack and here's the answer. The dream of an answer and River knows, knows that he is sleeping, and when he wakes up this key will be a line of code. The gift of a solution given him in dreams, a perfect, gleaming shell on the shore of consciousness, left there for him to find. A blade to cut through everything, the black curtain. A key, a key to every door. His father's secrets. One hundred rooms and a second master. Master River Baer of Versailles, USA.

47

They walked hand in hand, Missy and the boy with no name, this canvas city shifting in the summer breeze, but no music in the air; the meet was over, the trolls were heading home. Missy watched as people took down their tents, rolling black and silver poles up in dirty ground sheets, collecting trash, folding chairs and dousing smoking embers with the water from half-scrunched plastic bottles. They were moving on, taking care to leave the ground as they had found it. And Missy wanted to go with them, climb in the back of some car, anybody's car, drive north, west, east, it didn't matter anymore, anywhere but home. Somewhere in the moment, with people her own age. She just wanted to be in the back of some car, along for the ride.

The boy with no name was lagging behind. Missy would have given anything to go with these other guys, but right now she had to help this little boy find his father. He needed her. She'd planned it in her head. The moment they found Silas, the moment she set eyes on him, she would point the kid and run again, just like before, run as fast as she could before he saw her, and then find one of these other guys. She would find a nice person and get away in their car, these trees in the rear mirror, drive to the next place, wherever that was. Some inland city in the shadow of a mountain. Yeah, a quiet city, dark gray mountains in the background. They'd pull up outside the library, a modern building with large windows and an area of grass. *Here is fine*, she'd say, climb out of the car, thank them kindly for the food and the ride, step out onto the street and start walking. One foot in front of the other along the sidewalk. She was Missy Baer. She was smart, she was mature, she knew stuff, she would get a job, some money. A little apartment. She'd make friends. People seemed to like her. She would make friends, one by one, until there was a group of them. Shared jokes, private jokes, shared stories. Some inland city. She may never tell this story. The sword, Nora, Cass, the bikers, the boy with no name, Silas, the journey north, Crystal, Marchpane, the Molotov, Deep Sky ... She may never tell the story. How she got here. Maybe that could be her secret. All the pictures in her mind, saved there for another time.

They walked hand in hand, Missy pulling the boy after her by his arm. 'You're hurting me,' he said, twisting himself free.

'You're too slow,' Missy said.

'Why you being so mean?' the kid said, 'You weren't like this before.'

But Missy couldn't answer. They were all leaving without her, heading out, and she towards danger. Silas. The thought of him. Who was this guy? And Deep Sky. Scout's warning, the diamonds for eyes, all these people leaving, heading home or to the next adventure. She wanted to get in the back of one of their cars, half-open windows, the smell of their skin, their music less strange as the tarmac passed by underneath, the miles of road and the thrill of escape. Some

275

inland city. Shared memories, shared stories. But this little kid, all alone and because of her, because she ran away. This kid needed her right now. Like a big sister. He'd lost his rabbit. Not a day over seven.

They walked hand in hand, the boy with no name keeping pace. The burning man was now a pile of ash, white upon gray upon black. A perfect circle of charred wood at the outer edge. Missy could still smell burning but there wasn't much smoke, all this sky where her father had stood. It felt like a dream. All this sky and she remembered the black pill with the white star. This had all been Deep Sky. Silas, Crystal, Marchpane. They were all connected somehow. She adjusted her sunglasses against the bright sunlight.

She thought the boy with no name was lagging again, but he had changed direction. He was leading *her* now, trying to tell her something. 'Missy, please, Missy, *look*!'

She looked up and it was a hot air balloon, towering over them, slowly swaying, changing shape in the breeze. Looming and benevolent. Never been this close before. She'd only seen them on TV, and once or twice in the blue sky, high above Versailles. The balloon was orange, with a circle of triangular white flags one third of the way up. No sound except the lightest rippling of material, the soft roar of the blue flame, and the creak, creak of the giant basket below. There was a tent off to the side. *Balloon Rides* read the sign, yellow letters against sky blue.

'Missy, please, Missy, can we go in?' said the kid, pulling at her sleeve.

Flying crocodile. She found herself walking toward the entrance to the tent, the slow billowing of the balloon above, a continuous blossoming of fabric into this perfect thing, this great big, orange balloon with the pretty white flags and the roaring blue flame. All this sky, away, away from Versailles. One ride. No harm in that. *Twinkies.* They were on her mind but she could not think why. One ride. Flying crocodile. High above the turning earth, suspended there from a brightly colored air balloon and rising, Versailles too small to see, everything, the ocean waves unmoving, areas of blue, patches of green, yellow, brown and then— Missy continued walking, all reality left behind, only this balloon, the entrance to the perfectly pitched tent before her, the last tent standing in this field. *Balloon Rides,* the sign read. They walked hand in hand into the tent and that was it. A heavy cloth sack pulled down over Missy's head and two strong arms around her waist, lifting her from the ground momentarily. Even through the sack she could smell his sweat, hear the creak of the biker leathers. She struggled against his bear hug but it was no good. 'Now, Missy, don't fight,' Silas said. 'I gotcha, I gotcha. Now now.'

PART FOUR

Dark Profile

48

The monitor lizard is making his way along another empty corridor in Versailles. His teeth are bared but he is not angry. His yellow eyes look mean but he is not mean, he is a monitor lizard who has not eaten in over a week. Just then he passes a white door. According to Versailles' schematics, this is Room 50, the server room, and there is someone inside, though there is no way the monitor lizard could know that.

All of the footage from the thousands of cameras installed throughout the mansion is archived here in these servers: four cabinets constructed of carbon-fiber-reinforced black plastic, each standing eight feet tall. Every second of every minute of every day, month, year and decade that the family have lived in and outside this house is recorded here and in the same instant made available for live stream over any and all of Casey's multiple devices, his phones, tablets and various other computers. Conversations, altercations, their little hands and feet, their little mouths and deft articulations, their eyes and mouths and little ears for listening. And the process is ongoing. At this moment footage of Silas carrying Missy from the balloon tent over one shoulder is being archived as it happens, as are myriad other feeds of the rooms and corridors of Versailles where nothing at all is happening.

Space and time. Negative space. Silence. The silence is a roar. The space crackles with undirected electricity. Versailles as witness. Versailles as witness to itself. The miles of cable and the level of control, the choice of cameras.

Why here one might ask? Why not have the servers stationed elsewhere? Less chance of discovery. Because Casey likes the smell. It reminds him of the first time he stepped inside the server room for the social network. An entire building built in the shadow of a mountain in the north. The smell is of hot plastic. The smell is industrial. The smell is of power. Casey likes the smell and wanted the Versailles server situated here so he could come and go as he pleased. He's here now, returned to the house under cover of darkness, clothes damp through from walking in the hot city. He's in Room 50 now, the server room, breathing the smell of the hot plastic deep, deep into his lungs. Casey is breathing with his belly, his shoulders coming forward with the effort of each inhalation, his spine elongating like a lazily conceived creature of science fiction. The action is grotesque, almost sexual, like a cat arching its back to meet the stroking hand of its owner. Nothing less, only more.

In these moments Casey is like a machine, processing the smell of these other machines, turning it into this utterly banal sense of power, power over all the other creatures. Outside the food chain, the animal kingdom spread out before him like a living, breathing, squealing, squeaking banquet, all their eyes twinkling, twinkling like the blue lights of his network's server units, twinkle, twinkle, twinkle, twinkle, like stars in the deep sky, the deep, deep sky below, his darkness and the pleasure of this smell of hot plastic, motherboards warping under the stress of so much data, all your thoughts, your feelings, hopes, dreams, fear, fulfillment, disillusionment, all the photographs, the video, available right now, more, more, *more available than now*, all the data to be processed and only he knows, only Casey Baer could know what to make of it all. For he is the denominator, the innovator, the motivator, terminator, king of the castle, king of social, father of two. Father of two beautiful kids. His two little Baers. Missy & River. #pride&joy

River is intelligent. River is creative. River is good with computers. River reminds Casey very much of himself when he was a boy, a natural coder, logical, a problem-solver. But River has this creativeness behind it. His son could be whatever he wants to be, if only he would leave his bedroom fortress once in a while. Or not. These days you can invent yourself right there on your laptop. But maybe if his son got out of that room he would meet more girls, at least give them a chance. River is an attractive kid, what young girl wouldn't want to date someone like him? Rich, talented, athletic. The acne will pass, the bad skin will eventually give way to good skin. River has his mother's eyes, her yearning. All River has to do is get out of that room.

Missy is sensitive, beautiful, independent, willful. Missy reminds him of her mother when they first met. Always searching, always reaching for something better, something beyond the now. Forget about yesterday, what about tomorrow? And she has a dark side too. A secret life. She may look like an innocent young girl but she is more mature than other people know, more even than her mother knows. Sure she and her mother have been close in the past, but Casey has seen things, Casey has seen and heard things. It's all here on the server, collected, collated and indexed. The blinking blue lights. He knows his daughter, better perhaps than she knows herself.

Yes, his two little Baers. Missy & River. His pride & joy. He breathes the smell of the plastic deep into his lungs, the first-person footage of Missy being tied up in the back of the trailer playing out on his smartphone. She is still unconscious. Silas ties his knots a certain way. There's an economy to his movements, a soldier-like efficiency. He's done all this before.

Casey stops breathing so deep, sets his feet a fraction wider apart, straightens out his damp gray sweatshirt, smoothes out the wrinkles with the flats of his palms like he's preparing himself for company. But no one is coming. No one knows he is here, and that is as it should be for now.

49

River blinks against a shaft of sunlight coming through the canopy above. He looks down at the man and sees the tiara, although he doesn't really see a tiara because he is a black panther cat and doesn't know what one is. The sunlight reflects off the diamonds brightly and River has to blink again, only this time he was blinking in real life, opening his eyes and waking up, a shaft of sunlight coming in through the small, high window in his bedroom. *The bunker* his mom called it.

River got into a sitting position, saw the box of tricks. He set about carefully removing the seven pins from his forearm. They'd been in there too long. The pain now wasn't nice so much as dull and sickening, a bruised feeling that actually dovetailed pretty well with the way he felt every morning, self-harm or no. River wasn't quite awake, the taste of chocolate. The sparkling tiara and the line of code. A line of code. One hundred rooms and he'd dreamed a hack. Could it really be? This stuff only happened in books and movies. He shoved the box of tricks back into the low shelf with his foot and skated across the room to his workstation. It was only then that he noticed the time. Holy crap it was past midday, how could this have happened? He opened his email.

Congratulations, you are the competition winner! Please log in to scoutfan at 12:12 today for your one-on-one with Scout herself. This is a once-in-a-lifetime opportunity to get some private time with the most downloaded artist of her generation. Don't be late.

It was 12:03, he still had time, but not enough time for the tennis ball cannon. God*dammit*. He had to think. He still wasn't awake really, like, thirty to forty per cent of him was still in the dream as the black panther. He slapped his face from both sides with his hands. Not enough. He coiled his fist. The first punch was practically a knockout. He picked himself off the floor, climbed back into his chair for one more. Bam. He was bleeding now from his nose, this was messier than he'd hoped. He held the fleshy part of his nose to create a clot, wet some cotton buds in his mouth, rolled them between his hands and inserted one in each nostril. All good in the hood. 12:09. He was ready now. He clicked the link in his email and a dialogue box prompted him to log in to *scoutfan*. Next thing he was in an old-style chat room, no emoticons, just a white box that cast no shadow.

Scout is typing . . .

scout
Hey, pr1ncess, how are you? I'm touring right now and it's so nice to be able to take some time out with my

*laptop and chat to one of my amazing fans! So, where
are you from, pr1ncess?*

pr1ncess

*My name's River Baer and I'm not a fan, I'm here about
Deep Sky. I think they have my sister, Missy. My
question for you is this: Where have they taken her?
Where is Deep Sky? That's still one question, by the
way.*

River kicked away from his desk in the office chair but
went much further than he expected so he had to scoot back
a little bit. His arm was starting to bruise up pretty good.
Not his best work.

Scout is typing . . .

scout

*River you need to walk away from this thing. If your
sister's at Deep Sky it's because she wants to be there.*

pr1ncess

*I know my sister. If she was in trouble she'd come to me
first. There's no way she'd just disappear for no reason.*

scout

*River I don't want to speak out of turn but everybody
has their secrets. It's possible there was something Missy
didn't think she could share with anybody, not even her
little brother. Deep Sky is the perfect place for her right
now.*

pr1ncess

Well you're wrong. And I'm not her little brother, we're

twins, although it's weird that you'd say that. Just tell me where she is. I have a right to know.

scout

River, Missy has a right to her privacy. If she wanted you to know where she was, she would have told you.

pr1ncess

Nice talking, I'm calling the cops.

scout

River we told you what would happen if you tried involving the police. Like I said at the beginning of our little chat, it's best if you walk away from this thing. Missy is safe with us. You have my word.

pr1ncess

You're not Scout Rose, you're something else.

On another screen River tried running a location search on whoever this was. To his surprise it was working. He'd have something in the next few seconds.

Scout is typing . . .

scout

I can see what you're doing, River. It's fine, I don't mind you knowing where I am, not anymore. You're not going to like what you find. Happy hunting . . .

The satellite image was still loading, the image a pixelated wash of green, yellow, blue and white. And then it came into focus, and River's heart skipped a beat, the wounds in his forearm suddenly painful with the rush of adrenaline through his body. The green trees, the yellow beach, the blue ocean. The white was Versailles. Whoever this was they were here. Whoever this was chatting with him about Deep Sky, they were right here in the house, in one of Versailles' one hundred rooms.

50

They continued on the northbound highway. Every now and then the trailer went over a bump in the road and something fell off a shelf, but Missy couldn't do anything about it because she was tied up. She looked at the kid with no name. 'You tricked me,' she said. 'Don't you feel bad about tricking me?'

The kid carried on playing his video game. He wouldn't look at Missy because he didn't like to see her tied up like that.

'I thought we were friends,' continued Missy. 'I thought we made friends back there, but friends don't lie to each other, they help each other out. You lied to me and now I'm tied up and I don't know why. I'm scared and I need your help. Do you hear me?'

The kid died in his video game, waited to get spawned back in, and carried on playing.

'Can you untie me please?' Missy said. 'I've lost the circulation in my arms and can't feel my hands. It's not like I'm going anywhere if you untie me. We're on the highway.'

The kid flinched but carried on playing his video game. He liked Missy. She was cute and she was his friend, but she was a bad girl for running away like she did, real naughty, that's why Daddy tied her up. He felt sad when she went away but now she was back. He liked Missy because she was nice to him and pretty too, she had long blonde hair like a princess. But his dad told him: no matter what she tells you, you don't untie her. His dad made him promise. He said if he promised they would get him another rabbit, just like Bob.

'What does Bob say?' Missy said. 'Does he think you should untie me?'

How did she know that? How did she know he was thinking about Bob? Oh my God, she must have magic for that, how else could she know he was thinking about his rabbit Bob? How else could she know? He didn't look at her but he decided he should talk to Bob about it, quietly, in his head. 'Bob?'

'Hi.'

'Hi, Bob, how are you today?'

'I'm okay,' said Bob. 'I miss you.'

'I miss you too, Bob.'

'What video game are you playing?' said Bob.

'My favorite,' said the boy, 'but I keep dying over and over in the same place.'

'You're using the wrong gun.'

'How would you know, Bob? Rabbits don't know guns!'

'I know everything,' said Bob. 'I'm Bob.'

'Okay, so what should I do about Missy? She wants me to untie her but my dad told me no.'

'What do *you* think you should do?' said Bob.

'I want to untie her,' continued the boy in his head.

'But your dad told you no.'

'I *know*, but Missy's my *friend*. She took care of me when you died.'

'I'm not dead! I'm right here,' said Bob the rabbit.

'I know that but I like Missy, she's funny and she looks like a princess.'

'So what are you waiting for? Untie her!'

'But my dad told me no. He made me promise. He said if I did as I was told we could get a new rabbit that looked just like you, Bob.'

'I like your dad,' said Bob. 'He knows what's right.'

'I guess,' said the boy with no name. He said goodbye to Bob and spoke out loud to Missy. 'Bob says I should leave you tied up.'

'Well, Bob doesn't know what he's talking about,' said Missy.

'We're almost there, Missy, can't you wait a little longer? I can get you some apple juice. There's apple juice in the fridge. I could get you some of that . . .'

The boy with no name picked up his controller and carried on playing his video game. Missy waited a while before asking. 'Where's your momma?'

The boy didn't miss a beat. 'My dad says she dead but I don't believe 'm.'

'Why don't you believe him?'

'I see her at night sometimes,' sighed the boy lazily. He'd changed guns. Bob was right about the guns.

'What, like a ghost?' Missy said.

'No, not like a *ghost*,' said the boy. 'She real, she only come at night though, and she don't say nuthin'. She just sits on my bed and holds my hand. I can feel her hand and it's warm.'

292

'You think it could be a dream?' said Missy.

'Yeah, I guess,' said the boy, 'but it feels real. I can feel her hand and it's warm, I can smell her perfume and sometimes she'll kiss my cheek goodnight. Other times she doesn't do that.'

'You ever tried talking to her?' asked Missy.

'I always ask her, but she won't answer me. I ask her, *Are you real, Momma?* But she just sits there, lookin' at me. I can see her eyes in the dark and I know she can hear me, but she won't answer.'

'I'm sorry about that,' Missy said.

'It's okay. I like it when she visits.' He'd never talked about this to *anybody*, except Bob of course. Missy really was his friend and he felt badly about her being tied up.

'Where are we going?' said Missy. 'What's it like there?'

The boy didn't answer, the game controller clicking and squeaking in his hands.

Deep Sky. They had to be getting close. Deep Sky. Scout's warning. This feeling all through her body. This fear. It was the strangest thing, ever since she was tied up, this fear – a new sense that it belonged to her somehow, like, like – happiness. When something made you happy, you remembered what it was so you could have it again. Adults did it all the time. The choice of wine. The choice of music. The lighting of a cigarette. Their lives had *structure*. Control. This fear. The sword, Versailles in the rear mirror. Twinkies, balloon rides. These were choices. *Her* choices. Deep Sky. This fear. This must be what being an adult felt like. A waking dream. A dream of life. The degrees of control. You live by your choices. Her decision to run away. *Her* fear. Deep Sky. She was still curious. Scout's story about the diamonds

293

for eyes. Even if it was true, she would have a choice. Or maybe not. She remembered Silas's words after the bear encounter ... *Because once you start on this journey of ours, there's simply no turning back. There's no going home. Does that frighten you, Missy, when I say those words to you?* It still frightened her, but this fear belonged to her. She found herself relaxing. Bound by her choices. The rope Silas used to tie her up. It stopped cutting into her flesh so much. She felt the texture of the road, it vibrated through her bones.

It was all starting to make sense to Missy. When she felt fear, a part of that fear – it belonged to her. If she could just get through this, come out the other side alive, it would give her fear shape, like, it could become a story she told. Or didn't tell. Same with her anger. She was angry with her dad. She was angry with her mom. But if she could just stop feeling like a victim, like everything was happening *to* her, maybe she could be less angry. If she could take *control* ... She was her father's daughter. She was her mother's daughter. But she was also Missy Baer, and she was ready to face the world like an adult, sword by her side. Yes, Deep Sky were behind all this. Yes, she was kind of being kidnapped. But at the same time it was she who said yes to Silas when he asked her was she ready, way back in the trailer park.

Missy was ready. Ready to stop being the angry teenager, put all that energy into whatever was coming next. This *fear* belonged to her. It made her feel alive. Like no number of likes ever could, no single comment under her photo telling her how *perfect* she was. She wasn't perfect. She was Missy. Sixteen candles, an arc of quicksilver. For the first time since her kiss with Levon, she felt like she could do anything.

Missy wasn't missing, she was starting to find herself. Oh my God, that sounded lame, but it was true. She felt it in her bones. The bones inside her body inside her clothes. She felt the texture of the road. It was smooth. Not like a road at all. The rope Silas used to tie her up. It stopped cutting into her flesh so much. The road so smooth, the landscape playing like a movie. It felt like flying. *I'm flying — Like an arrow — My black feathers fluttering in the wind — My wings fluttering with black feathers — I'm flying, away from them, away from everything.*

51

A living daymare. A stranger in the house. Someone who knew about Missy, knew everything. River's nemesis. unknown_user, ruhin, InnerFame, whatever his real name was, he was inside these walls, breathing the same air, blood pumping round his body underneath his clothes. One hundred rooms. River sat before his seven screens, all windows minimized but one, his fingers resting lightly on the keyboard. Versailles' security mainframe. The taste of chocolate, the dream of an answer, a line of code, the key to every room in Versailles. It fell through him like rain. Pure inspiration.

```
01001101   01101001   01110011   01110011   01111001
00100000   00100110   00100000   01010010   01101001
01110110   01100101   01110010
```

Their names in binary. Missy and River. He pressed enter and the sound was a depth charge near the surface of the ocean; one hundred deadbolts throughout Versailles sliding back into one hundred doors. A rush of goosebumps, part fear, part excitement.

'Squawk!'

'Shut up, Money,' River said, 'that was all me, you're not

taking any credit, you little scumbag.' River thought for a second. 'You know what, Money, I take that back, the part about you being a scumbag. I got a lot on my mind, I'm sorry.'

'*Scumbag*,' repeated Money.

'Right,' said River, 'now shut up like I said, I gotta concentrate.'

What to wear. If he was going to save his sister, he had to look the part. The bear costume didn't feel right. Too childish. But just the headpiece. The head of a bear and his normal clothes. Really freak out the intruder. River kept on the headpiece and grabbed his potato gun from the box of tricks. It was made to look exactly like a Glock G21, only it shot potato pellets instead of real bullets. He tucked it inside the waistband of his skinny pants like an OG and headed out, an old green potato in each pocket. He opened the door to his bedroom and saw the folded paper on the floor. A note from his mother. He almost didn't read it, but he couldn't help himself. He heard her voice inside his head, delivering the lines like an actress.

River I came to you while you were sleeping. I came to tell you I love you that was all. I love you, River, and only want you to be happy. I came to tell you that. I also came to tell you that your sister is safe. Your father told me she is safe but would not tell me where. I was thinking maybe when she's back we should get together, the four of us, to eat something. It's so important for a family to sit together around a table once in a while. I don't know what happened. I don't know when we stopped doing that, but I would like it very much if you would join us. We could have gumbo and potato salad, it was always your favorite when you were a little boy. I love you so much, River. I know I haven't always been there. But I want to make it up to you and your sister. I would like very much to have the opportunity to make it up to you and Missy. So I was thinking we could go on vacation together, just the three of us. We could—

He didn't have time for this. River made a paper plane out of the letter and sent it flying down the corridor. The truth was he loved her back. But she was weak, she was weak and he hated to see her weak because she could be strong, she was strong, the most talented industrial designer of her generation. She'd designed some of the most iconic technology in the history of personal computing, but that was a long time ago and now . . . she was lost and no one was looking. He loved her back but— And he was weak because of her. Casey telling him he was nothing and his mother right across the room, right across the room saying nothing. She never protected him. That was all Missy, but Missy was his sister, she was just a kid like him. Synthea was their mother. He couldn't remember the last time he'd called her Synthea to punish her. Now he just called her that. She was weak and he was weak because of her. Standing right across the room and saying nothing.

And now Missy wasn't here and River was alone. Like a daymare. A stranger in the house who knew where Missy was. What was he going to do when he found this character? Jesus Christ, this wasn't a video game, this was real life and all he had was this potato gun from his box of tricks.

Important to be systematic. One room at a time. 'Later, Money,' he called, pulling the heavy door of the bunker closed behind him.

52

Click, click.

Push to open.

Another pill.

Synthea imagined it dissolving in her belly, behind the smooth white skin of her belly, deep inside, fizzing away seamlessly and entering her bloodstream. When she first started taking the pills she found the whole thing quite frightening. The delayed effect. The uncanny sense of smoothed edges, these missing segments of herself. A dissolving of self, her core replaced by one just like it, only molded out of white plastic this time, perfectly formed like one of her designs: no seams, no divides. No workings. A dull infinity. Her ego a white plastic orb reflecting no light whatsoever. They weren't messing around, the pharmas making this stuff, this opposite of magic.

She imagined the pill dissolving in her belly, deep inside her warm body, still warm under the covers, the silk sheets of the king-sized bed, the master bedroom, their bedroom. *I want to build you a house.* But this was never her house. She lived here like her children did, but this was never her home. *Versailles.* This was *his* life, *his* vision. Versailles had never felt like a home, this house, this monstrosity, this *blight* had never felt like a home, somewhere to bring up a family. *His* dream, her nightmare. *I want to build you a house by the ocean.* But as the years went by, the ocean seemed to have receded, a tidal retreat independent of the moon's influence.

The early years: her beautiful office with that impossible view. *It's everything you ever wanted. Isn't this everything you ever wanted? It's everything you ever wanted. I built it for you to make you happy, so you could be closer to your family.* It was where she did some of her best work – her life's work, as it turned out. But it was still working from home. It didn't matter that she had all the equipment she could ever need, they were still the same walls, always the same walls closing in. To create we must translocate. She remembered realizing one day that she hadn't left the grounds in several weeks. And that is exactly how Casey wanted it. Versailles was their prison, the scale deceptive, mirror on mirror. The painted perspective. The ocean framed and framed again. Walls within walls. One hundred rooms and the majority were locked.

No wonder her Missy wanted to run away. No wonder when, no wonder when— and then . . . a loss of concentration, the first effects of the tiny white pill, she feels it now, now no longer a pill but an altered state, a shift in perspective from *here* to there. The sense of something moving from the nape of her neck and over her head, of something like a cowl, an almost weightless hood being pulled forward over her head by another agency, across her scalp and ending over her forehead, eyes shielded from an invisible sun, this dull infinity, no start or end only flow, like a river seen from a great height, seemingly unmoving, a river flowing on and on toward the ocean, ever wider as the freshwater grows

heavy, the vast hulls of nameless cargo ships now like air-
ships in the summer haze, the river ever-widening until it is
the sea, the glittering ocean, the endless ocean.

The pill working its horror, but the love in her heart, the
warmth to her hands, she could still be herself – elbows to
fingertips – the concern for her daughter, the cold steel door
to River's bunker, her son asleep on the other side, her special, special boy, her only prince, the pill working its horror,
but the love in her heart, her role as their mother, her elegant
profile glimpsed in the closing French window, a once beautiful woman, the warmth to her hands and the coolness of
the water, the glittering ocean beyond the black curtains of
the master bedroom, these terrible black curtains. These terrible black curtains shielding her from the real sun outside,
the glittering ocean, the endless ocean, her only escape. The
pill working its horror, but the love in her heart, her role as
their mother. It was all her fault. Missy running away, River
locked away in his bunker. Synthea saw that now. All her
secrets and regrets, doubts and desires. Things about Casey,
things not meant for Missy's ears.

It was all her fault. Standing in the room as Casey called
their son names, told him he was good for nothing. Her
standing in the room and saying nothing. All these years.
Resting her head on Missy's shoulder. Missy always saying
the right things, but she was still a *child*, sixteen candles and
all the magic gone. Synthea saw it now. It was all her fault.
She let this happen. From the beginning. *I want to build you
a house by the ocean. I want to have your children.* She
knew Casey was manipulating her but there was no point
arguing, it would lead nowhere. She'd let Casey get his way,
she always had. Sometimes she was the mother, knowing the

right words to say. Other times she felt like a child. He frightened her. His shouting, his roaring, his own childishness turning to something monstrous. He was a monster. And there was nothing the good monsters in River's wardrobe could do about it. This was all her fault. She'd done nothing to protect her kids. Resting her head on Missy's shoulder. She closed her eyes and saw whiteness. 'I'm going swimming,' Synthea said out loud. Leticia opened her eyes. They were asleep only a few hours. Her over and she under the covers. 'I want to swim in the ocean today,' Synthea said.

'Are you sure?' said Leticia quietly, 'You have not been swimming in a long time.'

'I want to swim in the ocean,' Synthea said, 'Would you mind fetching me a fresh towel from the wardrobe, Leticia? I would like a fresh towel to dry myself afterwards.'

They walked awhile along the shoreline, it was like Mrs Synthea was looking for the right place where she should go in the ocean. The water so calm today, like a mirror for the sky. No boats, no birds. It was very quiet, like something was going to happen, not bad, not good. Something.

'But where will you go, Leticia?' Synthea said from nowhere.

'I'm here, Mrs Synthea, what's wrong?'

'Yes but where will you go . . . where will you go?'

'I have my apartment, my little place to live for now, it's nice, really. You can come visit if you like. I have my teddy bears all set up for when I come home. You remember my teddy bears, Mrs Synthea? You always said I was like a little kid. But they keep me safe and I like it in a way. It's my place and that's good for now.'

'You have an apartment? Where is your apartment?' Synthea said.

'In the city. Don't you remember, Mrs Synthea? You gave me the chairs and the table. That was very nice of you. The fancy chairs with the table. That was very nice. You were always good to me, Synthea. We looked after each other.'

'I remember, yes. Your new apartment. Yes, I do remember. The ocean today is so still,' Synthea said. 'It's like a mirror.'

'It's what I was thinking too,' Leticia said. 'Like a mirror for the sky. Very calm . . .'

'I would like to swim in it,' Synthea said.

'You should,' Leticia said. 'The ocean looks beautiful. You should enjoy it. I know how you like to go in the water, Mrs Synthea.'

'Yes, I do like to swim, very much.' Synthea came to a standstill and looked out over the water, out to the horizon where she thought she could see the shape of a boat, a cargo ship all the way out there. She shielded her eyes from the bright sunlight with the curve of her hand. She began undressing. Her movements were precise, very much like she was being careful to avoid some kind of pain, a terrible pain that might manifest itself at any moment. She unbuttoned her blouse and gave it to Leticia. She did the same with her skirt and when she slipped out of her shoes she was naked. Synthea looked down at her own body. A cluster of moles on her left shoulder. Funny, she didn't remember those.

Leticia thought she looked very beautiful as she walked into the ocean. Not just her body. Her spirit. She felt so sorry somehow, such a lovely lady, not the Synthea she remembers, not like when they first met. This was a broken lady, walking slowly and gracefully into the ocean, her feet disappearing, her naked body more naked than it should be, her fingertips touching the surface as the water grew deeper around her, a swell so subtle as to go unnoticed.

53

Missy blinked in the bright sunlight. She opened and closed her hands to get the blood flowing again. They had arrived, whatever that meant. They were on the edge of some kind of town, low mountains in the background, standing outside the entrance to what looked like a public swimming baths. The sky was a deep, azure blue. There were people here, walking along the sidewalk and driving slowly in their cars, but it was quiet as a daydream. This had to be a swimming pool, Missy even thought she could smell the chlorine, but then where were all the people? It was a beautiful day and this far from the ocean Missy couldn't imagine anything she'd rather do. The pleasure of swimming, her body moving through the cool water.

'I'm not going in there, Dad. I'm scared.'

'Don't be ridiculous, boy. If you don't pull yourself together right this minute, there's not going to be another rabbit. And you can forget about fixing up that motorcycle in the fall.'

The boy with no name fell silent.

'That's better. Now.' Silas tossed Missy her sword like it was a rifle, and she a fellow soldier. 'You're going to need this. Don't get any ideas.' Next he pulled a long, heavy chain from his pocket revealing a single, black key. At least Missy thought it was a key. This thing was pure S&M, like something designed to elicit answers. Silas inserted the black key into the door and pushed it open with one hand. 'After you, Missy.'

It was a swimming pool, but there was no swimming pool. A cavernous room defined by a single pane of curving glass that framed a view of the sky so total it felt like you were still outside. Three diving platforms. The walls bedecked with white tiles. But where the swimming pool should be there was only carpet, a vast, powder-blue carpet that looked brand new.

'What is this place?' said Missy.

'Anteroom to the unknown,' Silas smiled. He walked into the room and opened a trapdoor, a square yard of carpet lifted away to reveal a dark aperture.

'The head torches,' Silas said. 'In my backpack.' The kid with no name unzipped the bag on his father's back and fished out the three head torches. 'You first, son. Missy'll be right behind you so there's nothing to be scared of. We're doing this together.'

The kid walked over to the hole in the ground and looked at Missy. 'You coming?'

Avoiding eye contact with Silas, Missy walked over to the trapdoor and switched on her head torch. There was a ladder and – the bottom of a swimming pool. It was still here. A strange thought. To be standing over a swimming pool like this, as though on the surface of the water. Missy watched the boy with no name descend and followed after.

Missy took the boy's hand in hers and looked around. A swimming pool, you could still smell the chlorine. All the tiny blue tiles, the change in depth from one end to the other. It gave her butterflies in her stomach. There was a dull slam as the trapdoor closed above them. Utter silence. The combined light from their three head torches created enough ambient light that Missy could see a door. Goosebumps. A door at the bottom of a swimming pool. It gave Missy a very bad feeling, like a dream turning into a nightmare.

54

River was *hyped*, dancing along the corridor like a boxer, one foot to the other. Dancing to the beats in his head inside the grizzly headpiece. Somewhere in this house, in one of these rooms: the key to Missy's disappearance. Someone with all the answers and River ready to show them what time it is. That's right. Left-right-left-left-right. But that wasn't the whole story. River was hyped because . . . well . . . he'd waited his whole life for this. These rooms. Their secrets. Their sum total was who his father really was. Versailles. Versailles was *Casey's* box of tricks.

These rooms. Casey Baer, CEO of the internet's pre-eminent social network. A man for his times. But his own profile online was pure fiction, an extension of the company's corporate identity. The pictures. The updates. There was nothing there but an all-American greatest hits, all straight edges and no blood, no mess. A gilded cipher. The real Casey Baer? In River's dreams, Casey was a reptile, skirting the curtained borders of his subconscious, a continuous billowing of black silk. The real Casey Baer was in these rooms, behind these white doors. Versailles. His life's work. His testing ground. His box of tricks. River stopped in front of his first door. He'd lived in this house most of his life and had never set foot inside this room. Wild. He reached out and took hold of the handle, the rest of his body was still dancing. The rest of his body was still the old River. The one about to open this door—

Inside the room was pitch black . . .

And then a spotlight.

For a delirious second River thought he was going to die, and his death was lion-shaped. It reared up at him, over him, its two mighty paws poised to tear him a new existence. And in that moment River saw his life, the unfolding perspective. His whole life, no pictures this time, no sequence. His death was lion-shaped, but River saw his life, his true self, and his life was panther-shaped, full-blood, his black fur gleaming in this light, the infinity still before him, his will to live in this new body, his strength of vision, to leap, descend with gravity and sink his teeth, his black fur gleaming, the will to live, two sets of claws out front, the lion still before him. For a delirious second he thought he was going to die, and in that moment River stepped forward, not back, toward the lion, like, what, you want some of this? This was River Baer, making up, shaping up, waking up. He closed his eyes against the mayhem, ready for his bloodbath.

Nothing. No sound or fury. River opened his eyes and saw the lion on all four paws, his mouth wide open in a silent roar. And then he realized. Another step forward and he could reach out and touch the glass. Non-reflective glass, almost invisible to the naked eye. Pre-market, it had to be, he'd never seen anything like this before. River ran his fingertips in a rainbow arc across the uncanny surface and the lion went berserk, a vortex of violence beyond. River watched on as the lion did everything it could to destroy him. It was strange, River held his ground, but it was like facing off ten car crashes at once, the adrenaline, his heart and hands, this readiness to fight, to fly, and fight again. River felt naked, his clothes fallen away like a shrugged cape. Himself an animal, but he knew the glass would hold. This glass, this room. A room designed for just this feeling – a dream of death, a brush with life. River turned away from the lion as it continued to paw at the glass, its sharp claws making no sound, its roars that might as well be yawns. River turned and walked away without looking back, this new feeling throughout his body. A newfound courage. In the corridor he removed the grizzly bear headpiece. Not a kid anymore. He wiped the sweat from his brow and tossed his longish hair. He was *River* Baer, prince of the internet, ready to bring his mad skills offline.

55

Mrs Synthea waved from the water and Leticia waved back. It was good to see her like this, swimming in the ocean. Almost happy. She felt the vibration against her thigh. Her cellphone. It was vibrating in her pocket. Leticia angled it away from the sun so she could tell who it was. Mr Casey. Calling her on the phone. Why? It was never good with this man. She didn't want to answer but what could she do? The waves breaking gentle at her feet. She touched the green button and breathed.

His voice was calm. He told her to come back to the house. There were people waiting at the house. Visitors. And Synthea must come, she was expected. His voice was calm and Leticia said okay. She put the phone in her pocket and took a step into the ocean. She called out to Synthea to come back. Too far. She was too far out to hear so she called again, louder this time. She hoped it wasn't bad. She hoped Mrs Synthea was not in trouble. His voice was calm, but he was like this, Mr Casey. He knew how to talk to people. She called out and Synthea seemed to change direction.

As Synthea swam, she forgot everything else, even her daughter, even her son. The effects of the pill. It didn't matter anymore because she was in the water. This was the first time, the first time in a long time. She could not remember why. Swimming was dreaming. Synthea dipped her head under the surface and when she came up again couldn't help smiling. Her hair wet now, eyes stinging with the salt water, she might never see her children again. What kind of thought is that? What kind of thought . . . ? She divided the water with her hands and arms and kicked out with her legs. Forward motion. Swimming was a great pleasure. Swimming was dreaming. She waved to Leticia on the beach, not long enough for her to see. She would miss Leticia, the water reflecting the sun between them, she would miss this woman. What kind of thought? The effects of the pill. Fade out. It didn't matter anymore because she was swimming. Her arms, her arms, this time alone was precious, the feeling of her body moving through the salt water, this time before her feet must find the sand again. Synthea swam a little further out, out of her depth, the colder water on her feet, Leticia standing on the beach with the soft towel waiting, the sun reflecting off the water between them. She waved to Leticia and swam a little further out. Still further. Swimming was her time alone, her only escape. Her two beautiful children, but this was time alone, Versailles beyond the tall palms, the dark window of her office, the colder water on her feet and knees and thighs. Someone calling her. Calling distance. Leticia on the beach. Okay, too far. *Okay, I'm coming.* Synthea turned in the water and swam back towards the shore. Swimming she was young again. A little girl, her mother standing on the beach, calling her back, the ocean glittering between them, a swell so subtle as to go unnoticed. The pull of the ocean, this time before her feet must find the sand. Something made her stop. Leticia waving for her to come back, but why, why should she when out here she was not a little girl anymore, she could swim as long as she wanted. Synthea turned on her back and spread out her limbs wide, the sky above so blue, bluer than anything she'd ever seen. A swell so subtle as to go unnoticed.

56

He reached out and took hold of the handle, but he wasn't scared this time. This was the new River, bubbling over the surface, ready for anything. He pushed on the white door and walked over the threshold. Like entering the reptile house at the zoo. This room was warm with technology, three custom-built LCD screens occupying every inch of three adjacent walls. A chapel hush. He looked to his right and froze. It was him, at that very moment. The image on the screen was a live security feed of him from above having entered this room. He looked up and saw the glint of a lens. He waved. He looked left and saw Leticia on the beach out-side Versailles. A long lens shot of Leticia standing on the beach and looking out at the water, hand raised in salute but no, she was shielding her eyes from the sun, looking for something. There. His mother, swimming in the ocean. She was pretty far out from the beach, he hoped she was okay. River shifted from his left to his right foot. He didn't know it but he had his hands in his pockets. The fidelity of these cameras was insane, like nothing he had seen before. This technology was like, two, maybe even three years away. River turned his attention to the screen straight ahead. This he didn't recognize. A cavernous room defined by a single pane of curving glass that framed a view of the sky so total it almost looked outdoors. It was a swimming pool, but there was no swimming pool. A vast, powder-blue carpet where the water should be and – River walked closer to the LCD to get a better look – a trapdoor? He stepped back again. It was like a surrealist painting. A swimming pool with a trapdoor leading beyond the surface of the water. But this wasn't a painting. It was a real place. Whatever this was, it was happening now, and the logic of this room told River it was happening to his sister.

The logic of this room and the truth hit River like a bear attack. He nearly lost his footing where he stood. His father. All this time he'd known. Casey. Tracking Missy's every move. She was running, but not away. Her every move caught on camera, and relayed back to Versailles. His multiple devices. Missy running, but not away, away from what, though? That was the question. And Deep Sky. His father willing to hand his daughter over to a cult? Working with them somehow? For what . . .? Oh, Jesus *Christ*.

A second pawswipe. unknown_user, ruhin, InnerFame. They *were* all the same person. Casey himself. His father diverting River all this time while those bastards kidnapped his sister. No announcements on the network, unknown_user said, no cops. Deep Sky. Casey Baer, CEO of the internet's pre-eminent social network. Missy knew something about their father that he didn't want made public and this was his solution. Hand her over to some crazy secretive cult, make her disappear. Worse. Missy running, but not away. Deep Sky. A trap. A series of traps designed to look like an adventure, a rebellion. But why? What was so bad that he had to send Missy away? It couldn't be. His father?

Abusing his own daughter? It couldn't be. But really what *did* he know about his father? Less than Wikipedia. Zip. A continuous billowing of black silk. His father was the most powerful man on the internet, one of the richest people on the planet. Who knew what that did to a person? That kind of power? His father, Casey Baer. Just another man playing God with porn on the other screen.

But he was somewhere in this house. His father was in one of these rooms and River had to find him and confront him. The logic of this room. Three screens, three Baers. Three lives played out on film and relayed back. It chilled him to the bone. His beautiful sister, flying crocodile. The whole thing caught on film. Captured. Motherfucker, he thought. The level of control. His sister flying like an arrow from Casey's bow, her black feathers fluttering in the wind, her wings fluttering with black feathers. That motherfucker, River thought. He aimed his potato gun at the camera above and pulled the trigger. *Crack.* He checked the screen and yes: a long, diagonal crack, bottom left to top right, his likeness behind a thin film of potato juice. River replaced the gun inside the waistband of his jeans and went to look for his father.

An abandoned subway station. No signs, no maps, no color down here. But there were lights, and a train waiting on the platform.

'This is it,' Silas said. 'The last stage of your journey. We can go no further.'

'You mean you're just going to leave me here?' said Missy.

The boy with no name walked toward Missy and put his arms around her waist. 'I'm gonna miss you,' he said.

317

'I'm going to miss you too,' said Missy. She knelt down and kissed him on his cheek.

Silas gestured for her to enter the train and Missy did so without thinking.

'Remember, Missy,' Silas said. 'You're here because you've been chosen. You were chosen out of millions of other people because you possess certain qualities, and it's these characteristics that we think will stand you in good stead for the next phase of your journey.'

Next thing the doors were closing and the train began to move. Just like that. An explosion of butterflies and Missy waved to the boy with no name and he waved back. Silas had already disappeared from the platform.

It was a driverless train and Missy thought she recognized the pattern on the seats. The darkness in the tunnel made it difficult to know how fast or far she was going, the train's wheels screeching to find the metal tracks. She saw her reflection in the window opposite. The last of the leopard make-up. She looked scary. Wild. Like someone on film, looking back at her from the scratched-up glass of the window, a character in a story, a girl with a story, something to say and a way of saying it, the reflection in the window was who she was now, her story, her darkness, the leopard in the window was who she was, sparks lighting up the walls outside the train.

She wondered what was above her right now. Streets? Water? Fields? Mountains? Before entering the swimming pool, she'd seen those low mountains in the distance. Deep Sky. She imagined her train going deep into those mountains, the sky darkening. She pictured another subway station, entirely hewn out of the black rock of the mountain, the walls raw and glistening with moisture. Someone waiting for her. Someone dressed in strange dark clothes, a fabric like no fabric she had seen before. White gloves. It played like a movie in her mind. The black button with white star set into the wall. An elevator to the surface, so fast it would make her ears pop. Deep Sky. She remembered Silas talking about it by the light of the campfire. *I've seen it, Missy, the night sky as it should be, and when I saw it I knew who I was, I knew my purpose in life. True dark. I was there when he built Deep Sky, his monument to the true dark. I was there, Missy, and soon you will see it for yourself.*

She imagined the elevator doors opening and finding herself at the top of a tall tower, reaching way up into the sky, a night sky, because by then it would have gotten dark. Millions upon millions of stars and this feeling she was falling, falling up into the darkness until there was no light, no one, nothing but her.

And then a voice, the same voice that had guided her in the beginning, speaking to her now over the train's intercom:

Welcome, Missy, to Deep Sky, where one journey ends and another begins. We know things have been hard for you, Missy, we know why you ran away. We want you to know you came to the right place. You made the right decision to come here, because if there's one thing we know at Deep Sky, it's how to keep a secret. But enough with the formalities, why speak like this when we can do so face to face in just a few minutes? Have no fear, Missy Baer, you're in safe hands.

They were slowing down. Another station. No signs, no maps, no color down here. And no one waiting. The platform looked identical to the first, so much so that when Missy got off the train and found herself in front of another wooden door, she half expected to find an empty swimming pool on the other side.

Instead it was a corridor, completely bedecked with wood paneling. It felt like a ship, a luxury liner. There were rooms off to the sides but the door at the end of the corridor had already caught her attention. It was dark, almost black, but as Missy drew closer she saw that it too was made of wood, a dark, dark wood that could only have been illegal. At head height there was a white star, no bigger than the palm of her hand, set into the door so that it was perfectly flush with the surface. It looked like it was made of bone. Or maybe ivory. The idea gave her a bad feeling but she couldn't help herself. Missy reached out and touched it, felt the uncanny smoothness of the finish with her fingertips.

57

He could hear them talking inside. River put the soft flesh of his ear up against another white door, closed his eyes and listened. It couldn't be . . . but it was. Missy's voice, clear as glass. Then Synthea. His mother's voice, responding in turn. River turned the handle and slowly opened the door with his shoulder.

'Missy?' She didn't respond, but carried on talking to their mother across the way. River couldn't hear the words at first, so taken aback was he by the visual effect. His sister and Synthea. They looked real, like they were really in this space, only something wasn't quite right, some kind of light shining through them. A greenish light, like bioluminescence. They looked like ghosts. He'd seen this before: dead rappers conjured back to life on stage in front of thousands in the open air, a visual trick. Forced perspective, a sheet of glass at forty-five degrees. This was home video, footage from the recent past, a scene taking place in the garden at night. Missy and Synthea, the dark grass of the vast lawn all around them, his mother sitting cross-legged inside a circle of candles in her swimming costume, her wet hair twisted like a rope over one shoulder. River closed the white door behind him, bringing everything into sharper focus. Synthea was drunk, the candlelight picking up the beads of moisture all over her body. He could tell she was drunk from the way she was talking. Missy was outside the circle of candles. His sister saying something, her voice quiet with concern. River listened carefully to every word.

'I saw lights in the garden, the candles, from my bedroom window,' Missy said. 'I didn't know if it was you. What are you doing out here, all on your own? It's late and you know there are snakes, Mom, and you're all wet, you're dripping wet. Come on, Mom, you should come inside. Please?'

'Missy, Missy, calm down and come and sit with me. You'll be safe, Missy, inside this circle, you'll be safe.'

'But you're all wet, Mom, you'll catch a cold out here.'

'I went for a swim. Yes, I often go for a swim late at night.'

'I know you do, Mom, but it's really late, it's like three in the morning.'

'Why are *you* up so late, Missy?'

'I was . . . I was out with my friends, Mom, but now I'm back and I want you to come to bed.'

'Are you drunk, Missy?'

'No, Mom, I'm not drunk, I just went to a friend's house and now I'm back.'

'Was it Levon? Did you guys have sex? Because if you guys have sex you need to use protection. It's okay if you have sex with Levon, Missy, I'm not going to stop my daughter doing what she wants, but please be safe.'

'Oh my *God*, Mom, what's *wrong* with you? What the hell is wrong with you, Mom? Can't you just not do that? Can't you just not be like that for once and listen to me?'

'Don't raise your voice, Missy, that's what your father

does. He does it to get his way. And he does get his way, he always—'

'I'm not raising my voice, Mom, I just wish sometimes . . . I just wish sometimes you would listen to me.'

'I do listen to you, my darling, I love to listen to you. You're young, you're young, you're full of life, you tell me things, I love to listen to you. We talk all the time, you tell me everything.'

'I know I do, Mom, I know you listen to me, so why not now? I'm not drunk, I didn't sleep with Levon, not that it's any of your business, and all I want is for you to come inside, *please*, it's really late and you're all wet and I just want you to take my hand and come inside with me.'

'Ow, that hurts. Don't grab me, Missy. Don't grab me, I'm not a child. STOP.'

'Alright, fine.' Missy turned to go.

'Sit here with me, Missy. Sit here inside this circle of light. We're safe here. As long as these candles are burning, we're safe. Just us. No snakes, no bugs, just us.'

'But it's cold.'

'Are you cold, Missy?'

'No.'

'*I'm* not cold. I'm *warm*. I've been swimming under the stars and now I'm *warm*. And it's a beautiful night. Look up, Missy, look at the stars. So many stars. Sometimes I wish a spaceship would come down – sometimes I wish a spaceship would come down and take me far away, far, far away from this place so that when I look back, when I look out of the window of the spaceship, I see our sun, and it's no bigger than one of these stars, just a tiny point of light and I'm headed somewhere completely *different*, somewhere *other*, somewhere beautiful, unwatched, unhindered. Myself, Missy, out from under all these cameras, this *place* . . .'

'That's so dark, Mom, that's so totally dark.'

'But it's not, Missy, it's me being totally honest with you. Missy, please, don't close your eyes, don't turn away, I didn't mean to upset you, it's the last thing I want in the world. That wasn't a dark thing I said, Missy, these are just thoughts, they're just thoughts.'

'They're not just thoughts, Mom, because you're telling me what you're thinking so now it's real. You want to leave us. You want to—'

'I didn't say that, Missy, and I understand that you're upset.'

'So it *is* happening? You *are* leaving us? Are you and Dad getting a divorce?'

'No, Missy, stop putting words in my mouth. These really were just thoughts and I shouldn't be talking to you about this, it was wrong of me to do this. I just had this feeling of happiness and—'

'What about *my* happiness, Mom? What about *my* happiness? Look, I'm not angry with you, Mom. I want you to be happy, I really do, but did you ever think about how it makes me feel when I find you like this?'

'Like what?'

'I'm just worried about you, Mom, okay? I'm worried about you, and the more I worry, the more I can't sleep at night.'

'You always slept like a princess. I remember—'

'Oh my *God*, Mom, I'm trying to tell you something, and it's really hard for me to do this, so could you just *hear me out.*'

'Don't raise your voice, Missy.'

'Why, because I sound like *him*? Because I sound like *HIM*, Mom? Well maybe I do sound like him because I'm, like, his *daughter*, aren't I? I'm *his* daughter just like I'm *your* daughter and, honestly, I don't want to be anybody's daughter, I want to be *myself*. You think you're the only one who wants out of this house? *I* want out of this house.'

'Missy, don't say that.'

'That's the thing, Mom, you only hear what you want to hear. I *am* worried about you. How could I not when you're walking around the house naked at night, when you're always . . . I *am* worried, Mom. And then you tell me that you want to leave, but when are you going to understand that you're not the only person in the world?'

'I don't think that, Missy, you know I don't. But you're right, it's late, and now I *am* cold. It's this breeze, blowing out the candles. Let's go inside. Let's go inside, Missy, continue our discussion in the house. Come on, Missy, we could eat a midnight snack if you wanted.'

'You go, Mom. I'm going to stay out here for a minute.'

'No, Missy, like you said, it's cold out here, there are snakes and bugs and it's late . . . Please, Missy, take my hand and come inside with me.'

'Mom, just give me a minute. I need to be by myself for a second. Please just go to bed, Mom. I'll see you at breakfast. I love you.'

'I love you too, Missy. Please let's continue this discussion tomorrow. I don't want you to worry, Missy. Everything's going to be okay, Missy. Trust me as I say those words . . . Look me in my eyes. Everything's going to be okay.'

'I didn't mean to upset you, Mom, please.'

Missy remained alone inside the circle of candles, her legs out to one side. River watched his sister gaze after their mother as she zigzagged into the background, back to Versailles. Exit stage right. A sudden gust of wind blew out all but one of the candles, the last flame flickering in the persistent breeze. A fade to black. A fade to black followed by a menu screen.

River felt the sting in his nose. He rubbed his eyes with the balls of his hands. A menu screen. A user interface. That had to mean some kind of input device, a remote control or— River took a step forward into the semi-darkness and there it was. A barrier, and set into the barrier there was a tablet computer. River touched the capacitive screen and he was looking at the same menu, a dynamic list of past events, all meticulously tagged and archived. River's heart began to race. He'd always known about the cameras, but never dreamed their true purpose. Versailles as recording device. Here was a total archive of his childhood, Missy's childhood. Every conversation, every monologue. Everything that ever took place inside these walls. River's mind began to race. He started typing keywords into the search box and then stopped himself. This last video. Missy and the circle of candles. This last video was part of a playlist. River touched the next item and watched the scene unfold.

Casey's Versailles office this time, somewhere River hadn't been since childhood. There were cables everywhere, the walls covered in curtains of code, black biro on white. The effect was like heavy rain as seen from a great distance. Scripting for the social network, a work in progress. The only furnishings were a desk and a chair. Casey was sitting behind a desk staring into a cheap, 23" LCD monitor in gray

326

plastic. The lighting was bright, strikingly so. There was no atmosphere in this room, no shadows, nowhere to hide. Missy standing by the doorframe in her nightdress.

'Dad?'

'Missy.'

'Dad, do you believe in God?'

'Why don't you come in, Missy, instead of standing in the doorway?'

'I can come back if you're busy.'

'No, nothing's more important than spending time with my daughter. Come . . . Now, to answer your question. No, I don't believe in God.'

'Why not?' says Missy.

'Well . . . because I have you, Missy, I have you and I have River and I have your mom, and you guys are the most important thing to me. I believe in the power of love. I believe in people, Missy. The human experience. Sharing that with another person, with my friends, my family. I believe we make our own destiny. We act, we make, we determine. The human experience, Missy. It's all *us*, *our* destiny, *our* world. It's why I built the website. So that people could share their experiences, while they had the chance. I don't need God to tell me what to look for. I want to see everything, experience *everything*. All the color and the sound. All the feelings and emotions. I don't need God to tell me what I *should* and *shouldn't* be doing. I'm an adult, I can think for myself. I have a family who I love and who love me. I built a website that lets people find out who and what matters to *them*, that lets them be who they want to be. Because we're nothing without each other, Missy. Nothing.'

'Dad.'

'What is it, princess?'

'I prayed last night, Dad.'

'You're crying, Missy, what's wrong?'

'I prayed because . . . I prayed that Mom wouldn't go away because . . . and I don't know if she means . . . she said . . .'

'Come here, Missy, come here and tell me what happened.'

'Last night. You weren't there, Dad.'

'I'm here now, Missy. Tell me.'

'Okay, Dad, but you have to promise first. Dad, promise me you won't tell Mom I talked to you. Because I know what will happen, Dad. I'm like her best friend. Seriously, she thinks I'm her best friend and in a way she *is* my best friend so it would *really* upset her if she found out that I'd talked to you like this. She'd think everything she thought about us was true, her worst fears, that her family doesn't love her, that *I* don't love her. So you can't tell her that I talked to you about her. Promise me, Dad.'

'Missy, I give you my word.'

'Last night I found Mom in the garden and she was half-naked and all wet from swimming in the pool. I found her in the garden surrounded by these candles and she was half-naked, Dad, at, like, three in the morning, acting kind of drunk and high at the same time. I tried to make her come inside with me but she started talking all this weird stuff. She started talking like she wanted to leave this place, she was talking about wanting to be among the stars . . . I don't know if she meant she wanted to leave, like go live somewhere else, or . . . I just don't know, Dad, and I can't stop thinking . . . I can't stop thinking about what she might do . . .'

'Missy, listen to me. Missy, your mom's not going anywhere. Your mom's not going anywhere because I'm going to take care of her, *we're* going to take care of her, alright? Now look, I know you're upset, I understand why you're upset, but you have to trust me on this. Your mom's going to be okay. We're going to take care of her. Together. And you know what, Missy? It's okay that you prayed. It's okay that you prayed, I understand why you did it. You did it because you were scared. You were scared for your mother because your mother can be unpredictable, and when people are unpredictable we don't feel safe. We get scared because we don't know what they want anymore, we can't give them what they want because we don't know what they're thinking. Now, I know this is hard, Missy, but it's important you know there is somebody else you can turn to, besides God! Missy, seriously, listen to me. Whenever you need to talk. About Mom, school, boys, anything, I'll be here. And let me tell you something else. Your mom? I'm going to take care of her. She may be your mom, Missy, but she's also my wife, and I love my wife. If she's in trouble I'm going to get her the help she needs.'

'But you promised, Dad. You promised me you wouldn't tell her that I talked to you.'

'Missy, I told you, whatever you tell me doesn't leave this room, I give you my word. But you have to promise me something in return.'

'What?'

'You have to promise to trust *me*. I can be there for you, Missy. You don't have to feel alone. You're my daughter too and I want to know your life. Pray if you want, but you can always come to me, Missy. Promise me.'

'I promise,' says Missy.

A fade to black followed by the menu screen. River felt very tired, he wished he could just go to bed, rest his head a while, close his eyes and sleep for an hour. He thought he understood now, but there were still pieces missing from this puzzle. He scrolled through the playlist with his index finger, a seemingly endless list of past events. He saw one tagged *brown horse*. The tip of his finger hovered over the capacitive screen but what was the point? *brown horse*. It meant someone had gone in and tagged every one of these things. Casey. Whatever Casey did that made his sister want to run away and join a cult . . . Whatever Casey did that needed to be kept a secret, he wouldn't find it here, in this room. It would have been erased long ago, perhaps never even caught on tape. Outside the frame. Blind spots everywhere.

River rubbed his eyes with the balls of his hands, but he was awake again. He had to find his father. Find out the truth. He opened the white door and scoped the corridor with his potato gun. He looked the part. He felt the part. A newfound courage, his life was panther-shaped. He gripped the gun like it was real. It felt real. Brat. Brat-brat.

58

The boy at school. Levon would come to school every day wearing a different costume, complete with persona. Nothing too obvious, no lion tamers or superheroes. Levon specialized in characters you might pass on the street without looking twice, but always with some kind of modifier. Off-duty traffic cop, chilled-out garbage collector, new father butcher, murderous train operator, out-of-work dog walker . . . Whoever Levon chose it was full commitment every time, right up until he went to bed at night. It made it kind of hard to get to know him, but it was worth it to get close. Missy fell in love with Levon the afternoon of out-of-work dog walker. He turned up to school wearing these real specific clothes, again nothing fancy, just clothes an average dude that wasn't Levon might wear, and trailing a bunch of dog leads behind him with no dogs. His character was this mix of dejected yet hopeful that started Missy on a fit of giggles so epic the teacher had to throw her out of class. Levon liked her too and they started dating, which pissed off River at first but he was okay with it.

Missy wasn't like other girlfriends he'd had. Missy was special. Missy was the best. Missy was awesome, like, you could talk to her about *anything*. And he did. They'd walk on the beach outside her house and he'd tell her all this stuff he'd never told anybody, like, ever. He told her things he'd never told *himself*, you know? Maybe that's why. Maybe she thought he was too weird or something like that, maybe he scared her off with all that stupid nonsense he talked about his characters and where he got his 'inspiration'. What a douche. But somehow it didn't fit. Missy was different from the other girls. Missy was like, a *very* cool chick. So why'd she stop answering his calls? One day they were hanging out, having a great time, the next she wouldn't answer his frankly hilarious text messages. And at school. She pretended like he didn't exist. It hurt, man. It hurt real bad, and Levon couldn't stop thinking about her. He was heartbroken.

All summer long he'd thought about nothing else but this girl. Day in, day out. He couldn't sleep. So he made her a dress. That's right. Before they'd even kissed he'd started working on this incredible dress for Missy Baer. He *made* her a dress, dude. Part of Levon's thing was making all his characters' costumes at home on his sewing machine. He refused even to buy underwear from the store, nothing off the rack. But it was like everything that came before, all the work he'd done on his machine up until this point, had been training for Missy's dress. And he never got a chance to give it to her. All summer long he'd thought about nothing else but this girl. He was, like, *obsessed* with this girl, and the damn thing was? He knew Missy would love the dress.

So today he thought *fuck it*, I'm going to go over to her house. I'm going to go over to that house in *disguise*, dude. That's right, I'm going to rock up to those gates as, like, *the pool cleaner* or some shit, and those fools are going to invite me right in, they're gonna be like, *sure, Mr Pool Cleaner, come right in, sir and, like, clean our pool, please.* It wasn't gonna work but it was totally worth a shot.

So here he was outside the double gates to the largest private residence in the United States. Versailles. It wasn't his first time here, but it was his first time here as a pool cleaner. He rang the buzzer and tried to look casual. Now Levon thought of himself as something of a master of disguise, but this pool cleaner thing had him second-guessing. Should he go with the whole jumpsuit, utility belt, dirty baseball cap thing, or just go all-out sexy pool boy who winds up having an affair with the lonely lady of the house? In the end he'd opted for something in between. He didn't really have the body to go topless so he went with the neon orange vest and tropical-theme Bermuda shorts. And sunglasses. A pair of iridescent sunglasses with matte black frames and bright green arms. Okay, and a fake moustache. It was real subtle though. Thin, with a gap in the middle. He actually may grow one of these, he thought, who knows. He looked up at the camera and tried to look casual. He knew the gatekeeper, Angel. Nice guy, they'd had some good talks in the past, but right now Levon needed Angel not to recognize him.

'Levon?' said Angel.

'Goddammit, Angel.'

'Levon, she's not here,' rejoined Angel.

'I don't believe you,' said Levon. 'I just want to give her something.'

'No gifts, *cabrón*. Just go home, kid, it's not your day.'

Levon knew better than to argue with Angel so he walked back down the drive, out of camera shot. But this wasn't over. The truth was, he'd been planning this for weeks. Levon had a Plan B.

Versailles. Biggest private residence in the US, and with a security system to match. But there was a way in, and it was so simple. Levon knew this because River told him one time: all you had to do was swim up to the speedboat moored on that beach and wait till nightfall. Then there was a route through the garden. A corridor of blind spots. *It's like, join the dots!* River had said, *You're never on camera. I spent my whole childhood in this place, trust me, I know the angles!*

The current was stronger than he'd anticipated, but Levon had been swimming lengths these past weeks in preparation. He'd brought a waterproof backpack for the dress, and that was kind of helping with keeping him afloat. It was a long swim too, almost a mile he guessed, but he could see the boat now, Versailles' million dollar MTI 40 series speedboat with custom bolstered seating, wraparound windshield and twin Mercury 575 horsepower engines. He'd read about it on the internet.

He could see the tall palms now, the beginning of Versailles' private beach. Levon swam up alongside the beautiful white and canary-yellow speedboat. There was a small silver ladder at the back. If he could just climb up that ladder and keep low, the camera wouldn't see him. He took a peek. Versailles. Its southern edifice glowed in the bright sunshine, its darkened windows seeming to watch him. Levon ducked back behind the speedboat and expelled all the air in his lungs through pursed lips. *For Missy*, he said out loud. He climbed the ladder and slithered into the boat. It was a six-seater, two at the front, four at the back. Levon was in the rear footwell. Right away he wrapped himself in the rain cover he found there. This was great. A little hot, a little sweaty, but this way he could stay completely hidden until nightfall, and that's when he would run the gauntlet to the house and throw a coin up at Missy's window. A goofy plan, but what can you do? He was in love.

And as Levon lay there in the back of the speedboat, wrapped up like a giant burrito, he thought of Missy, her smile, her laugh, her long blonde hair, and with these sunny images, and the gentle rocking of the boat, he fell into a deep, afternoon sleep.

PART FIVE
Deep Sky

59

What Casey did. A broken promise. Missy had been the one to find Synthea, floating face down in the swimming pool, the water only pink with her blood. She dived under the surface and brought her mother to the edge, ripped her T-shirt and tied the wrists. She looked so young at first, her wet hair and the bathing costume coming off one shoulder. This was Casey. Missy knew it in her bones. He'd broken his promise and said something. She held her mother in her arms as they waited for the ambulance. He had said something to her and now this. Her mother, her beautiful mother, she looked so young, her wet hair and the bathing costume coming off one shoulder. The water only pink with blood. All that lost time. She had lost a lot of blood but she would survive.

And then the rest. What Casey did. He didn't send her away but he'd kept her prisoner in Versailles. The medication came in the form of pills. Nameless pills. The packaging was white boxes. No name, no disclaimers. She took the pills and she was not their mother. She took the pills because . . . she took the pills because he told her to. This was not her mother. Missy tried talking to her but she wouldn't talk to anybody, only stare out of the window in her office, smoking those cigarettes without the filters, staring out at the endless ocean as Missy stood behind her, asking her to come back, to come away from the window, asking, *Why won't you look at me, Mom? I never meant to hurt you. I never meant to hurt you, Mom. I get it now. You remember the candles? Do you remember us talking with the candles all around us, what you told me? You said you wished you could go away, far away from here, and I understand. It was him. You wanted to be far away from him, from this, from what's happening to you now. His control. But it's all my fault, Mom. I told him what you said. I told him because I thought you meant . . . because I was scared. And then you did hurt yourself, and it's all because of me, because I thought I could trust him. I thought I could trust Casey but I know what he is now. I can see what he's done to you, what he's doing. Where he wants you. But it's not too late, Mom. I'm still here, I'm still your daughter, I'm still your Missy and you can tell me anything. You can trust me. I know I messed up, but I promise, Mom. I promise it will never happen again. Please, Mom, stop staring out the window and look at me, turn around and look at me.*

She hated him. Her hate for him a perfect thing. She hated him for doing this to her mother, her talented mother, so full of love, and all her vision, all this color faded to black. She hated him so much she'd wanted to destroy him. She lay awake at night, thought about the worst thing she could do. The company. The network. Everything he had built. His reputation. She would take to the social networks and tell them everything, her friends, their friends, people she didn't know. It would take the internet by storm. CEO of the internet's pre-eminent social network and his wife was suicidal? Not a good look for a captain of industry. Any sign of weakness. The stock would take a massive hit, he might even be forced to sell up.

She had sat in front of her laptop, mouse pointer poised over the 'post' button. Post this and it would all be over: life as they knew it. Versailles, this dream of life. A dream of life was still a dream. She clicked and nothing happened. The button on the screen wasn't animating, like it was dead or something. Click-click-click. Then her phone, lighting up on the desk. *Unknown caller.* She touched the green button and held the phone to her ear. It was ringing. Her father answered, told her to come to his office, they needed to talk.

He told her to sit, no eye contact at first, the desk between. He asked her if she ever considered what it would do to her mother if people found out. 'Did you ever think about that, Missy? Did you?'

'What, are you tracking my online activities now?' Missy said. 'What happened to privacy?'

'I know you're angry, Missy, but I'm your father and you need to listen to what I have to say.' His voice was gentle but instructive. 'We cannot afford to upset your mother at this time. I know you blame me for what happened, but telling the world our most intimate affairs is not the answer.'

'You don't care about *her*, all you care about is your company.'

'That's a terrible thing to say, Missy, and I want you to take it back.'

'I'm nearly sixteen, Dad, it's going to take more than that to shut me up. You can't *control* me.'

'Don't do this, Missy. You're making a mistake. I don't know if your mother can be saved a second time. You don't want blood on your hands.'

'You didn't *save* her,' Missy screamed. 'She's a *ghost*. Oh my *God*. I *hate* you.'

That was the last time Missy saw her father. But she did as she was told. Her mother's silence became Missy's silence. She didn't want to talk about what happened to anyone, not even Levon. She wouldn't know where to begin. It was all her fault. It was all her fault and her dreams were of falling, falling upwards into a dark, dark sky, and when she opened her eyes the light from outside would tell her it was late, too late for Saturday, for swimming or seeing friends. Her friends told her she had changed, they didn't know about her mom, the swimming pool. She stopped updating her profile, stopped caring how people saw her. But they cared. They loved Missy. They kept calling, even when she didn't answer, her phone set to silent.

And then one night her dream of falling turned to a dream of flying, into the sky and out again, along a beach lined with tall palms, and the dream set her down at the entrance to a cave, and from that night forward she dreamed only of exploring that cave, of finding treasure, crystalline fragments of memory, desire, hope, anger, all different colors, all different shapes, but they were beautiful and they had *weight* and they felt important, more important than anything else. She wanted to bring them back into the waking world, assemble them into a new whole, like a new armor for herself, a new look for her waking life.

The sword video had come at the right time. The sword video, the *Level Up!* email, the voice on her phone and then the boy with no name, Silas and the epic journey *north*. She had eaten a cheeseburger for breakfast, shoplifted a bag of Twinkies, faced down a bear in the shadow of a mountain, thrown a Molotov cocktail at a wicker effigy of her father, kissed a girl and got stupid drunk with Scout *Rose*.

And now here she was, at the door to Deep Sky, sword at her side, black baseball cap pulled down low over her eyes. This was where the journey ended. It felt like two worlds, like this door was a portal between two worlds. She was far from Versailles, but this side of the door was still her world, the world of her father and her mother, of everybody telling her what to do, who to be, and how to feel. And *needing* her. Her trust, her friendship, her perspective. The other side was the another world, one she wasn't born into. Unwitnessed. On the other side of this door was *her* world, one glittering with possibility. This is where her childhood ended, teenage-hood, whatever. Her choice to delete her profile on the social network. Her choice to take up the sword. Her choice to start the engine of her SUV and drive out the gates of Versailles, out of frame. No status update. No pictures of her to *like* or comment on. Her choice not to call her mom. Her choice to steal the Twinkies. Silas told her all along. There was no turning back, no going home. This is where her childhood ended. Time to grow up. Deep Sky. Deep Sky was danger. Deep Sky was the unknown. Deep Sky was the furthest from her father she could think of. Her guilt changed color. Her hate no longer hate. Why hate when she could live? Deep Sky was the furthest from the internet she could think of, somewhere she could pass unwitnessed, see what that looked like, see what that felt like. She wasn't perfect. She was Missy. And right now she was no one's daughter, no one's friend, this was all her, her hands, her heart, her blood, her pulse, her choice. Entering Deep Sky was diving from the highest of three platforms for the first time, arms out straight, that one mortal moment longer in the air. A moment of sheer terror and anticipation. Deep Sky was ... Missy didn't know, but she wanted to. After everything she'd been through she *had* to know.

She touched the door again, the wood felt warm. A dark wood, but there was a redness deep inside the varnish. She saw the button. To the left of the door, a translucent white button with a black 'up' arrow. This was an elevator. She held on to the hilt of her sword with her left hand. This was the unknown, her door into the darkness, but it was *her* darkness, her fear and the pleasure of this feeling, of feeling like *herself*, of having *character*. She guessed this is what people meant when they talked about feeling comfortable in your skin.

Her fear, her darkness. What Casey did had cast a shadow but now it was her shadow. She was scared. Opening this door meant meeting someone. This time alone was precious, this time before she opened the door and stepped into another world. This time was precious, this time in the real world. Right now it was all she knew. Versailles. Missy was scared. She thought of her mom, brother, far, far away in Versailles, alone without her. The thought nearly made her turn around in the corridor, her mother and River still in Versailles, still trapped in that house and not know-ing where she was. The guilt nearly made her turn around in the corridor, but she didn't. Missy pushed the white button and the door slid open with a ping.

The inside of the elevator was emerald green, soft walls and no mirror but there was a piece of candy on the floor. A piece of candy in a bright pink wrapper. She picked it up and looked at it. She twisted the twisted ends and it squeaked, like a tiny creature it squeaked as she twisted. Missy felt spaced out. This was new candy. Not old candy. There was no logo but she could tell. It was new and when she untwisted the wrapper and put the candy in her mouth she could taste that it was new. The sugar made her feel better. She didn't feel spaced out anymore, but somebody had left this candy here on purpose.

There was one button in the elevator, so Missy pressed it. Butterflies. Like when she was a kid and her parents had people over for a dinner party. This was in the days before she and River where allowed to go to school. Sitting at the top of the stairs and waiting for the guests to arrive. Listening for the cars in the driveway, and when they came, when she heard the tires roll in and slowly crush up the gravel in the driveway, she got so excited, the sounds of different cars arriving in front of the house, the sense of excitement, of *guests* arriving, of new people arriving and ringing the bell to the mansion, more guests and the ringing of the bell, Missy remembered that feeling well. Sitting at the top of the stairs, the slow crush of gravel and the bell. And later, much later, when she couldn't sleep – long after Leticia had put her to bed and sung her a lullaby – she would get up again and walk downstairs, follow the distant sound of voices, people talking, people laughing, her bare feet on the cold marble stairs. People shouting at each other but they weren't angry, Missy watched them from the doorway and she could see. They weren't angry with each other, they were laughing and shouting and smoking, and some of them she knew, some of them she recognized from the daytime, but they didn't see her there, not right away. All their faces, their wet eyes and glistening white teeth, her father, her mother,

her beautiful mother in the electric blue dress. Missy's favorite dress. She wished she could see her mother one last time. Like that, in her electric blue dress, talking to another man, Casey at the other end of the table, smoking a cigarette with half-closed eyes as people talked across.

The elevator had arrived. Deep Sky. Missy put a hand to her sword as the door slid open.

60

The monitor lizard makes his way along another empty corridor in Versailles. His teeth are bared but he is not angry.
His yellow eyes look mean but he is not mean, he is a monitor lizard who has not eaten in over a week. Just then he
passes a white door. According to Versailles' schematics, this
is Room 1, Casey's office. The lighting is bright, strikingly so.
Utilitarian. All this *stuff*. It's like stepping behind the scenes
on a television set, a nightmare of technology beyond the
patterned wallpaper, doors leading nowhere, doors leading
everywhere. The smell of hot plastic, all these cables feeding
an alternate reality, tiny red lights, tiny blue lights, all these
switches, dials, sliders, slots and drives. Dirty keyboards.
Greasy trackpads. All this plastic, all this grime and dust, old
computers, new computers still in their packaging, plastic
within plastic within plastic within cardboard
within cardboard. Everything in this room is there to serve a
purpose, nothing more. There is no atmosphere in this room,
no shadows, nowhere to hide. At the same time, it's like
looking into a lizard enclosure at the zoo and waiting for
movement . . . There. A doorway slides across and in steps
– Missy.

She draws her sword. It's all she can do to stop herself

blacking out. This can't be. Her breath knocked out. Versailles in the rear mirror. The looming mountains. The northbound highway. The idea of north. Deep Sky . . . She draws her sword and it gleams in the white neon light. This can't be. *Like Disney World, but no Mickey Mouse.* This can't be happening. Casey. Casey. She is ready to kill, her musculature reorganized into that of a wild animal, this sword her dark talon, this sword is who she is now, the betrayal complete, the blood rushing to her hands and feet, replete with new hate. Casey Baer. She is ready to strike. Wide-eyed and ready to scream, but she cannot scream. This is like a dream, more like a nightmare.

She moves in slow motion toward his desk, the main terminal, around his desk, the curtains of code on every wall, progressing downwards and across the floor like a trillion ants in her peripheral vision. Teeming. They crawl towards her feet from every direction but she continues moving, around his desk, a 23" LCD monitor in gray plastic and all the folders on his screen, hundreds upon hundreds of little icons on his desktop, all layered on top of each other like spilled coins. For a moment she is spellbound. So this is how her father really works, this is what his mind looks like, a view deep inside, deep underground, where buried treasure lies on top of buried shit, a mass of dirty gold, but something glints at her, one coin among the others winks up at her like a sun disappearing in a black hole. One little folder and two words underneath: *Free Missy.*

She doesn't need to touch a thing, she knows what she will find inside. Deep Sky. The adrenaline coursing through her body, she's thinking fast. It all makes sense. Deep Sky is real, but she was never headed there. Silas, the boy with no name. Silas could be anybody, a Deep Sky agent, a gun for hire, it doesn't matter. He'd talked the talk, said all the right things, things Missy wanted to hear. True dark. The idea of north – Deep Sky as lure, as carrot. The antithesis of everything her father stood for. Deep Sky as escape from modern life, her father's cameras. His control. A manufactured rite of passage. A roller coaster rebellion. Full circle. Running, but not away. The emails, the video, the sword, the Molotov, everything. Placed there. Hidden in plain sight like an Easter egg hunt. But why? So she could get it all out of her *system*? So she will love him again? After what he did to her mother? Did he really think he could make her forget, make her feel better by taking her to the goddamned fun fair? Here, take this, Missy, buy yourself some fucking candy floss? What Casey doesn't know about his daughter. The sum total of what Casey doesn't understand. It would break the internet.

A roller coaster rebellion and here she is, back where she began. Versailles. Versailles as mission control. Mission Missy now. She shifts her weight and wields her sword, a swing so true she rends the monitor in two, a perfect fountain of sparks and tiny flames to celebrate the act. Casey. She is ready to kill, tears streaming down her cheeks, her musculature reorganized into that of a wild animal, this sword her dark talon, this sword is who she is now, the blood rushing to her hands and feet, replete with hate. She wants to cry bitter, but revenge is sweet. She sees the candy. A trail of brightly colored candy leading from the elevator to the other door in this room. Some of it is crushed. Some of the candy she crushed underfoot as she entered Versailles from the elevator. Some of the candy is crushed, but the rest is intact.

She bends to pick up a piece of candy. This one has a blue

wrapper. She twists the twisted ends and it squeaks, like a tiny creature it squeaks as she twists. Missy feels spaced out. This is new candy. Not old candy. New candy. Newly placed. Her father was just here. She can feel it in her bones. She follows the trail of candy to the white door and opens it. There is no hesitation, only in the telling. Missy steps into the corridor, into Versailles.

There is more candy in the corridor, a trail of brightly colored candy leading her around the corner. All this time. A trail of candy at her feet, she just couldn't see it. She follows her sword, the blade reading the overhead lighting like it's musical notation, she follows the sword, her musculature that of a wild animal, her body ready to kill, her mind on the trail of candy, the idea of candy, she never liked it much, even as a kid. Missy was never a candy kind of girl, but there's no denying this trail, this pretty trail of brightly colored candy leading somewhere. There's no denying the story so far. The looming mountains. The northbound highway. The idea of north. Her adventure into the unknown. What her father doesn't know.

Her clothes smell of woodsmoke, her hands are dirty from collecting wood for a fire. Her heart is full, her mind is full of ideas, images, new memories, feelings she might never have again, but she must, she must. She is human, so in love with being. But she is also a leopard cat, her musculature reorganized into that of a wild animal. Human, so full of love, her mind on the trail of candy, the idea of candy. A tiny squeaking creature and she the leopard cat. This isn't a hunt, this is pursuit. Missy following the trail of candy deeper and deeper into Versailles, the unknown.

61

unknown_user, ruhin, InnerFame, Casey Baer, whatever he was calling himself just now, he was inside these walls, breathing the same air, blood pumping round his body underneath his brand new casual wear. Versailles. One hundred rooms. Another white door. River reached out for the handle and thought again. No. This time he was going in hard. He took a step back and kicked out with all his strength, the door giving way like in the movies.

Wow ... A mountain of toys. Thousands upon thousands of toys piled high, all the way to the ceiling of this cavernous space. A dragon's lair of plastic toys and stuffed animals, metal cars and broken consoles, tangled cables, action figures, naked dolls and neon water rifles. River took a step closer, breathed in deep through his nose. All these things, he recognized every one of them. He'd played with every ... These were his toys, Missy's toys, every Christmas, every birthday, every birthday in this house, all the rejects, all the things bought twice, far too many, way too many, all in one place for him to see. It brought tears and he didn't know why. All this colored plastic, a million grooves and screws, every surface, gleaming, shining, glowing in the artificial light of this room. Nothing ever thrown away. Two billionaire kids and all they ever wanted, when all they ever wanted was to play, to swim all day in the bright sunshine. The light catching every surface, a glittering present tense, the stillness of this room, a deathly silence. A toy cupboard. That's what this was. A toy cupboard of horrendous proportions. Another archive, another warning, another bad dream of life. Reality turned in on itself, reflected back again and again and again. Versailles as witness. Versailles as witness to itself. And Casey behind it all, a regular Wizard of Oz, playing God behind a heavy black curtain.

River's gaze cut a switchback trail of memory and association from the bottom to the top of the mountain of toys, and at the very top, perched there all alone like a special prize, he saw something that filled his heart with pure joy and delight, it brought a smile – Croc – his pea-green dinosaur friend with the purple tail spikes. Without a second thought River made toward the mountain, wading forward through the sea of part-deflated balloon animals and swimming pool inflatables that made up the foothills. And then he was climbing, actually *climbing* up the face of this intricate monstrosity, this dune of high indulgence. A tricky climb because this mountain was unstable, a mass of fragile objects, all different shapes and sizes and textures. But River was an excellent climber, lithe, with a natural instinct for footholds and where to put his hands next, his center of gravity that of a monkey accustomed to navigating the thinner branches of the jungle's upper canopy.

The mountain creaked with his ascent, but he was making steady progress. And as he climbed he thought of Synthea. All these hundreds of toys, massed together like this, it made him think of her. Every birthday, every Christmas.

Every trip to the toy store. The buying, the endless buying, her baskets filled but never full. Every wish fulfilled, every need, every want. As he climbed he felt sick. He thought of her role all these years. Making sure they were happy. Making up for all their lost hours in the mansion. Their whole childhood had been Versailles, no contact with the outside world, and this was her way of making it all okay. All the colored plastic, shoring up this island existence. It was all for them, her kids. Her own life, her life's work, drowned out, muted, buried somewhere deep inside this haunted mountain. Her soul flickering, flickering out. No magic now. Her non-existence reflected back again and again. The mountain creaked but he was almost there, one more thrust with his left leg and he would get there, and then he was, grabbing hold of Croc with his right hand and that was it, he felt something give under his weight, one toy balancing on two, two on four and then – cause and effect – the mountain gave, swallowing River like a volcano, the sound of a hundred thousand toys crashing to the hard floor beneath, a crash so great you could hear it from across Versailles.

It hurt. It really, really hurt, but he wasn't dead. Darkness all around but these pin-pricks of light. He knew there would be blood before he felt it trickle down his cheek and neck, the white-blue sting that says your skin is open. He felt the softness in his right hand and squeezed.

'*Happy Birthday, River!*' Croc said. River twisted violently where he lay, breaking free of the toys so that he could get a better look at his old friend. He squeezed again. *Happy Birthday, River!*' He never said that before, not part of his repertoire. And his voice wasn't quite right. This was Casey saying these things. His father all along. He looked about him. This mess of toys. He was four years old again, surrounded by everything he'd ever wanted. River burst into tears, a deep, breath-taking sob that took over his body. When all he ever wanted was to play, to swim all day in the bright sunshine. He missed his sister, his mother, had for a long time. His father elsewhere, the white-blue sting that says your skin is open. He felt the softness in his right hand and squeezed again.

'Go *find her!*' Croc said, and that made River lose his temper. He threw Croc hard across the room, Croc still talking as he flew through the air: '*Go find your sistuuuuuuuur.*'

When Leticia told her about the phone call with Casey, Synthea knew. Her daughter was coming back. She could just feel it. Missy was somewhere nearby, perhaps even inside the compound. Before Leticia could finish her sentence Synthea was running up Versailles' beach, between the tall palms, across the lawn, past the swimming pool and up the marble stairs into the mansion. By the time Leticia caught up with her in the master bedroom, Synthea was frantic. She was pulling clothes from the wardrobe, tears rolling down her cheeks.

'I can't let her see me like this,' Synthea said. 'I'm a mess, I can't, I have to find my dress, I want my dress, I want to find my dress, the one she likes, I always wear it on her birthday. I can't let her see me like this, Leticia, my hair all wet, my make-up all down my face and I can't find this dress anywhere, she'll be here any minute and I can't, I just can't . . . I can hear them downstairs, she may already be here . . . but my dress, I have to find it, it's the one she said makes me look ... it's the one she said ... but I just can't, I just can't—'

'Sit down on the bed, Mrs Synthea, and I will find your dress,' Leticia said.

Missy walks along another empty corridor. Just then she passes a white door. On the other side of that white door is her brother, shoulder deep in toys, but there is no way Missy could know that. She follows her sword, the blade reading the overhead lighting like it's musical notation. A landing. A flight of stairs. The entrance hall. Back where she began. Missy realizes she is barefoot, she does not know how long. Her bare feet on the cold marble as she descends the stairs. The trail of candy, one on each step, placed there by her father, Casey Baer, by someone Missy doesn't really know. Her every step. He watched her every move, controlled her every move like a video game. Her every step, but now she is out of step, side-stepping, hot-stepper, sword in her right hand and this is all her. Her hands, her heart, her blood, her anger. The fullness of her anger. What Casey doesn't know about his daughter. It was her stole the Twinkies. Flying crocodile. Her impulse, her pulse. Her sword, her self given new shape, black baseball cap pulled low like she's feeling the future. What Casey doesn't know. This fairy trail, each candy being crushed underfoot, a storm of candy could not stop her now. This is all her. The man who placed this candy thinks he knows. That she is coming – everything that's happened – what she is feeling, right at this moment – but he doesn't, this is all her, and the thought makes her tighten her grip on the hilt of the sword. The thought nearly makes her lose her balance on the marble staircase. She doesn't know what she'll do when she sees him, this sword her dark talon, this sword is who she is now, the betrayal complete, the blood rushing to her hands and feet, replete with hate. What Casey is. Their lives a game.

The candy trail ends at the double doors. On the other side is the dining room and Missy can hear movement. There are others. She can hear movement. The candy trail has led her here. Whoever placed the candy is on the other side. Whoever placed this candy knows everything. The leopard make-up faded. But she looks scary. Wide-eyed and full of hate, this sword is who she is now. Missy kicks away the last gold candy and throws open the double doors.

62

Versailles as seen from a hot air balloon, its ramparts glowing white in the late afternoon sun. The God angle. Versailles. A great ship ready to cast off across an alien ocean, its towering A/C stacks breathing out, only out into the vanishing world. Versailles, USA. Palace for an American King, a thousand cameras pointed *out*. The miles of cable and the level of control. Versailles, a fortress for his family, a lock is not a lock when it is sprung. Versailles. His box of tricks, his apparatus, his grand machine.

Yet Casey is no different, no different from the rest. All the people on his network, all their devices. They frame, perceive, the landscape playing like a movie outside their windows. Inside their screens. They frame, record, review the tape, the infinite tape, infinite so long as they are there to eat the world, the vanishing world. They frame, record, review the tape, they view the tape. They view, they watch, they see. Each other on film, playing, sleeping, eating, fighting, their children eating what they give them. Yet they are older than these pictures have them, much older than these pictures, still pictures, moving. They frame, they frame, forget to breathe, to look above the camera at the world before them, outside the screen and then beyond, past the distant horizon to the emptiness beyond, the empty universe that waits patiently, they frame impatiently, review the tape, delete the images that make them old and only keep the ones that make them young, forever young.

Versailles. An American dream, a dream of life. Home to the four Baers. Missy. Her generation witnessed like no other, their every action reflected on the social networks, the internet as molten mirror, a primordial balm. Yes you are, *yes* you can. You are, you are, I am, I am. The sheer determination of this youth. To be somebody. Liked and unlike. And liked again, no time, no pause, no time to breathe, this generation witnessed like no other, this anxiety beneath the surface, the surface glittering like an open ocean. These pharma companies, these pharma companies conjuring their sick magic. White horses, white horses out there. This generation, her generation, the children of the internet, their lives mapped out on the shimmering social networks, Casey's network. When Casey was their age. When Casey was their age he wanted more. *His* generation. They are no different. They built the internet, this summer palace, they wove the social networks for themselves. They equip themselves. They frame, perceive, the world rushing by outside their forward windshield as they take the kids to school, a windowless building at the edge of the city, some inland city. *His* generation, and every one that came before. The sheer determination of this race, the human race across a vast lawn of gleaming grass, the coolness of the water as we dive.

Versailles. An American dream, a dream of life. Home to the four Baers. River. Intrepid explorer without a compass. His looking glass is one-way. Through the looking glass and then another. And never looking back, pressing forward toward the distant horizon, toward the emptiness beyond, an emptiness that he will flood with meaning, his very own big bang, an explosion so great that it might catch the attention of the boy across the classroom, the girl across the way. River. An old soul seeking older souls. Light to dark. When all he ever wanted. When all he ever wanted was to be told. That he was a good boy. You *are* a good boy, River Baer. When all he ever wanted was to play, to swim all day in the bright sunshine over Versailles.

An American dream, a dream of life. Home to the four Baers. Synthea. Roaming the grounds like a day spirit, a woman without witness, a dream of life. A dream of life is no life at all, her clothes falling away like burning paper, like burning paper in a cold flame. She gave her life to someone else. Till death she gave the life that she had made, her hands, her hand, the gold band on her ring finger, the silver watch of her own design now missing from her wrist. He put a ring on it, no doubt, encircled her with words. He wanted children. She wanted children. A dream of life. Versailles, a fortress for their family, a prison from reality. A dream of life is no life at all. The water only pink with blood, her blood, her heart. He stole her heart and put it in a black box. Their marriage had a black box. There, in amongst the wreckage. And really, that was all she ever did. Boxes. Beautiful boxes to house the technology driving the new world, a less courageous world but nonetheless. She made these things, designed these objects, and then one day she could not think. No new ideas. Pushing off the concrete wall and swimming underwater. And when nothing came she saw no point, swam beyond the horizon and over the waterfall at the edge of the world, the world unfurled. Over the edge and into the darkness. So dark she could not see, could not remember. And for a moment she forgot her children, her most beautiful creation. The water only pink with blood. A dream of life is not a life but when she woke it was Missy that she saw, her daughter, all this meaning suddenly, everything brought into the present. Her daughter holding her at the edge of the pool, consoling her, telling her it would be okay, that she was loved, the ambulance on its way. The water only pink with blood, sparkling in the moonlight over Versailles. Versailles, an American dream, a dream of life.

Versailles as seen from a hot air balloon, its ramparts glowing white in the late afternoon sun. And more balloons, colored balloons, tied with white string to the black double gates. Birthday balloons trembling in the summer breeze. This can only mean . . . This can only mean—

63

All their eyes, sparkling like jewels, all their clothes, their skin, covering their flesh just right, no blood, no blood in sight, and all their smiles, their teeth, their parted lips and open arms, arms in sleeves and wrists with shiny watches, their eyes sparkling like jewels and all their clothes, her friends, their friends, all singing the same song.

They are singing Happy Birthday. Filling their lungs with all the air and singing, the sound of people singing, a room of people singing Missy Happy Birthday, no blood in sight, her sword reflecting all the light like it's musical notation, the sound of people singing Happy Birthday all around her, all their eyes around her, their eyes like sparkling jewels and the sword leaving her hand, her sword gently taken from her grasp and passed around, her muscles softening as she finds herself in all their arms, their clothes, their skin, their lips on her skin. These are birthday kisses. Her friends, but these were never her friends. She looks around for her mom, her sword caught in the beam of a projector, a movie projected on a white sheet behind her. Missy turns and sees herself, her image cast on the taut, white sheet, her moving image. She runs her fingertips over the white fabric. A shallow undulation.

The picture abstract. She takes a step back. She watches along with everyone.

This is her running through a crowd of painted faces, her leopard make-up still fresh. Some guy just filming her on his phone. And now a long lens shot through the glass at the roadside truck stop. She has her elbows on the counter, Nora placing a coffee in front of her. Cut to security cam footage of her dancing with Cass in the motel parking lot, and now the kiss with Crystal, slowed right down as the explosion engulfs the wicker man, one hundred smartphones capturing the same moment. The effect is dirty bullet time, her kiss from every angle. These cuts are rough, random, no story, no progression. These images are background, ugly washes of color and no sound. Long lenses and mud-flung artifacts. These images are stolen, zipped, shared and shared again, reality lost in the upload, in transition, these images are dirty, bastard pictures, projected on this white sheet in no particular order, no story, no rhyme, no meaning, no focus, everything bleeding into everything else. What Casey doesn't know about his daughter. It would break the internet.

Missy bunches her fists inside her sleeves. *My sword, I want my sword back,* she says out loud, but no one seems to hear. *I want my sword, give me my sword*, she says, only louder this time, her birthday voice. The room falls silent, their eyes sparkling like jewels, their clothes, their skin, covering their flesh just right, no blood, no blood in sight, their parted lips, and it is Casey himself comes forward, her father, the sword across his palms like it's a ritual. *Happy Birthday, Missy*, he says. His eyes. She's seen those eyes on television. It's like he's not quite there, like he's wearing a mask of his own face. Like a celebrity you wish you'd never seen in real life. Her hate for him a perfect thing, the edges smoothed to infinity.

The gasps as Missy takes the sword, the weight of her sword as she turns and brings it over her head, then down across the white sheet, the sharpness of this blade as it cuts through the moving image, the sheet falling away along the diagonal, the hum of the projector as the film continues, out-of-focus now against the blue wall beyond. A moment's hush. All their eyes, sparkling like jewels, all their clothes, their skin, covering their flesh just right, no blood, no blood in sight, and all their smiles, their teeth, their parted lips. A moment's panic. Missy surrounded. Her musculature reorganized into that of a wild animal, this sword her dark talon, this sword is who she is now, the betrayal complete, the blood rushing to her hands and feet, replete with hate. But she can't move. All these people, their eyes on her, and she can feel herself transforming back into the old Missy. Before them. Before her. Her mother's daughter. Her father's daughter. All these people, they aren't her friends. All of it. It's all an illusion, and in that moment she can't remember how to break the spell. The magic word. Her name. She can't even remember her name.

A moment's hush, the hum and hush before the door bursts open and Missy turns and sees her brother. The sight of River coming in the door like a cop, coming in through the double doors like a soldier only with longish hair, securing the room, training his potato gun first this way and then that, but they don't know it's a potato gun, they think it's real, her beautiful brother River, a rare appearance out of costume, yet he's securing the room like a real-life marine, her friends screaming for their lives, the party over, the fear on River's face, the dark rings under his eyes and her heart is full of love. She crosses to him, says *Let's get out of here* and they flee, brother and sister fleeing the scene hand in hand, running for the front door like when they were kids, like two wild animals, running and laughing at the same time, almost falling over, but then they are out the front door, tearing down the stairs and through the garden like there's no tomorrow, past the swimming pool and across the green grass, running and laughing and then they fall, they fall as one, flying crocodile, tumbling on the grass and laughing, Missy laughs so hard she's crying, but she gets to her feet and pulls her brother with her. They have to get away. Their father. She can feel his eyes on her even now. Missy looks over her shoulder and it's not her father. It's something else.

Versailles. Glowing gold in the late afternoon sun, so bright she almost doesn't see at first. The figure in the window. Master bedroom on the second floor. The black curtains drawn back and there's someone there. It's her mother and she's waving. Even from this distance Missy can see. The electric blue dress. Even from this distance Missy can tell it's okay, it's all okay. She waves back, blows a kiss. Synthea does the same and feels the sting in her nose. Leticia zips up the back of the dress and Synthea touches the glass as Missy turns to catch up with her brother.

They have to keep moving, the grass turning to sand underfoot. And then Missy's bright idea. The speedboat. If there is magic in the world, the key will be in the ignition. She runs along the pontoon, River close behind, and if there is magic, and there is magic, she turns the key in the ignition, the engine vibrating through their bones, the roar of the engine telling them it will be okay, and she can't stop laughing, River laughing with her, Versailles in the rear mirror, sword on the back seat, the ocean wider than a dream.

Epilogue

The monitor lizard makes his way along another empty corridor in Versailles. His teeth are bared but he is not angry. His yellow eyes look mean but he is not mean, he is a monitor lizard who has not eaten in some time.

Just then he passes a white door. According to Versailles' schematics, this is Room 43, which houses a collection of more than 10,000 love letters. The room is 13'8 × 8'10. Walls are taupe suede with a satin finish. The room is furnished with six identical heavy-duty, three-bay, five-tier steel shelving units. The boxes used to contain the love letters are custom made to Mr Baer's exacting specifications.

Some arrived here unopened, others were bought in bulk from across the ocean. Some are long, others brief. There is no system of classification. The letters are in boxes and the boxes are on shelves and the shelves are in Room 43. Casey has read them all but there is one letter, one amongst the thousands that he wrote himself. A letter to his wife, Synthea, before they were married, before Missy and River were born, a young couple trying to make it work long distance, different colleges on opposite coasts, across America to another ocean, a great love worthy of the canvas.

Dear Synthea,

I almost died today and I love you. I guess I'll talk to you later on the phone but I thought I should write this down, everything that happened, so I remember all the details. I'm still shaking, my hands are shaking and they're dirty, my clothes are covered in dirt and I smell of woodsmoke and kerosene, but before I take a shower I thought I should write it all down.

Me and the guys went camping this weekend. The four of us. We went camping in the mountains, I think I told you we were doing that. We went out and bought all the stuff we needed, I never had a tent before, a sleeping bag, stove, food, everything we needed, we were so excited. We got it all in the car, put on some music and headed north-east for the mountains.

The weather was perfect, the sky was, like, cartoon blue. We made camp at the edge of the woods, the view was incredible, I wish you could have seen it, right across the valley, I thought I could see the ocean, it felt so good to be out of the city. We got pretty drunk, I'll admit things got a little out of control but we were camping, right? Under the stars, four guys, no girls, so things got kind of crazy.

I don't remember going to sleep, but I woke up next to my tent, headphones in my ears playing ambient music and the sun already high, it had to be late morning and my foot felt really hot, burning hot. I'd fallen asleep with my foot in the embers, melted the toe of my sneaker right off! That got me wide awake and I saw the bear. A goddamned grizzly bear on the other side of my yellow tent, real casual with

367

its snout in the long grass, like it was just grazing and I happened to be watching, no big deal. But he was thin. A thin bear and he looked mean, his fur all dreaded up under his empty belly.

Ambient music in my ears, I was on all fours and I saw the food, loose hotdogs in the dirt by the fire, candy wrappers and tossed beer cans. Thin bear like that, I thought, you must be hungry, and that's when he picks up his huge head, takes his muzzle out the long grass and looks right at me, like, wassup? I'm ready to run, but I can't move, the other guys must still be asleep and the bear does this thing like dogs do when they don't understand, like a head tilt to the side. I'd think it was totally cute if this wasn't a hungry bear looking at me right in my eyes like he's ready to delete me with one swipe of his epic paw. I take the headphones out my ears and hang them over my neck.

I stand to my full height and fill my lungs with mountain air. Bear vs Baer and I'm only thinking about one thing. You. I'm thinking about you, Synthea. The love of my life. All I can think about is you and the kids we're going to have together. I'm looking at the bear and imagining myself playing on the grass with our kids, a girl and a boy, and we're in the garden of our house, a beautiful white mansion I built for you and our children with all the money I'm going to make.

The bear looks right through me with those amber eyes, his big fluffy ears glowing in the morning sun. He could tear me to pieces, but I'm relaxed, I swear to

God I'm so relaxed I nearly close my eyes. I can feel your love, my heart pumping the blood around my body something animal, but I'm relaxed, ready for whatever happens next, something like faith but this isn't faith in God, it's in love, with you, across America to another ocean, my love, my heart, our future.

I was ready to die and the bear turns his head to one side, like he's heard something. Then he turns and bumbles away, back into the forest, disappearing between the tall pines. I don't move for a long time, our half-pitched tents fluttering in the cool breeze, it's blowing ash from the fire over my shoes. I hear the screech of an eagle, the music from my headphones playing quietly around my neck. I crouch to tie my laces, my hands are shaking but I feel great, my heart is full of love and I felt you right there with me, on the side of the mountain. Now I'm home and my hands are still shaking. I was going to write you an e-mail but I wanted this on paper.

I'm okay now, not a scratch on me, I'm better than okay. Matter of fact, I miss the bear. I know that sounds dumb but I feel like I made a new friend on that mountain today. I doubt he sees it that way, I doubt he thinks much of anything, but I miss him like a brother, being out there in the open air, I hope I dream about him. I have this feeling it's not the last I'll see of him. And I miss you too, I can't wait to see you again and hold you in my arms, my love, my queen,

Your Casey Baer

The forest monitor makes his way along another empty corridor in Versailles. His teeth are bared but he is not angry. His yellow eyes look mean but he is not mean, he is an ultra-rare, six-foot Filipino monitor lizard who has not eaten since before this story began.

He makes a decision on direction based on a special kind of smell. The scent is human. He knows this one, but the monitor is not good with names so we will help him out. It is Casey. Casey Baer, main man of Versailles, CEO of the internet's pre-eminent social network, father to Missy and River. The monitor is determined. It is dinnertime. His lizard eyes dart from thing to thing but there is no meaning really, only forward movement and a hunger that is fast turning a tame animal into one ready to bite the exposed flesh of his master.

He is in the entrance hallway now, at the top of the marble staircase. There are people down below. The monitor can only count to six but there are a great many more than that. He watches all the people. Their noises are high-pitched, like those made by the bigger rats when he crunches them between his teeth for lunchtime. He watches as these larger, upright creatures move towards the bright light. They are moving quickly. The monitor can smell new smells. He is smelling trees. He is smelling ocean. Perfume. Cut grass. Exhaust fumes. Chlorine. He has never known these scents before because he has lived all his life in Versailles, inside a makeshift cage of chicken wire and rough cuts. But there is one smell among the many he can still discern. His master. The man of the house. He descends the marble stairs one at a time, but when he loses his footing seven from the bottom he is forced to slither the remainder. But all is well, the monitor knows nothing of indignity. The entrance hall is empty now. The monitor makes his way towards the bright light and then down a further flight of stairs. Pretty soon he is on the lawn outside Versailles.

He settles for a moment on the grass, enjoying the cool, soft sensation on his belly. He resists the urge to roll. Roll and bask in the lovely sunshine. He blinks instead. He blinks again. A swish of the tail and a sideways glance. He has seen the swimming pool, the water disturbed by a persistent breeze. It looks tempting, an old instinct pulling him toward the water, this dynamic new element, so blue, so white, so blue. But even this is not enough to dissuade the monitor from his original goal: to find his master and eat him whole. He raises his head and finds the scent again, follows it deeper into the garden. He moves slowly, without a care, his tail sweeping the ground lazily behind him. He is just a six-foot monitor lizard ready to rip his master limb from limb.

And he is getting closer. He senses Casey close by, the grass turning to sand underfoot. The sun is brighter here. An old instinct to remain here a moment, take on the sun's powerful rays, restore the energy to his lizard body. And as his strange little eyes adjust to the brighter light he sees the outline of a human not so far away.

It is Casey Baer, standing at the end of the pontoon, oblivious to the monster behind, his hand raised in a salute, but really he is shielding his eyes from the sun, looking for something. His daughter and his son, but they are out of sight, the speedboat now only an idea on the horizon. Beyond the lens. Now that they were gone ... now that they were gone,

Casey had the clearest sense of being their father. Nothing more.

When all he ever wanted was to see them happy, live their lives to the fullest, their American lives, take everything the world had to offer, taste, see, smell, hear and feel *everything* in front of them. Make it their own. Eat the darkness and swim into the light. Before it was too late. Before they grew too old to see it all with open eyes. When all he ever wanted was a family. All eyes on. When all he ever wanted was a family to return home to, eat together, drink together, play, read, make, swim, fight, sleep, wake, and be. When all he ever wanted was a family to love and love him right back. All the people on his network, signed up, signed in, switched on, acting out, all their data passing through his vast, air-conditioned server farms, in and out, their love and hate, their boredom and anxiety, hopes and bad dreams, all the millions of people around the world, all witnessing as one, none of this meant anything when compared to the whims of his two children, their hidden motivations, their deft articulations.

He remembered in kaleidoscope. Missy's favorite constellation. River's favorite dinosaur. Missy's unexplained funeral for Barbie. River's tunnels in the sand, not a castle in sight, always shoulder-deep in beach. Their tortoises with the monster truck wheels out back, still going strong somewhere. The week River built a space rocket, the explosion at 200 feet bringing a dozen fire trucks, a special task force and local news crews. Missy & River. His two gorgeous children. They came from him, they came from her. Fatherhood. This thing was animal. The loss of control. The perfect gain. He remembered their birth, he had the whole thing on file. But he remembered everything he felt. Real time. These creatures came from him, their little hands and dark, dark eyes. His children. A truth as clear as daylight over ocean waves. The darkness coming soon, they called it twilight. His fatherhood a line of trees set back from the water, way back from the beach, a buffer between his children and the rest of the world, an ugly inland empire of danger and unpredictability. His role as father. To build his family a house. A fortress for his family. Versailles. One hundred rooms. A world unto itself. Where they could have everything. Sleep safe. Sweet dreams. Bad dreams but nothing more. Like Disney World with no Mickey Mouse. When all he ever wanted was to see them happy, healthy, still alive at twenty, bear-tough and ready to face the outside world, live their American lives. *Versailles*, the ocean seems to say, *Versailles*.

Casey steps to the edge of the pontoon and looks down into the water, the surface too disturbed to serve as mirror, but he knows himself, he knows that face. He sees it in his kids. Missy's eyes. River's mouth. His fatherhood a line of trees set back. He is one of a tribe. A group of people who know you even if they don't know what you do, what you're thinking. He is Casey Baer, American King, father of the online social network, a sum of all their parts. More than human, and so much less. A man playing God with porn on the other screen. He is Casey Baer, father of two. Now that they are gone. Now that they are gone, he's never had a clearer sense of being. When all he ever wanted was to love and be loved. When all he ever—

The water only pink with blood.

APPENDIX

THE ROOMS

A love story

Room 7

The money room. A place Casey would come to experience his wealth in the form of a kind of permanent, interactive conceptual art installation. A gigantic animatronic dragon guards a cavern filled with actual gold and treasure. Gold bullion, diamonds, rubies, sapphires, various precious artifacts, large chests brimming over with shiny coins. It's the real deal, the dragon so convincing Casey has to hold his breath on entering.

A sleeping dragon. It dominates the space, its long, finned tail encircling much of the sparkling riches. There is a routine, a primitive AI at work under the hood, the thousands of iridescent scales that make up its fantastic hide. There are certain things Casey can do to trigger the robotics. If he makes a sound, even the smallest sound, the dragon will wake, raise its monstrous head and look from side to side, scanning the room for intruders. Its emerald green eyes are ultra-sensitive light sensors that can detect even the slightest movement. If the dragon senses there is someone there it will fairly quickly rearrange itself into a terrifying upright position – hydraulic wings spread as wide as the room – and give a ground-shaking roar that in reality is the pitched-up, heavily amplified roar of a Bengal tiger combined with the bellow of a wounded African forest elephant.

Casey has only triggered the sequence once, and once was enough, so harrowing was the spectacle. Since then he has taken the greatest care not to wake the dragon, entering the room in soft-soled shoes, his movements almost balletic in his efforts to remain undetected. He is genuinely scared, a fear woven tightly together with his greed, a desire to have something in his hands, take something in his hands, just one of those brilliant diamonds between his index finger and thumb, to hold it up against the light and let it sparkle, sparkle just for him.

One day recently. The night before Missy ran away, as a matter of fact. He did it. He entered the dragon's lair. A sleeping dragon. A cave filled to its borders with gold and treasure, *his* treasure. He moved into the room like a panther cat, almost on all fours, eyes always trained on the dragon, those heavy eyelids like theater drapes, the dim light reflecting off its iridescent scales. Quiet yet confident, he made his way into the room and straight for a stray diamond, a brilliant diamond that seemed to have rolled a short way from the shoreline of shining gold coins. One last glance up at the sleeping dragon and – he closed his hand on the stone, felt its brilliant edges digging into the soft tissue of his palm. There, he had it. And the dragon still asleep. All he had to do now was retrace his steps. Get out of here. He could feel his heart beating hard in his chest. He got it.

He'd been planning this for some time, gathering the courage. He wanted this diamond for a ring. A ring for Synthea as reward for sticking to the program, for continuing to take the medication as he'd asked. For months now she had done as she was told, seemed to understand that this was the only way. A suicide attempt must be taken seriously. She seemed to see that now. The pills a necessary evil. And this diamond in his hand was the reward. He would have it set into a gold band for her ring finger, replace the one she said she lost in the swimming pool.

This diamond in his hand, and all he has to do is retrace his steps. So that's exactly what he does. He moves slowly back across the space, stealthy as a panther cat, brilliant diamond gripped tightly in one hand, his other finding the handle to the white door. And the dragon sleeps, a dreamless sleep.

Room 17

Every Wednesday, under cover of darkness, a black minibus with tinted windows and no license plates pulls into Versailles' staff car park out back of the compound. Twelve young men, all varsity athletes in peak physical condition, climb out of the vehicle and enter the mansion in silence. They walk through the empty kitchens in solemn single file, heads down like they're entering a stadium for the big game.

They assemble in Room 17, a large, square, windowless space with a rough, concrete floor and no furnishings. Each of these young men has been generously compensated for their attendance at this weekly event because in participating they may well incur serious injury, in some unfortunate cases, career-ending. For these men have to fight each other.

Not one-on-one. This is no fight club. There are no rules down here. Room 17 is a controlled free-for-all. Controlled in the sense that there is a time limit. It's every man for himself. Any style. No style. They're there to kick the living shit out of each other till Casey sees fit to put a stop to proceedings. Bare fists and open wounds.

Casey sits back in an original Eames armchair constructed of stainless steel and black Italian leather, watching a small, old-fashioned monitor, one deeper than it is wide to accommodate the sizeable cathode ray tube relaying the images of men doing their best to take one another apart.

These sessions have produced several stars, the men who walk away more or less in one piece, their clothes soaked

380

with sweat instead of blood. Once a season Casey will invite this all-star group back to the mansion and take his turn in the ring, rolling up the sleeves of his designer hoodie and going in hard. Both times this has happened he has won the bout, won in the sense that he has made at least one of the other participants cry quietly as a lost child. Casey fights dirty. He fights cruel, vicious as a cornered animal, no rhyme, no thought for the consequences of his actions. After the fight they can all enjoy a cold beer together, maybe sit around and watch reruns of famous moments in American sporting history on a large, flat-panel television screen. But Casey's dilettante appreciation for the various sporting disciplines does not go unnoticed, and fairly soon he will be subjected to a subtle form of psychological bullying by the other guys, to the point where, on the last occasion, Casey made his excuses and walked along the empty corridor to his bedroom, to where his lovely wife was quietly sleeping. He slipped under the sheets, careful not to wake her.

Hours later, Casey woke from a bad dream and didn't know where he was. The silver shaft of light from between the black curtains told him it was early morning and he was next to his wife in their bed in the master bedroom of Versailles, the mansion he built for his family, set back from the Pacific Ocean. Versailles. The house he built for her, his beloved Synthea. He saw now she had turned in her sleep to face him. He wanted to take her hand, make sure she was really here, the bad dream pulling at him still. He wanted to take her hand, make sure he was really here, but she needed this sleep. She needed this sleep.

Room 27

Room 27 is a plane crash on repeat. A faithful reconstruction of a Boeing 767 cabin and cockpit, complete with full crew and passengers, all professional actors on Casey's payroll. They might go for months without hearing from his people and then suddenly it's every day for a fortnight.

Sometimes Casey takes on the role of drunken captain, but mostly he is a member of the public, taking his seat like everyone else at the beginning of the flight, asking for a glass of iced water before take-off. He looks out of the window at the landscape beyond the edge of the runway, high-resolution footage of a real airport somewhere in America, played back in Cinerama outside the plane.

Casey actually loves to fly, has since he was a kid. He loves take-off, he loves landing, he loves everything about it. Airplane food. He's a sucker for airplane food. These days he has a personal chef prepare him his heart's desire at 35,000 feet in the network jet, but in the old days he would take anything that was put in front of him and devour every morsel. Something about traveling great distances. Gets him hungry as ten bears put together.

But Room 27 is a simulated plane crash, designed to feel just like the real thing. Sometimes the actors don't come back a second time because they find it too upsetting. The reason for the crash varies from one performance to the next. Human error. Mechanical error. Weather. Sabotage. Whatever the variable, the plane will end up crashing to the earth, killing everyone onboard.

A violent death. Things start going wrong about an hour into the flight. A member of the cabin crew or captain will make an announcement over the public address system, the tone pitched somewhere between innocuous and pragmatic. Casey likes to act out at this point. Sometimes he will play the hero, gently reassuring those around him that there is nothing to worry about, he's a frequent flier and it's just a little turbulence. Other times he'll go the other way and lose his shit completely, demanding the cabin crew give them more information, removing his seatbelt with a flourish and getting to his feet in the aisle, generally making a dangerous nuisance of himself. When Casey gets like this, the actors have been instructed to treat him as a genuine threat, restrain and handcuff him, if necessary, for the remainder of the simulation.

Casey likes the cuffs. Even under these make-believe conditions they seem to have a sobering effect. But it's more than that. He's dreamed up some of his best new features for the website while apprehended like this, sitting near the back of the plane next to the actor playing the air marshal (Florian, a regular player, he loves his job), the plane continuing to lose altitude. Something about being taken prisoner amidst the chaos, the inevitability of the crash, the appalling shudder of the cabin walls and the screams of his fellow passengers – it really gets Casey's creative juices flowing.

The crash itself. This simulator is designed to take everyone on board to the very brink of feeling like they are going to die. When Casey is playing the captain – a rare treat – it's the way the landscape fills the cockpit windows that really captures his imagination: no sky, only land, everything down there growing bigger and then bigger still, as though God himself were zooming in.

Room 30

The quietest room in the world. Its 99.99 per cent acoustic absorbency is achieved through a system of fiberglass acoustic fins and double walls of insulated steel and thick concrete. It smells ancient, and that's because Casey had a notable Paris perfumer work with illegal samples from King Tut's underground tomb in Luxor, Egypt, to create a scent for his beloved quiet room in Versailles, USA.

Casey comes here every day, strips down to just his dirty white socks and listens. To his heartbeat. His lungs. Stomach. The click and crunch of bones inside his skin. And he does so in the pitch black. The sounds his body makes. A hymn to only him. Casey Baer. Just Casey on his own. The room so quiet his thoughts take on a viscous quality, mingling with the flow of blood throughout his body, until he isn't thinking anymore, just being, the way a monitor might bask in the midday sun, but Casey's blood is warm, his lion heart, all the love for his family, his family the only thing. He'd die, he'd kill. He'd die, he'd kill, his thoughts becoming viscous, the flow of blood, his heart, his heart, this time alone is who he is now, his thoughts giving way to impulse, he'd die, he'd kill.

Room 30 is a test chamber. Casey brings in members of the public now and then, has them sit for him in darkness, then pays them in bananas. After forty-five minutes of close to utter silence, most humans will hallucinate, hear voices, even wish to strike up conversation. And some do. Our need for narrative, structure, interaction. After forty-five minutes in the chamber most test subjects will ask to leave, they cannot stand it any longer.

Not Casey. After seventy minutes in the quiet room, Casey has been hallucinating for some time, but these are not voices in his head, at least not human. Animal. Animals. Hundreds, thousands. A jungle-wide spectrum and he is lion king, his lion heart, the flow of blood, he'd die, he'd kill, his family the only thing. Missy, River and Synthea.

Synthea. She would like it here in the quiet room. It might help her focus. Like her swims out into the ocean. He remembers watching her from his own office in the mansion, swimming out, way out into the deeper waters. He never liked it, her all the way out there with the strong ocean currents, beyond calling distance. She would like it here, in the quiet room, with him. Just the two of them.

Room 39

In Room 39, Casey can be a woman. It is not so much a
need as a very pleasurable bimonthly indulgence, like smoking a single, secret cigarette by a French window opening out
onto an impossible desert palace garden. Bethany has been
part of his life for some years now, or is it the other way
round? He is never quite sure.

There is a small, adjoining walk-in wardrobe. This time
before entering the main space is precious. There is no rush.
No nerves. His audience is very patient, more than prepared
to wait. A black-sequined backless evening gown designed
for his body. He stands in front of the full-length mirror and
turns to check out his shapely ass, the arch of his spine
framed by the glittering fabric. Were Synthea to see this. He
doesn't know what would happen. He applies the make-up
last, already in character, he has his brief routine down to a
fine art. Nothing too crazy, just a little mascara and a touch
of red lipstick that complements his cool skin tone.

When Casey feels ready, he steps through a black curtain
and onto a raised stage area where a grand piano stands
ready. The light is silver, tuned to resemble moonlight as seen
through a wisp of cloud. Casey cannot play the piano. He
has never been musical in that sense, but that is not what
this is about. The performance takes place in complete
silence. Casey begins by climbing up on the instrument and
lying down on his side, arms stretched out above his head.

His movements are languid, controlled, like a professional dancer.

Casey proceeds to vogue slowly yet deliberately for the camera, a routine vaguely suggestive of a captive panther cat, stretching out lazily in the sun, and under the watchful gaze of those members of the public that happen to be passing by. But this live feed is far from public. Casey's audience are a highly select group. Subscription to the webcam is invitation only, and the price of entry would make all but the wealthiest individuals on the planet blush from head to toe.

Room 44

Casey's childhood bedroom. The same dimensions, wallpaper, curtains, a false window onto a neighborhood that no longer exists. Every object, all the furniture taken from the original room and transplanted here. The mood is undisturbed crime scene. And yet when Casey visits, he acts as though he were returning from playing out on the street, or spending Saturday afternoon at a friend's house. He takes up a comic book and flops down on the bed. The bedclothes have a repeating pattern of grizzly bears with friendly cartoon eyes. Casey slept under this duvet when he was a boy, and more besides. When he's bored with the book, he gets down from the bed on his knees and reaches underneath for the shallow wooden box hidden there towards the wall. He lifts off the lid. An unsmoked cigarette. A matchbox. Flick knife. Catapult. *Playboy*. Hand mirror. Potato gun. The matchbox contains nothing but a woodlouse. A reminder.

The woodlouse is alive at the moment. It is not the first to live inside this box. The woodlouse does not have a name because it is not a pet as such. The woodlouse is a reminder of something Casey did when he was six years old, he might even have been five, he can't remember now. What he does remember is finding a great many woodlice under a rock at the bottom of the drive of his childhood home in the suburbs of the city. He never told his wife this story. The rock was heavy, its underbelly caked with damp soil. He rolled the rock on its side and found the teeming creatures, not only woodlice, but the woodlice were the easiest to catch, and they didn't hurt him when he did, picking them up between his thumb and forefinger and watching as they moved their tiny, tiny legs, trying to gain traction in the thin air. Yikes. Casey remembers thinking what would happen if . . . Casey remembers thinking: how come these little creatures can live right under this big rock and not get squished like bugs? No space between. How come they can move around under this big rock when there's no space. Well, Casey thinks, if they can live under this big rock then they can do the same under a red brick. Right? He never told his wife this story. He remembers taking a wiggling woodlouse between his thumb and forefinger and walking around the dark side of the house to the back yard. No adults around just now. He remembers sitting cross-legged on the warm paving stones and getting hold of a red brick and placing it flat-end first on the scurrying woodlouse. A little red tower. The little red tower.

Now what he *can't* remember. It doesn't matter how hard he tries. What he can't recall is whether he truly expected the woodlouse to be alive when he lifted the brick away again a few seconds later. Or whether it was always his intention to squash the little creature flat, find it surrounded by a tiny coin of gore. Unmoving. In his more reflective moods, when Casey comes into Room 44 and doesn't read the comic book, lies down on the bed and closes his eyes, he will always draw the same conclusion: that moment, when one hard surface met the other, and the living creature between was no longer living, its continuum brought to an abrupt close – that moment was intentional, satisfying as a well-placed comma in a sentence about nothing.

He never told his wife this story. One of many secrets. But what would they be without secrets, without stories to tell that as yet were untold? They would be one, fallen into one another, not falling. And Casey never wanted that kind of love. He remembers, in the early years, flying across America to see her, lying next to her in the narrow bed of her dorm, her roommate already asleep. He remembers kissing her neck and saying things to her he only dared say in the relative dark. These things about the future. He remembers telling her he wanted to have kids, that he wanted to build her a beautiful house, and that he loved her. And he remembers the silence after, her reply coming only much later, years later, on a trip into the mountains, where the sky was so dark you could see the Milky Way.

Room 53

The delivery room. Casey has watched a great many births take place in this white space. He has the animals brought in at the apex of pregnancy, then watches them give birth right in front of him.

There are no cameras allowed. Casey likes to be involved. The rush of being right there at the moment of birth. But there are no cameras. He must rely on his senses to record the experience, his memory. It requires a presence of mind. He likes to be involved, the blood on his hands and clothes, the strangely wonderful smells. One expert – the lion man – said Casey was a natural, showing no fear. Says he would make a fine zookeeper.

That day. The birth of his own Transvaal lion. And yet his memory of this event is fragmented somehow. He remembers wanting very much to take the cub and show his wife, a powerful impulse. His beautiful wife. He wished she had been there for the lion, a sense that without her there the experience was incomplete.

The love for his wife. A powerful impulse to have her share in this private ritual of his, go back to when they shared most everything, their innermost thoughts and feelings. He remembers. Reaching for the Transvaal cub and the terrible roar from the mother. A warning. An almost overwhelming impulse to steal the cub away so he could show his wife. Something so real as this.

His once beautiful wife. The birth of their own children,

little Missy & River Baer. Their pride & joy. Every second caught on film, Synthea's smile as she holds the two babies in her arms, their heads nestled in her elbows. No need to rely on memory when every second of every minute is captured on videotape. A film long since transferred to digital, an undulating curtain of ones and zeroes, her smile as she begins to see things as they truly are. All this meaning, everything brought into the present. Console. A blinking cursor. Code unknown.

Room 61

The cache. A room full of drugs and guns. It is set out like a post-raid police exhibit, the guns lined up lovingly on folding tables like show and tell, the drugs piled high in their compact, bulbous bundles of shiny brown tape. Floor to ceiling. These are real drugs, real guns, from bona fide seizures around the world. There are even a couple of grenades. All this. Street value: $100 million. And while Casey has fired many guns in his life, he has never taken drugs. He's frightened: the delayed effect, the lack of control. But something about being in this room, in amongst all this shit, all this danger – there's no identifiable scent in this room, just this feeling that you're completely out of your depth in the cold water. Darkness over ocean.

Casey feels alive in this room, but he takes no pleasure. The knowledge he would go to prison for the rest of his life should they discover his cache, have everything taken away from him, his family, his house, his company, everything – it leaves him in a state of extreme anxiety, no question. He doesn't want to go to prison, of course not. He wants to survive. But more than wanting to live he wants to feel alive. Money can't buy you love, but it can buy you fear, and fear is all Casey has left.

Room 61 is an altered state. Casey doesn't need to touch anything to get there. These are real drugs, real guns, dark materials acquired by nefarious means. He won't touch but he breathes deep, drinks in every detail, pupils fully dilated and yet Casey has never taken a drug in his life . . . alright, one time. But it was long ago, when he was still in college. And it was her idea.

First summer at college and Synthea was visiting. A bunch of them went out to the beach and built a fire on her last night before flying back. All his friends, all theirs. They all loved Synthea. She wasn't like the other girls, they told him. They thought she was funny. Her deep voice and deadpan delivery. They thought she was sexy and, of course, that made her more sexy. At some point, fairly early in the evening, Synthea chose a moment when no one else was looking and stuck out her tongue for Casey. A small, blue pill. Cyan, he remembered. *You want one?* Casey looked into her sparkling eyes and she looked back into his. He trusted her, by now he was in love with this girl. *Sure*, he said, but he wasn't. *What is it?* he asked. She shook her head and barely shrugged her shoulders, like, *does it matter?* And at the time it didn't. He loved this girl and she was smoking hot and it was their first summer at college. Casey put the pill in his mouth and they kissed long enough that people started watching.

And it was beautiful. A real experience. He remembers them swimming together in the dark ocean, her breasts pushed up close against his chest. He remembers the dark, dark ocean, swimming under the moon and turning to look back at the fire on the beach. Too far, they were too far out, but this danger, he was sharing it with Synthea, this girl who wanted him and only him.

This room, all the danger in this room, all the suffering and bloodshed, all the history. Product. Bulbous, shiny packages, a fraction of whose contents is enough to destroy a life.

All this. Street value: $100 million. One hundred million dollars, but it is never enough. This cache. It grows a little every year. A garden of death. Too far, too far, but Casey likes to keep the danger close. Room 61. No light in the gap.

Room 77

A room of brief encounters. A different set up every time. A pretty girl as seen across a hotel lobby. At the beach, waves breaking gentle in the background. On a high-speed train, America a blur. On each occasion, Casey must gather the courage to approach the actress playing opposite. Participants are encouraged to improvise, but within certain parameters. The end game: Casey gets the girl.

There is never any physical contact, only talking, each scenario designed to feel like a chance meeting, an instant attraction. And while these episodes might take place in different time periods, Casey will always turn up dressed in his anachronistic yet comfortable sneakers, slacks and zipped hoodie, the same clothes he has been wearing since he was a teenager, in and out of the boardroom.

Participants are encouraged to improvise, largely because Casey is a terrible actor and can't remember the few trigger lines he is given at the beginning of each session. He has been known to show up drunk, but he is always respectful of the girls. Despite appearances he takes this project very seriously. He is charming, he listens, he wears his heart on his sleeve where appropriate. Some of the girls come away having genuinely enjoyed their time in his presence. Because Casey really opens up in this room. He enjoys the frisson, but it's something more. He feels he can talk to these women, frame his life how he likes, speak freely about what's on his mind. They take him seriously.

They used to have this. He could talk to Synthea like no one else. Those long periods apart in the early years. Always so much to talk about. Endless conversations deep into the night. No one subject. Holding hands in sleep. Then later money. The kids. Events unfolding. *Should I wear the blue dress or the black dress?* These days she could not look him in the eye. They used to have— They used to be in love. Now it's like they had nothing. Her hate for him a perfect thing. The long encounter an endless goodbye.

Room 84

Like shuffle mode for your music. Every time Casey enters this room it is a different experience. An incredible team of artists and technicians collaborating on the ultimate art form: life.

Every month they are given this space to work with and an organic budget. Sometimes the event will be very elaborate in nature, requiring long hours of preparation and the kind of ad hoc inventiveness only found on big studio film sets at the eleventh hour of shooting. Other times the team comes up with a very simple concept: lean, yet poetic. Minimalist, but effective. The last one, for example, turned out perfect. The boss seemed real happy which makes the team happy. They love their jobs, the creativity involved, the pressure, balanced with the relative freedom. No studio executives breathing down their necks. But anyway the last event: a real success story.

Here's the set up: a generous lawn of gleaming green grass. An almost imperceptible slope up towards the house, a white Regency mansion nestled somewhere in the English countryside. Only the very tops of the trees are moving in the light summer breeze. The 8K screens depicting everything beyond the edge of the lawn render the scene utterly lifelike, an upgrade from reality if anything. And now the scenario as it played out: Casey must lie down in the middle of the lawn and wait. He has been briefed in advance about what is going to happen, but unlike most events taking place

in Room 84, this one does not have a fixed narrative structure. It is up to Casey to make it work. And his task is this:
tame a wild animal.

A white rabbit enters the space via a hatch concealed
somewhere in the artificial horizon. Casey is lying on his
back on the grass. It takes some time before he can see
movement in his peripheral vision. The rabbit is very scared.
It spends the first twenty minutes of the event jumping up at
the screens making up the walls of the room, unable to rec-
oncile the truth of these images with their impossibility. The
team – huddled around a monitor in a separate annex –
think this thing isn't going to go their way. The rabbit is too
frightened, they whisper. There's no way this is going to
work. They had a professional hunter shoot to maim this
poor little creature in the woods outside the city a few days
ago. There's no way. This rabbit's just too crazy, too far
gone. But then something changes in the rabbit's behavior.
Its spasmodic efforts to penetrate Room 84's four invisible
walls have left it somewhat exhausted so it has switched to
hopping about at the fringes of the lawn and occasionally
stopping to nibble at the greenery. For one of the team
behind this event has thought to include some delicious dandelions in the spectrum of flora allocated to the experiment.

Yes, the rabbit likes dandelions very much. Casey continues to lie on his back as instructed, barely moving a muscle.
Once in a while he will tilt his head to the side a fraction,
just so he can get a better look at the little creature, its circles
around the room growing gradually smaller. The team can't
believe it. There's no way the rabbit hasn't clocked the boss,
and yet here it is, getting ever closer. Hop-hop – dandelion
– up on its hind legs for a quick look around, and then down

again – more dandelion – hop-hop-hop – grass. The team are leaning closer to the monitor, they can't believe this is really happening. Hop-hop – dandelion – more dandelion – hop-hop. Casey turns his head and the rabbit is no more than four feet from his head. He watches as the last of the dandelion disappears in its little mouth, a flash of its pink tongue. He never thought of rabbits having a tongue.

And then the moment. In the wrap party afterwards they still can't believe how it happened, but it did. The rabbit turns and hops towards Casey's shoes. It just stands there for a few seconds, apparently forgetting what it was doing. Then it turns again and hops right up on Casey's stomach. He's quite ticklish so it takes a tremendous effort not to burst out laughing, but Casey manages, lifting his head so that he can get a better look at this thing. *Hello, little buddy*, he says softly. The rabbit's ears prick up momentarily, but it doesn't seem too worried. Next thing it is doing that thing where it washes its face with its front paws and the team in the annex cheer and pump the air with their fists like someone just scored a touchdown.

Casey cannot resist. He reaches out with his hand, slowly so as not to frighten the little fella, but that's exactly what he does. The moment the rabbit sees the hand coming towards him he leaps away and fairly quickly resumes his dandelion routine, albeit in ever-increasing circles this time. But the event has been a success, and that night Casey kisses Synthea on her cheek as she sleeps. She wakes to his kiss but will never know why.

Room 100

The aquarium is an unfinished love letter to his wife. Even by Casey's standards this was an ambitious project, but money was never the problem. The truth is Casey sent the contractors home long ago, told them he changed his mind about the whole thing.

The aquarium. He'd hired the world's leading experts on experimental concrete structures, pre-ordered several million dollars' worth of thick, curving glass. It would be the most beautiful aquarium on earth, and all for his gorgeous Synthea. His wife, who loved the ocean and was fascinated by all life beneath it, the undiscovered country. His wife, who loved to swim, to dive under the surface of the water and forget about the world above. Her wet hair twisted over one shoulder, the smell of chlorine on her skin. This aquarium was to be her sanctuary, a place where she could get away, relax her mind and observe some of the planet's weirdest creatures, their colors and behaviors a dynamic inspiration for her working life, her dreaming life, her life with him. But one day, something went wrong. Not with the contract itself. In fact, the build was ahead of schedule and in-budget, the morale among the construction team never better. This was something else.

They were days away. Three days and they would be ready to fill the tanks with water. It was to be the moment of truth, not only in terms of everything being watertight. For the architect, but most importantly Casey, this would be the moment when they knew whether their original vision for the space had been fulfilled. The light, the shadows, the play of light on every surface, the *ambience* of the place. They wouldn't know for sure until the tanks were filled. Everyone was excited. Even the younger guys on the site interrupted their conversations about girls to guess what kind of animals Casey planned to introduce once the tanks were full. Odds were high on a great white, with dolphins coming in a close second favorite. But something happened that turned the whole thing on its head.

Casey was in attendance on the day in question, discussing something with one of the structural engineers, when the door opened behind him. The unlocked door to Room 100 opened and in walked Synthea. And that was the end. Casey lost it right there and then, screaming for her to get out of here, *you can't see this, get out.* But even then it was too late. It didn't matter that she didn't know what she had seen. Afterwards when they were arguing she begged him to listen to her, she begged him to listen but he wouldn't. *I don't know what it is, Casey, it can still be a surprise.* But Casey's blood was boiling, the words spilling from him like an oil slick, and then he told her, told her exactly what it was that she had seen. An aquarium, it was to be her own aquarium, *and now you've seen it and it's all over.* And so it was. The next day he told them to go home, he paid them all in full and sent them home. And so it is, an unfinished love letter to his wife.

Years later, long after Missy and River's escape by speedboat, Synthea returns to Room 100, the aquarium. Even in its unfinished state it is a breathtaking space, these impossible concrete structures framing the tanks, like a series of volcanic eruptions deep beneath the surface of the ocean, the lava forming and solidifying in the ice-cold water. These panes of glass, each one curving, curving by degrees of love, all for her, to witness life under the ocean. Even without the water, without the creatures present, she feels Casey's love as she runs her fingers over the surface of the glass in a rainbow arc. The dust gathered there. *I love you too*, she writes.

Acknowledgements

I wrote *Versailles* in the months following my mother's death. It was only when she was gone that I realised how much of the world was hers. And when her vibrations ceased, when the music that I didn't know was everywhere came to an end, the silence for a time felt total. *Versailles* was my attempt to make some noise. So while the novel isn't about Milena, I dedicate it to her.

It's also for all my friends and family, particularly my legendary little sister, Egg.

And I couldn't have got here without Tilti, my grandparents Babi and Oko, my dad Peter Hill, Sally James, Michael Gleeson, Tony Dixon, Chris Wellbelove, Nicola Barr, Angharad Hill, Naomi Alderman, Patricia Dunker, Stephen Bass, Xander Cansell, Isobel Frankish, my brilliant editor Jamie Groves, the Unbound crew and all the people who turned up to pledge for the novel. Big up.

I'd like to thank the Society of Authors for kindly allowing me to quote from Virginia Woolf's *To the Lighthouse*. I'd also like to acknowledge the Cahuilla people of California, whose *Climbing the Mountain* folk tale Silas recounts for Missy and the boy with no name.

And thank you so much Yehrin Tong for creating a cover design that so intuitively and gorgeously captures the spirit of the novel.

Supporters

Unbound is a new kind of publishing house. Our books are funded directly by readers. This was a very popular idea during the late eighteenth and early nineteenth centuries. Now we have revived it for the internet age. It allows authors to write the books they really want to write and readers to support the writing they would most like to see published.

The names listed below are of readers who have pledged their support and made this book happen. If you'd like to join them, visit: www.unbound.co.uk.

Jody Aberdein

Ladan Ahmed

Naomi Alderman

Tanya Andrew

Tom Andrew

Paul Angus

Leonie Anning

Beckie Arden

James Aylett

Lucy Ayre

Raya Herzig Babi

Corinne Bailey

Duncan Bailey

Joanne Bain

Craig Baker-Austin

Jason Ballinger

Nicola Barr

Thomas Bartlett

James Basham

Stephen Bass

Katy Bassett

Jaimie Batchan

Kay Bathke

Antony Bayman

Dan Benton

Claudia Bernold

William Bonwitt

Mitchell Bornstein

Tamar Bourne

Joanna Bowen

Phil Brachi

Richard W H Bray

Catherine Breslin

Stephen Bristow

David Bristowe

Jim and Pauline Bristowe

Karen Bristowe

Mark Bristowe

Rachel Bristowe

Erwin Brunner

Cristina Burke-Trees

Emma Burns

Jaspar Cadenhead

Aifric Campbell

Andrew Campling

Xander Cansell

Austin Cantu

Judith Carlton

John and Valerie Carne

Nick Carter

David Charles

Joe Chilton

Melanie Chrysostomou

Joanna Ciechanowska

Michelle Clark

Ross Clark

Brian Clarke

Elanor Clarke

Garrett Coakley

Elizabeth Coleman

Stevyn Colgan

Sara Concejal

Philip Connor

Maia Conran

Manuel Rodriguez Contra

Phil Craggs

Amie Crago-Graham

John Crawford

Richard Cresswell

Jess Croll-Knight

J-F Cuvillier

Kate Dawson

The Days

Miranda de Freston

Annie de Maintenon

Orjon de Roo

IVH de Whitkirk

TTH de Whitkirk

Paul Dembina

Kevin Donnellon

Connor Doyle

Hamish Dunbar

Patricia Duncker

Katherine Dunhill

Stephen Dunhill

Jack Ettinger

Sarah Farley

Peter Faulkner

Blanca Fellows

Nicholas Flint

Hantverk Found

Paula J. Francisco

Brutal Frank

Alan Franks

Graham Fulcher

Mark Gamble

John Gartside

David Geaney

Amro Gebreel

Bert Gilbert

Christopher Gill

Natascha Glauser

Margaret Gleeson

Michael Gleeson

Susan Godfrey

Caroline Goldthorpe

Peter Gordon

Jonathan Gosling

Veronica Gosling

David Graham

Alice Grainger

Clemency Green

Kate Green

Andrew Groves

Emile Guertin

Kenan Guler

Jessica Gulliver

Katherine Hackworthy

Phoebe Haertner

Helena Haimes

Vic Haimes

Elliott Hall

Alison Hand

Stephanie Hand

Vladimír Handl

Anne and Adrian Hansell

Joe Harling

Camelia Hart

Caitlin Harvey

Chris Hassan

Michael Hatchett

Peter Haveland

Mark Henderson

Milena Herzig

Martin Hicklin

Sarah Higgins

Helen Hildebrand

Angharad Hill

Josette Baer Hill

Ben Hill

Eleanor Hill

Peter Hill

Sophia Hill

Yannick Hill

Adam Hinks

Vivien and Nigel Hinks

Holly Howells

Emma Hughes

Hannah Hughes

Justine Hyde

Rivka Isaacson

Maxim Jakubowski

Matt James

Verity James

Woody James

Zaborsky Jan

Jennie Jiricny

Michael Johnson

Sheila & Richard Johnston

Henryk Kalinski

Judith Kavanagh

David Keane

Mike Kennedy

Dan Kieran

Julian King

Graham Knox

Sally Knyvette

Georg Kohler

Andrzej Kowalski

Alfred Lampart

Jimmy Leach

Lewis, Cooper and Amy

John Little

Marina MacKay

Allison Maclenzie

Margot Maidment

Annuska Manzini

Julian Mash

Jethro Massey

Bozena masters

Daniel Mattson

Ross Maylor

John Mc Dermott

Cassie McCallin

Niki McCann

Huey McEvoy

Joel McIlven

Ewan Mee

Luka Melon

Claire Menzies

Reena Merali

Adis Merdzanovic

Senada Merdzanovic

Billy Meyer

Jean Mi

Daniel E. Miller

John Mitchinson

Diego Montoyer

Gabi Moody

Iain Moore

Shona Morley

Suzannah Musson

D N

Rulf Neigenfind

Christopher Nelson

Katie Nixon

Jam Norman

Zoe North

Kevin O'Connor

Cairbre O'Donnell

Jenny O'Gorman

Janet Obl

Georgia Odd

Walter Schneider Oko

Par Olsson

Alan Outten

Eiron Page

Phoebe Pallotti

Claire Parry

Janice Parsons

Laura Pathe

Jiri Pavel

Agata Peksa

Red Pender

John Pentreath

David Pettet

Luisa Plaja

Justin Pollard

Rose Popham

Samuel Porritt

Willem K. Posthumus

Jean Power

Sophie Pratt

Juliet Price

Alexander Prout

Vinnie Quinn

Margaret Reeves

Juraj Rehak

Claire Reynolds

James Reynolds

Michelle Reynolds

Thomas Richers

Thogdin Ripley

Devon Gleeson Roe

John Roslingon

Gilly Ross

Martin Ross

Michael Rowley

Benjamin Russell

Michelle Salomons

Amy Sayer

Walter Schneider

Rosanna Schura

Hannah Scott

Annemarie Shaughnessy

Georgia Lee Wright Shaw

Hilary Sheers

William Simpson

Ross Sleight

Craig Smith

Philippa Snow

David Somers

Richard Sowman

Aaron Starum

Gabriel Stebbing

Sarah Stephen

Philip Stewart

Mandy Street

Stephen Street

Claudia E. Suter

Pete Sutton

David Swettenham

Ezra Tassone

Shireen Taylor

Eleanor Teasdale

Michael Thackray

Graham & Alison Thompson

Daniel Thorens

Garth & Sheila Thorne

Eva Tjajkovski

Margaret Todd

T & N Todorovic

Julia Trocme-Latter

Michael Tucker

Laura Upton

Cara Usher

Lotte van Buuren

Daniela Verzaro

Gert Vonhoff

Madlaina and Michael Wachtl

Tig Wallace

Sophie Walton

Luke Waterson

Alyson & Nigel Waterson

Gail Watson

James Watts

Ewa Webb

Chris Wellbelove

Jonathan Wellbelove

Siboy Wellbelove

Andrea Welti

Sam Werner

Angela Wiggan

Derek Wilson

Robert Witkin

James Wright

Jon Wright

Lucy Wright

Maggie Wright

Sally Wright